MELTING THE SNOW ON
HESTER STREET

MELTING THE SNOW ON HESTER STREET

Daisy Waugh

WINDSOR
PARAGON

First published 2013
by HarperCollins*Publishers*
This Large Print edition published 2013
by AudioGO Ltd
by arrangement with
HarperCollins*Publishers*

Hardcover   ISBN: 978 1 4713 4557 9
Softcover   ISBN: 978 1 4713 4558 6

British Library Cataloguing in Publication Data available

Printed and bound in Great Britain by
MPG Books Group Limited

Darling Bashie,
movie star in the making (maybe)
This book is for you

Max & Eleanor Beecham's
October Supper Party

1

Santa Monica, 17 October 1929

'What did he say, Charlie? Did he say it was gonna be just f-fine? Did he say it was OK?'

She was sitting at her dressing table, watching Charlie's approach with anxious eyes, blue as the sapphires round her throat. But Charlie didn't reply at once. He was thinking how graceful it was, the line of her neck: the nape, did they call it? He was sauntering towards her, across perhaps the most opulent bedroom in America. The sound of softly lapping waves filtered through the open windows and, beyond them, a long white beach gleamed in the early evening moonlight. Not bad, Charlie thought, as he often did. Not bad for a workhouse boy. And a chorus girl not so young as she pretended.

Beneath the sweet smells of her innumerable lotions, and the particular perfume, flown in from the fragrant hills of Tuscany, there was still a faint whiff of newness to the room: new fabrics and paints; new draperies and furniture . . . Marion's beachside house (if you could call it a house) was only recently completed. One hundred and eighteen rooms in all, her lover had built for her. Thirty-five bedrooms, fifty-five bathrooms, a brace of swimming pools, a private movie theatre . . . everything, really, a woman's heart could desire, so her lover believed. Wanted to believe.

And somehow Marion pulled it off: transformed this preposterous white elephant, into—not a home, exactly, but a place of merriment and warmth. A place where, despite the marble and the gold and the high ceilings and important stairways curling this direction and that, people could have a good time. They could feel relaxed. Charlie Chaplin felt very relaxed. At Marion Davies's beachside palace. More relaxed, perhaps, than Marion's long-time lover would have preferred.

But what can you do?

Charlie came to a stop just behind her, and then, absently, he dropped a warm kiss on that part of her—the nape?—which had been so distracting him, and breathed in the familiar perfume.

'I didn't ask,' he replied at last.

'You didn't ask? Charlie! Why ever not?'

He kissed her again: inhaled the smell of her skin. 'You really are . . . very lovely,' he murmured.

'Why didn't you ask him, Charlie? I thought you were going to do that. Because I'm all ch-changed now, and ready to l-l-leave. You can see for yourself! I thought you were going to ask him!'

'Well I didn't ask, I informed. I told him that I would be bringing you along.'

'No!'

'In fact—now I think about it, I didn't even do that . . . I informed whoever it was picked up the telephone. The maid, I guess—'

'Oh God. Charlie!'

'Sweetheart—it's a small party. Max and Eleanor Beecham are splendid people . . . Smart people. You know them well enough. What do you think they're going to say? The biggest movie star in history wants to come to their party, bringing with him the reigning Queen of Hollywood—'

'It's not funny . . .'

4

'. . . The finest hostess, the most beautiful and talented actress—'

'I'm not laughing, Charlie. Because you're not being funny. Why's everything got to be a joke with you?'

'And a movie star, too—in her own right . . .'

'Ha! If you don't count it's WR who pays for the movies.'

'And—without wishing to put too fine a point on it—the beloved mistress of the most powerful man in the most powerful nation . . . in the world . . .'

'Oh Charlie, no he's not!'

'Well, you may not think so.'

'He's the s-second. S-second most powerful. It's what he says. After President Hoover. WR says . . .'

'HA! He says that, does he?'

'Because he's more modest than you are, Mr Charlie Chaplin. So it's no use your laughing. In any case, I don't like it when you talk that way. It's vulgar. It's not attractive to me. And who says you're the biggest star in America, anyway?' She flashed him a provocative smile. 'Your good friend Douglas Fairbanks certainly wouldn't agree with you . . .'

'Because my good friend Dougie is a fool . . .'

'Mary Pickford wouldn't agree.'

'She's a floozy.'

'Jack Gilbert, John Barrymore, Gary Cooper, Thomas Mix . . .'

Charlie laughed aloud. 'Sweetie, you insult me!'

'. . . Rudolph Valentino . . .'

'Ah! . . . But you're vicious, Marion. Merciless. Cruel. Rudy may once have been more adored than I am, but in case you didn't notice it, honey, Rudy is dead.'

She sighed. Bored of the game, now. 'Well. I suppose I shall just have to change out of my fancy clothes then. Since you haven't asked if I can come along. And you can go on your own. See how much I care . . .'

But Marion did care. More than she would ever let on to anyone: Not to her ageing lover, the newspaper magnate, multimillionaire, and possibly the second most powerful man in America, William Randolph Hearst. Nor even to Charlie Chaplin. Keeper of everyone's secrets, including his own, and probably her best friend in the whole world. No.

She hated to moan, so she never did. But she was careful. There was never any knowing, even in this crazy town, who thought what about anybody else's business. With Marion's standing in Hollywood society being what it was—ever so high and yet ever so low and, frankly, internationally notorious— there was always a risk when she ventured out in public, and she preferred not to go where there might be a scene. As a result Marion rarely attended other people's parties. And since her own were notoriously the wildest, most extravagant and most glamorous in the city, she didn't generally feel she was losing out.

Even so, Max and Eleanor Beecham's annual shindy had quite a reputation, and she'd never been to it yet. The couple had been holding the party at their house every 17 October since the building was completed, eight long years ago. The party was as close to a tradition as the Hollywood Movie Colony yet knew and, for that alone, it would have been treasured. Added to which, people said it was fun.

No one could compete with Marion when it

6

came to scale: the Beechams were too smart to try. Their party was exquisite and select—never more than fifty people, but always the best (in a manner of speaking). Moguls and movie stars. Sometimes even a sprinkling of European royalty. One year, somehow, they'd managed to produce Mr and Mrs Albert Einstein.

Marion Davies imagined, correctly, that she would know just about every person present. Added to which, WR was out of town and she was tired of staying in. She felt like dressing up and getting canned in some decent company.

None of which would have been enough, ordinarily, to make such a difference. But last week a piece of information regarding the Beecham host and hostess had been brought to her attention and, before Marion acted on it, as she longed to do, she wanted to investigate further.

Most stars never touched their fan mail. But it was well known and often commented upon that Marion Davies read and replied to every one. This particular letter had been delivered, along with the usual weekly sackload, to her bungalow at the MGM studio lot. She was waiting to be called onto set, and it was lying at the top of a large pile of unopened letters on her assistant's desk.

Dear Miss Davies [the letter began], *I hope sincerely that you will forgive me for intruding in this way upon your precious time . . . I have long been a fan of all your movies, and I adored you in Tillie the Toiler . . .*

It was a harmless beginning: crazy, perhaps—because everybody who wrote was crazy—but polite enough. She read on.

. . . However this is not why I am writing. I have a

7

most unusual request . . .

After she had finished reading it, Marion wondered if it was luck or something more sinister which had persuaded the writer to approach her for help. For sure, she and Eleanor had been photographed together at a handful of Hollywood gatherings: they were indeed friends, at least up to a point. And they were of similar ages, perhaps a little older than most of the leading ladies. But since they both lied about that, it was hardly relevant.

There were the rumours about Marion, too, of course, which would have made her an appealing target. But the fans shouldn't have known about them: not even a whisper. The fans shouldn't have known anything—not about her, nor about Eleanor—except what their studio publicists put out.

Of course it was possible—likely, even— that similar letters were languishing, unread or disbelieved, on the desks of film stars' assistants all over town. In any case, it so happened that on this occasion, such a letter could not have been better directed.

When Marion read it, it touched a raw nerve: broke open a secret sore. She did something she only ever did alone, and then only rarely: she wept. Not for herself, but for the Beechams. Later, when they came to fetch her onto set, she locked the letter inside a small jewel box and said not a word about it to anyone.

'What do we know about M-Max and Eleanor Beecham, Charlie?' Marion asked him suddenly. 'I mean to say, just for example, do you imagine it's their real name?

8

'Beecham?' Charlie laughed. 'It would make them quite a rarity in this town if it were. Why don't you ask them tonight?'

'I might j-just do that . . .'

Charlie let it hang there. She would do no such thing, of course. Say what you like about Marion— and people did—but she was never intentionally impolite or unkind.

Even so, Charlie noted, she was on edge this evening. Something was bothering her. 'What's the trouble?'

'Nothing's the trouble, Charlie. We can be curious about each other every once in a while. That's all . . .' She stopped. 'Only, don't you wonder sometimes, what draws us all to . . . w-wash up w-where we do? The way we do? The Beechams, for an example. There they are, y'know? Part of the scenery since I don't even know how long. Can you remember? When you f-first laid eyes on the Beechams? They've just *been there*. Beautiful and clever and on top of the world . . . But where did they come from?'

'He was at Keystone when I first came to Hollywood. Playing piano on set . . . They all adored him there.'

'Well, I know that.'

'Then they teamed up with Butch Menken, didn't they? . . . They made some very fine movies. Between them. You can't say they're not talented.'

'Of c-course I'm not saying it, Charlie. Max Beecham is terrific. One of the best in the wide world . . . Everybody knows that.'

'Let's not go too far.'

'Well I think he is. I think he's a great director, and even if it wasn't such a hit as some of his other

9

ones, I think *Beautiful Day* was the best—the best t-talkie—of last year. Including mine—and you didn't bring any out, Charlie, and I specially said t-talkie—so I can say that. C-can't I?'

'Of course you can, sweetheart.'

'. . . I also think Eleanor is a g-great actress.'

'No better than you are, Marion.'

'But where did they *come from*? Who in hell are they? They seem so . . . together. They've got that beautiful, perfect house, and everybody knows they just adore each other—they're probably the happiest couple in Hollywood . . .'

'It's not saying so much.'

'But you can see the way they look at each other.'

'They seem . . .' Charlie thought about it. 'They do seem to care for each other. Yes.'

'And I mean to say they're a *mystery*. Don't you think?' She stopped. 'I just wonder . . .'

'Wonder about them especially? Or about everyone?'

'What's that?'

'You could ask the same questions about any of us. We all have secrets.'

'Huh? I thought you and I were pretty close friends.'

'Of course we are. But we don't know everything about each other.'

'I should certainly hope not!'

'Exactly. We all embellish. It would be dull if we didn't. Look at Von Stroheim! One of our greatest directors, yes. But do you suppose he's really a count, as he pretends to be?'

'Oh, forget it,' Marion said, suddenly sullen. 'It doesn't even m-matter, anyway.'

'Why ever not?'

10

'I shouldn't have b-brought it up. Eleanor Beecham's a terrific lady. That's all I'm saying . . . Let's get going, shall we? Are you taking me to this stupid party or aren't you?

Charlie checked his not-bad-for-a-workhouse wristwatch. Heavy gold, it was. Cartier. A gift from Marion. 'We're too early yet,' he replied. 'In any case, Marion, the mood you're in, I'm not taking you anywhere. You're so damn miserable you'd reduce the entire party to blubbering tears in less than a minute.'

'Ha! I would not!'

'Nobody'd want to talk to you.'

'Very funny.'

'Except for me of course . . . I always want to talk to you.'

'Well, that's not true— Oh!' she interrupted herself. 'But you know what we need, Ch-Charlie?' she cried, brightening all at once. 'Cocktails! Don't you think so, h-honey? Then we'll *definitely* be in the mood for a party!'

2

High up in the Hollywood Hills, at home in their splendid *Castillo del Mimosa*, Max and Eleanor Beecham were nicely ahead of schedule. Between them, as always, they had everything for the evening under good control. Max had paid sweeteners to all the necessary people to ensure the hooch flowed freely all night. Cases of champagne, vodka, Scotch and gin, and the correct ingredients for every cocktail known to Hollywood man had

11

been delivered discreetly in the early hours of the morning, and tonight the place was heaving with the finest liquor money could buy. Al Capone himself would have been pushed to provide better.

Meanwhile Eleanor had seen to it that the halls, the pool and garden were decked in sweet-smelling and nautically themed California lilacs: white and blue—a subtle reminder to everyone of Max's nautically themed latest movie, *Lost At Sea*. There was a jazz band running through its numbers in the furthest drawing room, where carpets had been removed and furniture carted away; and in front of the house, on the Italianate terrace, beneath a canopy of blue and white nautically themed silk flags, there stood a long banqueting table. It was swathed in silver threaded linen, with a plait of bluebells curling between silver candelabras. The table shimmered under the marching candles and the artful electric light-work of Max's chief gaffer— the most sought-after lighting technician in the business—fresh from the set of *Lost At Sea*.

Eleanor was longing for a drink. But she was of an age now—somewhere in her mid- to late thirties—where even the one drink made her face wilt just a bit, and like any professional actress she knew it well. She also understood how much it mattered. So she was holding out on the liquor until all the guests had arrived and they could move onto the artfully lit terrace.

She was holding out changing into her evening dress, too, for fear of creasing the damn thing. In the meantime—though her short dark hair, shorn into an Eton crop, was perfectly coiffed, and her finely arched eyebrows, her full, wide mouth, her green eyes were perfectly painted—she was still

12

wrapped in an old silk bathrobe.

She had already busied herself with a final, unnecessary tour of the house: just to be extra certain that everything was in place. And so it was. A fleet of waiting staff had already reported for duty and were in the hall, receiving final instructions from the Beecham housekeeper.

And so she stood: at a loose end on her Italianate terrace, gazing at those silken flags, fluttering like bunting in the electric light. They'd been Max's idea—because of the movie. Had he seen them yet? She supposed not. Eleanor hadn't realized, when the designers described them to her, quite how low they would hang, nor quite how they would resemble . . . Gosh, she hated them. But it was too late. It was just too bad. Max had said he wanted them. She wondered if he'd had any idea . . .

Eleanor had nothing much to do. The last few lobsters were being boiled in their shells in the kitchen: she could hear the squeak. The scream. She could hear the scream and it made her shiver. The cook had prepared the hollandaise—the oysters were set in aspic. It was done. Everything was done. She sighed. Nervous as hell: of course. Nervous as ever—but this time, somehow, she was nervous without being excited. When had this wonderful party—this highlight of the Hollywood social calendar, this manifestation of her and Max's extraordinary success—when had it lost its magic and turned into a chore?

She wondered briefly, bitterly, was it a chore to Max too? Who the hell knew?

She'd left him upstairs, changing, but she needed to discuss with him various things. She needed to tell him about the problem with the ice sculptures in the front hallway. And she needed to say something about the far arc light, behind the mimosa on the eastern end of the terrace. It looked as if it might be dipping slightly . . . She wandered up to join him.

He was already bathed and dressed: bending awkwardly over the looking glass at her dressing table, slicking back his dark hair with one hand, smoking a cigarette with the other. He was wearing a white evening jacket and matching, loose-fitting pants. Handsome as ever. It always struck her, even now, in spite of everything, just how handsome he was: fit, slim, well built, dark, elegant—good enough to be a movie star himself, if he'd wanted it. She still loved the look of him. Sometimes. And it still took her by surprise.

'Hello, handsome,' she said, putting her two arms around his waist—sensing his body tense at the intrusion, and hating him for it—hating herself for not having remembered, once again, how painful it was, to try to breathe warmth on his coldness. 'Nice jacket! I've not seen that get-up before—have I?'

He glanced at her reflection as she stood behind him; at the green eyes, not really smiling at him. He turned and pecked her on the end of her nose. 'You've seen it often,' he said smoothly, removing her hands. 'By the way,' he added, 'did Teresa tell you? Chaplin called.'

'He did?' She sighed, exasperated. 'When? This evening? Because if he's not coming, he might have told us so before this evening.'

'Sure he's coming! He called to say he was bringing Marion.'

'Oh! . . . You mean Marion Davies?'

14

'Of course, Marion Davies. What other Marion?'

'Well . . . that's a bit awkward . . .'

'I don't see why. Marion's all right.'

'I didn't say she wasn't.' Eleanor turned away from her husband, sat herself on the edge of the marital bed: a bed so wide they could have fitted a lover in there each, and hardly bumped elbows. She sighed again. Who in hell could she put beside Marion for dinner?

'I thought it was kind of flattering,' he said, smiling a little, elegantly shamefaced. 'Maybe now she's gatecrashing our party, she and Mr Hearst will finally invite us up to San Simeon.'

'Hah . . .' Eleanor offered up a soft, half-laugh. 'Yes indeed . . . Wouldn't that be something?'

The beauty of San Simeon was legend. The luxury of Randolph Hearst's fairytale castle 200 miles north of Los Angeles, perched high on a fairytale hill overlooking San Simeon bay was legend, too. But the house parties he and Marion held there were the greatest part of the legend of all—not just in Hollywood but around the world. Invitations were delivered by chauffeur, in envelopes so fine, so deliciously soft and fragrant they might been pulled from Marion Davies's own underclothing drawer. Nobody turned them down.

'And in the meantime,' Eleanor added, 'I guess I'm going to have to rearrange the whole damn seating plan . . .'

Max looked down at his wife, watching as she absently gathered the silk robe around her, and crossed her smooth brown legs, one over the other. It shocked him every time, after all these years, but there were moments when her sensuality moved him still. 'What is that thing, a bath gown?' he

15

asked her.

She looked down at the robe. Didn't bother to reply. He'd seen it a hundred times before. And then—yet again—he surprised her, swooped suddenly and kissed her. She moved her face before he could reach her, and his lips caught the edge of her cheek. 'You'll have every guy in the place swooning, just as you are,' he said. And it sounded tender. As if he meant it.

She gave him a tight smile, refused to return his gaze for fear he might notice his effect, the hopeless burst of happiness—and pushed him away. 'Only, it's rather difficult, isn't it?' she said, just as if he hadn't spoken, 'especially with so little notice. Because you never really know who's going to turn out to be the most terrible bluenose. Not really. The oddest people go funny around Marion . . . especially after a few drinks. I don't want her coming to our house to be insulted.'

'Nobody's going to insult her,' he said, turning back to the dressing table.

'Well. They had better not. Poor girl.' Eleanor pulled herself up, glanced vaguely around her, sighed lightly '. . . I guess I'd better do something about the seating. Come down, Max. When you can. Come and see. They've finished on the terrace. It's looking . . .' She stopped, uncertain how to finish. 'Have you seen it?' she asked instead. 'Have you seen the bunting? The flags?'

'I have,' he replied. A short silence. Hardly noticeable. 'Very nautical,' he added, with a little smile.

'Yes. Nautical . . . Lovely,' Eleanor added quickly. 'Don't you think?'

He didn't disagree.

16

She told him about the problem with the ice sculptures, and the dipping arc light in the far eastern corner, but he wasn't really listening.

'By the way, El,' he shouted after her. 'For God's sake don't put Marion beside Von Stroheim. He's pretty crazy at the moment. And he never could stand the sight of her . . .'

3

Three hours later, the Beechams' famous 17 October Supper Party was in full and boisterous swing. Eleanor's aquamarine satin sheath dress, which brought out the magical green in her eyes had, indeed, become a little creased. And Eleanor knew quite well that after the third glass of champagne—or was it the fourth?—her face was more than a fraction wilted. But, as she kept reminding herself, it didn't matter. Not any more. In the softly falling terrace lights, and with the liquor freely flowing, no one was going to notice anyway. Everyone was canned. For the hundredth time that evening, she told herself to relax.

There had been an incident with one of the waitresses shortly before the guests arrived which hadn't helped to ease her mood. But she really ought to have shaken it off by now. These sort of things happened to movie stars all the time. Thomas Mix found one in his bathtub. Gary Cooper (who lived in the house next door) was constantly encountering them roaming his private grounds. Mary Pickford found one splashing about in her swimming pool. It came with the territory . . . There

17

were always stories of stray fans slipping through the stars' careful barricades, and it wasn't the first time it had happened to Eleanor, either. Perhaps, Eleanor considered, if the wretched girl had been anywhere else, holding anything else, on any night but this one, it would have felt less threatening: simply an amusing story to tell. But Eleanor found her right there in the bedroom—standing, guilty as a thief, at the same dressing table she'd left Max at only half an hour earlier. In the girl's hand was a heavy gold photograph frame; and in her eyes— Eleanor shuddered—dark pools of emotion and fear: all the madness of a fan obsessed. Eleanor had never seen it so close, and it frightened her. She had shouted for help, and within moments, Joseph the houseman had been there, standing beside her, and then, just a little later, Max had come, too. The wretched girl, sobbing uncontrollably, clutching Eleanor's precious gold photograph frame until it was taken from her hand, had been escorted safely from the property.

It was nothing. A hazard of the job. Poor girl . . . Max had brushed it off; told Eleanor not to fuss. She should take comfort, he teased, considering some of the notices for her last picture, that there were still fans out there who cared enough to bother. And he was right of course. These things happened.

In the meantime here she sat, the Queen of her own fairy tale. She should try to enjoy it. The evening's guests were seated at the long banquet table before her, deep in noisy conversation, and from what she could tell, they were happy to be there. The freshly boiled lobster had been eaten and carried away, and so, by now, had all remnants

18

of the perfectly judged, entirely exquisite Beecham Supper Party feast . . . She could hear the sound of the jazz band filtering delightfully through the open windows. Soon, after coffee, and more drinking, she would slip quietly inside and ask them to snazz up the tempo, and there would be dancing. Everything was just as it was supposed to be. Everything was Lovely.

Eleanor had decided, finally, to put Marion in place of honour, beside clever, gently spoken Irving Thalberg, whom Marion knew well. She had placed herself on Irving's other side. Not because she liked him (although it happened that she did), but because, as chief executive producer at MGM, the largest and most profitable studio in Hollywood, he was the most powerful man at the table, if not the industry. And since her seven-year contract with the almost as large, but not quite so magnificent, Lionsfiel Pictures was shortly up for renewal, it seemed like a good time to foster relationships with the alternatives.

On her right side she put Douglas Fairbanks, who was tiresome in all sorts of ways, but a big star—and he would have been offended if she hadn't. Max, far away at the other end of the table, had Gloria Swanson on his right side, for the same reason.

But he must have switched round the name cards on his left, because where Irving's wife, Norma, was meant to be sitting, there sat none other than Blanche Williams, chief feature writer for *Photoplay* magazine.

Eleanor knew, because Butch Menken had told her; and Butch knew because . . . Butch made it his business to know everything. Also because he knew a German actress who lived in the same block, and the German actress had spotted Max going in and out of Blanche Williams's apartment on numerous occasions. So Eleanor knew. Or she almost knew. And she had known (or almost known) for a couple of years now.

Did Max know she knew? Did he even care? She could never be sure, not about anything, any more, let alone who knew what about anyone else . . . Christ.

She could leave him, of course. And maybe one day she would. But not today . . . Eleanor needed to think of something else.

She wondered if Irving Thalberg was aware that her deal with Lionsfiel was up for renewal. Probably not. Should she tell him? Or would it be just too awkward? And if he already knew, would he perhaps suggest she came across to MGM?

Of course he wouldn't.

Why would he do that? *Why would he do that?* Perhaps she should boast to him about the fan she'd only just encountered in her own bedroom? He might be impressed. He might even think— Eleanor pinched herself. She was drunk. Any minute now, if she wasn't careful, she was going to burst into tears.

A passing waiter refilled her glass. She swallowed it back without tasting it, fixed a blank smile to her beautiful, full lips, and allowed her gaze to travel down the table. Stars, stars—and more stars . . . Buster Keaton and Natalie Talmadge . . . Gary Cooper from just next door, John Gilbert, Greta Garbo, Charlie Chaplin, Cecil DeMille . . . and Mary Pickford, of course, sitting beside her husband, Douglas Fairbanks, because tiresome

20

Douglas would never have it any other way . . .
And sprinkled between the stars were the others:
the studio executives, the producers, the writers;
all the big cheeses who helped to make Hollywood
the money factory it had now become. Yes, Eleanor
reassured herself once again, it was a good crowd.
She and Max could certainly pull them in . . .

Everything was just fine.

. . . Were the flags hanging too low, so close to
the candlelight . . .?

Concentrate.

Max was—was he?—was he running a finger
along Blanche Williams's cheek? He should stop it!
She should put a stop—

Concentrate.

Dougie Fairbanks was talking to her.
He was saying something as if it were quite
fascinating . . . Someone's chauffeur had made
a killing on the stock market . . . She hardly
needed to listen. These days, everyone knew
someone who knew a chauffeur who'd made a
killing. In fact conversation around Eleanor's
star-studded banqueting table wasn't much
different from conversation at a million dining
tables across America that night. There was
only one thing anyone ever seemed to want to
talk about any more: who'd made how much on
what stock and at what margin . . . the increase in
values of Bethlehem Steel versus General Motors,
National Waterworks versus United Founders . . .
The stock market was everyone's obsession.

Added to which, it happened that the day of the
Beecham Supper Party, 17 October 1929, had been
a reassuringly good day on Wall Street: an excellent
day, after a disconcertingly bad one, at the end of a

21

record-breaking summer. There had been a couple of serious wobbles at the beginning of the month, 'just to keep things exciting', Max and his friends confidently agreed, but that morning, newspapers had been filled with the comforting forecasts of the experts:

'Stock prices,' declared Professor Fisher of the University of Yale, 'look as if they have reached a permanently high plateau.' His respected voice was just one of a chorus of bullish experts, academics, business moguls and financiers, and the markets had taken comfort. Up, up and up went the stock prices again, back on their apparently relentless rise. It meant that anyone who'd put in a call to their brokers before sitting down to dinner— and that included most of Eleanor's guests and Eleanor's husband, too—would be wanting to chew over their successes this evening.

But not Eleanor. On this particular night, 17 October, with fifty-one guests to worry about, and a dipping arc light, and Marion Davies, and the flags, and bloody Max, kissing her so tenderly one minute that her heart swelled with hope, and talking so animatedly with Blanche Williams the next, Eleanor was finding the usual subject less than compelling.

'Well that's just too fantastic, Dougie,' she said blandly. 'He must be one happy chauffeur.'

'Isn't it terrific!' Douglas Fairbanks shouted. Because Douglas always shouted. Because he hated not to be the centre of attention. 'And isn't that such a terrific feeling!' He turned to the rest of the table: 'Doesn't everyone think? Don't you think so, Von Stroheim? Isn't it great to know we live in a country where your average Joe can turn

22

himself into a millionaire just by . . . *knowing how to do it*? Mr So-and-So from Nowheres-Ville can make a million! Just like that! Just like you and me! *That's* why I love America!' He thumped the table with such emphasis it made Eleanor jump. '*That's* why I'm proud to be an American! Charlie-boy, c'mon. Admit it!' he shouted. 'You heard Professor What-Not, Tuesday. You heard what the man said! Are you telling me you know better than the professor from Yale?'

But on this, as Douglas knew well, his friend Charlie Chaplin would never agree with him, nor with Professor What-Not from Yale. Charlie— an Englishman, in any case—was, that night, the solitary voice of caution among them. 'You know exactly what I think, Dougie,' Charlie said wearily. He'd said it many times before. 'You got people making money out of money that never even existed in the first place! It's a trick of the light, I keep telling you. It's a whole pile of nothing, built on a mountain of Zilch. It can't go on.'

'Aw, Charlie!' groaned Marion. 'Don't go getting started on that again! . . . J-just *nobody* wants to hear it!'

Charlie smiled at her. Shrugged. 'Dougie asked me,' he said. 'In any case, I'm only passing on what I've been told by the experts . . .'

'By ONE expert!' Douglas Fairbanks shouted. 'And you know, you keep on about your "expert" like the guy's some kind of oracle . . . but he's a solitary, single voice, Charlie-boy. There's no one out there supporting him . . .'

'There's going to be a crash.' Charlie shrugged. 'It's what he told me. And it's going to be catastrophic. It's only a matter of when . . .

23

Personally—as you know, Dougie—I'm out.' He looked up and down the table. 'I'm guessing I must be the only person round this table without a stock to my name. Ha! Maybe I'm the only person in the entire business!'

'Butch Menken's sold out,' someone commented. Not Eleanor.

'Butch sold up, did he?' Charlie said. He looked at Mary Pickford, whose voice had provided the information. 'When, I wonder? Do you know?'

'Oh, a couple of weeks back. I considered following him . . .' She smiled. 'Where Butch Menken leads . . .' she said.

'. . . We all should follow,' Charlie finished for her wryly. 'Well. He's a smart man.' Eleanor said nothing. She examined the silver-plated dessert fork in her hand, didn't glance up. There was a tiny lull, hardly perceptible—because of the history: Butch, Max and Eleanor used to be thicker than thieves. It was quickly, tactfully, broken by Marion.

'Made a killing though, dintcha, Charlie?' she called out. 'Every s-single stock he owned. Sold the lot. Pretty much, huh? Imagine it! And now he's sore, because if he'd stayed in just one more day, or two more days, he would have made another k-killing, same as all the rest of us! Isn't it so, Charlie!'

'All I'm saying . . .' Charlie paused, sighed, and apparently thought better of continuing. '. . . Just don't come crying to me when all the money's gone . . .'

'Ha! It won't be for m-money that M-Marion comes crying to you, Charlie boy . . .' declared Douglas.

He looked around to collect the laughter—

24

but was met instead with a brief, shocked silence. His wife, beside him, put a quietening hand on his shoulder. 'Isn't that right, Mary?' he said to her weakly.

He was drunk. Clearly. And a fool. Everybody knew it. Even so . . . Eleanor glanced nervously at Marion.

'Such beautiful candelabra,' Mary Pickford said smoothly, in her sweet, steely voice. 'Tell me, Eleanor, did you pick them up in Europe?'

Eleanor turned to her gratefully. She was about to say yes, to tell Mary a touching story of how she'd discovered them—all eighteen of them—covered in dust in a little antique market on a side street in *Roma*—

'Oh, they're terrific little antiques!' broke in Douglas. 'They remind me of a funny incident a few years ago . . .'

Eleanor longed to lean across and apologize to Marion, but so long as the stupid *shoyte* continued to jabber at her, it seemed quite impossible.

'. . . I had the candelabra in the one hand and there was I,' he bellowed, 'a hundred foot up on the rigging, the whole damn thing swaying. Next thing—WHOOSH! . . . The entire set's up in flames and I'm thinking to myself—I kid you not—I AM GOING TO DIE! Right here, right now. And I'm dressed as Robin Hood of Sherwood Forest!'

Eleanor, not really listening, offered him only the wannest of smiles.

'Imagine me, El!' he cried stubbornly, determined to get a better response, 'I'm a hundred foot in the air . . .' He stood up, grasping the nearest candelabra as he rose, his infuriating, actorish laughter filling the air. He held the flames

25

aloft, waving them this way and that—

'. . . I'm holding onto that rigging for grim death! . . .'

Eleanor watched him. Felt the cold, wet fear crawling slowly over her skin. Felt her lungs tighten, making it hard for her to breathe.

She saw only the tip of the candle, the flame, and the tip of the flag . . .

'. . . Next thing, WHOOSH! . . .' Douglas shouted.

She sat quite still as he and the light swayed this way and that, from side to side and back again, flickering flame against dainty, deadly silken flag. She opened her mouth to protest . . .

'HA HA HA! Can you *imagine* it, El?'

But she couldn't hear him any more.

'There I am. A man in tights!'

Her lungs had filled . . .

'In *tights*, I tell you!' shouted Douglas, laughing and swaying. She couldn't breathe . . .

'A *man* in *tights*! HA HA HA!'

There was a taste of smoke in her mouth, in her throat, and she could feel it . . . blackening her insides as it burned its path through her chest, scorching, melting, choking—

'WHOOSH! WHOOSH! FIRE! HA HA!'

And then, somehow, Max was beside her, taking the candelabra from Dougie's fist, placing it back on the table. 'Eleanor,' he said loud and clear, his strong hand on her shoulder . . . 'Honey. I think it's time we were on that dance floor, don't you? They got the best Charleston playing . . . can you hear it? . . . It's got my feet tip-tapping like nothing else . . .'

Eleanor smiled. Quickly, gratefully, feeling his touch, willing herself to recover. 'I can hear it!' she said, in the mellifluous voice she could use. 'It's too perfect! Let's not sit a moment longer!' But she was shaking. Max could feel it. He could feel her shoulder convulsing beneath his hand.

He bent across the table and kissed her. There and then. In front of everyone. Someone sighed, '*Awwww* . . .', possibly Marion. The kiss lasted a second or two longer than expected, giving Eleanor time to collect herself. Douglas Fairbanks, observing it disconsolately, leaned down to Mary Pickford and kissed her on the lips, too.

'Mary, my darling wife, I adore you!' he cried.

'Oh, for crying out l-loud, Dougie!' Marion said. 'P-pipe down for once in your life, why dontcha?'

And then Max and Eleanor pulled apart, Eleanor smiling at her husband. She stood up. 'I hesitate to imagine what you've been discussing at this end of the table,' Max said to everyone, but looking only at his wife. 'I'm afraid we've been talking nothing but Investment Trusts, down our end . . .'

'Eleanor, darling, you can't even imagine how dull we've been!' drawled Gloria Swanson.

'Humblest apologies, Gloria,' Max flashed her a smile. 'We'll do better next year, I promise.'

'Except of course, if we're to believe Charlie Chaplin,' Eleanor said, with her lovely light smile, her beautiful soft voice, flirtatious and humouring to everyone around, 'we shall all be in the poorhouse next year, anyway. There won't be any parties!'

There followed plenty of laughter, and the scraping of chairs: chairs which, had Douglas bothered to look at them closely, he might have noticed were as familiar as the terrific little antique candelabra, and the terrific banqueting table, too.

27

Every scrap was due to be returned to the studio props department first thing in the morning.

'No more dullness!' declared Max, 'or Gloria Swanson might go home in a sulk. And none of us wants that! It's a party, for God's sakes. Added to which—except for Charlie—we all made a fortune today!'

'God Bless America!' cried Douglas Fairbanks.

Max ignored him. 'Let's dance!' he commanded. And for a brief, uplifting moment the brilliant director, handsome as the devil himself, and his dazzling movie-star wife, were united again; and they were happy. He squeezed her hand and led her across their nautically themed, Italianate terrace, through the sweet-smelling hallway decked in blue and white lilies, onto the centre of the dance floor . . . And though they hardly noticed it, alone in their fragile cocoon, the cream of America's fame and beauty followed close behind . . .

Nobody talked about Investment Trusts for the rest of the evening. And they danced until five in the morning.

4

Too often, in a soured marriage, such uplifting moments do more harm than good, and only serve to make the thud of the landing more painful.

Max was gone by the time the maid came in with Eleanor's tea the next day. It arrived on a tray at eleven thirty, with the usual glass of freshly squeezed lemon juice, unsweetened, the usual small pile of pre-selected mail; and a

28

small, square, leather jewel box. She took a gulp of the juice. Shuddered. And opened the box.

Every year, on the morning after the party, he gave her something precious. This—a large ruby pendant in the shape of a heart—was larger and more precious than last year's jewel; she imagined because of their recent successes on the stock market. And beautiful, too. No doubt about that. Max had excellent taste. She shuddered once again as the last of the juice went down, laid the ruby heart back in its box, set it aside. She could hardly bring herself to touch it. Why a heart, of all things? A heart—how absurd! She wondered—what did he give to Blanche? A ruby pendant in the shape of a goddamn *putz*?

She laughed to herself, though she didn't find it funny, and looked about for the accompanying envelope. There was always an envelope. She wished she could ignore it, simply not open it, because what could he say that would ever make it all right again? What could he say that wouldn't hurt?

Darling,
Another wonderful night!
Enjoy your morning. You certainly earned it.
Your ever-loving,
Max

She put the letter down. *Ever-loving.* Indeed. Had he forgotten what it was all for? This night of nights? He never mentioned it. Never said a word . . . Gosh, her head was throbbing so—she must have drunk more than she realized.

She could hear the people downstairs, still

clearing away the residue of the party. If she stayed up here long enough, as she fully intended, there'd be no evidence of the party at all by the time she went down there. The bunting, the flowers—the eighteen candelabra, the silver-threaded linen table cloth, the banqueting table, too—all of it borrowed, all of it gone. And she could forget about it until next year came round again. If it ever did.

She wallowed, briefly, in the pleasure of not having to get out of bed. Her last picture only wrapped at the weekend—so she'd enjoyed a few days to herself. And she knew well to treasure them. In fact . . . she glanced at the post on her tray and saw, with a familiar twist of anxiety, a familiar-looking package tucked away at the bottom of the pile.

Already, then. That was too bad.

There would be a one-page synopsis at the top, first of the plot, and then of her character's part in it. And through the following eighty-odd pages of film script, her designated role in whatever movie had been chosen for her would have been underlined. And there it would be. No message, no discussion. Just a whole lot of new lines to be learned. And a reminder to Eleanor that, though she may be a star in Main Street America, not to mention in the hearts of the odd stray, crazy fan, at Lionsfiel Pictures she was only an employee—a single, shiny cog in a very large, very shiny machine. It was how the system worked. She did as she was told. They paid her handsomely. Eleanor had learned long ago that you could never win against the might of the Studio.

And no matter what, no matter how good she was, one day, it would surely happen, because one day it happened to them all—and to the women sooner than the men. One fine morning Eleanor would open up that familiar-looking package, delivered to her by her maid on her sunny breakfast tray, and discover that her moment in the limelight was passed. The screenplay's leading role would not be underlined for her, having been underlined for somebody else—somebody younger, fresher, more beautiful, more alluring, *better* . . . It was a morning every contract movie star learned to dread.

Eleanor was—how old? She'd lied about it so often, she honestly didn't know any more. What did it matter? She still looked young. They could make her look young: with the best flat lighting, she didn't look a day over twenty-five.

There was absolutely nothing to worry about.

Even so, she chose not to open the package. Not just yet. Instead she leaned back against her lovely plumped-up pillows, on her magnificent, giant bed, in her beautiful sun-filled bedroom; sipped the tea which her maid had delivered, and mulled over the events of the previous evening.

Max was quite right about the party's success. Except for the unpleasant interlude with Dougie— Dougie, of all people!—and then the dreadful moment with the candelabra, it had been a splendid night: better than previous years, for all sorts of reasons, not least the unexpected presence of Marion Davies. Which was quite a coup, whatever way you looked at it.

Not just a coup: a pleasure.

Marion had pulled Eleanor aside after dinner, pulled her right off the dance floor, thrust a cocktail glass into her hand, clinked their two glasses together, winked at her. And downed her drink in

31

one. 'That was a lovely thing you did b-back then,' she said, wiping her mouth with the back of her hand.

'It was?' Eleanor was confused. She hadn't done anything. 'W-what you said to Dougie . . .'

'But I didn't! I didn't say anything!'

'I mean to say, the way you looked at him. The way you refused to laugh.'

'Oh! But I wanted to do so much more! Only I wasn't sure if you had even heard him, and then I thought it was better not to fuss—I am so sorry, Marion. I can't apologize enough . . .'

'You m-made him feel like a sap.'

'You think so?'

'Ha!'

There was a long pause, a peculiar pause, as if Marion were on the point of saying something else, something terribly important. But then, at the last second, she seemed to balk at it. '. . . I just wanted to tell you, th-thank you,' she said instead. 'That's all. And I was thinking. Well, I was thinking it *anyway*. But I wanted to ask you up to San Simeon. Would you come to San Simeon if I asked?'

'Of course!' Eleanor had replied. 'We would love that, Marion.'

'Next week or something,' she mumbled. 'Real soon. I'll fix it up for the week after next. Are you free?'

'Well . . .' Eleanor laughed. 'Absolutely. We're free. We've both just wrapped.'

'I know you just wrapped.' Marion winked at her. 'It's too perfect, isn't it? Next Monday then. How about it? I'll get a good crowd up, I promise. And I'll send you all the stuff you need. Tickets and so on . . . Don't worry about any of it.'

'Next Monday . . . Max will be delighted.' And then, suddenly, with the smallest hiccup, Marion had lurched forward and enfolded Eleanor in the tightest, warmest embrace. It lasted several seconds. She rested her head on Eleanor's shoulder, squeezed her, clung to her and then, just as abruptly, released her and without looking at Eleanor again, quickly swung away.

It was, Eleanor decided, looking back, a most peculiar moment and, because of the warmth, one of the high points of her evening. Marion had mentioned the invitation to San Simeon again as she was leaving. She would send a car round with the train tickets later on in the week. So maybe, Eleanor thought—maybe she actually meant it?

Other than that, Marion had kept herself perfectly busy, of course: smooched half the night with Charlie Chaplin, until Charlie spotted the little Von Stroheim protégée, barely in her teens, poor little thing . . .

She'd danced with Gary Cooper for a while, but he was in the middle of a movie and had slipped away early; staggered across the garden in the moonlight, and taken a back route home through the Beecham grounds to avoid fans at his own gateway. After that, she'd latched onto John Gilbert. It would have been perfect—except of course then La Garbo decided to kick up the usual stink, which was pretty rich, reflected Eleanor, considering Greta hadn't even arrived with John Gilbert that night. Considering Greta had actually spent most of the night in a hot, dark corner with Miss Lilyan Tashman . . . Eleanor smiled to herself. Holy cow, if her public could have seen her! If *Irving* could have seen her! Too bad he'd already left . . . The girl only had a handful of movies behind her—and not even a talkie among them, yet Greta Garbo acted like the Queen of Sheba.

Eleanor glanced again at the script package on her breakfast tray. Greta was ten years younger than she was, that was the truth. And beautiful. Just too damn beautiful. Nobody could compete. Nobody stood a goddamn chance . . .

She wouldn't open it. Not yet.

Her mind turned, before she could stop it, to Little Miss Blanche Williams, chief feature writer—

Much better to open the script.

There it still was, lying there. So what was stopping her? *Mermaids* had grossed over $1.3 million, for crying out loud.

Meanwhile Greta hadn't even made the transition to talkies.

Over $1.3 million!

There'd been three other pictures since, of course, each one grossing less than the one before. And then came the last, the real turkey, disdained by viewers and reviewers both.

'Whatever has become of this once vibrant actress?' wrote the critic in *American Mercury*. *'Eleanor Beecham's performance is her most dull and lifeless yet. Maybe it's time the good people at Lionsfiel pulled the curtain on a talent long since spent, before La Beecham's name becomes a by-word for Films You Definitely Want to Miss!'*

Fuck.

Fuck all of them. Eleanor felt sick.

What was Blanche Williams doing, sitting in place of honour, anyway? Why had she come at all?

Because Max had insisted upon it. That was why. He'd told Eleanor he owed it to Blanche, after the write-up Blanche gave his last movie. So maybe he did owe it to her. He owed all sorts of people all sorts of things. He hadn't invited them and it wasn't why he invited her. He invited her because he was screwing her. And probably because she insisted on it. And because she had the sort of hold on him any woman has on a man when he particularly, especially, enjoys screwing her.

Eleanor didn't want to think about that. Not this morning. Not today. She didn't want to think about Max. She didn't want to think about the studio. She didn't want to think about her failing career, her fading looks, her philandering husband . . .

Deliberately, she turned her mind to Butch.

Sometimes it helped to think about him. But not this morning. This morning his name conjured nothing but guilt and sadness—and a churning of lust—and nothing . . .

And then unbidden, inescapable, always in her mind, always there, always waiting, came the face of Isha, three years old, waxy with the fever, sobbin

—Only the nice letters made it to Eleanor's breakfast tray, generally. Invitations were allowed through, and personal notes (and the scripts, of course, because they were unavoidable). And then, every few months—less and less often, actually— This.

Her heart missed a beat.

5

Eleanor stared at the letter. Postmarked Reno, as it always was, wrapped in the same dull brown envelope, and with no name above the address. She tore it open.

Dear Miss Kappelman,

As one of our most valued clients [she read], I am writing to inform you of sad recent events.

After 25 years' devoted service to this Bureau, which Bureau, you are no doubt aware, he himself founded, my beloved father sadly passed away last month. Since then, as he and I had always arranged, I have left my employment with Reno City Police and taken up the reins. It is a sad point in time for me, but also a point in time I have long awaited and I am eager for the challenges that lie ahead . . .

Eleanor skipped on impatiently.

. . . Madam, you will observe from the enclosed that our rates have increased . . .

Yes, yes, yes.

. . . I note that progress in the case has, to date, been somewhat slow. Not least as a consequence of the limited information you have provided. Nevertheless, please rest assured that we are dedicated to discovering the truth, and continue to work tirelessly, leaving no stone unturned. I can tell you that already we are making definite strides forward.

Please do not hesitate to contact me here at your convenience, should you have any questions regarding the case, or should any further information come to light that you feel

36

*might aid us in our work. Or, if you would
like to pay a visit to us at the bureau here in
Reno, I can assure you of a warm welcome. Of
course I understand however that it is a long
way to travel. In the meantime I will make it my
business to keep you abreast of each and every
development by post.*

*I would be grateful if you could attend to the
enclosed invoice at your earliest convenience.*

Respectfully yours,

Mr. Matthew Gregory

Eleanor reread the letter once, twice, three times,
desperate to discover any hidden message behind
the lines—but it seemed the more she read it, the
more cryptic it became. So Gregory Senior was
dead. She had never met him. She didn't feel much
sorrow at the news. Perhaps the new man would be
more efficient? He sounded as though he might.
He certainly sounded optimistic—didn't he? Yes he
did. And it was wonderful.

Perhaps a fresh pair of eyes might yet be able to
see something new, something they had all been
missing? Perhaps he truly had made some strides
forward? Perhaps . . . Perhaps . . . After all, a fresh
pair of eyes . . .

Perhaps, after all, it might even do some good
for her to visit him in Reno?

She laughed at the idea. And then suddenly
stopped. Asked herself again—after all, why not?

He would recognize her. That was one reason
why not. He would know who she was. There would
be questions. It would be dangerous . . . But she
would find a way around them, after all these years.
Of course she could.

Why not?

Why not indeed? A minute ago it had seemed like sheer madness. Now, suddenly, it was not only possible, but imperative.

She could feel, from nowhere, the slow burning of hope—the faintest trace of the tidal wave she had been keeping in check for so long. She needed to talk to Max. She needed to explain . . . He didn't know about Mr Gregory—Junior or Senior. But she would tell him. Now. This morning. She would tell him—that she had never given up. Even if he had.

And he could come with her or not. She wanted him to come more than almost anything. But if he wouldn't come, she would travel alone. She had waited long enough. Suddenly she could not wait a moment longer.

She called him at work, though she didn't like to, and was put through to his secretary. 'Why Mrs Beecham!' the woman cried when she heard Eleanor's voice, 'I've been longing for you to telephone us, all this time! Only so I could say to you in person how much I adored your last picture. And I know Mr Beecham mentioned it didn't do so well as some of the others. Well, I know it didn't because of course we keep a track on all that sort of thing here. It's our business, isn't it? Who's doing what, where. It's all madness, isn't it! But I swear, I thought it was splendid! You had me weeping from start to finish.'

'My gosh—thank you,' said Eleanor, with her beautiful manners. 'That's so good of you . . . Always so good to hear. Thank you . . . Could you—'

'And the lilac dress in the final scene! I never

saw anything so stunning!'

'Yes it was a lovely dress—'

'And how was the party last night? It was last night, wasn't it? Mr Beecham was pleased as punch with his new jacket—we had the costume girls in doing last-minute adjustments yesterday morning. You should have seen them—running around like little crazy things. Yes, Mr Beecham, no Mr Beecham. Anything for you, Mr Beecham!'

'Mrs Monroe—Is he about?'

'Is he about?' She sounded confused.

'Only I need to speak to him rather urgently. Could you—can you possibly find him for me? Please.'

'Well. I can certainly try . . .'

'That would be so kind.'

'But you know he's not here.'

'Not in the office?'

'Why, no! He's not coming in today. I thought he was with you.'

'With me?'

Too late, Mrs Monroe realized her mistake.

'Oh, but what am I saying? I'm nothing but a butter brain, Mrs Beecham! He's probably in with . . . probably just bashing something out with Mr Silverman right next door, just like he always is! Shall I take a quick peek? If you wait right there . . .'

'No,' Eleanor said quickly. 'Thank you, Mrs Monroe. It doesn't matter at all. I'll find him later.'

She hung up. Took a deep breath, and another. It was nothing new. There was nothing new about it.

After that, she didn't allow herself to wallow. Eleanor never allowed herself to wallow. She simply dressed and packed. She fetched one of her personalized cards from the drawer of her dressing table, and beneath their curly, gold-embossed initials, entwined, wrote her husband a note:

Darling,
I called the studio, but you were busy, busy! Mrs Monroe offered to go in search, but then she said you might have gone out of town on reconnaissance and really I couldn't wait. Darling, you remember I showed you a letter once from a little detective I had found in Reno and you thought so little of him? Well, I never mentioned him again because I knew it made you so cross but I went ahead and employed him, because . . . well, of course you know why. Matz, he died. But now his son has written, and I think he has something important to tell us. He has asked me to Reno to meet with him and of course I must go. I will call you the first moment I have any news.
Your ever-loving wife,
Eleana

She placed it, carefully, at a jaunty angle on her sunny dressing table, paused, and looked at it again. She looked at it for a long time.

When had she last called him Matz? Seeing it written, and her own, Eleana, beneath it, took her by surprise; brought a stab of pain. She had no idea what had possessed her to use their old names. She snatched up the card and ripped it into pieces. She opened the drawer, took out a fresh card, and started again:

M,
I shall be gone for a few days. I think it's about
time we talked, don't you?
E

She placed the card, carefully, at a less jaunty angle, on the same sunny dressing table, pinned beneath the heavy gold-framed photograph. She picked up her bag, leaving the rest of her post unopened, the script unread, the forgotten jewel, more precious than last year's, half hidden beneath a cold, dry piece of toast. And then she left the house before she had a chance to think better of it.

6

'It's probably gonna sound funny,' Blanche Williams was saying, a couple of miles down the road. 'But I have respect for your wife. I have a lot of respect for her. I thought she looked just about as classy and dazzling as a girl can look in that emerald-green get-up last night.'

He had his head between her legs; his tongue inside her sweet, juicy *knish* . . . Half a second ago she'd been purring like a pussycat . . . Dammit. He put a soothing hand on her stomach, gave her ass a little pinch, and stayed right where he was, just as if she hadn't spoken.

But once Blanche started on a topic, as by now he knew quite well, there was rarely any chance of her dropping it.

'She's beautiful,' Miss Williams continued, 'she's mysterious. God knows, she's a terrific actress . . . at

41

least, that is, when she wants to be. And you know with all that, I got to ask myself—' Blanche hoiked herself onto an elbow to look at him—'what in hell you're doing spending your time with a Little Miss Nobody like me?'

He paused. Stopped. Lifted his head. 'What's that, sweetie?' he muttered.

'I was just saying . . .'

Max gave up. He stretched across her naked body for the cigarette pack, lit up two, one for each of them, and lay back on the pillow beside her. '. . . I heard what you were saying, baby.'

'So?'

Max exhaled, disguising a small, dull sigh inside the smoke: 'So . . . what?'

'So . . . what are you kicking around with a dozy little broad like me for? When you have a class act like Eleanor Beecham waiting for you back home?'

It took a beat before Max replied. Blanche noticed it, even if he didn't. 'Baby,' he said, 'because I love "kicking around" with you.' He laughed. 'And you're hardly "a dozy little broad".'

'But you never talk about her.'

'Why would I talk about her?'

'Because she's your wife. Is why. And because I am your lover. And everybody knows you two adore each other. And because of the way you kissed her last night. And the way you two looked at each other. And because I am just jealous as hell. Is why.'

Max smiled into her pretty, honest eyes, and dropped a kiss on her pretty shoulder. 'You have nothing to be jealous about, sweetheart. If you did, I wouldn't be here.' His hand returned to her slim stomach, and slowly continued on down. She paused—before reluctantly pushing his hand away. 'You're not being fair, Max.'

'Baby,' he murmured, not giving up just yet; nuzzling her neck, returning his hand. '. . . And nor are you . . . what are you fretting for, hmm? You have nothing to fret about, baby . . . just enjoy yourself . . .'

She pushed him away again, with more conviction this time, and climbed out of the bed. They'd spent the whole morning enjoying themselves in her bed already. And much as she would have loved to spend the rest of the day there with him, she needed to check in with the office. She had an interview with a new girl over at Columbia at three o'clock—some soon-to-be-big, Little-Miss-Girl-from-Nowhere, with a freshly invented life story to plug—and the Columbia people were keen for Blanche to do the big write-up. Added to which, she was determined that she and Max didn't part company without having had at least a semblance of a conversation. In bed, Blanche was more than happy to be treated like a dirty little sex machine. Actually it suited her just fine. But out of bed, there had to be something between them to make her feel like a decent human being again.

Blanche was ten years Max's junior, easily young enough to produce a litter of children if she wanted them, except she was adamant she didn't. Her independence, so hard fought and still so fresh, was something she could never envisage surrendering. Blanche was a woman of her time, and proud of it. She paid her own way, made her own path—lived alone in her snazzy little apartment (very *moderne* she told her disapproving family, back home in

43

Oregon), in a spanking new apartment block just above Sunset. She and Max had been lovers, on and off—with two short breaks during which Blanche attempted to wean herself from him—since she interviewed him for the magazine five years ago.

7

Nineteen twenty-four, it would have been. Or thereabouts. Almost a year after he joined Silverman. They met for lunch at Musso & Frank—without the marketing guys, because Max insisted on it. He was supposed to be telling her about his first picture since being lured away from Lionsfiel. The film was called *The Girl Who Couldn't Smile*, and it went on to gross more for Silverman Pictures than any movie they had yet released. But Blanche had been instructed by her editor not to 'go too heavy' on the new movie angle, since readers were unlikely to be terribly interested, and instead to concentrate her questions on the Big Split.

Max's move from Lionsfiel to Silverman had astonished the Movie Colony because he left behind not only his long-time producer and friend, Butch Menken; but—even more intriguing, at least to Blanche's readers—his movie-star wife. Until then the three of them—producer, director and star—had made not a single film without each other. They were a winning formula—no one doubted that, and everyone had always assumed the trio was inseparable.

So Max had talked to Miss Blanche Williams about the Split that Rocked Hollywood (as her magazine later entitled the article). And with or without the marketing men to prompt him, he had stuck to the official version of events. Which, with a few vital omissions, wasn't, after all, entirely divorced from the truth. And Blanche was a good listener—an accomplished interviewer. Over steaming, unwanted bowls of the famous Musso & Frank pasta, and a bottle of Château Margaux, provided by Max and poured by him, under the table, into Musso tea mugs, Max talked with disarming warmth and eloquence about his sadness not to be working with his beloved wife any longer. He and Eleanor had agreed that the moment had come for them both to spread their wings . . . It was time for Eleanor to experiment with different directors and, for Max, with different actors and actresses. He didn't mention Butch Menken.

'What about Butch?'

'Butch Menken?' Max waved a dismissive arm. 'Butch is a good guy.'

'That's what I heard.'

'But creatively, we had taken it as far as we could. Butch is good guy. I have a lot of respect for him.'

'So there was no fall-out?'

'There was no fall-out. Whatsoever. Butch and I remain the greatest of pals.'

'So the rumours . . .'

He cocked a smile, looked his little interrogator dead in the eye. 'What rumours would they be?'

She blushed, which didn't happen often. His gaze was disconcertingly direct. Made her want to wriggle in her chair. He was, she reflected as she recovered herself, without doubt the most attractive man she had ever had lunch with.

'Well, the rumours that . . . Heck, Mr Beecham, I'm sure you know what people are saying! That you dumped him. Despite being the oldest and best of friends. Because he just wasn't up to it . . . You had creatively outgrown him.'

'Ahh. Those rumours.' He smiled. She would never have known it, never have guessed. Under the table, he refilled her mug with red wine, and felt his heart begin to beat again. 'Butch is a fine producer,' he said, making a show of picking his words with great care. 'It goes without saying. Butch is a good producer. But as filmmakers we were travelling different paths. That's all. We wanted to make different kinds of movies. And consequently we were finding it difficult to agree . . .'

In any case, Max explained, redirecting the conversation, the offer to join Silverman Pictures was too exciting to turn down. Joel Silverman had promised him more autonomy, bigger budgets, freedom to choose his own scripts. 'And I have to tell you, Joel Silverman has kept to his word! Ha! And it's not so often you hear that said, is it? Not in this town!'

'But why didn't Mrs Beecham come with you?' Blanche persisted. 'She's such a great actress. Didn't you want her to come with you? Or was it her? Maybe she didn't want to come?'

Max shrugged. 'Of course I wanted her to come. Of course . . .'

'But you . . . Maybe you wanted to create some space between the two of you. Is that it?' Blanche asked, aware that she needed some sort of explanation for the piece, and that he didn't seem willing to offer one himself. 'A separation between work and home,' she said, already writing it down.

46

'Yes. I think I can understand that.'

He didn't know what it meant, and neither—when she thought about it—did Blanche. What 'space' between them? The space between them was already immeasurable.

'That's right,' he said vaguely. 'Creatively.'

She scribbled it down. 'And tell me,' she added, still scribbling. 'Tell me how it happened. Did the two of you sit down and discuss it? Were there tears? Or was it . . . kind of civilized? Can you tell me a little bit about how it all went down? My readers are longing to know.'

He looked at Blanche, her honest, pretty face so eager to hear whatever he might say next—no matter what. The problem was, he couldn't remember. Couldn't remember having the discussion—or even if there had been one. One day it was the three of them working together. And the next day—nothing. He had left them. Both. And he was on his own.

'Lionsfiel has always been like a family to her,' he mumbled. 'That's what you have to remember. She was never going to leave Lionsfiel. But—' he added, looking again into those honest eyes, and feeling suddenly, inexplicably compelled to reciprocate, to say something to her that actually had some meaning—'I have to tell you,' he said, surprising himself, not only by its truth but also by the fact of his sharing it with her, 'I miss her. I miss having her with me on set. I miss spending my days with her. I miss our working together. There was something very, very wonderful about that . . .' He paused, thinking about it: the old days. It wasn't something he allowed himself to do often. And it hadn't always been wonderful. Of course not. But there had been

47

wonderful moments. Many of them. 'I'm not sure I realized quite how wonderful,' he added, 'until it was gone . . . Hey. But that's life, huh?'

'It sure is,' she said, scribbling away.

'Sometimes,' he added, unwilling to leave the memories just yet, his mind briefly awash with images from good times, the early days—the old nickelodeon on Hester Street, the journey West, the long, slow climb together, 'when I contemplate a future, making movies without Eleanor . . . It's like imagining a world . . .' and he paused, searching for the truth—any truth at all—that he might be able to share with her, '. . . it's like imagining a world without music. Without birdsong . . .'

'That's very, very pretty,' sighed Blanche. 'Gosh. I wish someone would say that about me one day.'

He laughed, tilted back in his seat, looked across at her appreciatively. 'I'll bet you have guys murmuring stuff like that in your ear just about every day of your life, Miss Williams,' he said, and he meant it. She was sweet—sweet enough to blush, he noticed. For the second time, too. He watched as she recovered herself; watched as she busily pretended to scribble in her little reporter notebook . . .

'But you have to understand, Blanche—may I call you Blanche?' He leaned across the table toward her. 'That in spite of everything—really, everything—I had to go to Silverman. Silverman Pictures are making the most exciting—the best— movies in Hollywood right now. I believe that. I truly do believe that. And I make movies, Blanche. I'm a filmmaker. I'm a director. It's what I do. What I am. There's nothing else . . .'

He stopped abruptly, aware that he was revealing

too much. He smiled. 'Any case,' he continued, 'I sincerely hope that when you finally get to see the finished cut, you will agree with me that this new picture has been worth the . . . the pain . . .' He paused. Added, more to himself than to Blanche, 'And of course it has. You know, Blanche, I think, if you don't mind my saying it, I think it's my best picture yet.'

And then, somehow, she had looked up from her notebook, gazed back at him with such smitten warmth, that . . . in the intensity of the moment, the excitement and passion of talking about his beloved project to such a pretty, sympathetic, innocent, intelligent woman, he'd asked Blanche what she was doing later.

And they had spent the rest of that hot August afternoon in Blanche's bed.

It wasn't the first time he'd been unfaithful to his wife. Not strictly speaking—not by any stretch. But (if you didn't count the move to Silverman Pictures), it was the first time Max felt that he was betraying her. Because Blanche was not Eleanor. But she was quite a find. And Max could appreciate that. And he knew from the very beginning that he would be coming back for more.

That was the last time he talked to Blanche about his wife at any length, or in any detail. And it was difficult for Blanche. Always, very difficult. Because Eleanor was a big star. And, if not classically beautiful—her features were irregular; everything was too large, too vital, too wild—there was no question that she shone. Something shone from her on screen—and in life, too. She was a big star. And—yes—Blanche was right. In a city of cheats and shrews, Eleanor's beauty, her small

49

kindnesses, her beautiful manners, made her a class act. Nobody had a bad word to say about Eleanor.

Max was very fond of Blanche. Blanche knew that. In fact, he loved her. And she knew that, too. But whereas Max Beecham loved Blanche Williams, Blanche Williams was in love with Max.

So it was difficult for her.

8

'I bumped into Butch Menken yesterday,' Blanche said suddenly. Changing tack. She was sitting on the edge of the bed looking vaguely for her clothes.

'I'm sorry to hear it,' Max replied.

'Oh, he's not so bad!'

'Whatever you say, baby.'

'And you know what he told me?'

'Tell me. What did you he tell you?'

'You don't know already?'

'I don't know if I know. I don't know what he told you.'

She considered him, the handsome man in her bed, the love of her life, lying there beside her, checking his wristwatch. Already thinking about his next appointment, his next battle, his next . . . whatever it was he had to do, which had nothing whatsoever to do with Blanche Williams. She was jealous—only a little jealous, she told herself. She was ferociously jealous—and not just of his wife, but of all the beautiful women who surrounded him. To be fair, he had never given her any reason to suppose that his attention wandered. But he cheated on his wife, and that was enough. If he cheated on his wife, why wouldn't he cheat on Blanche?

She pushed the thought aside. It was pointless. Self-defeating.

'So?' Max glanced across at her, noticed her troubled expression. He placed a thumb between her brows and gently creased out the small frown. 'Baby? You still here? . . . What did Butch tell you?'

'Butch told me . . . only I thought you might already know. Because it so directly affects you. But I guess not.'

'What?'

'Well. That Butch is joining you at Silverman.'

Max dropped his thumb, looked at her sharply. 'Nonsense.'

'That's what he told me, Max. He said—because of Eleanor's role in *PostBoy*. Being partly the reason . . . But I'm not sure if I believe that. Except he probably feels pretty bad, with Eleanor being left behind again, after you already did it once . . . But I'm telling you he's leaving Lionsfiel and he's going over to Silverman.'

Max gazed at her. 'Blanche,' he said coldly, 'you're talking in riddles. What about Eleanor's role? What has that to do with Butch coming to—?'

'Butch Menken is joining Silverman as executive head of production,' she said, patiently, despite his tone. 'I'm sorry, Max. They should have told you. Joel Silverman should've told you. Should've . . . involved you in the decision.' She leaned over and kissed him, as an apology—for the news itself, and for being the one to tell him. She offered him a perky, uncomfortable smile. 'So I guess that means he's going to be your boss.'

Without another word, Max climbed out of bed.

'Hey! . . . Max?'

He ignored her.

She followed his naked shape through to the small sitting room, where their clothes were still strewn over the couch. (Scarlet velvet, it was. Very *moderne*. Her proudest possession.) 'Max? It's not the end of the world . . . C'mon! . . . You two worked well together before. You made some great pictures together. You, Eleanor, Butch: you were a *tour de force*. Pardon my French. Gosh—maybe he'll bring Eleanor across with him. Wouldn't that be something?'

'He's not going to do that.'

'Well, but he might.'

'No. He's not.'

'Especially now. She has her contract up for renewal. And with the casting on *PostBoy*, and it all looking so shaky and all . . . you know?'

'I don't, Blanche. No. I don't know. Unlike you I don't know everything about everyone else's business. Because I have enough business of my own to keep me occupied.'

'It *is* my business to know everyone's business. And you benefit from that.' She told him levelly, her feelings hurt.

Max collected himself. 'I'm sorry, baby. Of course it is. That was rude of me.'

'In any case,' she continued, brushing his apology aside, 'you and Butch—you worked well together before. Didn't you? You'll work well together again!'

He smiled grimly. 'Somehow I doubt that.'

'Max—I hate to say it, but you haven't had a sensation since *The Girl Who Couldn't*—'

'Every film I make is a sensation.'

'Well, I know that. But you know what I mean...'

'If by "sensation" you mean "sensational ticket receipts",' he said, childishly, as if, in Hollywood, 'sensation' could ever mean anything else, 'well, baby, you go right ahead and say it.'

'OK, I will.'

'Because it so happens I've had more goddamn box-office hits than just about any other director in this town.'

Blanche, unselfconsciously naked, leaning against the doorframe, watching him dress, wondered, sometimes, what she saw in the man. She sighed. 'That's not actually true, Max. And you know it and I know it. And you know I know it. And actually I could give you a list of the ten—hell—the top twenty grossing directors in this town these past two years. You don't even come close.'

He didn't reply.

She relented, just a little. 'OK—1927, you came close. But we're near to finishing 1929! That's almost three years, Max. Don't pretend you don't know. I'm only saying, maybe Butch doesn't have to be such a bad thing for you. What's the big deal?'

Max didn't answer. She watched him, shaking out his pants—scowling at them, at her—at everything ... And still so damn handsome. She softened, but not only because of that. Because, in spite of everything—his temper, his director's vanity—he cared so much about the movies he made. It was noble, foolish—doomed. And she sensed that, underneath the machismo and the bluster, he knew it. He was a talented filmmaker, yes. A talented and dedicated filmmaker, whose films would probably one day be forgotten. And she loved him for it.

53

'By the way,' she said, 'I was touched, you know. When you wore the white jacket last night. Didn't think you'd do it.'

He chuckled, in spite of everything. 'The fuss you made about that goddamn jacket. You would have killed me if I hadn't.'

She'd given him the jacket as a birthday present, way back in May. And then, even before he'd pulled it out from its elaborate ribbon and wrapping, she was fighting with him, working herself into a state about how he'd never be able to wear it without questions being asked, perfectly arched movie-star eyebrows being raised. If he couldn't even wear a jacket she gave to him, what small space could she ever hope to occupy in his busy, complicated life? All roads led the same way. She tried to stop herself from careering down each and every one of them. But it was hard for her to be in love with him all this time, and never to be making any progress.

'I thought you looked very handsome in it,' she said. 'Eleanor did too, I expect? Huh? What did you tell her? Did you tell her you'd bought it for yourself?'

'Honey, have you seen my wallet? I could swear I put it on the side here.' He stopped. He knew he was being rude, again, and he knew she'd done nothing to deserve it. Except he couldn't stand it when she talked about Eleanor. It made him wilt inside, for both of them: him and Blanche—and for Eleanor, too. It took every grain of good manners he possessed not to put a hand over each ear and walk right out of the room.

Most of all, he wanted to get to his desk, get on the telephone to Butch Menken—and find out

54

what in hell was going on.

Instead, he came across to his lover, took her pretty face in his hands, and kissed her. He said, 'You're a girl in a million, Blanche Williams. You really are . . . But you understand, don't you? I have to go now. I have to get back to the office. Maybe you're wrong about Butch . . .'

But she never was wrong. Not about this kind of thing. 'Or maybe I can put a stop to it . . .'

She hesitated because she was not unkind and, in fact, in spite of everything, she bore no bad feeling towards Eleanor. Quite the opposite. She was, if anything, in awe of her. 'But you should probably know about *PostBoy*,' she said solemnly. 'Before you go charging in there making a scene.'

'Tell me,' he said wearily, dropping his hands, 'about *PostBoy*.'

'It's your wife's next picture. They sent the script to her yesterday. She will have got it this morning.'

He laughed—impressed, in spite of himself. 'How in hell do you know this stuff?'

She shrugged. 'I told you, Butch told me . . .' Again, she hesitated.

'Would you spit it out—please, baby? Put me out of my misery.'

'Eleanor's not the lead . . .'

'Oh!' he said, slowly, gave a soft groan. He wondered how Eleanor would take it. Realized, with a small shock, that he had no idea how she would take it. She might even be a little relieved. Either way, the news hardly came as a surprise. 'Poor El,' he said.

'I mean to say, Max,' she continued, 'it's not even the second lead. Nowhere near. The fact is, she's a great actress, and we all know that. But her numbers have been dropping. People don't turn out to see her. And they haven't and you know this, Max. They haven't, not like they used to—except for *Mermaids*, not since you left for Silverman. And that's the fact. And you probably don't want to hear it. But I'm sorry.'

'*Mermaids* was a smash,' he muttered. Yes, it had been a smash, but everyone knew that it was no thanks to Eleanor. Eleanor might have played the lead, but the notices hardly mentioned her. They were all raving about the new kid on the block, Joan Crawford.

Blanche was right, of course. As usual. Eleanor was half the actress she used to be. Because she didn't care enough, it seemed to Max. Not about anything, not any more. And if she didn't care— if she couldn't remember how far they had come, how hard they'd fought, how tightly they needed to cling on—then why should he fight for her? He felt a prickling, not of pity, but of anger, of rage at his wife, for abandoning him mid-game— mid-everything—when there was still so much to fight for. Perhaps this would wake her up. Perhaps it might shake her out of the torpor. He glanced at Blanche, who was watching him so closely, trying so hard to read something, the smallest clue, from his perfectly unreadable expression. He kissed her. Thanked her for telling him the news—and left the apartment.

Too bad, he told himself, as he started his engine. It was Eleanor's problem. He would try to help, if she turned to him. Which she wouldn't, because she never turned to him any more. In the meantime, he had problems of his own.

56

9

October 1929. As America helterskeltered through those last few ecstatic days of the greatest economic boom in its short history, Hollywood offered a matching heartbeat. In its confidence, its joyous vulgarity, it was a perfect fit for a bold new universe. The Movie Business was big business. Hollywood was the centre of the world: and in Hollywood, just five enormous film studios reigned supreme.

Silverman Pictures, where Max Beecham worked as one of three contracted directors, was not one of those studios. In a good year, it produced no more than ten films (as opposed to eighty or more, for example, over at MGM). Even so, it had a fine reputation. More than any other studio, large or small, it was known for the quality of its productions. Not all Silverman films made money. But once every eighteen months or so, Silverman Pictures produced what Blanche called 'a sensation'—a box-office triumph; and that was how, against the giants, it continued to survive.

Its founder, Joel Silverman, had come to Hollywood in 1910 with nothing, so he always claimed, except $100 and ten years' experience in the scrap-metal business. But he was a man who put more thought, effort and intelligence into a single day than most people put into a lifetime, and he had made a fortune. Along the way he had lost his only son, killed by a German sniper in the swamps at Malancourt just six weeks before the end of the War. Joel Silverman had no other children. Now he only wanted two things: he wanted his studio to make a play for a place in the big league. And he wanted to find a worthy heir to help him take it there, so that one day, before he died, he might consider the possibility of retiring. It was with these two ambitions in mind that he approached Butch Menken.

If Max had been capable of thinking rationally, which on this matter he was not, he would have had to acknowledge that his boss of six years, Joel Silverman, was not simply a clever man, but as sure-footed as any in the business; and that, of all the talent available to him, in Butch he could not have made a smarter choice.

'Married to the movies,' Butch used to say, when anybody asked him (as they constantly did) how it was that such an attractive man, already forty and with no shortage of willing candidates, had thus far evaded the efforts of so many beautiful women, and not yet taken a wife. The phrase, glibly reiterated, was truer than he realized: truer than he would have liked to acknowledge, even to himself. Butch Menken's work was his first passion: the last thing he thought of at night; the first thing he thought of in the morning. It was also true that the only woman he had ever truly wanted for a wife was already spoken for and, try as he might, he could not wean her away.

He was handsome: blond and square-jawed, blue-eyed and broad-shouldered; in manner and in dress he resembled an upmarket East Coast lawyer more than the West Coast movie producer he was. Succinct, soft-spoken, clever, understated in every way, Butch rarely uttered a wasted word, or offered a wasted smile, or moved a well-honed, athletic limb without having a reason for it in mind. Nevertheless, the sheer size of him—he was six foot three—meant that even in a crowded bar, or a large party packed with stars, it was hard not to be conscious of his presence. Added to which, Butch's reputation was already part of Hollywood legend. It seemed, for the past few years, that every film he touched turned to gold. He had an instinct—verging on magic, so it seemed—for what and who was going to work up there on the big screen.

When Joel Silverman approached him with his partnership offer, Butch was one of six senior producers under contract at the gargantuan Lionsfiel Studios. Which six senior producers (along with thirty junior producers) answered to an executive producer who, in turn, answered not only to the Studio's founder, but to his two very capable and ambitious sons. Too many chiefs. Whether or not Max chose to acknowledge the fact, it could only have been a matter of time before a man with Butch's record was lured to a more promising position elsewhere.

On that afternoon, while Eleanor was racing toward Reno, and Max was racing across town from his lover's bed, Butch was sitting at his desk at Lionsfiel thinking—with quiet satisfaction—about his encounter with Blanche Williams the previous afternoon. She was a sharp enough cookie, and he liked her. But if she thought for one minute she'd wheedled anything out of him he hadn't expressly intended for her to wheedle, she was a fool. A fool—though she didn't know it—with a predicament so similar to his. He might perhaps have felt a little human sympathy for her, had it crossed his brilliant mind to do so. It did not.

His brilliant mind wandered, instead, to Eleanor. She hadn't called. And she must have seen the script by now. She must have seen the small and unflattering role she'd been given—and with just three months before her contract was due for renewal, she would know how it augured for her future at Lionsfiel. So why wasn't she on the telephone haranguing him, sobbing, begging him to help? It bothered Butch Menken. Under normal circumstances the histrionics of his actresses left him cold—just rolled right off him. But with Eleanor—obviously—things were different.

Like Butch, Eleanor never lost her cool. That was the thing about Eleanor. One of the things. Not once, not in all the years he'd known her. Sometimes, when she was upset, or excited—she shook. Her entire body shook. Which was beautiful. Made her even more beautiful.

Why hadn't she called him?

He buzzed through to his secretary, asked her to check again that the script had been sent to Eleanor yesterday. His secretary confirmed that it had.

'And she hasn't called?'

'Not to my knowledge, Mr Menken. And I've been here by the telephone since nine o'clock.'

'And it was made clear, which role she was to play?'

'Yes, sir. Her lines were underscored in red. As usual. I saw it for myself before Mrs Broadbent sent it out, and I was with Mrs Broadbent when she was placing the script in the envelope. Because we were both saying what a shame it was. Because really Mrs Beecham is still so lovely, and it seems such a waste . . .'

All the staff at Lionsfiel loved Eleanor. They

60

always had. It wasn't something you could claim about many of the studio's stars. And it said something about her, Butch reflected sourly. Too much self-control. For an artist. Not enough passion. Always so damn polite—would nothing rattle her?

He returned the handset, brilliant mind briefly befuddled. There was plenty of passion there. He knew it. It was that tension between passion and control, which she no longer revealed for the camera but which had once made her so compelling on screen. It was the same mix which, in bed together, still made her so irresistible in the flesh.

And he should have called her. He should have warned her the script was on its way. Why hadn't he done that?

Butch glanced at his clean, clear desk: he actually did have five minutes to spare. Why hadn't he called her? He checked the time on his immaculately unnoticeable $25,000 white-gold wristwatch.

Because he was afraid. And he knew it. Because, in matters of emotion—real emotion, as opposed to the magic created for screen—Butch was lost. Like a child. He simply didn't know how to deal with it. Not with Eleanor. All the shaking that was going to go on. The passion and control. The swirling, silent hurt, the unspoken accusations. Dammit. Damn her. Damn Max. Damn everyone.

At the production meeting yesterday he'd fought for her. He'd taken on the senior producers, the executive producer, the whole lot of them, one by one. But by then, by the time they told him what was planned for her, Butch had already informed them he was leaving. Their decision regarding

Eleanor's future—or lack of it—was, of course, in large part retaliation for that, and he knew it.

'Why don't you take her with you, Butch, huh?' Mr Carrascosa (Senior) had suggested—sneered, actually: it was closer to a sneer. 'She's lost the magic. Lost it so long I can hardly remember she even had it.'

'But she did have it,' Butch said defensively, more quickly than he would have liked. She and he—and Max—had together made the finest films. And though the men had gone on to make more hits, not one of the three had made a film of the same quality since the split. He knew it. Everyone knew it. 'The magic is still there,' he said. 'We only need to fix her up with the right director.'

'So you've been saying for some time,' replied Mr Carrascosa.

Butch had looked across the boardroom table to the Carrascosa Son and Holy Spirit, sitting on either side of their founding Father—but they said not a word. He looked at Mr Stiles, Executive Producer of the studio, and Eleanor's friend:

'Tony?' Butch asked him. 'She's still beautiful. She still has so much to offer . . . Why don't you give her another chance?'

Tony Stiles shuffled his papers, shrugged, slowly shook his head.

'Hell, Butch—why don't you sign her!' Mr Carrascosa called out again. Pleased with the joke. 'You're so goddamn fond of her! . . . She's costing us an arm and a leg—and for what? She's finished here, my friend. She's all yours!'

Butch smiled at them—one of his rare smiles. They had done it to spite him, without doubt. But they would have found another way to spite him if getting rid of Eleanor didn't also happen to make good business sense. And the numbers were against her: her age, for one; her ticket receipts, for two. And Butch knew—everyone in the business knew—she just wasn't as good as she used to be. On set, she was professional. She knew what was her best angle and where the kindest light shone; she knew her lines: like an efficient machine, she did everything right. But the tension was gone. She put no heart into it—and somehow, the camera could always pick it up. It's what Butch had told her, more than once. He'd said it again only a couple of weeks ago.

'You have to care, Eleanor. You have to care as Max does. As much as I do. As much as you care about life itself . . .'

'Of course I care,' she'd said—beautiful, trained voice crackling with the sound of caring.

It was Butch, then, who'd shaken his head. 'I can't protect you from them, Eleanor. You know that. Not if . . .' But he couldn't bring himself to mention it. Two weeks later, he still hadn't told her he was leaving the studio.

'I don't need you to protect me,' she said. And then, unkindly—she regretted it at once: 'I have Max to do that.'

But Max had not protected her. Max had gone to Silverman. The truth of it rang out in the silence. Butch, his own guilt hanging heavily, left her statement unchallenged.

'In any case,' she added, and kissed him. 'You mustn't worry. I'm tougher than I seem.' And she smiled, and seemed, to Butch, in that instant, to be quite unbearably fragile. He could protect her. If she would only let him.

63

He kissed her: 'Eleanor, things might be going to change for me soon. Everything's going to change. It's going to be different.' He stopped. Still, he couldn't say it. Instead, to fill the silence, he said: 'I think you should come live with me . . .'

Eleanor gave him a throaty chuckle: 'Watch out, Butch Menken,' she laughed at him. 'One of these days I may just take you up on the offer . . .'

They were in his bed, in his new apartment at the Chateau Marmont, an apartment Eleanor had helped him to arrange. It was a beautiful, sultry afternoon. The ceiling fan had kept them cool and, from behind the half-closed louvre shutters, softening the whir of traffic as it chugged down Sunset Boulevard far below, the smallest, sweetest, softest breezes had caressed their warm, naked skin. They were a little drunk, both of them. And she wasn't listening. She never listened.

10

Butch looked at his watch. Four thirty in the afternoon already. Even taking into account the party last night, to which, of course, he had not been invited, she must have woken and checked her post by now. Why hadn't she called?

He should call her. He should tell her he was leaving Silverman—if she didn't know it already. He should talk to her. There was really no way out of it. He knew that. And so, finally, he geared himself to do it. He would call before Max got home and had a chance to break the news to her himself. He would check up on her, make her feel better, soothe her with promises to help . . .

Grimly, he leaned to pick up the telephone. As he did so his secretary buzzed through on the intercom. Max Beecham was on the line.

HA! It was, Butch realized, the very call he had been waiting not to take all the long afternoon. All day, actually. Ever since his cocktail with Blanche Williams the previous afternoon.

'Thank you, Mrs Rowse,' said Butch, soft and succinct as ever. 'You can tell the son of a bitch I'm out of town.'

'Out of town. Right you are,' Mrs Rowse said primly. 'Shall I say when you'll be returning?'

'Tell him I'm back after the weekend. I'm on vacation.'

'Mr Menken, you'll be on a reconnaissance out at Palm Springs this coming Monday. Shall I tell him you'll be back Tuesday?'

'You tell him that. And tell him you've no idea where to find me.'

'I'll do that.'

Butch stood up, feeling satisfied. Trying to feel satisfied. The job was done. The son of a bitch could take care of his beautiful wife himself, for once in his lousy, cheating life. Butch had a date with a cute little actress named . . . Melanie . . . No, Bethany. From Savannah. Maybe Charleston.

In any case, he was heading home to shower.

11

On those very rare occasions when Max allowed himself to think about it, the truth seemed to shine out like a beacon: the most immutable fact in the universe. Butch Menken had always been in love with his wife. During all the years the three had been working together, Max used to see Butch, watching her, from behind his clever, blue, predatory eyes. And then Max had moved to Silverman. And because she reminded him of so many things he needed to forget, he had turned away from her long before and he had left the two of them together. He never quite knew how long she held out—not quite as long as he might have hoped, perhaps. They were as lonely as each other. But he knew one thing, always. She never stood a chance.

It was all such a long time ago now. But the months and years rolled by—and he knew the affair rumbled on. Or he didn't know. But he knew. Because Eleanor almost never mentioned Butch's name, though they worked together; and because Eleanor lied so well, about everything, always, and because she seemed always to be wrapped in an invisible, impenetrable shell. Just as he was.

After his failed attempt to get through to Butch, Max had thrown down his telephone in disgust and immediately, blindly, stormed along the corridor to fight it out with his boss.

Silverman glanced up from his work as Max burst in. 'Ha!' he barked cheerfully. 'Well, I was wondering when you'd finally show your handsome face in here. And before you even start, Max— listen to me. You're gonna get used to him. Trust me. He's good news for the studio. Which means he's good news for you and he's good news for me.' And that was it.

When Max tried to present the case against

Butch: that he was untrustworthy and extravagant; that his artistic taste was vacuous and shallow; that the sort of big budget films he produced were anathema to all that Silverman Pictures stood for, his employer and friend held up a hand to shush him. And when that didn't work, and Max continued shouting, he stood up from behind his desk (something he didn't do often) and simply pushed him from the room.

'It'll be good for us,' was all Joel Silverman would say. 'Don't whine, Max. Men should never whine. Butch Menken's the best producer in the business. He's just the tonic we need. And if you cared about this studio as much you ought to, you'd be celebrating. Just as I am. Now go home, Max. Lighten up. Enjoy a pleasant weekend with your beautiful wife . . . And while you're at it, would you thank her please for a beautiful party last night. Tell her Margaret wants to know where she found those lobster . . .'

Max returned to the *Castillo* not long afterwards. Feeling bruised and foolish, and in a filthy mood, he went directly to his study, where he stayed, hidden away, drinking heavily to dull the myriad of pains—among them the ache, ever present, in the palms of his two hands. It was always more acute when he was tired. He sat at his desk and pulled out the old screenplay, the one he turned to whenever his hands burned, or his heart ached, and which one day he swore he would make into a film. After several hours of failing to make any progress with it, he staggered to bed.

All the time he had imagined his wife's brooding presence somewhere in the house, and was torn between resenting her failure to engage with him, and delighting in not being required to engage with her. But then the bedroom was empty. And then there it was, the miserable little note:

> *M,*
> *I shall be gone for a few days. I think it's about time we talked, don't you?*
> *E*

He stared at it stupidly, mind throbbing, trying to work out what in hell it meant. Time to talk? About what? He was tempted to laugh.

Where did she imagine they could possibly begin?

The Nickelodeon on
Hester Street

12

New York City, December 1909

Thick snow had settled above the city grime on Hester Street. During the day, the two had mingled under a million tired feet, and this evening the resulting soup had frozen over once again. Eleana's boots had been restitched so often there was barely anything left to hold them together. They had sucked in the filthy, icy mire, numbed her feet as she stood on Greene Street—and now, in the steaming warmth of the picture house, they were itching and aching as they thawed. It didn't matter. Not really. It was such a relief to be inside—somewhere warm and cheerful at last—and with Matz at the piano, smiling at her through the crowd. There was neat gin running warm through Eleana's veins, and hot potato soup in her belly, and the new movie, *Frankenstein*, playing on a loop on the screen above her head. Her feet could have detached themselves completely and she might not have complained.

Maybe 'picture house' was too grand a name for the place. It was a five-cent Lower East Side nickelodeon, a dirty little store front, nothing more, and nothing like the big, fancy theatres opening further uptown. There was a screen at one end, a hand-turned projector at the other, and not enough benches for the boisterous audience between the two. It was packed, as it was every night, even now, with the garment strike—and thick with the smells of tobacco and sweat, and hot, unwashed bodies.

The projection screen was too small, or the film was too large. Something wasn't right. As always, at the nickelodeon on Hester Street, the top half of the image was bouncing lopsided off the ceiling. But nobody complained. In the normal run of things, such a detail wouldn't stop the audience from screaming with merry terror: it was Matz Beekman, up to his tricks at the piano keyboard, who was so blithely sabotaging the mood.

Matz was employed five evenings a week (at seventy-five cents a night) to provide musical accompaniment to whatever film was showing. Tonight he had cast aside the official score, as he did from time to time, and was improvising a comic soundtrack of his own—turning what was meant to be a horror show into a ludicrous romp—and the crowd was loving it. Their bellows of laughter could be heard outside on the frozen street, bursting from the room, beckoning more people to join the hot, boisterous crush. Looking at them all, as Eleana did just then, it would have been hard to guess just what and whom they were up against. The garment workers' general strike, into its third week now, was more widespread—and more successful—than anyone had expected it would be, including the strike organizers. And now the city authorities were turning savage. In cahoots with the factory owners, they were letting their thugs loose on the picket lines, and for the mass of the Lower East Side, garment-manufacturing centre of the world, life had become not merely a struggle to stay warm and to find enough to eat, but a battle—bloody, violent, lawless. To the hunger and the grind, the anonymity and the squalor, there had been added a tang of actual, mortal fear.

Eleana turned her mind from it, from all of it. Everything to do with the strike, and everything connected with it. She concentrated instead on the here and now: the nickelodeon on Hester Street. And Matz at his piano. And Frankenstein and his monster, bouncing off the ceiling.

The film was only sixteen minutes long and Matz knew every frame. He watched movies differently from other people—with the same concentration and passion that he did everything, but with a filmmaker's instinct, too; though he couldn't know it yet. It meant he only needed to watch something once, and he could break it down, scene by scene, shot by shot.

No matter what the film was showing, in just a handful of notes, and simply to keep himself amused, Matz could take possession of it, transform the mood. He could send the audience lurching from horror to tears and then to laughter, and carry every soul in the room with him. It was magical. Matz was magical. Eleana loved him most when he was at the piano, hitting the keys, playing the audience—happy and free. He was a different man from the one who stood on stage at the Union halls and called on his fellow workers to strike, or to keep striking, or to keep up the fighting. She loved him then, too—of course. She loved and admired him in the halls. But she loved and desired him at the piano. He would look up suddenly, in the middle of it all, his audience weeping or laughing at his musical command— he would glance up through the crowd, with that look of ferocious concentration, search out Eleana, catch her eye, and his face would break into a wild grin. Often, more and more often, he would beckon her over, forget the film entirely, and instead start hammering out one of the popular songs, in the hope that she might sing along . . .

Give My Regards to Broadway . . ., Take Me Out to the Ball Game . . ., Keep on the Sunny Side . . .

The crowd never objected. The regulars would holler for her until she came forward to stand beside him.

She didn't do much. A song and dance. A little routine. The usual *schtick*. The sort of acts pretty young girls were running through in cheap bars and crowded nickelodeons all over the city. Except, when it came to it, Eleana was anything but usual. Her dark features were too large to be conventionally pretty, and there was a wildness about her, as if she were permanently searching, in hope and fear—and, above all, in vain—for an exit from whatever situation she was in. She was rough hewn, yet: still only a teenager. But she was beautiful. Matz saw it. The crowd saw it, when she sang. In years to come, the camera would see it. She was as magical as Matz up there, standing by that piano: a born performer. Her rich voice, her expressive face, her timing, her intensity, her humour, her lightness of touch—something and everything about her cast a spell. Matz told her so, endlessly. He knew she was a star, all along. He used to say so. And she must have believed it, just a little, or she wouldn't have continued to stand up there, night after night. She wouldn't have followed him to the ends of the earth . . . And she must have heard the applause, felt the warmth. She loved it back then, in the beginning. It made her feel alive.

Tonight, after she sang, they would be passing a hat for the strike fund. And when Matz stopped

74

playing for the evening, when she'd done her song and dance, and the customers were heading home, she might pull him into the cupboard behind that beaten-up piano. Or he might pull her, probably: either way. It was where the proprietor, Mr Listig, stored any reels of film overnight. Not such a big cupboard then: no space to lie down. But big enough. At the end of the evening they always helped to put the reels away, and then—what the hell? Mr Lustig pretended not to notice. He didn't care (so long as the reels weren't ruined). Seventy-five cents an evening wasn't much, after all, and Eleana didn't even get that. She received nothing, except a wave-through at the door. A little bit of privacy at the end of the night wasn't much, but it was a luxury not many young couples enjoyed back then, not on the Lower East Side. The use of his cupboard was a perk of the job.

13

She and Matz had been together for three years by then, since Eleana was fifteen. And Matz was eighteen, perhaps. Or seventeen. Nineteen . . . Matz always travelled light on such details. Until he met Eleana, he seemed to travel entirely alone. He came to America—he said—ten years earlier, alone with his mother, who had died since, to be reunited with his father, who never appeared at the dock to claim him. It was a daily tragedy in New York back then, when so many thousands of immigrants were pouring in every day.

And, to Matz, it was a mystery still. His father

had sent the money home, enough for their passage to join him. It had taken him four years to collect enough together: four long, hungry years, saving, scrimping, living no better than a dog in the Lower East slums.

But when wife and son disembarked at last, the Statue of Liberty behind them, and a free life in the New World in front, he wasn't at the pier to greet them, and though they waited for three days, returned every morning and every afternoon for many more, he never did come. Matz and Matz's mother never laid eyes on him again.

So that was Matz.

He couldn't remember his father, anyway. Couldn't remember his home country, not really. But he remembered this and that: a grandmother, plenty of cousins, and a great crowd—the whole *shtetl*, his mother said, turning out to wave them off on their journey. He remembered the ship, and the long days at sea: the cramped, stale air on the lower deck, the seasickness—and the lice inspectors at Ellis Island, who had dragged him off, yanked him, screaming, from his mother's arms. He remembered the wild, overwhelming relief when he was allowed to fall back into her arms again. He would never forget that.

And then . . . nothing much. The shock of the Lower East Side. The tenement flats, six storeys high, one after the other to the horizon end, blocking the sun, hiding the sky—and the teeming streets, the dirt, the smell of rotting garbage and horse manure, the roar of metal wheels on cobbled roads, the soot that rained from the elevated trains, the endless noise . . . And his mother finding work, and then working, and working, and never stopping

76

. . . Someone used to bring vast bundles of materials to the apartment where they boarded, and then she—and the lady who took the rent, and her three daughters and an old man and someone else, and sometimes Matz, too—would sit in silence, too tired to talk, constructing silken flowers for ladies' hats, by the hundreds, by the thousands, night after night . . . Someone took the bundles away when the work was completed, and brought back more bundles: a never-ending stream of bundles, squatting in the space, piled high, stealing the daylight . . .

What he remembers most is that airless August, when she lay dying.

They were boarding with a family on Essex Street, and the family was kind. There was tuberculosis rampant through the block that summer. With so many bodies existing so close together, when the sickness visited a building, as it did from time to time, it took with it whole families, it swept away whole floors of human life. But on this occasion, in Matz's small apartment, only Matz's mother fell prey—and the family they boarded with took pity. They let her stay on the only bed, they moved it to the room with the only window, and for those last few weeks, and even for a week or so afterwards, they wouldn't take any rent from him, and they fed Matz free of charge.

After that—after that—Matz had survived. That was the main thing. He stole food from the carts on Hester Street, collected coal fallen from the back of the coal carts and sold it, or exchanged it, piece by piece. He constructed silk flowers, carried bundles, took work where he could; did whatever he had to do. And in fact he did far better than simply

77

survive. Somehow, between the struggle to earn enough to eat, the struggle to find a place to sleep, Matz achieved what his parents had brought him to the New World to achieve: there was a charitable night school on East Broadway, founded to help little immigrant boys just like him. Without it, who knows what might have happened?

Matz learned English. He learned to read and write. Learned the piano. Discovered Karl Marx. Learned, above all, that life didn't have to be this way; that it wasn't this way for everyone.

When he first came to live at Eleana's tenement flat on Allen Street—his fifth move in a year—he was a member of the Socialist Party of America, and a vocal and active member of the Garment Workers' Union. He worked ten hours a day as a cutter at the Triangle Waist Company, already one of the largest and most productive garment factories in the city—where, because his job required skill as well as masculine brawn, he earned $12 a week; three times what the young female machinists were paid, working the same hours. He kept only what he needed to survive, and divided the rest between the Party, the Union, and the little boys on the Lower East Side who roamed the streets just as he had, whose fathers never came to meet them at the dock, whose mothers died of consumption by a small window in a filthy street, in a crowded tenement a world away from home.

That was Matz.

By comparison, Eleana had enjoyed an easy life. Who hadn't? She was born a few crowded streets away, on Orchard Street, five years after her parents arrived off the ship. By the time she was born, her parents were fully Americanized, and took care to speak to Eleana, almost always, in English. Her sister, two years her elder, died of tuberculosis when Eleana was one. Her father, Jethro, shared a lease on a six-by-four feet pickled food store, in the hallway of a neighbouring tenement block. He died of pneumonia, aged thirty-nine, in the winter of 1905, a year or so before she and Matz met. But Eleana often remembered her father: learned, affectionate and kind, always with the smell of pickled herring hanging over him, and—like everyone she knew—always working.

After he died, life grew much tougher. The shop, such that it was, was quickly appropriated by the other lessee, leaving Jethro's widow and daughter to fend for themselves: Eleana abandoned her education and set to work making up the family income. Easier than Matz's life, perhaps. But never easy. Before Jethro died, their tiny apartment had been shared only with one uncle and two cousins. Afterwards, innumerable more were crammed in. The apartment, like so many of their neighbours', became home and sweatshop both, and a flop house for an ever-changing roster of boarders and fellow workers. They sewed buttons onto feathers, or feathers onto ribbons or ribbons onto hats . . . Whatever piecework was going, they took it in, and sewed—too tired to talk—and sewed—too poorly paid to stop—and sewed, and only paused to sleep.

It was how Matz first encountered her. Old for her years, and with the roster of boarders always passing through, no longer quite the untarnished maiden of good romantic fiction, a toughened daughter of the Lower East Side, but with a bloom that nothing and no one could dim.

79

There was a heat between them from the moment they met. No doubt about it. She was fifteen. He was eighteen. Maybe. He came back from the Triangle factory that first night. He sat down at the small kitchen table, where the boarders had to eat in shifts. Her mother passed Eleana a plate of *schmaltz*—chicken fat—and cornbread, which Eleana set before him without a word. He looked up at her—she looked back at him. If it wasn't love, it was desire at first sight: hot, thick, rich. They gazed at each other, and felt a rush of something wonderful flow through them. They gazed at each other, in no hurry to look away; allowed their eyes to roam each other's faces as if they were quite alone in the room, as if it were the most natural thing in the world. After a minute, when the current between them seemed to stifle everything else—and there seemed to be no question where it would lead, Eleana's mother leaned across from the stove and smacked her soup ladle against Matz's bowl. That was all. She said nothing. Nobody said anything. And, for the instant at least, the spell was partially broken.

There were eight bodies sleeping in that small and crumbling 'old law' Allen Street apartment then. Lower East Side was still filled with them—tenements with conditions so foul, with so little light and space, that they were no longer legal. Slowly, they were being replaced. But too slowly. In this small apartment, there lived five family members, loosely connected—not everyone could say quite how—and three boarders, connected only by the fact of the rent. At the end of each day, ten dog-tired bodies returned from their workplaces to be fed by their landlady: pickled herring and cornbread, pickled herring *or* cornbread, *schmaltz*, potatoes . . . mostly potatoes . . . Eleven bodies squeezed into the four small rooms: a parlour, a windowless kitchen, two windowless bedrooms. Directly outside ran the track for the Second Avenue elevated railroad, which meant a constant thunder and rumble of passing trains, and cinders from the engines floating through the only window, coating the parlour and everything inside it with dust. There was a water faucet in the hallway and a couple of toilets, which serviced all six floors, all seventeen apartments, each one as crammed as the one above, and the one below, and opposite, and on either side . . .

They slept sardine-like, side by side on wooden pallets—no room for niceties here; no single-sex wards. On the sixth night, the two of them lay together in the same hot, slumbering room, separated only by a few unwanted bodies, a few feet of space. Neither could have stood it much longer: the proximity and the distance. But Eleana waited, her mind and body restless with longing. She knew he would come to her, and so he did.

Matz clambered over the two sleeping figures between them—Eleana's young cousin was one, and the other was somebody else. Matz squeezed in beside her. And she regarded him in the semi-darkness. A long time it was they lay like that: a minute or two, or more. And in the beautiful hush, when the noisy world receded, he touched her face—and she touched his, and they saw in each other all that they needed to see, at least for the moment: more than they ever knew it was possible to see in another human being—acceptance, trust, curiosity, desire . . . Finally, he whispered:

81

'You—this moment—no, *you, Eleana*. This is all I have been able to think of . . .'

She nodded, curved him a slow, warm smile: 'I was hoping so,' she murmured, 'but my goodness you took your time!'

He laughed—they both did, a whispered laugh—and they made love to each other—they fucked each other—just there and then. Quietly. *So quietly.* Beside them, the sleeping man—the one who wasn't the cousin—grunted in his sleep, a half-conscious protest at his small space being disturbed; and shunted up as best he could. But he didn't wake.

It was a stolen moment: a moment of enchantment and fierce perfection, shared by two people for whom life had only ever offered struggle. It was a moment which amazed them both.

'*Kishefdik!*' Matz whispered. 'I am a lucky man.'

And she giggled. '*Kishefdik!* Magical. Yes, yes. It was. You are. Let's do it again.'

He gazed at her, through the tenement gloom. There was a small light shining from the parlour, where a few of them were still at work, attaching mother-of-pearl buttons to a heap of child-sized pantaloons, sixty little buttons an hour, ninety child-sized pantaloons a night, fourteen hours a day. Three dollars more a week. '*Sheyn maydl,* Eleana,' he whispered, over the hum of the sweatshop sewing machines, the hum which never stopped; over the snores and grunts of his fellow boarders. 'You're beautiful . . . The most beautiful girl I ever saw.' And she was. He believed she was. Cat's eyes, green as emeralds, warm as a summer moon; and that soft, smiling mouth, that long slim neck, and those eyes . . .

'Your eyes . . .' he whispered. 'All week, all I see are those eyes . . .'

She didn't giggle. She looked at him, looking at her, through the tenement gloom. 'I am not really beautiful,' she said simply. 'But you make me feel as though I were.'

That was how it began. And now, three years on, Matz still worked at the Triangle Waist Company factory during the day and, five nights a week, he worked (though it hardly counted as work) at the Hester Street nickelodeon. During the strike, of course, he and Eleana earned nothing from the factory. But thanks to the nickelodeon, they were better off than many. They had moved to another apartment on the same street, no less cramped or dark or crumbling, and even smaller than the last, but without the elevated railway right outside the window, at least, and with fewer roommates. They lived with Eleana's mother, Batia Kappelman, and Eleana's pregnant cousin, Sarah Kessler, and Sarah's brown-eyed baby Tzivia, and (sometimes) with Sarah's husband Samuel Kessler, who came and went. There was also, temporarily, a greenhorn boarder living with them, a cousin of Sarah's, fresh from the old country and still finding his feet.

And best of all, of course, there was a daughter, Isha. Two years old—eighteen months older than her cousin Tzivia. The girls were as alike as two peas in a pod, so their grandmother always said. But of course they weren't. In any case, Matz and Eleana quietly, confidently noted, Isha was not like anyone, not really. She was their golden child. She could walk and talk already, and she had a smile that could melt all the snow on Hester Street, and eyes as wild and green as her mother's. Her parents

83

wanted nothing less than the world for her: but a different world—one that was kinder and fairer, and which didn't smell of pickled herring and horse manure and rotting vegetables. And where food was plentiful and the air was clean, and where their baby girl didn't have to fight for every soot-filled little breath, and wheeze through every airless night, but where she could sleep comfortably, breathe easily, and know that she was safe.

Isha was never strong—not from the first day. But she had bright green eyes, like her mother, and thick dark curly hair, like her father. And laughter that was so easy, so warm, so infectious, it lightened the burden of all and any who were lucky enough to hear it.

So. They were blessed. They had a roof over their heads and enough food on the table—always enough for Isha, and enough, just about, for them. Unlike his fellow strikers, Matz still brought money home from his work at the nickelodeon and there was just enough, after he had given half of it away, to pay the rent. Better than that, in the apartment they shared with only five others, it had been agreed that when the strike was over, and the greenhorn had found his feet, Eleana, Matz and Isha would have a room of their own.

14

Last night, as she had been making her way home from the Greene Street picket line, Eleana had been approached—ambushed, rather—by Mr Blumenkranz, one of the supervisors at Triangle and someone who, when she wasn't striking, she was forced to deal with on a daily basis. He was a small man, no taller than Eleana, in his late forties, with an unhappy wife at home. Mr Blumenkranz was standing in wait for her, hiding behind a stationary coal cart, because he sensed, quite rightly, that if Eleana had seen him she would have quickly turned and walked the other way. He fell into step as she bustled by, causing her to jump, and offering her no choice but to acknowledge his presence. She glanced about her, unhappy that anyone should spot her fraternizing with the management, and tried to walk on by. But he was quite determined.

'Eleana!' he said, panting slightly to keep pace, struggling for a foothold on the ice.

'Good evening Mr Blumenkranz,' she replied, cool but polite, not glancing at him, walking faster. Since when, she wondered, had he thought to call her Eleana?

He rarely bothered to learn the machinists' names—not first names or second names. Most came and went so fast, why would he bother? But there was generally one girl who caught his eye, whose name he always remembered. Eleana was the one. Everybody noticed it. All the girls. And Matz, too. Mr Blumenkranz's crushes were a long-running joke at Triangle. Sometimes the girl he fixated upon simply left. Couldn't cope with it. Sometimes, when they wouldn't submit to his advances, he fired them. Sometimes they accepted his little gifts, his offers of money and stayed for a little while. Until they were fired. Sometimes, rumours circulated about a girl getting herself in trouble. One way or another, nothing good ever seemed to come of his crushes. To their recipients, it was generally deemed, they were less of a blessing than a curse.

But Eleana was clever, in her quiet way. And somehow she had survived Blumenkranz's cloying attention for longer than the rest, while still keeping him at bay. Her pleasant refusal to engage with him, her ability to slip so innocuously through his fingers, only left him panting for more. Mr Blumenkranz had taken to standing behind her as she bent over her sewing machine, which whirred from the same motor under the same floorboards and at the same speed as the machine beside her, and the machine beside that, and all two hundred machines on the factory's eighth floor . . .

'Ah, Miss Beekman!' he would sigh, above all the racket of the whirring. 'A born machinist, if ever there was one!' As if that were any kind of compliment. And he would turn to the rest of the row, heads bowed, necks and backs twisted over their work: 'If only all you girls could work as efficiently as the lovely Miss Beekman!'

She corrected him once. 'It's Mrs Beekman, Mr Blumenkranz.' Though, strictly speaking, it wasn't. She was still Miss Kappelman. She and Matz weren't yet married. It was something Eleana's mother protested about from time to time. But somehow they had never quite got around to it. There was always something else more urgent to be done, some other more essential way to spend the time and money.

Mr Blumenkranz knew perfectly well she lived with Matz Beekman the cutter—Union sympathist and nothing but trouble, as far as Blumenkranz was concerned. If he could have his way the man would be fired. But a good cutter was hard to find. And everyone knew, Matz was the best they had. So Blumenkranz ignored Eleana's comment. He laid a plump, yearning hand on her thin shoulder. 'Continue your work like this, Miss Beekman,' he said to her, 'and before long we shall make you head of the line!'

Head of the line. Meant an extra $1 a week.

'Head of the line, Miss Beekman! I don't need to remind you—it's another dollar a week!'

She let his hand rest on her shoulder—glanced across at Matz briefly, at the far end of the same floor, where the cutters stood. But Matz was oblivious—busy with his knife, slashing away, muttering Marxist revolution into the ear of the cutter beside him. She let Blumenkranz's finger touch the skin at the top of her neck. Felt nothing—not a shiver of revulsion, because after all, the moment would pass.

When he finally wandered away, Dora, working beside Eleana, glowered at her closest friend.

'*Dershtikt zolstu vern!*' she said furiously. 'You're such a fool.'

'You think so?' Eleana giggled. 'Why's that? The stupid man is driving me crazy!'

'"Miss" Beekman. "Mrs" Beekman. Who the hell cares? Not you! That's for sure. Or you might have done something about it.'

'Oh!' Eleana tutted mildly. 'For sure I care.'

'Blumenkranz adores you, Miss Eleana Kappelman. You're his One and Only.'

'Nonsense! Shh!'

Dora chortled. 'For sure—you're his Chosen One, Ellie! The Only Girl for Him.'

'Shut up, Dora!'

'He loves you better than his own life!'

'You'll have us both fired!'

'Carry on treating him as you do, Eleana, and pretty soon *you* shall be out of a job. That's for certain.'

Eleana tipped her head to imply disagreement, but said nothing.

'You want another a dollar a week? Or don't you?' her friend burst out impatiently.

'Of course I want an extra dollar a week.'

'Because if *you* don't want it, "Mrs" Beekman, I surely do! Mr Blumenkranz can call me anything he likes! I'll take an extra dollar for it, gladly.'

'I'm sure you would, my friend,' Eleana smiled.

'You think I'm a *kurve*? Very well. Perhaps it's so. I am a survivor. That's what I am.'

'And a *kurve*,' Eleana added, laughing now. 'And I shall tell your mama, too. The very next time I see her.'

Dora smiled. 'You think my mama was any better in her day?'

'Well . . . yes, Dora.' Eleana looked at her, quite startled. 'Indeed I do! And you know it too! You're mother is a good woman.'

'Well, Eleana, and so am I. That is exactly my point. I, too, am a good woman. And so are you. But a "good woman" needs to survive. And these are different times. This is America. Life isn't what it was in the Old—'

'Oh, please don't start . . .'

It wasn't that Eleana disagreed with her. Far from it. She only wished that all roads, all conversations—everything—didn't have to lead to the same point. Dora's socialism was becoming

88

more irksome, more all-consuming than even Matz's.

Nevertheless, Eleana didn't correct Mr Blumenkranz again. She put up with his calling her Miss Beekman, leaning over her shoulder so his warm breath ran damp down her spine, and always smiled brightly when he passed. By the time of the strike neither the salary raise, nor the promised head-of-line advancement had materialized. On the other hand, she still had a job at the factory.

And here he was still, all these months later, slip-sliding after her over the ice as she returned from the Greene Street picket line. 'Wait, Eleana!' he panted, skidding in the frozen grime. 'Can't you stop a moment? I have something terribly important—'

'I have to get home, sir,' she said, still walking. 'I have a small daughter waiting. Unless . . .' Away from the factory floor, in these teeming streets, it was harder to hide her disdain. She threw him a glance, mid-stride. 'Unless of course you have a message for the workers?' She smiled at him, without warmth. 'In which case, I'll be sure to pass it on.'

'Not for all the workers. No.'

'Oh. Well then.'

'Eleana.' He took hold of her sleeve and pulled her to a halt. She might have snatched it back. She fought the urge. Because—even now, in the street, with the pathetic, pleading look in his eye, he was still powerful. The strike would not last forever, and there was the life beyond it to consider, when Mr Blumenkranz would once again be standing behind her, his hand on her shoulder, his finger on her neck—choosing whether to fire her, or to make her head of the line.

'What is it, Mr Blumenkranz?' she snapped.

He seemed surprised, as if he hadn't really expected her to stop. 'I have an offer for you,' he said. 'I wrote it down . . .' He fumbled in the pockets of his thick winter coat. Eleana, standing still and wearing a jacket far thinner than his, began to shiver. 'Wait a moment,' he mumbled. 'Wait there . . .' But the paper could not be found, not in all the many pockets of his thick, warm coat and, finally, he abandoned the search. 'I simply wanted to say . . . that you're better than all this! It is irresponsible nonsense, what you are engaged in, and you can do better, Eleana. Much, much better.'

'Better than what?'

'Look at you—so cold. Your coat is so thin.'

'Certainly it is thinner than yours.'

'Eleana, my dear, you know you cannot win. None of you can win!'

'Several other factories have already settled. You know they have.'

'But not Triangle! Mr Blanck and Mr Harris have both said that they will fight you to the end. And they can because they have the rescources, and they have done so and, trust me, they will continue to do so. They will keep the factory working with or without you. They will never accept the Union. Never.'

He looked up at her, spotted the split-second of uncertainty in her eyes and, instinctively, he pressed his advantage. 'But I could help you,' he wheedled. 'If you would allow me, Eleana, I could help *you*. Did you have breakfast this morning? I'll bet you didn't.' His eyes were on her lips. 'I can organize a payment. *For you*. It would be our secret, just between us. I can do that . . . if you are willing . . .'

'What sort of payment, Mr Blumenkranz?' she asked him politely. 'Tell me, sir. What did you have in mind?'

But he didn't hear her, not properly. He was gazing at her lips, and imagining himself, with his arms around her—pushing her back into the alley, right there, behind the rubble, the pile of rotting . . . whatever it was, and pulling up her skirt—and he couldn't do all that and listen properly, not at the same time.

'. . . Fair pay for all,' she was saying. 'Union recognition. Fewer hours for all of us, Mr Blumenkranz, not just for me. It cannot continue . . .'

'But I can help you,' Mr Blumenkranz pleaded. 'You look hungry. Eleana. Of course you are hungry! What are you living off, while the strike is on? You cannot live on ideals! And nor can your child. Think of your child! Do you need money? I can give you money. How much do you need?' Again, he was fumbling in his pockets.

But this time, when he looked up, she was gone; vanished. And he was standing alone on the bustling, noisy street. Yearning. Burning.

Such is the lot of the small, plain man with an unhappy wife and a hateful job: neither in one camp nor the other, neither rich nor poor, and in thrall to a young woman who despises him, to whom he has promised a dollar-a-week raise, and from whom, until recently, there had rarely been anything but smiles. No wonder, by the following morning, after he'd tossed and turned and failed to sleep on her rejection, while his unhappy wife snored foully beside him—no wonder he was angry.

15

It had been agreed by strike organizers that the pickets should, as far as possible, consist of young and attractive women workers whose suffering elicited better public sympathy, and that the striking men would be more usefully put to work behind the scenes. So it was that the following morning Eleana was due back on the picket at Greene Street, outside the workers' entrance to her own factory. Meanwhile, Matz intended to spend the morning flitting between picket lines city-wide, informing strikers of the Union meeting later that day, boosting morale with his eloquent passion and, above all, keeping an eye on the police—who were less liable to erupt into violence when there were men about.

Eleana hadn't intended to mention the incident with Blumenkranz, but as she and Matz were leaving the apartment that morning—without breakfast, and with a sickly daughter clinging tearfully to Eleana's neck, the thought flitted through her mind: if she'd said yes to Blumenkranz, how different things would be. There would be breakfast for everyone. And a good breakfast for Isha. There might be a new coat for Isha, too; and warm blankets, a new coat for herself, and even for Matz. She spoke over her daughter's small, frail shoulder without pausing to think of the consequences:

'Blumenkranz stopped me as I was coming home.' She smiled, a shy smile. 'He took a hold of my sleeve, and wouldn't let go. And he called me

"Eleana"! Can you believe it?'

Matz, waiting impatiently for her at the door, didn't reply. He scowled.

A moment passed. Matz understood at once what Blumenkranz would have been after—of course, as she had intended he would. What on earth had possessed her to mention it? Silently, Eleana cursed herself. She turned back to Isha, wailing with surprising gusto for a sickly child. She stroked her daughter's face, embarrassed of herself, and relieved of the distraction. 'Enough,' she murmured, kissing the small, dark head—'You have to stay with your *bubbeh* today, my darling. I have to leave now. Try to help your *bubbeh*. Or you can play with Tzivia.'

'Tzivia is not kind to me.'

'Nonsense. She's a baby!'

'*Bubbeh* likes Tzivia better.'

'Oh, what nonsense!' Eleana laughed. Looked across at her mother. '*Bubbeh* doesn't like either of you much. And I don't blame her, the fuss you both make!'

Isha fell silent, uncertain whether her mother was teasing.

'. . . And I shall be back before you know it,' Eleana said, kissing her daughter's sweet, soft cheek, postponing the moment of departure.

Matz looked on, forcing himself to wait—but his anger with Eleana only added to his vast impatience. Every cell in his body longed to extricate itself from this small, domestic scene and to get back out into the world. It was eating up what little air there was in the room. 'Ishie, angel,' he said a moment later, 'let go of your mother. You'll see her in no time. Be brave, now. She has important work to do. Let go of her at once.'

He took a few steps back into the room, dropped a kiss on the girl's head. Disentangled her small arms from Eleana's neck and dumped her, without further ado, at the feet of her grandmother.

'Take her, *Bubbeh*! For goodness sake,' he said. 'We are already late, as it is.'

Leaving behind the small, crying child, and the crowded, airless flat, they walked quickly through the brittle cold. Beneath the lines of grey laundry, frozen stiff in the filthy city air, dodging pedlars and garbage heaps, Matz and Eleana walked through the clotted, squalid streets in angry silence, Eleana struggling to keep pace. Beside her, or just ahead of her, she could feel Matz's brooding fury, and it infuriated her. She had done nothing wrong. Nothing whatsoever. Except to inform him of an event for which she had absolutely no responsibility. If Matz wanted to be kept in the dark about such things, then he was a fool. More of a fool than she realized. And more of a child than Isha.

She didn't want to walk all the way to Greene Street with him, not in his current mood. 'Perhaps you should head over to the Bijou factory?' she suggested, panting behind him. 'I hear they had the police at the picket there yesterday.'

'Of course that's what you hear,' Matz snapped. 'I told you about it.'

'A couple of the girls were beaten to within an inch,' she persevered. 'And they arrested twenty more.'

'That's what I told you.'

'They'll be in need of a boost. After something like that . . .'

'You're trying to get rid of me, are you?'

She laughed, and shook her head.

'So you can cuddle up with Blumenkranz, I dare say. How much did he offer you?'

'Oh! You're being ridiculous.'

'How much?'

'"How much?"' she mimicked irritably to the back of his head—more to herself than to him. 'How much, indeed? *Es iz nit dayn gesheft . . .*'

'What's that?' he stopped abruptly, glared at her. *'Es iz nit dayn gesheft*? What, exactly, is not "my business", Eleana? When my own wife is offering herself like a whore! Tell me!'

She glanced at him and kept walking, too angry to speak.

They marched on through the teeming crowds, stepping around the scrawny, frozen carcass of an old horse on the corner of Essex Street without even noticing, too accustomed to the squalor to register it. They were oblivious to everything but their anger. At the end of the road, Matz stopped again. *'How much did he offer*?' he repeated. 'He must have offered something! Did he name a price?'

She gazed back at him, torn between laughter and pure, burning rage. How dared he even ask? 'He told me, any price,' she said. 'So I told him fifty dollars, Matz. Which would help us enormously, would it not? Since you insist on giving half your money away, and I am earning nothing at all, and we have a daughter who is sick. We could buy a warm jacket for Isha. Give her a decent meal . . .' They gazed at one another. She wondered, briefly, wildly, if he might hit her. And if he did—what she would do? Of course, she would hit him back. 'I told him fifty dollars,' she said again. She leaned a little closer to her husband. 'And he is considering it.' She turned, then, without another word, blood roaring in her ears.

By the time she reached Greene Street, twenty minutes later, she regretted having lost her temper. Of course. Bitterly regretted what she had said. He must have believed her. She must have hurt him. In any case, he had not followed her.

There were fifty or more of her fellow workers clustered together by the factory's locked grille gate, already in position, chanting slogans, their banners aloft.

At the sight of her friend, Dora Wiseman broke off at once. 'At last! I thought you were never coming!' she shouted, pulling at Eleana's arm. 'Where have you been? Have you heard what they have planned for us? Stand firm, mind! We must not rise to it, or they triumph. I swear, when they come, I shall laugh! I shall laugh in their filthy faces!'

'When *who* comes, Dora? What are you saying? Pass me a banner, won't you! And some leaflets. I hate to stand here empty handed—'

'Don't you see all the police, El? They have their paddy wagons parked just round the corner. They're only waiting to fill them up and cart us off to the Tombs!'

Yanking her mind, finally, from her stupid squabble, Eleana glanced about her—they were indeed surrounded. The city police were everywhere; and they were waiting for something, all right. They were standing in a semicircle around the women, arms folded and smirking, as if in possession of a secret and highly amusing joke.

96

Eleana could sense, as all the women could, that something was afoot. Something bad was surely about to happen.

The factory gates were due to open any moment. Mr Blumenkranz would be down, with his stopwatch, and then the strikebreakers would come shambling in. Shamefaced. Scooped from hunger and desperation—direct from the immigration office at Ellis Island, more often than not, before the poor souls had even made it to the mainland. Normally the sight of them, shuffling pathetically through the factory gates, only strengthened Eleana's resolve. It was the factory owners who were her enemy, not the bedraggled creatures they employed to keep their dirty, dangerous factories making money for them.

'They think they can insult us—'

'*Who*? Dora—'

'Why, the bosses, you fool! But they have no idea of the strength of our feelings. A fink is a fink no matter who or what else they are. What do we care? Oh! And there is Mr Blumenkranz—look! He's come down at last. They shall be arriving any minute. Look at him, with his secret smirk—he thinks he can shock us! Ha! But we already know!' She leaned forward and yelled though the crowd, '*Nothing will shock us, Mr Blumenkranz!* You cannot insult us! You only insult yourselves!'

Eleana nudged her. 'Dora—for goodness' sake. The day has hardly begun. Can't you calm down, just for a moment at least, and tell me what is happening?'

But by then some of the others had spotted him too. Fury erupted from the ranks of striking women, and their chanting drowned out everything

97

else.

'WE'D-RATHER-STARVE-QUICK-THAN-STARVE-SLOW, *BLUMENKRANZ*!

'WE FIGHT TO THE DEATH! AND WE FIGHT TO WIN!'

'DORA! Tell me!' Eleana yelled. 'In God's name, what is happening?'

'WE-FIGHT-TO-WIN, *BLUMENKRANZ*!' Dora yelled, and the veins stuck out on her thin neck. 'WE-FIGHT-TO-WIN!'

Blumenkranz scanned the crowed. Sweaty, in his thick woollen suit, despite the cold, he looked jittery—taken aback by the women's passion. His eyes found Eleana, and stopped still.

Dora pulled her friend's ear towards her. 'They have hired streetwalkers, Eleana!' she shouted. 'Filthy *kurve* from the Bowery! Yes, that's right! To replace us machinists—they have herded up the Bowery whores! And the pimps are in on it. And everyone is in on it. And they shall be here any minute. And Emma says they will be driven here in automobiles—'

'In automobiles!'

As she spoke the word, a fleet of cars appeared from around the corner of Washington Place. The cars pulled up, one by one, stopping in a neat line by the workers' entrance, directly in front of the striking women. Automobile doors opened—and from behind them the hated *kurve* emerged.

With their gaudy clothes and hard, painted faces, there was no mistaking what they were. Nor, indeed, their pimps, tripping out, smirking, behind them. It had all been staged, of course: an elaborate, expensive taunt, dreamed up by the two factory owners, Mr Harris and Mr Blanck, penniless immigrants themselves, once. A long little time ago. Not only would they keep their factory running in the face of the strike—they would illustrate to the picketers in what low esteem they held the workforce, and just how easily they could be replaced.

Max Blanck, snickering nervously from behind closed windows on the tenth floor, watched as their little stunt took effect. The ripples of hatred could be felt from ten floors above; so much so, indeed, that he turned to his brother-in-law beside him, and wondered aloud if they hadn't perhaps taken the thing too far?

His partner snapped for silence. He couldn't hear what was happening.

Far below them, before the still-locked gate, the strikers had closed in on the new arrivals and formed a seething, hissing line across the sidewalk, blocking the factory's entrance. Of its own accord, with no instructions shouted, a quite different kind of picket line had formed: one that nothing but physical force would break.

Torn between protecting their stock, and merry amusement at the unlikely drama unfolding, the pimps simply stood back to watch. So, too, for a little while, did the city police. Pimps, police, and factory-hired thugs mingled cheerfully together, and for several moments nothing happened. Hatred simmered. The women squared up to one another while the men stood still, smirking and goading. Violence simmered unexpressed in the air.

It was impossible to say exactly when or how it began, but quite suddenly the fighting erupted. It seemed to break out simultaneously all across the line. Eleana remembered one of the streetwalkers spitting in Dora's face. And then Dora lifting her hand to wipe the spittle away, or perhaps, Eleana feared, to lash out at her assailant. She remembered snatching Dora's wrist and holding it there, and shouting out—*yelling* at her:

'It's what they're waiting for, Dora! One wrong step . . .' Eleana motioned to the police surrounding them, arms crossed, eyes peeled. 'One wrong step, and they shall . . .' But she couldn't finish, because it appeared they had already taken it. From the left, the prostitute whose spit had landed in Dora's eye seized her advantage and laid her clenched fist on Dora's cheek. Eleana relinquished her grasp on Dora's wrist; Dora hit out; a police officer grabbed Eleana from behind.

. . . And then, pandemonium.

Eleana glanced through the scramble of bodies, the long skirts, broken banners, flying leaflets, lashing arms and legs. Someone yanked her backwards by the hair, her hat tumbled, her neck twisted . . . Wildly, she cast about her for something, someone to grasp hold of, some simple way to fight back. But she was helpless. From behind the grilles of his locked factory gate, she spotted Blumenkranz gazing at her, his eyes fixed, a look of pleasure—intense pleasure, revenge and desire—settled on his face. It was the last thing she saw before her head hit the sidewalk, and her assailant's club came down on her.

She lay still, face down in the snow, hands covering her bare head as the club beat down on her. Her arms were yanked from her head and into a shoulder lock, and she screamed in renewed pain, but still the blows rained down. Lying there, she believed her moment had come. She believed she was about to die. But then, suddenly, the pain stopped.

Her arms fell loose. And the body of her attacker dropped like a stone beside her. Fearfully, she opened her eyes, saw his uniformed bulk lying limp, his face frozen with surprise. She stared at him, waiting for the next blow, but it didn't come. He didn't move. And then two hands were lifting her gently to her feet.

'Forgive me,' Matz said to her, holding her to him. 'I'm a fool. I was a fool—Eleana. Can you forgive me?'

'Forgive you?' she repeated, confused.

He indicated the policeman, still at their feet: 'Did he hurt you?'

'I'm fine . . .'

Matz would have led her away. But the violence had reached a crescendo and he was yanked back into the vicious throng. She stood for a moment, disorientated in the midst of it all, her head spinning, blood seeping down her cheek, soaking her clean white collar. By now the pimps had launched themselves into the fray. They were trying to pull their women out. The factory-hired security, too, had come thundering in. Strikers were attacking the streetwalkers. Police were attacking strikers. Security, pimps and streetwalkers were attacking anyone and everyone in sight.

And there was Eleana in the heart of it, staggering for balance, the edges of her vision slowly turning to black until she lost the battle and quietly sank to the ground, exactly where she stood.

Somehow, from the chaos, the factory owners' will prevailed. The *kurve* were extricated from the rabble and shepherded into the building. The

101

factory doors slammed shut and the pimps slunk silently away. Yet the fighting between picket line and police continued unabated. Eleana lay in the midst of it, unconscious and ignored. A few yards away, a group of four officers had set to work on Matz.

She came round as they were lifting his battered body off the sidewalk, dragging it to the police wagons around the corner, and the voice of Dora was ringing in her ears. 'Eleana, WAKE UP! They're taking him off! They'll lock him in the Tombs! They'll put a fine on him so high we shall never have enough to pay it. They might just as well throw away the key. *Do something*! Think of something! Oh, El, *wake up*!'

With the prostitutes removed from the scene, and the police busy carting their crop of captives to the paddy wagons, the riot had lost its fire. Eleana looked on, helpless. She knew where they were taking him. Of course. And not for the first time, either. Matz was known to the police. Known to the city magistrates. Last time they took him, they fined him just $10 and he was able to walk free. This time, Dora was right, it wouldn't be so easy. Now that Union activities seemed to pose a genuine threat, the courts were flexing their muscles. Added to which, Max had taken out a city cop; brought him to the floor in front of hundreds of witnesses.

Eleana stood up, leaning her weight on Dora, and looked desperately through the crowd in search of someone who could help. But there were only women there, fighting for their own survival. She called after him, but he didn't turn; didn't appear to hear her.

'Do something!' Dora pleaded.

'I don't know what . . .' But then, standing by the factory door, quietly observing the scene, she spotted Mr Blumenkranz. He looked at Eleana, who looked back at him, and even then—from that position of power—there was a look of desperation about him.

Dora nudged her friend towards him and tactfully melted into the crowd.

16

Two cold, painful days passed before they transported Matz from the cells to the court that adjoined them. It was not the first time he had appeared in that courtroom—nor even, as luck would have it, his first appearance before that same, hostile judge. On this occasion, as he stood before Judge Olmsted, his face cut and swollen and with a ribcage cracked, he struggled to stand unaided, and the judge, infuriated by all that the prisoner's wounds implied about the men who had dragged him here, took exorbitant offence.

'Straighten up, Mr Beekman!' he said. 'Bear yourself like a man at least, when you stand before me!'

Matz Beekman did not attempt to bear himself any differently. He could not have done so anyway, even if he'd wished, which he did not. 'I have been clubbed and beaten, sir,' Matz replied. 'I have been kept in a cell for forty hours without food, and dragged to this court for what? For exercising what is my legal right to picket peaceably—'

'Silence. Stand up!'

'*I* bear myself like a man, Your Honour. But do you?'

'You are charged with—'

'*Do YOU?*' Matz yelled out, unable to contain his fury. And the thunder of it, from that broken body, made the courtroom jump.

It did not help his case. A fine was set at $100: an impossibly large amount, as the judge well understood. Matz would be held at the city jail until he paid it, Olmsted decreed, or for a maximum of three years.

As they yanked him, handcuffed, from the dock, every muscle and bone in his body protesting, he scoured the public gallery one last time. But Eleana was not there.

They put him in a cell with two other men: a Union member, in no better physical shape than he was, and a common house robber. Matz might have shared his own experiences with both, but he spoke to neither. The bars of their tiny cell, four floors up, overlooked the internal gangway, and for an hour each morning he watched his fellow inmates tramping past on their daily exercise, but his own body was too broken to join them. He lay on his cot, thinking.

He knew she would come. And he knew she would come with the money. Because he knew her. And that was what he thought about as he lay there, too battered to move or to speak. He thought of Eleana—doing what he knew she would do, because she loved him; what he prayed she would do, because he hated it here, and what he prayed she would not do, because she was his.

She came for him four days later, the money in her purse. After she had filled in the forms and

104

paid the dues in Blumenkranz's filthy dollar notes, she sat down to wait for him.

It was a long wait, but at length he emerged from behind the last of the heavy, locked doors. She leapt to her feet, unbearably nervous, and stood before him at the far end of that long, bleak room, waiting, holding their child to her hip, the tighter, the closer he approached. Behind her, at their high wooden counter, a couple of officials were busy at work. Behind him the heavy door slammed shut. There was no one else present but she held back, watching him on his painful journey through the room. The gash across his forehead was beginning to heal, she noticed, but the bruises—the edge of an imprint of a policeman's boot—were still livid on his face, and he was obviously weak.

He shuffled to a standstill before her without yet raising his eyes to meet hers. Instead he looked at his beautiful Isha, beaming up at him. He held out his arms, the child clambered into them and he buried his face in her hair, breathed her sweet smell. And collected himself.

'*Mayn Khaver,*' Eleana said softly. 'My friend. My good friend. Hello there, Matz . . . You look terrible.' She smiled.

He didn't reply.

'I missed you,' she said. 'We both missed you. And you see . . .' She stopped. 'I have missed you horribly, Matz. I couldn't have borne it. Not for three years. Thank God you are free.'

'It's not God I have to thank,' he said roughly, through his daughter's thick hair. She waited until he looked at her. A moment passed, when even Isha didn't speak. Standing alone in that long, barren room, the mundane echoes of officialdom

105

behind them, Matz and Eleana searched each other's faces.

He put the baby down. It was a long silence, longer than most people could have endured. Finally, he reached out, touched her: '*Mayn likhtik ponim*, my Eleana. No matter what. I love you . . .'

'No matter what,' she said, 'I love you too.'

And they kissed, and took the baby, and headed home.

Divorce Capital

17

Hollywood, 18 October 1929

M,
I shall be gone for a few days. I think it's about
time we talked, don't you?
E

Max laid her letter back on the dressing table just
as he found it and stood before it, at a loss, stunned
to inactivity. It was not his natural state. He was a
little drunk, he realized. Rather more than a little.
In any case, he returned downstairs, crossed the
yard to the staff bungalow and rapped on Teresa's
door.

Moments later the housekeeper stood nervously
before him, dressed in nightshirt and curling rags.
She held her front door barely ajar, alarmed to
see him at such a time, and in such a place. He
had never ventured to the staff bungalow before.
Alarmed, too—though of course she had seen his
wife's note when she came to take the breakfast
tray—by his dishevelled state. In her experience,
having worked for the Beechams since the house
was completed eight years before, Mr Beecham was
never dishevelled. Like his wife, he was always in
control.

'Teresa—my apologies. My apologies,' he
mumbled, aware—suddenly—of the awkwardness
of his presence. 'But I wondered if you might . . .
Do you or Joseph happen to know . . . Did Mrs
Beecham happen to mention . . .' He tried again.

'Teresa—do you know where she has gone?'

It was Teresa's husband, Joseph, who had driven Eleanor to the train station. Teresa called him to the door.

'Did she tell you where she was going, Joseph?'

'She didn't specify, sir.'

'You didn't ask?'

Joseph shrugged. 'She didn't seem to be in the mind for talking.'

Max thought about that. 'Was she . . . alone?'

Again Joseph seemed to hesitate. 'Joseph, *was she alone*?' Max asked again. 'Or did she . . . was she . . . For example, was Miss Gredson with her?'

'Miss Gredson?'

'Or one of her other girlfriends?' he suggested hopefully. Eleanor didn't have many girlfriends. 'One of the other girls. I don't know . . . Or perhaps—did she meet anyone at the station?'

'There was a young lady at the gate . . .'

'What kind of young lady?'

He shrugged. 'A young lady. I think she was a fan. She was waving some kind of an autograph paper.'

'And?'

'She was gone when I got back, so I guess she was after Mr Cooper.'

Impatiently, Max shook his head. 'But no one at the station, I'm asking you? For example . . .' He stopped, swallowed. 'There wasn't a tall, light-haired . . . gentleman?'

'No, sir! Absolutely not! Not that I saw. Mrs Beecham was all alone.'

But by then Max had decided not to believe him. 'Well,' he said. 'Thank you. I'm sorry. Very sorry to bother you. Good night to you both . . .'

He turned back towards the house, returned to the hall—his beautiful black and white marbled hall, smelling of lilies. How quiet it seemed, suddenly! He stood still, stared at the telephone, its silence thundering in his ears. His hands were burning. His head was aching. The telephone was quiet.

I think it's about time we talked, don't you?

He made two calls. The first, to Blanche. Because . . . He wasn't sure why. It felt better to hear her voice than to hear no one at all.

But Blanche wasn't home. Where in hell was she, he wondered—briefly, vaguely. And then, because he was drunk and desperate, and he had to do something and he couldn't think what else to do, he called Butch. It was the first time since he left for Silverman.

No answer. Max spoke to the night porter, who told him Butch was away for the weekend.

'Where is he?'

'I'm sorry sir?'

'I'm asking you where he is.'

'Well, sir, I have no idea.'

'Can't you find out?'

'No sir. He doesn't tell me where he goes. But would you like to leave a message for him?'

Max didn't bother to reply.

He couldn't face the empty house, or the curious looks of his housekeepers, or the silence of the goddamn telephone. Nor the note, declaring war: still sitting at its unjaunty angle beside the little jewel box with the ruby heart inside, which meant nothing to either of them. Less than nothing, actually. The memory of it—and the hurried vulgarity with which he had chosen it, fobbed her

111

off with it, was not comfortable for him. It wasn't something he wanted to dwell on.

He thought of dropping in at Blanche's. He was sorely tempted. But to do that, to turn up at her door without invitation, drunk, in the middle of the night, would be breaking all sorts of unspoken rules between them. She might be with someone else. Or she might not. Either way, she would take his appearance on her doorstep—in such a state, at such a time—to signify more than he wanted it to. And in any case, he realized, he didn't want to see her. He wanted to see Eleanor. He wanted her to tell him that nothing had changed. They didn't have to talk. He loved her. She loved him. There was nothing to talk about.

He needed to find her, he realized, so he could tell her that. They still loved each other. There was nothing to talk about.

So he climbed into his car and drove—nowhere and everywhere—zigzagging on a drunkard's mission. He almost hit someone on his way out— another dumb broad, leaping out at him: one of these days one of them was going to get killed. One of these days he'd get a plaque made: *Gary Cooper Lives Next Door*.

But not tonight.

Tonight, he drove to the filthy little hostel in downtown LA where he and Eleanor had stayed all those years ago, black smoke still clogging their lungs. Perhaps he would find her there?

But he couldn't find her there. The building was gone.

He drove up to the old studio at Edendale, where it all began, their dizzy journey to the dizzy heights . . . and then he drove back to Hollywood, to the bungalow on Poinsettia, where they were living when they signed the contract—him and her and Butch Menken. It was where they were living when they finally got married, and where they were living when they built the *Castillo* . . . Perhaps she would be waiting for him there.

But she was nowhere.

So he drove on, west again. Back towards home. That was the intention, but then somehow he found he'd pulled up outside Butch's apartment block. He parked the car by the main entrance and waited. It was a stupid idea. He hated it, every minute he sat there; despised himself. Butch wasn't home. The porter had already told him. Butch was somewhere else, with Max's wife.

The vigil kept him busy at least. It kept him away from the *Castillo* and its silent telephone and it kept him away from Blanche. Some small grain of chivalry told him how important it was that he didn't involve her in any of this. So he sat, biting his nails, nursing his aching hands and imagining Eleanor as she had been, as she was right now. This minute.

He woke in the early dawn, neck stiff, head throbbing and like a homing pigeon, he drove towards the only place he could bear to be: his desk at Silverman Pictures.

18

At the sight of Joel Silverman's Bugatti in the parking lot he felt a sour, unhappy twist. His sprightly, unsympathetic employer—whom, until yesterday, he'd believed was his unquestioning ally, was the last person on earth he wanted to deal with that morning.

He was tempted to drive away—but to where? Where else could he go this morning? He needed to be at his desk. It was the place he felt the safest, always; the only place where he was able to think.

So he parked up beside the Bugatti and headed across the sunny courtyard, hoping against hope and all experience that he might slip into the building, and past Silverman's door without being noticed.

'Max Beecham!' bellowed Silverman with the customary vigour from his desk, a room and two half-open doors away. The sound of his voice made Max wince. 'I *thought* that was your filthy, dishevelled shape I spotted shambling across my parking lot this early morning!'

Max wondered if he could perhaps tiptoe on past the door, pretend he hadn't heard him.

'No good cowering out there, Max! I've seen you! Get on in here!'

It was a long, wide room. A vast room, actually. Joel, not tall by any stretch, sat at the far end of it, a large window looking out over the barren Hollywood hills behind him, and an impressive walnut desk in front, oval, with solid gold edging, and the size of a large dining table. He looked small and neat behind it. His walnut-coloured oval head was perfectly framed by the matching, high-backed, gold-edged walnut throne. He sat quite still: a small, dense bundle of power and energy, watching Max as he loped unhappily towards him, not quite the angry man who had barged in to his office yesterday.

114

Joel sniffed the air. 'I can smell the liquor on you from here,' he said. 'What in hell did you get up to last night? You look like a tramp.'

Max gave a careless shrug and flopped into the seat opposite him. 'What's up?'

Joel considered him a moment or two. 'Everything OK?'

'Everything's fine.'

'You've been watching the markets?'

Max shook his head.

'Bad day yesterday . . . It's going to be bad again today . . .'

Max said carelessly. 'Maybe Charlie's right.'

'Charlie Chaplin is always right,' Joel said dryly.

'Ha! Ain't that just so . . .' Max should call his broker. He would do that. Later.

Joel shook his head. 'I hope you got yourself covered, Max, my friend. It's not going to be pretty today. I'm selling. Selling out. Just put in the orders . . .'

'It's only a hiccup,' Max said automatically. 'It's what everyone's saying.'

'You read the *Post* yesterday? And the *Times*? . . . It's time to get out, I'm telling you. The party's over. Take my advice. Charlie's right. *Butch Menken* is right. Take the hit. Make a loss if you have to. Sell while you can.'

But Max didn't want to talk about the markets. He didn't want to talk about Butch. He didn't want to sell. He gazed out of the window. Sulky. Nervous. He should call his broker. 'Beautiful morning,' he mumbled. It was all he could think to say.

'What are you doing in here on a Saturday, anyway? It's seven o'clock in the morning.'

Max looked at Joel. 'I could ask you the same

115

thing.'

'You could . . .' agreed Silverman.

'But I didn't.'

'Ha!'

Max gave him a thin smile. They liked each other. Trusted each other, up to a point—more or less. There weren't many you could say that about in this town.

'It's good you're here, anyway,' Silverman continued. 'I was looking at the test audience feedback from *Lost At Sea*.'

'Oh.'

Joel studied him, his difficult son: 'You thought I wouldn't see them?'

Max shrugged: 'I'm doing a second screening.'

'What? Just like that? With no changes?'

'No changes.'

Joel sighed. 'They didn't understand the end. *No one* understood the end.'

'They were morons.'

'All audiences are morons,' Joel said.

'Not the audiences I want.'

'Then pretty soon you won't have any audiences.'

Max didn't reply. He looked over Joel's shoulder at the hills beyond, and wondered where his wife was.

'Also . . .' Joel hesitated. 'Max, I have to tell you that Butch Menken has taken a look—'

'He what?'

'He came in and took a look at a couple of things . . .'

'Oh come on! You showed him my movie without telling me?'

'And he agrees . . . with me. It's a good film. Nobody's arguing with that.'

116

'That's mighty good of you both.'

'But Butch and I agree—'

'*Butch-and-I-agree* . . .' Max mimicked him childishly.

'—that we need to go with the test audience.'

'Is that right?'

'Yes, Max. That's right.'

'Dammit, Joel, I know what I'm doing. The audience we had was the wrong audience. We should have done the screening after work—it's not a movie aimed at dumb broads with nothing to do all day except ruin my test screenings. Of course they didn't like it! It's about men at sea. Fighting.'

'Also . . . we got feedback from the Catholic League of Ladies,' Joel continued.

Max held his throbbing head, and groaned.

'They don't like it.'

'Oh. You don't say.'

'They don't like the tone.'

'They never like the tone!'

'They don't like the whole idea of the mutiny. It upsets the—'

'Oh *come on!*'

Silverman shrugged. 'They're going to push for every state censor in the country to ban it. They want it banned. Max, I don't have to tell you what that means. We've got to change the end.'

'We can't change the end!'

'And the middle. And the beginning. We can't put it out like it is—because nobody's going to take it. Not a theatre outside Los Angeles. We have to take the whole thing apart and re-edit. So.'

He waited for Max to say something. Anything. But Max didn't oblige. 'So . . .' he said again. 'Max? What have you got?'

'Nothing.'

Silverman shook his head. 'Not good enough. Monday morning. You, me and Leeson. Get Leeson back in for a re-edit. We're going back to the beginning. Going through everything you and Leeson cut out and we're putting it back in again. In the right order, this time. And don't tell me it's impossible because I've seen the dailies. We have at least three different movies in the can.'

'On the floor.'

'We need to pick it all back up off the floor. And stick together the version that won't give the Catholic dames any nightmares . . .' Joel paused, looked briefly sheepish. 'Butch wants to stick in some singing numbers,' he added. 'Which means a few days reshooting . . .'

Max opened his mouth.

'Enough,' Joel Silverman snapped. 'Enough, Max.'

'Joel, this is the best movie I ever made. It's the big one. If this one's not a hit . . .'

'You said that about the last one.'

'But—'

'And the movie before that. Enough. Max, I like you. You know that. I love you. I love your movies. But we got stock prices dropping like a stone. We got the economy on a precipice here . . . No more risks. No more. This is not the time. We need a hit. *You* need a hit. Go home to your wife. Take a bath, for God's sake. Come back Monday morning with a new attitude. We're starting again.'

19

They had come to Reno together eleven years ago. It was a month after the War had ended and the first and last time she had ever visited. She and Max, with new identity papers, new contracts with one of the largest studios in Hollywood and an undreamed-of fortune in the bank; they had travelled across this same desert to this same small city at the foot of the Sierra Nevada mountains, to tie the marital knot—quickly, quietly—and at last.

As Eleanor sat quietly in her first-class carriage, she tried not to dwell on the previous visit. What a magical, delusional journey it had been; she and Matz with the world at their feet—all the hope they had carried with them then.

Hope, she reminded herself, which wasn't quite extinguished. Not yet. Not for her, or she would not be returning today. With or without Matz. *Max.* She was here in Reno again, full of hope—not to marry anyone, nor even to unmarry them, she assured herself. No.

Divorce may not have been what brought Eleanor to Reno. But it tended to be the reason most people in the Reno-bound first-class train carriages made the journey. A city in the middle of nowhere: 500 miles from Los Angeles, almost 3,000 miles from New York, it had little else to recommend it.

Reno, Nevada was famous for only one thing. It was the Divorce Capital of the World, and it had been for several years. Mary Pickford planted the fact onto the national consciousness when she came to Reno to take advantage of the state's uniquely liberal divorce laws, back in 1921 (only to return to Hollywood a few days later and marry that silly fool Dougie Fairbanks, Eleanor reflected; there was no accounting for taste). Until then, to most people, if they had heard of it at all, Reno represented nothing more than hicksville: a dusty pit stop for cowboys and silver prospectors.

By 1929 the streets twinkled with electric lights, gleamed with slick, modern luxury hotels, fashion stores, smart restaurants, casinos and expensive lawyers' offices. Movie stars, society figures, anyone who could afford it: they all came to Reno to avail themselves of Nevada's divorce laws, and the city had grown rich off the back of them.

Outside her train window, dawn broke on a new day. The long miles of desert scrub which Eleanor had been gazing on, unseeingly, through most of the night and through first glimmers of sunrise, had turned abruptly into the brutal green lines of suburban gardens, and the train was slowing to a stop. Eleanor had been dressed for hours— drinking coffee; staring into the darkness. She had barely slept with the thrill of what the next few days might yet bring.

Alone in her carriage in the middle of the desert, in the middle of the night, anything had seemed possible. But now she was here, the station platform awaiting her, and she wondered what madness had possessed her to come. It was a wild goose chase, one which Max had turned his back on long ago. Damn him. But she couldn't do it. For her, the search would never end.

Nervy as hell, she pulled her hat down onto her head, hid her eyes behind sunglasses—red from lack of sleep this morning; permanently red, in any case, like most movie actors', because of the harsh klieg lights the studios used for filming. She wrapped a silver fox fur around her chin— unneeded in the desert warmth, but it hid her face—and regretted very much having employed a detective agency in a city where reporters lurked on every corner and waited to greet every new train that came in.

Too late. It was done. There was no turning back. Employing an agency in Los Angeles would have been difficult, for fear of her identity being discovered: not only by the press, but by Max, who had expressly pleaded with her not to do it. New York would have been the obvious choice of course, except back then—God, even yesterday morning—she had still hoped, one day, to win Max over; that this day would arrive, and that Max would have been beside her.

But Max could never have come back with her to New York. So here she was in Reno, alone. It was Saturday morning. She'd called the bureau from the station, before her train rolled out of Los Angeles, and it had been really very obvious that Matthew Gregory had not been expecting to hear from her. He sounded quite put out. He had apologized— profusely—and explained to Eleanor that under no circumstances would he be available until after the weekend.

She might have turned back at that point. She considered it, but not for long. The train ticket was bought, after all. The note to her husband was written. She had left the house. The decision, put off for so long, had finally been made.

And now here she was in Reno. She would spend

the weekend alone, gathering her thoughts, and go to the bureau first thing Monday morning.

20

Gregory had taken a private apartment for her in the Riverside Hotel, a hotel Eleanor already knew by repute. Conveniently close to the courthouse (not for Eleanor, but for most of its clientele), the Riverside was the finest of a fine crop of hotels in the Divorce Capital of the World, and it had been designed, Gregory assured her, with client discretion uppermost in everyone's mind.

Her rooms were booked under the name of Miss E. B. Kappelman. Of course. For the same reason she had employed a detective agency five hundred miles from her and Max's home. Kappelman was the name she used in all her business dealings with the Gregory Bureau. And Mr Gregory's father had died, she assumed, none the wiser as to her true identity. She wondered what were the chances of Mr Gregory (Junior) meeting her in the flesh and failing to recognize her. Was it possible?

She didn't venture beyond the Film Colony much, not any more. Her studio contract, like all star contracts, dictated so much, from her clothes and hairstyle to the words she spoke in public, with whom and where, that it would have been almost impossible for her to lead a more ordinary life, even if she'd wanted to, and even without her famous face. Eleanor lived, for the most part, in a studio-choreographed bubble, and usually she forgot it was a bubble. It was her life.

But last night the ticket collector had asked for her autograph. So had the boy who brought her tea and biscuits in the first-class carriage. And of course, only the night before there had been the incident with the waitress in her own bedroom. It was possible that Gregory Junior would not recognize her. But it was unlikely. And she needed to be prepared for that.

In any case she was tired of the evasions, and tired of making no headway, and tired of living in false hope. How could the case proceed when she kept so much back from her own detective? Gregory's father had charged her thousands of dollars and uncovered nothing new. Now she had travelled all the way from Los Angeles to meet with the son, in the hope that he might, by some miracle, do better. Gregory Junior needed to know the truth. Something of the truth. *Something*. She smiled to herself, though she didn't know why. Come Monday morning, he was in for quite a surprise. She dreaded it.

21

At five minutes to nine on Monday morning, Matthew Gregory sat at his father's desk—*his* desk, now—gazing unhappily at the paltry array of papers related to the Kappelman case: papers so haphazardly organized and in such slim supply it made Matthew feel almost ashamed. He had not expected the client to reply to his letter, let alone to take him up on the—foolish—suggestion that she travel to Reno to discuss the case with him in person. But so it was. She had made the wretched journey, and he needed to make the best of things. Miss E. Kappelman was an excellent client. The bureau's best, actually. Not that it was saying much.

On the telephone she sounded sweet, he thought. Nervous. *Classy*. And full of hope. Almost as if . . .

He realized it immediately after he had posted the stupid thing. He realized it again—and with a vengeance—when her telephone call came through. He should never have sent her the letter. What had possessed him? It had been madness to stir the peaceful waters. He could ill afford to lose such a client—especially now, with stock markets behaving so erratically and the agency in hock, and his late father's broker calling in more margins every day.

Matthew Gregory glanced nervously at the stock-ticker in the foyer, just beyond the glass doors of his own office. A small glass dome perched on a brass base, with a thin strip of ticker tape snaking from it, the contraption spewed the latest stock prices in an apparently unending stream of symbols, most of which Gregory never could quite recognize. They came direct from the Wall Street stock exchange, and kept on coming, *ticker-tacker-ticker-tacker*—for as long as the market was open—longer, if trading was heavy. Sometimes it took a while for the tape to catch up.

He gazed at the paper strip coiling, forever coiling, onto the growing heap on the carpet below, and felt the usual prickle of angst. He could hear the thing now, tick-tacking incessantly. It used to stop in the mid-afternoon, Wall Street being three hours ahead, but recently trading had been so frenetic that the ticker tape never caught up, never seemed to stop—*ticker-tacker-ticker-tacker* . . . All day long. It had been a bad day at the stock exchange, Friday. A bad morning on Saturday. And now it was Monday, and the newspapers were predicting the worst. He would sell up—if only he could. But he couldn't afford it. Already his losses were such he had no choice but to cling on and pray that the market would improve again. As of course it would. As it always had before . . .

The machine was another absurd extravagance of his late father's, who in his last few years could think of almost nothing but the vagaries of Wall Street. He used to take his bourbon and drag his leather armchair, and sit in the foyer, reading that goddamn tape; watching his fortunes ebb and flow. Matthew Gregory longed to disconnect the thing. But it was part-owned by the law company opposite. Besides, there were stocks whose symbols he recognized and whose prices he needed to follow. With the information so close to hand, it was impossible not to get sucked in.

He felt a little sick. Slurped on the lukewarm bottle of Coke which, this morning, because of his nerves, was all he could manage for breakfast, and he waited.

Miss Kappelman was on her way. She would be here any minute, no doubt bursting with questions. Looking down at his late father's pathetic collection of notes yet again, notes Matthew had tried his best to pad out during the weekend, he was reminded, once again, what a fool he had been to write to her in the first place.

Matthew Gregory had always been kept at arm's length from the Gregory Investigative Specializations Bureau, which he knew he would one day inherit, and now that he had finally inherited it, he could understand why. His father's once-thriving concern—the Biggest Little Bureau in Reno—had in the last ten years been run into the ground.

Matthew had always suspected things were bad, but while his father still lived, and he earned his (reasonably) honest crust, as a junior detective with the Reno Police, he could do nothing. So he watched his father slip-sliding ever deeper into alcoholism, frittering the family fortunes on liquor and ticker-tape machines, and dreamed grandiose dreams of the day he could take over the reins.

Now he discovered that the reins were hardly worth taking over. Gregory Senior had sucked the business dry. Matthew Gregory considered selling up. And he might have done, despite the grandiose dreams, except after so long spent waiting, it seemed (his wife explained to him) a little feeble not at least to give the thing a go.

'This town is desperate for a decent detective agency,' she decreed, on what grounds no one could say. Except she'd always felt there might be a glamour attached to a husband with his own detective agency. She'd been looking forward to being the wife of that husband for years. 'Give the place a try!' she said. 'If it doesn't work they'll always take you back at the police department. And with all the added experience and connections you'll have made, I'll just bet they'll promote you. Right away.' So it was. The decision was made.

With his slicked-back sandy hair, his little hamster cheeks, his portly belly, buttoned tight into what he hoped was his trademark: the brightly

chequered waistcoat, Gregory Junior was not a
stylish man. He was thirty-three, deaf in one ear,
and slightly lame since his return from France in
1918. He was weak-willed, feeble-minded, vain and
idle. He loved his wife and he loved his daughter.
He loved America. In short he was a run-of-the-mill
man—easily bullied, easily fooled, a coward and
a buffoon, but moved from time to time by great
kindness and insight. His wife and daughter loved
him. And, on the whole, America loved him, too.

And he still dreamed. Vaguely. He dreamed
of one day returning the Gregory Investigative
Specializations Bureau to the bureau of its former
glory; a bureau which lived up to the company
motto: 'In Us you can trUst'.

Among the paltry collection of cases-ongoing
that he found on his late father's desk, Miss
Kappelman's seemed to wink at him with its
mystery and promise. Why, for example, after so
many years, and with so little to show for it, did
the inscrutable Miss Kappelman never question
the vast bills that had been sent her? And why,
given the cost and duration of the investigation,
were there still so few facts to work with? And why,
when the mystery began in New York, and probably
ended there, and since money was clearly no object,
why had Miss Kappelman not engaged an agency in
Manhattan?

The Kappelman client was living under a
different name. (That, at least, he had discovered
for himself. There were no E. Kappelmans listed
anywhere in Hollywood). But whoever she really
was, she was obviously rich, which meant she
probably had rich friends. And if he could impress
her sufficiently—heck, maybe even actually solve

the case—she might recommend him to them. He might get a foothold among the rich set in Hollywood. And if he could do that, who knew what exciting commissions might lie ahead?

In the meantime, while the ticker tape *ticker-tacked* in the foyer, and the stock market insisted on acting the giddy goat, and with the agency leveraged to five times its worth, it was vital that Miss Kappelman was protected from realizing quite what little progress had been made in the case to date. Or she would be a fool not to take her mysterious business elsewhere.

And now she was due to arrive. At any minute.

Ticker-tacker-ticker-tacker . . .

Another slurp of Coke. Didn't help much.

His secretary had arranged a vase of flowers beside the ticker-tape machine, and a second vase above the filing cabinet behind his desk. It was a warm day, but not unpleasantly so. He had the windows pulled open to dissipate the smell of his father's cigar smoke, forever embedded in the walls. There was coffee brewing. And there were cookies! His secretary had brought some home-baked cookies in this morning, especially for the honoured guest . . .

He heard the car drawing up outside and, simultaneously (it was how he remembered it later, although of course it wasn't really possible), smelled her expensive perfume wafting through the air.

Like the movie star she was, and ever was, when out in public, no matter how she felt inside, Eleanor Beecham swept through the foyer, past the ticker machine, sparing it barely a glance. He watched her hesitate, uncertain whether to turn left or right.

And then his secretary, who had gone to open the front door for her, came scurrying up behind, half bowing (it struck him as excessive) and directing her onwards, to the glass double doors that led directly into Matthew Gregory's father's office, to Matthew Gregory sitting at his father's desk.

Knock-out.

Those were the only words that came to mind. *Knock-out.* He hoped he hadn't uttered them—but he couldn't be sure . . .

A fox-fur wrap, draped over slim shoulders . . . and a dress, kind of blue, shimmering over those slim hips, and a little blue hat, pulled down over the eyes . . . and bright red lips . . . and sunglasses covering half of her face . . . and the intoxicating smell of an expensive, beautiful woman . . . She walked towards him, dainty, gloved arm outstretched. It was quite a distance—a good-sized office, with three large windows between them: distance enough for Matthew Gregory to notice her walk, her smell, her clothes, her little white teeth behind the wide mouth smile—and for his jaw to fall open.

He'd seen this woman before! A hundred times! She was a big star. One of the biggest. She was . . . who in the hell was she? It wasn't Gloria Swanson—no. This broad wasn't as big as Gloria. It was the other one! Not Norma Shearer. Oh, good God! Who was it? Louise Brookes? Clara Bow—no! She was a big star—but not one of *the* big stars. Oh, this was going to kill him! He knew this woman—

'Mr Gregory,' Eleanor said, in her soft voice, with her small teeth and her soft smile. He collected himself just enough to stand up from behind his desk and to take the hand that was offered to him.

'Mr Gregory,' Eleanor said again, wanting to put him at his ease; wanting to get this awkward moment over with. 'You know me by my maiden name, but—'

'Why!' he cried, too excited to hold back. 'But I know you better as—'

'Eleanor Beecham?'

'ELEANOR BEECHAM! That's it! I swear, I'm your greatest fan! I've watched all your movies. Every single one. That is to say, I have watched all your movies, and ha-ha! *So has my lovely wife!*'

'Oh . . . well. Thank you, Mr Gregory. That's always so good to hear.'

'My wife adores you!' he said, still pumping her hand, forgetting to let it go.

'She does? That is so kind of her!'

'We both—oh *absolutely*. Miss Kappelman. Mrs Beecham. May I call you Mrs Beecham?'

'You know—in these particular circumstances I think I would prefer—'

'Mrs Beecham, my wife is just going to go crazy if she doesn't get to meet you. She would never forgive me. Would you allow me to invite you . . . would you allow us? Why, if I'd known it was you . . . If I'd known it was you, I would have . . . I might have . . .' In his confusion, he fell silent, briefly.

Eleanor smiled at him sympathetically, masking the weariness, the loneliness such effusiveness always brought on. She raised one of her studio-tended eyebrows and waited nicely for him to finish the sentence. When it was clear he didn't know quite how, she prompted him, gently. 'What might you have done differently, Mr Gregory?' she asked, still smiling. 'Nothing, I hope! Nothing at all!'

'Why, no! Ha ha. How right you are. Nothing differently . . . Nothing at all . . . Would you do us the honour—My wife and I—would you dine with us tonight? Or tomorrow night? Or at least—I don't know how long you may be staying—gracing us here in Reno with your presence?'

'How kind of you. And what a very lovely idea,' she said vaguely. 'May I sit down here, Mr Gregory?' Eleanor, having taken off her sunglasses (much good they did her) and shaken off her fox fur, was gesturing to a small leather armchair in front of his desk.

'My goodness, of course. Please sit down. Would you like coffee? Where are my manners? Or perhaps—I know it's early. But would you prefer something stronger? I think I would. In the circumstances.'

'A cup of coffee would be perfect,' she said.

'Coffee!' he said. 'At once! What an excellent idea. Where is my secretary?' But she was standing right before him, a yard or so behind Eleanor's chair, rubbing her hands together nervously.

'Right over here, Mr Gregory,' she trilled. 'Welcome to the Gregory Investigative Specializations Bureau, Mrs Beecham. The best detective agency in Reno. And may I say it's an honour—'

'Could you perhaps fetch her some coffee?' interrupted Gregory Jnr. 'The poor lady has come all the way from Los Angeles . . . And some cake! Didn't you say you had cake, Mrs Davison?'

'No cake for me, thank you,' Eleanor said.

'Not cake. Cookies! I baked them especially when I discovered you were coming. Though little

131

did I know . . .'

'Oh—gosh. Cookies! You are kind. But no. Just some coffee would be perfect. Thank you.'

'Just coffee, then?'

'Thank you.'

'And for me too, please,' Gregory shouted after her.

'Oh, Mr Gregory, forgive me! I forgot all about you!'

He chuckled happily, rocking on his little heels. 'Not to worry,' he said, and winked at her.

The secretary left the room and Matthew Gregory began at last to collect himself. He sat down in his chair, opposite Eleanor, adjusted the button on his waistcoat and nodded self-consciously at her. His father's oak desk stretched out between them—vast, it seemed to him suddenly—and on top of the desk nothing but his father's silver pen, and a single thin cardboard file labelled in thick black print:

KAPPELMAN CHILD

Eleanor glanced at it. The words alone—stark as they were—stopped her short: hit her so she could feel the tears stinging.

'Mrs Davison makes truly excellent cookies,' Gregory was saying. 'I recommend them, Mrs Beecham. If I may, I would encourage you to taste one, only because—'

'Mr Gregory,' she said, her voice deep and heavy.

He stopped.

'Enough of this. Please. I am here now.'

Silence. The weight of it sent a small tremor through him. He dropped his gaze, wiped an

132

imagined dribble of sweat from his forehead. 'Yes. Indeed,' he muttered. 'Indeed you are.'

She indicated the thin file on the desktop between them. 'And that is my file?'

'Yes,' he said. Picking it up, tapping it. Placing it back on the desk again. Dear God, what had persuaded him to invite this woman to visit him? He had asked her to travel all the way to Reno, and she had come. And he had nothing to show for himself. 'Indeed it is. The file.'

'It is rather thin,' she said softly.

'It is—*slim* . . .' he said, tapping it one more time, not opening it yet. 'But I have recently been through it, thrown out bits and bobs of extraneous . . . information. I can assure you it represents a great deal of concentrated work. A great deal,' he repeated, as if to make it more believable.

'That's good.'

'Yes, it is.'

'. . . So?' she said.

He leaned forward. Felt the pinch of his waistcoat as he did so. 'Mrs Beecham. If I may. If you will permit me . . . Before we begin, *I must be brutally honest with you—*'

'NO!'

The word burst from her chest before she could stop it. 'NO!' It took them both by surprise.

22

And there it rested on the large, empty desk between them. NO! The expression on Mr Gregory's face turned slowly from astonishment to relief, without the hint of a glimmer of comprehension in between. He did not understand her. But for the moment, he didn't much care. *Ticker-tacker-ticker-tacker-tick-tack-tack.* The market was diving. But it would stabilize. It always did. Everything would all right.

Gently, because her distress combined with his own relief moved him greatly in that brief instant, he said: 'Mrs Beecham. You *don't want* me to be honest?'

'What?' She laughed and recovered herself with the swiftness only an actress of her calibre could. 'Well, of course I want you to be honest, Mr Gregory. I am so sorry. I do apologize. I thought you said something else entirely. I would hardly have come all the way to Reno . . .'

'No, of course,' he said. 'It would make no sense at all.' And he let it rest.

'So tell me,' she said, smiling, leaning forward, treating him to a small breeze of her deliciousness, 'what have you learned? Tell me everything you have uncovered!'

He slid the file across the desk without another word. She took it. He watched her pulling it open, with difficulty because her hands were shaking so. And he wondered, vaguely, when she cared so much that it made her hands shake, why had it taken her so long to come? Why had she left it so long?

A photograph of Isha gazed back at her. It was a copy of the same photograph which rested on her dressing table at home; so familiar to her, and yet—devoid of that precious, heavy gold frame, the very same she had wrested from that crazy waitress's paws only a few nights ago—the image

134

seemed so much fresher; more real. Looking at it now, Eleanor could remember the smell of Isha's skin, the warmth of her little body, the hope-filled softness of her childish voice.

It was the only photograph of Isha that Eleanor possessed. She was four years old, and smiling. Eleanor couldn't see the smile without hearing the laughter—so easy, so warm, so infectious. She looked into Isha's almond-shaped eyes— you couldn't see the colour, not from the picture, of course, but Eleanor knew the shade of green: turquoise green, they were; greener than her mother's. Witch's eyes. Almond, laughing, witch's eyes. The most beautiful eyes in America. Isha was sitting on her *bubbeh*'s knee in the old apartment on Allen Street; beside her, on *bubbeh*'s lap, the toddler Tzivia, Isha's cousin. Eleanor's mother had sent the photograph to her shortly before the letters stopped.

Eleanor set the photograph aside. Someone, presumably Gregory Snr, had put a small cross by Isha's figure, as if to differentiate her from her cousin, the baby. As Eleanor placed it back on the table, her eyes lingered. She knew the picture so well, and yet she hated to look away.

'The sheet you see there,' said Matthew Gregory, clearing his throat, breaking the silence, 'contains a précis of the facts, as given to my father at the time you engaged him . . . As you can see, they were— thin. Real thin.'

MISSING PERSON: ISHA KAPPELMAN
BORN: October 17th, 1907
LAST SEEN: September 15th, 1913, at Allen Street, New York City

PARENTS: DECEASED March 25th, 1911
LAST KNOWN CONTACT: The client, Miss
E. B. Kappelman of Hollywood, California
(MISSING PERSON's aunt and only known,
surviving relative) regularly received drawings
and letters purporting to come from MISSING
PERSON until November 2nd, 1914. Nothing
has been received, either from the MISSING
PERSON, nor from her grandmother/guardian,
Mrs B. Kappelman (DECEASED December
12th, 1914) since that date.

Eleanor glanced at Mr Gregory. 'It wasn't much to go on,' she said. 'Was it? I didn't give him very much.'

Gregory nodded, leaned across the desk and took the sheet from her hands. 'As you can see, between us, my father and later myself, have added considerably to that information . . .'

She turned her attention to the small bundle of sheets still tucked into the file.

There were photographs and press cuttings about the fire. But they didn't help. In any case, she couldn't look at them.

'As you can see,' he said again, disconcerted by the speed with which she flipped the sheets aside, 'we have been busy collecting background information—'

'Yes. But I know about the fire. Isha wasn't in the fire. I have seen her since the fire.'

'But these details help. You need to understand. They help to paint that all-important "picture". They "set a scene", you know? In my business you soon learn that you can't ever be sure when a clue is going to throw itself up, Mrs Beecham.

And we have uncovered a whole lot of interesting possibilities, I think you will agree. Just from getting a better fix on the background . . . So we can begin to understand . . .'

But he didn't understand. Didn't even begin to understand. How could he? She said, 'But do you have anything else? Anything new? Anything—'

'Of course.' He stretched across the desk once again, the button of his waistcoat catching uncomfortably on the ledge. 'Perhaps, if you would be kind enough to pass me the file . . .'

She continued to flip through the pages. There were other photographs, several she'd not seen before; photographs of the streets she had left behind all those years ago. She hated to look at them. 'This one,' she said suddenly. 'When was this photograph taken?'

'Ahh,' he said. 'Yes. That is a photograph of Allen Street, which you have in you hand.'

'It is. I know it. But the building—'

'As you are aware, the building in which Isha was last seen was razed to the ground in 1916.'

'Yes, I know.'

'What you see there is the building which replaced it. Isha's building was an old law tenement block—worse than most, from what I understand.'

'No. Not really . . .'

He didn't seem to hear her. 'And I'm pleased to say that it no longer exists. It was designated illegal, quite rightly. Unfit for human habitation—'

'Ha!' It was a bitter laugh that escaped her suddenly. 'But *we* lived in it, Mr Gregory. It was fit for us!'

He blinked. Had she? This beautiful woman: had she lived there too? He wasn't aware of it. It said nothing in the notes. 'Shortly after the outbreak of tuberculosis,' he continued, as if she hadn't spoken, 'which devastated the building in the winter of 1914 to 1915 and in which Batia Kappelman died . . .'

'There was always tuberculosis, Mr Gregory.'

'Yes indeed.'

Another silence. Eleanor's heart was pounding, and her breath came quick and angry as she flipped through the few remaining sheets. There were more photographs of the fire. And a copy of her mother's death certificate. Tuberculosis. New York City, 12 December 1914.

'This is all?' she asked him at last. 'This is all you have? Nothing new?'

Mr Gregory said: 'Miss Kappelman. I wish I could tell you otherwise. But—it's not so easy. Under the circumstances. We haven't got so very much to go on. You have really told us so little. And then, with every year that passes, the thing becomes harder.'

She laid down the papers and looked at him. 'Of course,' she said steadily. 'I apologize. You are quite right. I have not told you everything, have I? But I shall. I think it is time. I will be honest with you, Mr Gregory.'

'. . . Well then.' He nodded politely, hoping he hid his confusion. She offered nothing but contradictions, it seemed to him. And yet here she sat, with her disconcerting gaze, her intoxicating smell, and so many intriguing questions unanswered. 'Good then,' he muttered. 'Well, I think that would be an excellent beginning. And I think we need to start from the beginning, don't you?'

'I do.'

'For example, Miss Kappelman. Mrs Beecham. You will forgive me for saying so, but you have kept your personal details pretty tight until this point. I was not even aware that you had lived in the apartment on Allen Street. I was not aware of that.'

'No?' Eleanor affected surprise. She was a good actress, and she relied upon her acting skills unthinkingly: obfuscation, pretence, lies—all came to her automatically. But they hadn't helped. There came a point—and she realized suddenly that she had long since arrived at it—when you have waited fourteen years and travelled to Reno to unearth the truth, when the pretending simply had to stop. She swallowed. Smiled. Added, 'Of course you weren't aware of it. How could you have been? Because I never told you before.'

'Ah,' he said. And left it there. In half an hour he had discovered more than his father had uncovered in seven years. 'Thank you.'

Gregory's secretary rattled in with coffee and the unwanted cookies. They waited for her to leave.

'I want to help you, Miss Kappelman,' he said as the door closed behind her. 'But you have to help me. When I was studying my father's papers, it seemed crazy to me that in all these years you had given us almost nothing to work with and that we . . . well . . .' he shrugged. 'I'll be frank with you: we hadn't come back to you with so very much ourselves. But maybe . . . if we work together. If we come at it fresh. You and me. It's what I want to do for you. It's the very least I can do for you, Miss Kappelman. If you'll allow me. The Gregory Investigative Specializations Bureau. Absolutely one hundred per cent at your service . . .'

He waited. Watched his most valuable client looking down at her gloved hands, considering her options . . .

Tickety-tack, tickety-tack . . . These dips always corrected themselves. It was time to sell. He should sell. He should hold on. He would call his broker the minute the meeting was over.

'Miss Kappelman,' he pressed. 'Mrs Beecham. Why don't you tell me—from the beginning? Describe to me in the closest detail the last time you saw and spoke to your beloved niece, Isha.'

Tickety-tack, tickety-tack . . .

'But Isha is not my niece, Mr Gregory. Of course not. You must have worked it out already? Eleana Batia Kappelman was my maiden name. I am Eleana. And Isha Kappelman is my daughter.'

23

'Listen to me,' she said, not pausing for his reaction. 'And I will tell you about the last time I saw her. Because you may find something there. Something I have overlooked. And I have turned it over in my head—you can imagine. I have turned it over so many times that it becomes confused. *Did they see us? I ask myself. Did they follow us? Did they return to the apartment after we fled?* These are the questions that haunt me. Except of course they didn't see us! You understand? I know this, because, after that, when Isha understood I was still alive, I received letters from Mama, and little pictures from Isha. And then—' Eleanor laughed—'a little note from Isha: *Ich han dich lib, Mama.* I love you, Mama

. . . But she was supposed to be writing English, Mr Gregory. Can you imagine? How happy I was to receive it. Her *bubbeh* must have told her to write it . . . She knew how I longed for home. And then— nothing. Nothing. Nothing . . .'

'You need to start from the beginning.'

Eleanor took a deep breath. She had not quite planned for this. Of course she couldn't start from the beginning. That was impossible. She would start—from the middle. Where it was safe.

*   *   *

'We came back to New York the first moment we could. It was the longest eighteen months of my life. And not a day passed, not an hour passed, when I didn't long for my little Isha. But you know, times were different then. Or they were different for us. We left her with my mother, and I knew my darling mother would take good care of her, and we promised to be back the first moment we could . . .

'But it was eighteen months. We were moving around, you see, looking for work. Always, looking for work. And Matz played the piano, but his hands were still weak—and of course I sang. But we had to find a place that was safe. We couldn't simply take her away with us, when we had no roof above our heads. And then the day came. Matz found work—it was a job, a real *job*, you understand? Eleanor stopped, looked at the man before her, munching gently on his secretary's cookies. Of course he could not understand. Nobody could understand how hard it was back then.

'Keep talking!' he said, reading her thoughts, wiping a crumb from his chin. 'Just keep talking.

I'm going to try to understand. All right? It's the best I can do. I am not . . . one of your people. I did not . . . I mean to say, I've never been hungry. I'm sorry. I've never even been to New York. But it doesn't matter. You have to try to forget that. Because here I am. Matthew Gregory. At your service. Confidentiality guaranteed.'

'How can I be sure?'

'How can you be sure? Why, because if I started yelling around town all about my clients' secrets—pretty soon I'd be out of business!' He believed it. What use was an Investigative Specializations Bureau, after all, which didn't put client confidentiality first? 'So, how about this,' he continued. 'How about—you talk, and I listen? I'm going to take a few notes. OK? But no matter! Just keep talking! And afterwards, when you're done talking, I'll ask the questions. OK? How's that? Only whatever you do,' he waved an arm expansively, spraying cookie crumbs as he went, 'just keep talking. OK?'

Eleanor smiled. 'I'll keep talking,' she replied. 'But bear in mind, won't you, it's been a long while. And though I sometimes think every detail is burned on my mind—memories play tricks . . .'

'They sure do,' he said soothingly, pen at the ready.

'Well, I remember Matz on the day he got the job. They gave him a job at Keystone—the picture studios. You know? To play piano on set. Imagine that! Twenty-five dollars a week, to play piano while the camera turned. Nobody got to hear it except the actors, of course. But it helped the actors. He set the mood for them. And Matz,' she smiled. 'Matz . . . he could set a mood with that

142

piano like no one else . . . in twenty notes or less. He was a genius on that piano, Mr Gregory. I loved him . . . when he played piano. So . . .'

She glanced at Gregory, who was staring at her, goggle-eyed. 'I thought you were taking notes?' she said.

'Huh?'

'I thought you were—'

'So where's Matz now? Excuse for asking. But I'm guessing—is he deceased?'

'Is he *deceased*?' she repeated. Stupidly. 'Is he *deceased*? Why, yes. Matz is dead. Of course. But I thought you were keeping your questions to the end, Mr Gregory? I can't do this if you insist on interrupting.'

'Forgive me,' he said. 'Carry on. Only wait one moment—before we go on. The fire . . .'

'Yes?'

'The fire was in March 1911.'

'Yes it was. That's correct.'

'But he came with you, after the fire—and he got himself a job at Keystone Studios, playing piano?'

'Oh. I'm sorry,' Eleanor shook her head, and laughed. 'I didn't make myself clear. Matz died *as a result* of the fire. You understand? He died from "injuries sustained". That's what the doctor said. Except he didn't see a doctor. But he didn't die immediately. That's all. He died several years later . . . May I continue?'

Gregory nodded. Jotted something on his paper. It was going to be a long morning.

Tickety-tack . . . And he needed to speak to his broker before markets closed in New York.

143

24

'Matz came home to the boarding house. I was sleeping . . . I was sick. After the fire it took a while for me to feel healthy again. I couldn't find any work. I was trying to find work as a singer. But nobody wanted me. Matz said I looked like I carried the weight of the world on my shoulders, and it's true . . . I couldn't seem to shake it off, not in the way Matz could. Every time I closed my eyes, there it was again—and all the questions . . . how did *I* get to live when so many others didn't? . . . He said people took one look at my face, and they wanted to sob—so. Of course, they didn't want me to sing! Matz came back to the boarding house that night. And I never saw a man so happy! He lifted me up into the air, and it was—just for a moment— it seemed as if we could start again. Does it make any sense?'

'Not yet.'

'He said: "We're going home and we're going to bring back the baby!" But he didn't mean "we". Because of course he had to work. And in any case, Matz could never go back to New York. But *I* could go back. He had a job and we had money at last. We could get a place of our own. And I could go home and fetch the baby, and bring her with me back to Los Angeles. And we would be a family again.

'Well. After the first week, we had enough to buy a train ticket, and after three weeks, or maybe four, we had enough to put something down for a couple of rooms. Two rooms, all to ourselves. It was such a

144

luxury!

'Matz and I had never been apart. Not since the day of the fire. Not for a single night. We lived together. We did everything together. So he bought me the train ticket and he took me to the train station, and in spite of all the excitement, I wept when I left him. I didn't let him see it of course. What's to be gained from that? It was hard enough. But I feared I might never see him again. That fate might play its hand . . . After the fire, it was hard to see anything quite as it was. That is to say, quite as other people see it. There was an impermanence in everything, as if—you know—as soon as you turn away, it will be gone. But I had to turn away. I was going to fetch the baby. So I climbed onto the train. I said, "Next time you see me, Matz, there shall be two of us! There will be Isha. And there will be me."' Eleanor smiled. 'I wish you could have seen his face. I see it now, Mr Gregory. Matz has a wonderful face. So expressive. Everything he felt was right there in those warm brown eyes. The warmest eyes . . .' She fell silent. This time, Mr Gregory stayed quiet. He waited.

'. . . Shall I go on?' she asked.

'Please.'

'I sat on the train. Third class back then . . .' She laughed. 'I was lucky to get a seat. But I did get a seat. And of course, the thought of returning to New York after all that had happened—I dreaded it. The smell of burning. Do you know, even today, the sound of the words alone: New York City. They smell of the burning. And the . . . I mean to say, the smell of burning flesh, Mr Gregory.'

She looked at him, her green eyes vacant, expressionless, and he wondered, briefly, if she weren't a little cracked. Quite simply, off her head. Actresses often were, so he'd read.

'It must have been terrible,' he mumbled. 'Perhaps it's why you employed a detective in Reno. Of all places? As opposed to New York?'

'Yes.'

'I am so sorry . . .'

'But there were things I missed,' she continued, not really listening. 'My mother's cooking, of course. Who doesn't miss that? And even, somehow, the smell of the food carts on Hester Street. Not because they smelled *good*. God, no. Because they smelled of home . . . And I was going home . . .'

. . . Across the hall, through the glass double doors, a couple of lawyers from the offices opposite were standing at the ticker machine, slowly, carefully, examining the tape. From the way they stood, and the still, set expressions on their faces, they could only have been discussing the market. Were they selling up? Or were they going to sit tight? Suddenly he couldn't concentrate.

'You have to excuse me, Mrs Beecham,' he said abruptly. 'I have to make an important telephone call. I apologize. But I want to give you my fullest attention. And I really must make the call. Can you forgive me?'

'A telephone call?' She looked terrified. 'Why? Who are you calling?' Already, she was half on her feet.

'No one for you to worry about Mrs Beecham, I assure you.' He smiled at her. 'Please, sit back down. I shall only be a minute. Only I hear the ticker machine, and as you may be aware—'

'Oh!' she laughed. 'You too, huh?' She wondered

vaguely whether Max was on top of it all. 'Well then. If you must, you must. Will it take long?'

'Just a couple of minutes.'

But it took him almost half an hour. He returned to her looking and feeling like a new man. His broker had advised him to hold his nerve after all. Utility stocks were dropping so fast it was crazy not to snap them up, the broker said, and Gregory had taken his advice. As he settled back into his seat, the sound of that ticker machine took on a different ring: it sounded confident, upbeat, hopeful— *efficient.* So the stock might drop a little further yet, but the doom mongers would soon see. This was America, after all! Everything was going to be just fine.

Eleanor, oblivious to all this, deaf to the ticker machine, was impatient to start talking again. She'd stayed silent for so many years and now the dam had broken. She could hardly wait long enough for him to sit down.

'Mr Gregory,' she said, leaning across the desk, distracting him with another waft of her expensive beauty. 'Matz did the most wonderful thing! Twenty minutes after we pulled out of the station, the carriage door opened, and who should walk in—who should be standing there? Can you guess? It was Matz! You see? It was a surprise for me! Because he knew how painful it would be to have to return to the city alone. He'd only just started work at Keystone but there—that's his charm. People always melted for Matz. Because he was so talented, you see? And so handsome. And so funny. And so very, very warm . . .

'. . . But you see,' after a long silence, she continued, 'if Matz hadn't come with me that day,

147

if he had stayed in Los Angeles as we planned, I believe Isha would be with me today and there would be no need for me to be here. I could have waited until she was stronger, you see, and we could have travelled together. Matz would have had the little cot waiting for her, and I would have brought her safely home . . . It was her birthday on Thursday, Mr Gregory. Twenty-two years old. It's a beautiful age, isn't it? Twenty-two. Do you have children yet? I bet you do. A couple of beautiful kids . . .'

'I do,' he said, not quite able to hide his pride. 'I have one beautiful kid: Florence. She's five. And we have another one on the way.'

'Oh! One on the way!'

'I'm a lucky man.'

'Well,' Eleanor said. 'I should love to meet your family. Young Florence. Five years old? It's a beautiful age. Another beautiful age. They are all beautiful ages! Is she already at school?'

25

'Matz and I made our way there, from the train station to Allen Street, with our eyes down and our heads covered. It was important—it was terribly important, Mr Gregory—that nobody saw us. Mama didn't even know we were coming. Matz didn't want to put the news out. Just in case . . .'

'In case of what, Mrs Beecham?'

'Oh . . . there were people,' Eleanor said vaguely. 'I can't tell you everything. You have to understand that. There were people who were our enemies.

148

Matz's enemies. It was very dangerous for us . . . But you must let me tell the story. And keep your questions to the end.'

'I shall try my best,' he said. 'But if we're to make progress . . .'

'Please. Just listen.'

He sighed—a small sigh. She didn't notice it. Her mind was back in Allen Street, in the tiny tenement flat she had left behind.

'Sarah was dead. Of course. And Samuel— Mama didn't know where he'd gone. But he'd gone, all right. Mama said he came and went from one month to the next. So there wasn't only Isha for her to take care of. There was the baby, Tzivia, too. And no one else left to help her. The apartment was the same. Well, no. It wasn't. But it took me a while to notice . . . The little things that used to make it home: the flowers Mama grew by the window, they were gone; and drapes, and the walls, the tablecloth—Mama used to take pride, but they were dirty. Tired. The place didn't feel like home any more. Sarah was gone. Samuel, Matz and I— we were all gone. It was Mama, Isha, Tzivia—and new people. Boarders. She said they were cousins, but who cares? We didn't meet them in any case. They were out at work all day and, when they came home, we hid in our room. And of course she didn't tell them who we were.

'We arrived at the door dressed like a couple of greenhorns. Because nobody looks at the greenhorns. They all look the same, don't they?'

'Greenhorns?' he repeated, confused.

'Fresh off the boat, Mr Gregory. Still in their peasant clothes. The women in their wigs, the men in their big, ugly work boots . . . I wore a shawl over

149

my hair. Matz brought the clothes before we left. He had thought of everything. And when we came to the door, Mama didn't recognize us. She looked weary. Old. She almost shut the door in our faces!'

Eleanor smiled, remembering. '"We're full," she said. "Try over the way." I had to whisper to her: *"Mama! It's me. Us. We have come for Isha . . ."*'

'I loved my mother. Of course. Who doesn't? I loved her dearly. But right then, I only cared about getting to my baby. We stood in the hallway, people brushing past us, and I watched the haze lifting from Mama's face: the weariness, the sadness. I had never thought it before, but just then I thought for the first time—perhaps she suffered as I did, with her only daughter gone. "My little girl!" she cried. Her face lit up and she hugged me so tight . . . She wasn't expressive in that way. Not normally.

'Matz told her to shush—there were people everywhere. Of course. There always were people everywhere. You couldn't turn for *people* . . . It used to drive me half crazy. But I miss it sometimes . . . Well—she pulled us into the parlour.

'"Who is here?" Matz whispered.

'Nobody was there. Just Mama and Isha—and Tzivia. The boarders were all out at work. So.

'Tzivia was at the kitchen table, her little head just peering over the table ledge. She was preparing the potatoes. And she had grown! Not a baby any more—three years old or so. Of course. It was eighteen months since we had left . . . Unlike Mama, she saw right through our disguises. She recognized us at once. Her mouth fell open. She looked absolutely terrified, as if she had seen a ghost. There was a photograph on the wall—a portrait of Matz and me with little Isha on my knee

150

. . . And she looked from the picture, back to us, under our heavy disguises—and immediately burst into tears.

'Mama had told the children we were dead, you see. For her own safety, and for ours and for Isha's. For everyone's safety. Because if she hadn't . . . Tzivia called for her *bubbeh*, and her tears turned into wails.

'But Mr Gregory, you have a daughter of your own. You can imagine, I wasn't concerned about Tzivia. Poor darling. She was not my child. "Where is Isha?" It was all I could say. Why wasn't she in the kitchen preparing potatoes with her cousin? We had come to fetch her, and we had imagined taking her off with us, there and then. That same day. Bundling her up amd taking her back with us to the train station, back to Hollywood . . .

'My mother motioned to the bedroom and I turned towards it. She said, "But Eleana, you will frighten her. And she is sick. I must warn her first that you are not a ghost. She is so sick. Always. All the time. She is not strong enough for this sort of a shock. Wait a moment. I shall go in and prepare her . . . She will be so happy."

'So I had to wait. I could hardly stand it. "Please," I said to Tzivia. "Tzivia, stop. Your *bubbeh* has important business. Stop your crying at once!" But Tzivia would not stop. She wanted to know where her own mama was. But her own mama was dead. Oh, I should have been kinder. Poor little mite . . . But how could I? "Mama! Hurry!" I cried. Oh God—it was the longest wait of my life.

'Tzivia was quiet at last. She said to us, "Are you coming to take Isha away?" I said yes. She said: "Where are you taking her?" I told her—to the place where the sun shines every day. And where there is a beautiful ocean, full of fishes to eat, and where the oranges grow on trees, and the air is full of the scent of flowers . . . She listened to me in such wonder. As if this ghost before her were describing Paradise. And I was, of course! I was rehearsing it for my Isha. But when I saw Tzivia's little face I realized how cruel I was being. And I realized, too, that there was nothing to prevent her from coming with us. And Mama, of course. They could all come to California! I said it there and then! As I waited to be allowed in to see my Isha, I bent down and took little Tzivia's pretty face in my hands. I said, "Come with us, my darling! *Bubbeh* will bring you. Why don't you come too?" And for a moment her little face lit up. And then the cloud. She said, "But I can't come. When Papa comes to fetch me, how will he ever find me?"

'Matz spoke. He crouched down before her. He said, "Tzivia! Your papa will find you. We will make sure of it. You have nothing to worry about . . . We will be happy. We will be a family."

'You see?' Eleanor glanced at Gregory. 'You see? Matz was a fine man. Was he not? A fine man. You can see why a girl would fall in love with him . . .'

Gregory said, 'He sure as hell sounds like it, Mrs Beecham. I look forward to hearing more about him. But—hey—it's almost noon. Are you hungry? What do you say, we stop for something to eat? I could have some lunch sent in, if you like. Or, if you're not afraid of the crowds, I know an excellent little eaterie on Virginia Street. They can provide us with a quiet booth, and we could continue with our conversation there?'

152

Eleanor didn't want to stop. Not for food, nor for anything else. And she dreaded being seen in public. How would she explain her presence here, if the reporters were to spot her? What would Mr Carrascosa say? She felt a fluttering of panic, only remembering his name . . . . She had left the script on the bed unopened. Her contract was up for renewal. She wasn't even meant to leave town without his permission.

But Eleanor was polite. She was always polite. 'Forgive me, Mr Gregory,' she said. 'I'm sorry. I've been talking so long. But *lunch*. Yes. Of course. Perhaps if we travelled by car. And I walked through the restaurant quickly, with my head down. I have learned to do it quite well, you know! Sometimes, in Hollywood, I wear a large hat and go to the movies! I do, you know! And nobody notices me at all!' But she didn't. She had never, in fact, done any such thing. She had heard that others did. Bigger stars than she—Rudolph Valentino, before he died. But Eleanor had never dared. Somewhere along the way she had lost the ability, lost the will, lost the taste for ordinary freedom. It occurred to her, just then, as she tripped out the easy lie, that she had lost her nerve for life. Where had it gone? What had she done with it?

'Well, gosh,' she said suddenly, in a burst of something quite new; something almost resembling her old spirit: 'I should love it. Let's do it! Let's walk, for heaven's sake. If it's close enough! Let's feel the sun on our skin!'

26

The restaurant was only a couple of blocks away, and so far as Eleanor could tell, nobody spotted her. Anywhere else in the world, she and Mr Gregory might have made an incongruous pair. But in Reno—city of rich, elegant and newly detatched women—incongruous couplings were the name of the day. It wasn't only lawyers who were exploiting the city's chief source of income. And if Mr Gregory didn't quite fit the archetypal gigolo mould, in his cowboy hat and gaudy, ill-fitting waistcoat, walking along beside Eleanor he looked, at least, like a man on the make.

They ordered steak. Mr Gregory said he knew just how to ask for some under-the-counter hooch. Red wine, smuggled in across the Nevada desert, all the way from France, Gregory told her proudly. 'Only the real McCoy in Reno!' he said. But Eleanor only ever drank the real McCoy. Prohibition did not mean a hidden gin still in the bathroom, not to her. It meant Max seeing to it. Or Butch. Or whoever. Somebody else paying sweeteners, doing whatever needed to be done, keeping her champagne glasses full. In any case, she didn't like to say it, but the wine Gregory poured into her tea mug tasted like vinegar. There was no way it had been brought in from France.

'Exquisite!' she murmured, taking a sip, and then another, because she could see how much it pleased him. 'Too delicious for words!'

And her mind wandered back to the tenement flat, and her mother, so tired and old, and the smell of horse manure and rotting vegetables, the thunder of the elevated trains, and Tzivia, her face alive with the dream of California . . .

And her little Isha. Pale as snow, with the glisten of cold sweat on her cheeks.

'Mama returned to us in the parlour at last . . . and I could tell from her face it was bad news. "I have told her you are here," Mama whispered to me. "She wants to come out and greet you but I have told her to stay in the bed." I moved to pass her—but my mother held me back. She pulled at my arm and insisted that I stop. "Understand, daughter. She is not well. I don't think she really understands what I have said to her, but when she sees you by the bedside perhaps it will be clear . . . She talks of you."' Eleanor stopped there. Looked at her wine and took a careless gulp: because the words caught in her throat. '. . . "She talks of you all the time . . ." I didn't know that, Mr Gregory. You have a young one yourself. You can never be sure, can you, how quickly they forget? But my Isha had not forgotten. She talked of me all the time. It's what Mama said. Well. Mama released me at last. She said, "Approach softly. She is fragile."

'I approached softly. I could not have approached more softly if I had really been a ghost. She was lying on the mattress that had once been Matz' and mine. She slept on it with her *bubbeh* now, and her cousin Tzivia. Because all the rest of us were gone. Sarah, in the fire. Samuel—who knows where? Matz and I to California . . .

'But it was going to be different now. They were coming back with us! You see? We were bringing them all to California, and then that filthy city, our filthy, disease-ridden streets . . . and that

155

room with no light—we would leave it all behind. And never come back again.

'Isha was lying on the bed, and she looked so small, so pale. She watched me crossing the small room. It was almost dark. There was no window. She watched me in the half-light as I sat—so gently—onto the mattress beside her. But her face did not change. She didn't move. All I could hear was the wheezing . . . Her little chest, fighting for breath. Her dark hair was damp, sticking to her head so you couldn't see the curls. You would never have known, looking at her just then, that she had the most beautiful, bountiful, joyful curls . . . You couldn't have known it, Mr Gregory.

'She was sick. I bent over her little body—so limp—and I kissed her forehead. It was damp and cold. She raised her arms and put them around my neck, and I wept so that my tears were falling onto her poor face. She said *"Mama!"*'

Eleanor stopped.

Gregory looked at his plate. At the juicy steak growing cold in front of him. And pushed it away. Tentatively, in the silence, he reached a hand across the table and patted her sleeve.

'We will find her,' he said. 'I promise you. We will find her.' He wanted to believe it.

'Thank you,' she said.

*   *   *

After that, until lunch was over, they talked about the markets. It was much easier for Mr Gregory. She asked him what his opinion was, and gave every appearance of attending to the answer. Mr Gregory assured her that the market was bound to bounce

156

back. 'Simply, Mrs Beecham, because it always has.

'Why,' he said, pouring himself another cup of wine, growing expansive at the pleasure of his own voice—it was such a relief to be away from that poor child's bedroom, 'we only need to listen to the experts on the subject. They are quite convinced.'

'Charlie Chaplin has sold his interests,' she said casually. 'And on the advice of Jesse Livermore, no less. I think we must agree Mr Livermore is an expert.'

'Jesse Livermore! You don't say!'

'They are terrific pals.'

'Ha! The Tramp and the Greatest Stock Trader in America—are they indeed? Well, ain't that a thing? What can they have to say to one another?'

'Oh—but Charlie's nothing like he is in the movies!' Eleanor said. 'He's *terribly* smart, Mr Gregory. I mean to say he's one of the smartest men you'll ever meet.'

'Well,' Gregory laughed, 'I dare say I shall never meet him . . .'

'No,' she smiled at him. 'I suppose not.'

'So Charlie Chaplin has sold out his positions, has he?' Gregory muttered. 'And on Jesse Livermore's advice . . . But then again, Mr Livermore goes bust as often as he makes a fortune. We mustn't forget that!'

'It's true . . .'

'Believe me, Mrs Beecham. The market will recover. I say, hold firm.'

They returned to the bureau in something approaching companionable silence. It was a short walk and the sun was shining. In the hallway, he stopped at the ticker machine, picked up the paper coil at a point somewhere between floor and tabletop, scowled at it for a moment. Muttered under his breath.

'Do you understand it?' Eleanor asked. 'I can never understand any of the symbols.'

'Oh you get used to them,' Gregory said, dropping the tape, no wiser than when he lifted it. 'They're really very simple. Shall we get back to our work?'

His secretary bustled in with more coffee, and Eleanor returned to her tale.

27

'So, our idea to return that same day to California proved impossible. Isha would not have survived the journey. There is no doubt about it. Matz wanted to wrap her up warm and to leave right away. But I wouldn't allow him. My mother was in agreement. So we stayed. There was a pattern, generally, to Isha's illnesses; every few weeks she would relapse again, and return to bed for a day or two, sometimes for longer. Mama said that recently, since Matz and I had left, each bout of sickness had seemed a little worse than the last, and it seemed to return to her more quickly. Even so, we were full of hope. We had money—not much. But enough to buy her some good, healthy food, and to bring a doctor to see her, and even to pay for medication.

'Mother assured us that none of the boarders would know us. In any case, as soon as they returned from work, we kept to our room—Isha's room. And they barely paid us attention. I don't believe they knew who we were.

158

'There was a danger in little Tzivia of course. We had to impress on her the importance of telling no one who we were. And she seemed to understand. I think my stories of California had cast a little spell. She was terribly excited. She would have done anything, poor darling, if she knew it would help her to come to California.'

'She sounds like a sweet girl . . .'

Eleanor didn't hear him. 'No,' she said. 'It wasn't Tzivia. She was still a baby. Half of everything she said was gibberish, in any case. Nobody would have listened. Nobody would have believed her. I've thought about it so often, wondered again and again who it might have been . . . Because we were so careful. Matz was fanatical about it. We stayed inside. Spoke to no one but Mama. Not even the boarders heard us speak. We stayed in that small room, hidden away, talking in whispers . . . Poor Matz! It nearly killed him, being cooped up like that. But he loved her, just as I did. You see? We sat by her bedside, feeding her, talking to her, watching her sleep. She was so happy we were there. When she returned to herself and the fever dropped, she would look at us, one to the other—and that smile would light up her face. And then she would mutter something; sometimes we couldn't hear what she said . . . She would close her eyes, and that smile would still be lingering.

'It must have been the doctor. He came to visit us twice, but Matz and I took care—we didn't meet him. Or speak to him. But somehow . . . he must have wondered where the money came from to pay for him. And perhaps Isha said something, in her fever. Or perhaps one of the boarders. But it doesn't matter, does it? Not any more.

159

'We'd been there three days, and Isha was growing stronger. And that morning, when she woke, the breathing sounded easier—less painful. And the fever had dropped. She was still weak. But the delirium had gone. We were going to wait one more day . . . Maybe even leave that same evening . . . And then they came for us.'

'Who came for you?'

'The police, Mr Gregory. We couldn't stay. Mama heard them on the street. And she knew at once. They came thundering up the stairs. We were on the fifth floor, and we could hear them—the angry voices in the hallway as they stormed past, knocking everyone out of their path. They were heading directly for our door—'

'Why were the police after you, Mrs Beecham?'

'What's that?' she said. She sounded startled.

'I think you should tell me why the police were coming after you.'

'Why?'

'Well, because it might have some bearing—'

'I was collecting her things together, talking to her about the journey we were about to make. Maybe that very evening. Maybe the next day. And she was lying back on the pillow, too weak to sit up, but her eyes followed me. She was listening, I knew it—I was describing the beach at Santa Monica, and the mimosa trees, and the sweet smell of the California sunshine. And she smiled at me. She said . . .' Eleanor laughed suddenly. 'It was the most she had said in all the days we were together: *Sheyn vi di zibn velten.*" It means—'

'But why were the police coming after Matz?'

'"*Sheyn vi di zibn velten.*" As beautiful as the seven worlds. She was thinking of California. Mr

160

Gregory. My daughter is the only thing that's relevant. *This* is the last time we saw her. When the police were hammering on the door, yelling for Matz and me. And little Isha was in bed . . . "*Sheyn vi di zibn velten.*" Don't you see?'

'I don't. No. I don't see.'

'It was the last thing she said to me, Mr Gregory.'

'Why were the police coming after Matz?'

'They weren't coming for Matz. They were coming after both of us. But you asked me when I last saw my daughter. Please. I want to tell you. Listen to me.'

Gregory sighed. 'We'll come back to it,' he said. 'Keep talking then . . .'

'Mama came through the door. Only fear—pure fear—on her face. She said, "Go! Go now!"'

'At the back of the parlour there was a small air shaft. Not quite a window. An opening for air. There was one in every apartment, and everybody in the block used them as a shoot for the garbage. We had it covered most of the time because the reek from the garbage below was too sickening. The smell seeped through anyway—of course it did. But it stopped the flies. The smell was always dreadful.

'But we could climb through that and reach the fire stairs out back. It was our only way out of there. Matz wanted to take Isha with us, but I stopped him. I stopped him, Mr Gregory. I didn't think she was strong enough. She wouldn't have survived the journey. And I told him—we would come back for her. And come back for Mama, too. And for little Tzivia, if her father hadn't taken her by then. Matz wouldn't listen to me. But that's so typical of him! He said, "We have come for Isha. We're not leaving without her." He had Isha in his arms, and she was

161

whimpering and I could hear her chest tightening again. She couldn't breathe, and the sound of the policemen's boots was getting closer. The walls of that building might have been made from paper. You could hear everything. We could hear them, barking orders to each other. It was terrifying.

'Mama said "Go *now*!" And she held out her arms to take Isha. "Go!"

'I took the baby from Matz, held her tight, lay her back on the bed. She was sobbing. Her little body was shaking . . . I said to her: as soon as you are strong enough, we will come back for you.

'Mama said: "Don't come back for us. It's too dangerous. You must send money, and we will follow as soon as Isha is well. It won't be long. Just a few weeks. As soon as she is well, we will come! I promise you."

'Matz was tugging my sleeve: "We have to leave. Now. *Now*, Eleana!" I took a last look at my baby . . . "Goodbye, darling," I said to her. But she didn't reply to me. She turned away, sobbing still. She said, "*Mama . . . Mama . . . Mama . . .*" It was so faint . . . she was coughing, and the weight in her chest was squeezing the sound from her. She was fighting for every breath.

'And then Matz pulled me away. Finally. And that was the last time. It was the last time I saw her: the fifteenth of September 1913. It was the day we were meant to bring her home with us to California.

'She was five years old, Mr Gregory. And now she is twenty-two. And not a day has passed. Not one day . . .

The ticker tape had fallen silent at last. Except for the motor cars chugging down Virginia Street, all was quiet in the bureau. Awkwardly, Gregory

162

looked at his watch. Mrs Davison would be wanting to head home. And so did he. It was late. He was tired. He wanted to be at home with his wife. And his beautiful five-year-old daughter, Florence.

28

Eleanor took a car back to the hotel. Her lunchtime euphoria had evaporated in the long afternoon and the thought of being spotted—worse still, approached—filled her with horror and exhaustion. Wrung out, like the grey sheets that used to hang from the windows on Allen Street, she struggled to muster her usual good manners when bidding Mr Gregory good evening.

Looking at her, the pale of her cheeks, the limp expression in those beautiful green eyes, Matthew Gregory was torn between sympathy and intense personal discomfort. The sight of such raw unhappiness in that lovely, so-familiar face made him feel at odds, like the world was upside down.

'Hey—you're gonna be all right?' he asked awkwardly, as he wriggled into his mustard-coloured overcoat.

'That's quite some coat,' Eleanor replied irrelevantly.

'You like it?' He sounded pleased.

She nodded and sighed. It was all she could manage, and he was briefly overwhelmed by her sadness. 'Listen here, Mrs Beecham,' he said kindly, 'why don't you come back with me? Might do you good to be . . .' He was going to say 'at home with a family'. But of course that wouldn't strike the right note. 'Not to be on your own,' he said instead. 'It's been a difficult day for you, huh? Mrs Gregory cooks a beautiful . . .' He paused again. Couldn't quite think what. She was a lousy cook. 'She cooks a beautiful dinner . . .'

Eleanor smiled. The invitation lacked quite the enthusiasm of his morning's invitation. 'I'll be just fine, Mr Gregory. Thank you for asking. I think I shall go to my room and I shall probably fall asleep right away.'

'Excellent!' he said, too quickly. 'If you're sure?' He picked up his case, glanced at the clock on the wall. 'You sure look like you need the rest.'

'I'll be just fine,' she reassured him. He was already halfway out the door.

*   *   *

But Eleanor did not fall asleep right away. She hardly slept at all. She returned to her rooms and, for the first time in a very long time, took a moment to wonder at the extraordinary turn her life had taken. From Allen Street—to this! She had grown so accustomed to it, this life of preposterous luxury, that she only seemed to notice now when the luxury wasn't there for her.

It was there for her in Reno. The private drawing room in which she stood was already three times the size of the whole apartment back in Allen Street. Beyond it was a large bedroom, and a bathroom with marble bathtub. And through the hallway, adjoining the back of the drawing room, there was a personal maid's room (empty, since Eleanor had not brought one), with private kitchen and smaller bathroom. Nevada law required a state

164

residency of six weeks before any visitor's divorce could be granted, and though there was usually a way round even that, most guests expected to be stuck in Reno for a month or so. Eleanor's rooms were designed with longer visits in mind.

She had no idea how long she would be staying. Nor, until that instant, had she paused to wonder.

'For as long as it takes,' she muttered. Vaguely. Decisively.

For as long as it takes to achieve what? It's what Max would have asked, had he been with her tonight. She could hear him, spitting the question out. And she answered him aloud. 'To find Isha, of course. For as long as it takes to find Isha.'

She imagined him, turning away unconvinced. Not replying. Not saying what she knew he wanted to say, what she would never allow him to say. Because if the hope was gone, then what was left?

She missed him.

Did he miss her? Would he even notice she was gone?

Of course he would notice. They were expected for dinner with Dougie and Mary's tomorrow night. He would be needing her there with him, to present a united front. She wondered what would he tell them all when he turned up alone. That she was too sick to come? That she was in Reno, seeking a divorce? Ha. Or maybe that she was in Reno, seeking their long-lost daughter? Twenty-two years old last week, Mary! (Have we never mentioned her before?) *Older than the candelabra! Older than Hollywood, almost . . . It's what we've been celebrating all these years. At our famous Beecham Supper Party. Celebrating little Isha. Fighting for breath. Alone on her bed. Sobbing. Her back turned.*

165

Was he alone? All alone at the *Castillo del Mimosa*, which they built together. Or was he at the studio, perhaps? Working. Always damn well working. Or was he . . . ?

She imagined Blanche, young and naked, lying with her husband in their enormous bed. Sweet and bright and very ambitious, by all accounts. It's what people said about her. With a loving family back in Oregon, hoping she would come home. Have kids. Be sensible. Settle down. Of course he wasn't on his own at the *Castillo*.

Eleanor wished, suddenly, fervently, that she hadn't left her husband behind. What did she expect him to do with himself while she was gone? Set up a shrine to her memory? She laughed aloud. Or would he simply persuade himself she had never existed, just as he had apparently persuaded himself with Isha?

There was a tap at the door. Eleanor—accustomed to staff answering doors for her, or Max, or Butch—didn't think to answer it herself. She heard the soft scratching sound of something being slid onto the carpet and it jolted her out of her reverie.

She found a wire, addressed to 'Miss Cappalmann':

Baby, what are you doing in Reno? Please, darling, don't be rash. I miss you. Come home!

She felt a thud of disappointment.

It was from Butch. Of course it was. Aside from Matthew Gregory, only two people in the world knew it was her maiden name. And Max would remember how to spell it.

How did Butch find her? How did he guess she would be booked in under her maiden name?

166

Stupid questions, both. Butch wasn't stupid. Butch knew everything, or nearly everything, and a simple little thing like who climbs out of the first-class carriages at Reno? That was Butch's business. Rather, it was Lionsfiel business. The studio probably had half the reporters in Reno on its payroll. Of course. All the studios probably did. It was how they kept a lid on the scandals. How they kept an eye on their stars, and how they controlled them. But if Butch knew where she was, she supposed Mr Carrascosa knew it too. They would no doubt all be assuming the same thing. Which was OK. Actually. They could assume whatever they liked. It was better than the truth.

She dropped the telegram on the side table. Yes, she would call Butch. Maybe tomorrow. She would think up some excuse for being here. In the divorce capital of the world. She'd think of something . . . But she was so tired. She only wanted to sleep. And she wanted Max to find her. Except, of course, he never would. The time had long since passed, it occurred to her, when he would even think to try.

29

'Mama rented a post-office box and, as soon as she sent us the details, we began to send money to it. We started a few weeks after we returned to Hollywood, and we never stopped. I sent letters, too—and Mama wrote to me . . .' Eleanor indicated the slim file lying open before Mr Gregory, and tried not to look at him. Emboldened by her admiration of his mustard overcoat, she imagined,

167

his apparel this morning—mauve tartan waistcoat, even tighter than yesterday's, with shirt peeping through gaping buttonholes—was proving mildly distracting. 'You have the first letter there, I think. Where she tells us about the PO box.'

'I do indeed. I have it right here.' Mr Gregory picked up a single, flimsy sheet of paper, worn more flimsy still over the years. The letter was short and littered with spelling mistakes. 'If I may say . . . the letter makes a whole lot more sense, now I understand she was writing to her daughter.'

'Does it really?' Eleanor smiled. 'She was always cautious. And she meant to be cryptic. She believed the authorities might be reading her letters. She always thought it—even before we had anything to hide from them. It was a hangover from the old country, I suppose. In any case—the situation wasn't simple. She needed to be careful.'

'This little letter—this was the first you heard from her, was it? After you and Matz skipped town?' He turned the sheet over. 'She wasn't a great communicator.'

'I told you. She had to be careful,' replied Eleanor. 'And she was writing in English, too. She was trying to reassure us . . . that Isha was being educated properly. That she was teaching her written English, as we asked her to—you see?'

He didn't, but he nodded.

'We wanted Isha to be an *American*. First of all.'

'I admire the sentiment,' said Gregory primly.

'In any case, the letter must have taken her so much time, poor darling, because you can see all the crossings out . . .' Eleanor smiled. 'It didn't reassure us at all! You can imagine. Matz wouldn't stop nagging about it. But we were so happy to

168

hear from her. It was such a relief . . .' She broke off suddenly, unable to resist the urge to defend her family from this man, who didn't know and who didn't care and whose opinion of them hardly mattered. But she couldn't let it rest. 'Papa was different,' she said.

'Papa was as learned as anyone you ever met. As a young man, before he came to America— he would have been a lawyer if they had allowed him . . . But there were quotas. For the Jews. You probably heard about them. My father knew the law better than anyone.'

'Quotas?' Mr Gregory was confused.

Eleanor waved it aside. 'I'm sorry. Forgive me. It has nothing to do with . . . anything. I only meant. My family was poor—but we weren't uneducated. And the letter—Mama's letter . . . English wasn't her first language. When she wrote to me in English it was a gesture of love. You understand? English— she spoke it perfectly but the writing never came easily to her. She used to freeze up. Lose her confidence. But she knew how important it was to Matz and me. And she loved us. She loved Isha . . .' Eleanor smiled. 'She even loved Matz! She would have done anything for us. Anything.'

Mr Gregory nodded, politely. It crossed his mind that he and Eleanor had not yet discussed a final fee. Were they working on an hourly rate at this juncture? Or a daily rate? He wondered whether he should broach the subject of an hourly fee . . . It didn't seem unreasonable. He should certainly mention it. Perhaps over lunch. Not now.

'You know what I picked up from this letter?' he asked her. And answered before she had a chance to reply: 'I got a sense she didn't really want to

169

make the journey west. She was safe in New York. The kid was OK.'

'Of course she wanted to make the journey,' snapped Eleanor. 'Of course she did.'

'I think she had already made one long journey in her life—to America. And she was elderly. And perhaps—you say English was difficult for her. Perhaps she dreaded making yet another long journey, starting all over, yet again.'

'No,' Eleanor snapped back. 'You are quite wrong.'

'Look, I'm not pretending I can understand. Me, I've always known where my home was. I am not . . . one of your people . . .' It was the second time he had said it.

'We are all people, Mr Gregory,' she snapped. 'Some of us are Jews. And some of us are movie stars. But we are all people.'

'Yes indeed. Of course.'

She leaned across the desk, smiled at him more kindly. 'I only say it,' she said, with that soft voice again, aware of the effect she could have, 'not to alarm you, Mr Gregory. But I think if we are to work together, if I am to pour my heart out to you, as I seem to be doing—and I apologize, because sometimes, I know, I leave the subject behind, I forget where I am. But—I think, if we are to work together, we need to establish certain things. Any . . . awkward differences between us. We can talk about them, if you like. Get them out of the way.'

'No, no! No need for that,' he cried. 'We are here to find your daughter, after all. Not to set the world to rights.'

'I quite agree.' Eleanor sat back in her seat again. 'Good. So where were we? Mama's letter.'

He passed the flimsy sheet across the desk to her. 'I have read it several times, of course. Plenty of times. But the ink is smudged. And the paper's awfully thin. And the handwriting—I'll be frank with you, Mrs Beecham, it's not an easy read. Seeing as you're here, maybe you could read it out. Just in case—maybe I missed a word, you know?'

So Eleanor took it from him. As she gazed at the familiar page, she felt a thrill to be touching it again, and a flood of old emotions washed through her: the wild relief when she opened her Hollywood post-office box and first saw the letter lying there. Here it was, all these years later, back in her hand again. It smelled of the apartment on Allen Street. Or did she imagine that? She felt a wave of longing—for her home, and for her mother, who had loved her as well as any mother could, and whose death, in all that followed, Eleanor had never paused to grieve.

The letter gave a post-office box number in Manhattan, to which Eleana could send money; it related the story of the police, as if Eleana herself had not been present:

I tell them again and again, poor dear Matz is ded. My Eleana is ded. I am not so shure they beleved me. What more can I say to them? My baby is ded! But in any case, they are gon for now . . .

The letter warned, too, that Isha's health remained poor. She said Isha was longing to come west, and could talk of nothing else. But now it was December—bitterly cold in New York. She wanted to wait until spring before they made the journey.

171

Eleanor stopped, rested the letter on her lap. 'I wanted to tell her, "but it's sunny and warm in California!" Can you imagine? Spending the winter in New York when your mama and papa have a warm, bright home waiting for you in California? Matz was making twenty-five dollars a week! Sometimes even more, because all the stars adored him at Keystone. Whatever they were shooting, no matter: sometimes even on the street, in the desert, they insisted on Matz and his piano being there. Everyone always asked for Matz.'

'He must have been very talented . . .'

'And we were rich, Mr Gregory. Rich! Not like now—it was different. It was better! Every penny he brought home felt like a million dollars! Matz sent half back to Allen Street, to care for Isha, and half we spent preparing our home for their arrival. We were happy.

'Week after week, Matz sent the money back. And for a while, each week, we received three letters. One from Mama, one from Isha—and one from little Tzivia. Poor darling. She always said the same thing. "Isha is getting stronger every day. Love from Tzivia." She could have said more. She could have told us other things. I would have liked to know her news . . . I was fond of her. But . . .' Eleanor shrugged. 'She would have loved it in California. But—what can you do? Her papa came back for her. Once, twice, three times. He came for her and he left that poor girl again—I lost count of the times. And then that was the end of it. I received no more letters from Tzivia. Her father, my cousin, was not a good man. I don't know what became of either of them.'

Gregory said, 'But the letters from your mother

and Isha—they kept on coming?'

'Yes. Yes, they did. December finished, then January, February . . . We sent the money back each week. Mama said she and Isha would come in March. But then, there was snow in March. She told me to be patient. And I was patient! We prepared the apartment. Matz was working at Keystone. I was working more and more as an extra girl at Keystone, and then at the other studios, too. It was good. It was exciting. And I knew Isha and Mama would come. But then the spring came and went, and still Mama said Isha was too sick to make the journey. And spring turned to summer. I wrote to my mother that she and Isha simply had to come, or it would be fall again, and it would be too cold to travel. I told her I would come to New York myself, risk everything, and take Isha no matter what. But I was bluffing. Of course. Matz said I should go— he missed her too. But I trusted my mother. And I would never have made Isha travel unless she was strong. Of course not . . .' Eleanor's face twisted suddenly, in doubt and regret. 'It was almost a year since I had seen her, Mr Gregory. A whole year. And I began to think Isha would forget me.

'Finally, at the end of August, I received a letter from Mama telling me that the train tickets were bought, and that she and Isha would be arriving in Los Angeles at the beginning of September.

'Can you imagine, Mr Gregory? Can you imagine my happiness?' Mr Gregory grinned at her: 'Mrs Beecham, I think I almost can!'

'September came . . . And then another letter from Mama. Isha had suffered a relapse. The doctor advised two weeks' further rest. Oh God, I was beside myself! October, November. By

173

then we had enough money saved they could travel in second class—in warmth and comfort. Mama booked two more tickets. She sent a letter—you have it in front of you. Dated the second of November. They would arrive on the twenty-seventh of November 1914. It was done. There was money for blankets and coats, and a berth on the second-class sleeper. Isha had been strong for a whole month.

'On the twenty-seventh of November Matz and I set out for the train station. Matz had taken a day off work. Of course. And so had I. I didn't envisage ever returning to it . . . The apartment was ready. The beds were made. There was a little doll house I had bought, and I furnished it with . . . oh, never mind. We had filled the decking with flowers; fresh California lilacs, because I thought she would be amazed by them, the way I had been when I first came. And I had prepared a feast, Mr Gregory. All the foods I knew she loved—*babke* and *blintz* and . . .' She glanced at Mr Gregory. 'In any case, it was a feast . . .

'She never arrived. We waited, just as Matz had waited for his papa at the dock—and the train pulled in, but they never stepped off it. We waited for the next train. And the next. Matz had to go back to his work. But I waited for seven days. Each day I returned to the station. I travelled back and forwards from the train station to my post-office box. Nothing. Nothing. Nothing.

'The flowers wilted. Of course. And the food . . . well. And the doll house,' she smiled, 'I still have it. At the *Castillo*. Hidden away. So.

'But I never heard from Mama or from Isha again.

174

'I waited a whole month. Even longer. God knows—I thought they would come. I couldn't bear to leave, in case they . . . That was November. In the beginning of January, I left Matz in Los Angeles to work. He had a wonderful new job by then. Not playing piano, which he loved so much— that was all behind him by then. He had joined up with Butch . . . Butch Menken,' she amended. 'Anyway, his rise to becoming the big Hot Shot was just beginning.'

Eleanor could hear the tang of sourness in her voice—and felt shocked, a little ashamed. Because what he had achieved was remarkable. Not something to belittle, no matter the cost. It was exceptional. He was exceptional, and—yes, of course she was proud of him. 'That same week, he was hired by Mr Griffith. Second Unit, third assistant director. They were making *The Birth of a Nation*,' she added, a little shyly. 'You know it?

'Goodness.' Mr Gregory shuffled in his seat, blushed a little. 'I most certainly do . . .'

'He was assisting Mr Griffith himself!' She smiled.

'My goodness.'

'It sounds better than it was, of course. Really, he was just a dogsbody. But it was the beginning—and he was in love with his work. Why shouldn't he be? Of course—every man should be in love with his work. Isn't that right, Mr Gregory?'

'That's quite correct,' Gregory nodded keenly. He had been thinking perhaps they might take a break for lunch, see what news the tickertape heralded on the way out. And perhaps he and Mrs Beecham might enjoy a pleasant glass of wine again today? Perhaps she might tell him a few more

175

amusing stories about Hollywood. His wife had found it most amusing when he'd told her about Chaplin no longer believing in the great stock market of America. 'The little English tramp!' she had laughed. 'That's some nerve! Thinks he knows better than all the experts in America!' They'd enjoyed quite a little chuckle about that. 'A man should always love his work,' he said to Eleanor. 'That's how it should be.'

But she wasn't really listening. 'In any case, Matz couldn't leave Los Angeles. That's the point. And I understand it. I do. In any case—New York was too dangerous for him. It really was. There was no question about that. Not after the last time. So I made the journey alone . . .' There was a long pause.

'I should have made it earlier, Mr Gregory.'

30

He asked her to lunch, but she declined. 'It's probably best for both of us, don't you think? If we take a break. You have my voice, drilling into your head all day!' she smiled at him ruefully. 'I'm sure it would drive any man to distraction.'

'Hardly a drill,' he said, blushing. How did she do that, he wondered—transform herself like that? Lighten the mood, and herself, and the very air around her from one short second to the next? 'You have a lovely voice, Mrs Beecham. If I may say so . . .'

'You're very kind.'

'Not at all.'

176

'Well then. If it's all right with you, Mr Gregory, might we continue, just for a little while? And then perhaps we could break for the day and you could take a late lunch and I could return to the hotel . . . only I'm not sure I can keep this up all afternoon.'

'Yes of course,' he said. 'An excellent idea. Keep talking, Mrs Beecham. Forgive my interruption. You just keep talking until you want to stop.'

*   *   *

'Two months had passed since I received her last letter, and not a word. So I turned the corner into Allen Street and the place was boarded up, Mr Gregory. There was a notice on the door. The building had been condemned . . . They were bringing it up to date, somebody said.'

'That's right. Allen Street, Delancey Street— several streets in the triangle. As you know, the "old law" tenements had been rendered unfit for habitation,' Gregory chipped in, tapping his notes. It was something material to show for his father's investigations. 'And the process had been accelerated by the added health hazard attached to your particular building, because of the tuberculosis.'

'But there was always tuberculosis! Pneumonia. Consumption. Whatever you want to call it! It was part of life. It's simply how it was, Mr Gregory! People died every day. Don't you understand it yet? So *why*? Why that particular building? On that particular month. Why?'

It was an outburst, and it shocked them both to silence for a moment.

Ticker-tacker-ticker-tacker.

177

They gazed at each other, miles apart: 'I wish I knew,' he muttered at last.

'Yes. I wish you did too. But you don't know, do you?'

He opened his mouth, shocked. Thought better and closed it again.

'All these years I've been paying you,' Eleanor spat out, 'but you can't tell me. Can you? You can't tell me anything at all. Nothing that I don't already know! My mother was dead. I know that. There was a record at the City Hall. God knows, in those few weeks, before they shut down the whole goddamn building—what happened to everyone? One minute the building was swarming with us, hundreds of us, crushed in together, and we were dying like flies . . . And the next, nothing! Can you imagine it, Mr Gregory? *Can you?* In your fine offices here in Reno? With the sun shining outside—can you imagine what it felt like?

'My mother was dead. There were records. You have them. There were *records* of her death. Records of exactly sixty-three deaths, in that one building, in those few weeks. But do you know how many people were living in that building? Of course you don't. Because *nobody ever knew*. We were uncountable, Mr Gregory. Because there were swarms of us, in our peasant clothes and our wigs, pouring into the city every day. Learning the American way, from our little tenement hutches! We were all the same! Interchangeable. Uncountable. And not only to you, Mr Gregory. But to ourselves! We came, we went, we lived, we died. But where, Mr Gregory, *where did they put my daughter?*'

Matthew Gregory—Reno born, and Reno bred,

with a wife at home and a child on the way, and a garden which needed watering—opened his mouth, and closed it again. He had seen the war. He had seen his father drink himself to an early grave. And now . . . he had seen this. He was not a cruel man— and not stupid. Or not entirely stupid. But such depth of feeling—such wild and deep emotion— left him confused. Listening to her, it was as if his most valuable client had suddenly launched into a made-up language. It left him confused and, above all, irritated. She had no business to yell at him. As if it were his fault. He spoke into the silence, while she glared at him, waiting for an answer which she knew he could not give:

'Mrs Beecham. I understand your anger. I would feel angry, too, in your position. I surely would. But there comes a time, you know . . . when you have to ask yourself some real hard, cruel, bad questions—'

'No. I disagree. I disagree. We haven't reached that time yet. We have only just begun.'

'Your daughter had a history of illness, and, most especially, of a weak chest and lungs. There was an outbreak of tuberculosis in the building which killed most of the inhabitants, many of them previously fit and healthy . . . What happened to your daughter? . . . Mrs Beecham, do you really want me to tell you what I believe happened to your daughter?'

'But you can't *know*, Mr Gregory. You can't possibly know!'

'But I believe—'

'But we have only just begun; I have so much more to tell you. We're both tired. That's it, that's all it is. Perhaps we should break for lunch after all? It's too early to guess at what happened! We simply

179

cannot know—'

'*I disagree* . . .' he said. And was surprised by his courage. 'We have been working on the case for seven long years.'

'Not really. You haven't.' She sounded desperate. 'It doesn't matter. Not any more. I'm not *complaining* about it. And before—just now—I didn't mean to be rude. Forgive me. Please. I beg you. I'm only saying that your father—he didn't work on it. He wasn't working on it all these years. I'm not a fool. I can see—look at your file! There is nothing in it!'

'There is nothing in it. I can't argue with that. But, Mrs Beecham . . . I have to put it to you that there may be nothing in that file because, after all, there is really nothing left to put in it.'

'No!'

'Your daughter—by your own admission, was a very sick little girl. The building in which she lived suffered an epidemic that killed seventy—' he looked at his notes—'I beg your pardon, *sixty*-three unfortunate inhabitants—'

'And Isha's name is not among them! Isha Kappelman. Born 17 October 1907. Do you see it? Did you see a record of her death, during all those years of research?'

'Batia Esther Kappelman—'

'Was my *mother*!'

'I am aware of that.'

'Yes. Of course. I'm sorry. I apologize.'

'Mrs Beecham. Forgive me. But I can't simply sit here and fail to say what I know is on both of our minds. Is it not highly likely, Mrs Beecham, is it not *as good as certain* that little Isha died that same December, while that dreadful illness was

180

rampant in her home; and that, in the tragic and chaotic circumstances, your poor mother was in no fit state to trouble herself with the demands of City bureaucracy—or perhaps, by then, may even have passed away herself already—'

'Stop it!'

But he couldn't quite, not now. He leaned across the table, put out a hand but failed to reach her. 'Do you not think,' he asked her gently, 'fifteen years after these tragic events, that it's time to confront the very real possibility—that little Isha is at peace? That she has been at peace for a long, long time . . . And that it time for *you* to find some peace now, and to try to accept . . . that life is cruel, and life is short?'

He thought, briefly, of the two friends he had left behind him in France, and quickly, through force of well-practised habit, blinked their memory away again. 'I think your daughter is dead, Mrs Beecham. I believe she died of tuberculosis in December 1914. I also believe that you believe it too, or you would never have tolerated my father's . . . lack of . . .' He shook his head, unwilling to finish the sentence. 'But—I am happy to continue with the search, if you feel it will help you. If you feel there may be a small chance—'

'There is a small chance.'

He sat back and looked at her. 'Yes,' he sighed. 'Indeed.'

'She might have been taken up by someone. Don't you see? A small girl, all alone . . . After her grandmother died, someone might have taken pity. They might have believed she was all alone in the world. Someone might have taken her. Or perhaps the authorities, after they closed the building.

They might have taken her and put her into an orphanage. Have you checked? Did you ask the orphanages?

'Every orphanage in the state. Yes. My father did that.'

'Batia Isha Kappelman?'

'Yes. Of course. But I can do it again. If you would like me to.'

'Someone might have taken care of her. Or perhaps taken her out of State? She might be anywhere—don't you see? Or she might be just like her father, Mr Gregory! Her father survived alone on the streets. And look at him now!'

Gregory opened his mouth—and closed it again.

Belatedly, she noticed her mistake: 'I mean to say . . .' she said. 'That is . . .' She fell silent.

'Is Mr Kappelman still alive?' Gregory asked at last.

'Mr Kappelman?' She looked at him blankly.

'Is Matz Kappelman still alive?'

She took a long time to answer. She thought about it. Finally she said, 'Oh no. Matz has been dead for years.'

31

Tuesday 22 October 1929

Max Beecham didn't make an appearance at Silverman Pictures until the Tuesday afternoon. He called in to his secretary late on the morning that he, Silverman and the editor Mr Leeson were meant to have been re-cutting his precious film. He

182

explained he was heading out of town. There was an actor he needed to woo in Palm Springs, he said, and a location he wanted to check out along the route.

She sounded worried. 'Mr Silverman has been asking for you since nine o'clock. He's on the warpath, Mr Beecham. He's got that look in his eye . . . What shall I tell him?'

'Tell him you can't reach me,' said Max. 'Tell him I'm out of town.' He hung up.

But by Tuesday afternoon he was ready to face the music. He sauntered into the studio, freshly shaven and sleek as he ever was, an athletic spring to his step which belied . . . everything. It seemed to him that even the receptionist trembled just a little when she greeted him. She said, 'Oh Mr Beecham! You're here at last!'

'I sure am,' he said, bestowing on her his famous smile.

She said, 'Well—good luck!'

'Bad as that, huh?' He winked at her and she blushed.

'He was making a stink all yesterday . . . Making life hell for all of us, Mr Beecham. You're going to need all the luck you can get.'

He took the elevator to the first floor and again hoped—against all experience—that he might be able to sneak along the corridor to his office unobserved. But God knows—Silverman must have had some kind of sixth sense. Before Max had even taken a step out of the elevator, he could hear his name being roared.

'Max Beecham, is that you?' bellowed his employer, shaking every pot plant along the corridor. 'Get your ass in here!'

183

Max paused, just for a second. Took a small breath. And followed the sound of the roar.

As he passed her desk, he nodded at Silverman's secretary, gave her a cockeyed kind of a grimace. Ordinarily so collected, she could think of nothing to say to him, and as he reached for the door that opened into the lion's den, she released a tiny, empathetic whimper. 'Oh dear,' she whispered.

He grinned at her and walked on in.

Silverman sat at his desk as usual. His small, round face was angrier than Max had ever seen it, the pate of his small, round head shining in the early sunlight. Max had heard it said of people before—but he'd never observed it so literally: Joel Silverman's compact outline stood out against the morning sun behind him, and it really did look as if it was ready to explode. Even so, as Max travelled the long, long length of his office, beams of sunlight reflecting off the floating dust particles between them and causing Max to screw up his eyes and squint, Silverman did not stand up, or even speak.

He looked tiny, Max thought. As if to reassure himself. The desk was far too big for him. It looked absurd. He looked absurd. Like Humpty Dumpty at a dining table.

'You should get a smaller desk,' Max said. 'The proportions are all wrong. Don't you think?' He sat down in the low leather seat—too low—in front of the desk which so offended him. And immediately regretted having spoken. They looked at one another. Max crossed his legs. Sat forward. And then: 'But I guess that's not top of your concerns right now.'

Joel Silverman glared at him.

Max said: 'So. Here I am. A day late. I apologize

for that. Stuff I had to do down in Palm Springs. But I think I found a perfect spot for *Wishing You Joy*. I think we could shoot the whole thing right there on a single location. It's driving distance from LA, so no overnights. It's going to halve the cost. We have the lake right there. It's absolutely—'

'Max. What the hell are you talking about?'

'*Wishing You Joy*?'

'Never mind *Wishing You Joy*. I wish you anything but. What did you do with the dailies, Max?

'Hm?'

'All the outtakes from *Lost At Sea*. Where are they? I sent down for them yesterday—and guess what? They've vanished. Last seen, *signed out by you*—on Saturday morning. What in hell did you do with them, Max? I got the vaults being turned upside down. Nobody knows where they are. Except you.'

Max opened his eyes wide. 'You're kidding me? Where have they gone?'

'You tell me.'

'Hey, I've come in this morning to go through them with you. You know that. We're starting from the beginning, just like you said. You, me, Leeson and every bit of footage I have. Remember? Butch Menken didn't like what we made. So we're starting again.'

'Where the hell is it all, Max? Where's the old footage? What have you done with it? How can we start again, if we've got no extra footage?'

'Joel, I wasn't even here yesterday! Why the hell are you asking me? How should I know?'

'You think I'm running a goddamn fucking *art school* here? I am running a *business*. What did you do with them, Max? I'm asking you one last time.'

There was a long silence.

'Honestly, I wish I could help you,' Max said solemnly. 'But I don't know what you're talking about. Hell. I want those rushes as much anyone else does. Now you and Butch have decided the movie's got to change. Well, it's got to change. Here I am to re-edit. Get my movie out in the theatres. That's what matters. That's what it's all about . . .'

Joel Silverman gazed at Max, long and hard and, finally, he shrugged. He'd expected nothing else. 'I don't know what you've done with them, Max. But you'd better get them back here. Fast. Or you've just wasted half a million bucks. *My* bucks. Get those dailies back here. On my desk. By eleven o'clock. Or I'm firing you, Max. You understand? I don't want to do it. But you're making me do it. We get *Lost At Sea* into a shape that'll satisfy the censors—'

'I think you mean satisfy Butch Menken.'

'Or there's no *Lost At Sea*.'

'Oh, come on!'

'*COME ON?*' he repeated, incredulous. '*A kholere af dir*, Max Beecham. You piss my money away. The end. Now get out of here!'

But Max didn't move.

'Get out!'

He said, 'Joel—I'm not getting you the dailies.'

'Yes, you are.'

'No. I'm not . . . I cut them up.'

'You did *what*?'

'After we talked. Case by case. I cut them up. The Catholic ladies are wrong. The test screening was wrong. And most of all Butch Menken—'

'Don't talk to me about Butch.'

186

'He's wrong. And he knows he's wrong. And so do you know he's wrong.'

'The test screening is never wrong.'

'It was the wrong audience. It's a great film. You said it yourself—before the screening. It's a beautiful film. That's what you said. Remember?'

Joel didn't reply. Of course he remembered.

'I know you remember it, Joel. You said it. You said, "Max—it's the best movie you've put together in three years!" How can you let the Catholic ladies trample over that—huh? Huh?'

Joel didn't reply.

'What *happened* to you, Joel? Don't you care any more? You used to care! You used to be the only goddamn producer in Hollywood who looked beyond the bottom buck. And now look at you! You've got Butch Menken coming in here to make his crumby, filthy, dumb, stupid goddamn musicals. Everything this studio ever stood for, Butch Menken stands against. Did you even see his last film?'

'Did you see the receipts?'

Max considered his boss. Despite the bluster, he knew he had struck a note. *'A kholere af dir*, Joel Silverman! A plague on you too!'

'Hey!'

'I give you the best film I ever made. It's yours. It's out of my hands now. You're the boss. You can leave it in the vault and leave it to rot. If that's what you want to do. But at least I didn't let you trash it—for the sake of a few extra bucks from the Catholic Morality bitches—'

'Hey!'

'—who wouldn't know a decent movie if it smacked them on the nose and bust every blue-ass,

187

blue-nose bone in their dumb-ass bodies . . . And maybe, one day, when Butch has been and gone, and left this studio the pile of shit he'll turn it into, you'll thank me for standing up . . . and for *remembering* why at least some of us ever got into this business in the first place.'

A moment of pure silence followed. And then— in his outrage, Joel Silverman laughed aloud. 'You piss half a million of my dollars down the pan, and you think I'm going to thank you for it? Get outta here. Hey! And before you go, listen to me.' Silverman raised a finger, pointed it at him and— though Max was already standing by then, and though Silverman still sat, and though it was only one small, fat finger—the menace of that single movement brought Max to a halt. 'One more stunt like that—any kind of stunt; one false move, you leave a cigarette butt in the wrong place—and I don't care how good your movies are. I don't care how much money you've made me in the past. I don't care how much you kick and squeal—you're finished here. Fired. Out. I'll make it my personal goal—my only goal—that you never make another movie. Not for me, and not for anyone else in this town.'

'I understand,' Max said solemnly. He did, too. Actually, he couldn't believe his luck. As he walked back out of that long room, with all the dignity he could muster, he was tensed for one final missile— verbal or otherwise—to come hurling towards the back of his head, but it didn't come.

He longed to know what Joel would do with *Lost At Sea*. Whether he would take on the censors, or leave the film to rot. He longed to ask, but it wasn't the moment. That he managed to be walking out of that room with his job intact was astonishing enough. He would enquire after the film's fate a little later. And he would fight for it, at every step. Because that was what Max did. When he cared about something. He fought for it.

32

'So . . . when you discovered the building was boarded up, and there was no sign of your daughter?' Mr Gregory handed his menu back to the waiter and settled back into his chair. Eleanor had agreed to go to lunch with him after all. Anything to keep him from closing the file altogether. 'What did you do?'

'Well. I made enquiries. I found out what had happened to the building. I went to City Hall and found Mama's death recorded . . . and then . . . I didn't know what to do, Mr Gregory. There was no one in the city I could go to, not safely. And wherever I turned, there were always people who might know me.'

'You needed to be careful?'

'I needed somebody to make the enquiries for me—that's all. I had money, but not much. I did what I could. I searched for her. All the hospitals, the orphanages, the warm little corners of the city where kids with nowhere to go used to sleep sometimes. Matz had shown them to us—the places where he'd sometimes hidden when he was a little boy. They hadn't changed. I thought perhaps Isha might have . . . But she was so small then. Only three-and-a-half when we left her. Of course she wouldn't have remembered them. She was nowhere. There was no sign of her. Not anywhere, Mr Gregory. She had simply vanished.'

Gregory kept his eyes lowered, and scribbled something—anything—onto the sheet in front of him. It was tragic. Of course it was. But the more he listened to her story, the clearer the truth became. His father should have put a stop to this inquiry years ago. It was a disgrace, really, that he had strung her along all these years. And now here was he, still listening to her tale of woe. *I'm a shrink*, he thought to himself in disgust. *Not a detective*. Yesterday they had agreed a fee of seven dollars per hour. Just now, before they came to lunch, she had agreed to double it. Fourteen dollars per hour. It was astronomical.

He knew he should stop her. Set her straight. Put her back on the train to Los Angeles.

On the other hand . . .

She didn't want to stop. She didn't want to be set straight. She wanted to talk and talk and talk . . . until some kind of miracle occurred.

'Vanished,' he repeated, finally. 'You couldn't find her anywhere. There was no sign of her. So . . . What did you do?'

'I stayed for three months. Matz sent me money. But then—something happened. Nothing important. I was on Hester Street, searching, searching—and somebody called out to me. I looked up and there was Dora's little sister gazing up at me! Dora—my beloved friend. From the factory. Her sister was not so little any more. I heard my name:

'"*Eleana?*"

'God! You can't imagine what it felt like! Just to

190

have it confirmed that I had indeed existed in this place. And there she was! Izzie. Dora's baby sister! Staring right up at me, her eyes looking directly into mine. And she knew it was me, just as well as she knew her own name. I could see the smile just waiting to break across her face.

'God, and how I longed to embrace her.'

'And did you embrace her?' Gregory heard himself asking. Carried away, for an instant, by a grain of hope. 'Perhaps she might have known where Isha was?'

'I did not. No. I couldn't. She wept—because of course she thought she had seen a ghost. I shook her by her little shoulders. I said, *"Where is my Isha?"* And she stopped crying. She looked at me as if I was quite, quite stupid . . .'

'And what did Isha say, Mrs Beecham?'

'She said, "Why, Eleana, Isha is dead."'

'That's exactly what she said . . . ?'

'I left the city the following day. Matz had already written, begging me to come home. He was frightened for me. And he was right to be frightened. After Izzie had seen me, it wasn't safe. I had the ticket for the train in my pocket already. Matz had told me to hire a detective before I left. And so I did that.'

'May I ask, how did you find him?'

She shrugged. 'He was just a man—with a card, Mr Gregory.' Eleanor smiled at him. 'Rather like you . . . I don't remember how I found him. After I saw Izzie, it was a blur. I was so frightened. For me and for Matz, too. Of course. They would have tracked him to Hollywood eventually.

'I asked the detective to discover the fate of every person who had lived in the block . . .

everyone who was living in the block, when they shut it down. And I gave him the post-office box number in Los Angeles . . .'

'And?'

Eleanor laughed. 'Well what do you think? Here I sit. Still trying to find out.'

33

Matthew Gregory might have had a megaphone attached his brain, Eleanor reflected; it's how easy it was to know what was running through his mind. She knew what he thought of her story, and what he thought of her, too: noticed the flickers of electricity, every now and then, when he remembered that the woman before him was not simply any woman, but a woman who had dined with Charlie Chaplin . . . She saw that. She saw bewilderment, impatience, disbelief—of course. And restlessness and inattention . . . Sometimes she spotted him glancing up at the clock on the wall, or maybe the ticker machine in the hallway, and she knew he was quietly totting up her bill.

She saw, also—that sometimes his attention wandered to her voice, her face, her throat, her slim limbs. She would sit away from him. Speak faster and louder until his attention returned. And she saw that there were also moments, many of them, when he was moved by her story.

He had a kind face, she decided, beneath the oiled hair, the Arbuckle hamster cheeks. And when she talked about Isha, lying ill in her cot—or perhaps in an orphanage somewhere, or perhaps in the same gutter Matz had used for refuge, fifteen years before her—she could see that he was imagining his own daughter: five years old, playing safely in her bright green suburban back yard, only a couple of miles away.

All of this, she noted and understood. Greedy, lustful, incurious, impressionable . . . but not unkind. He was not a wicked man. And above all he was someone to talk to. Someone who would sit and listen. What she needed to escape was the pity.

Finally, she said: 'You must be hungry, Mr Gregory. I am so sorry—I keep talking and you don't get a chance to eat your lunch.'

'Not at all!' he said politely.

She looked down at her own plate, the food on it untouched, the sight of it turning her stomach a little bit. Really, she didn't want to eat. 'If it's all right with you, Mr Gregory, I'm feeling rather ill. I may leave you here in the restaurant. Would it be very rude? I might just leave you in peace to enjoy your lunch. And perhaps I will head back to my hotel after all. I'm sure you have a whole lot of other business to attend to this afternoon in any case—or perhaps,' she added hopefully, pointlessly, 'maybe something I've said might have encouraged you to make some fresh enquiries?'

He shook his head. He said he would wait until she had told him 'everything' before he launched into any new investigations. 'However,' he added, already standing up (the poor man was indeed quite peckish), 'you are right, I do have other business to attend to. And of course I won't be charging you for the afternoon. Please don't concern yourself with that.'

'Thank you,' she replied. It was the last thing that

193

concerned her.

They shook hands over their congealing lunch plates. 'I think I may drop in with my broker this afternoon, Mrs Beecham. As soon as I have eaten. See what he has to say about your friend Mr Chaplin's theories on the market . . .'

'But Mr Gregory,' she frowned. 'I'm sure I don't need to mention . . . I hope you wouldn't . . .'

He held up a paw to stop her. 'Don't even imagine it, Mrs Beecham! Neither the name of "The Tramp", ha-ha, nor your own shall escape from my lips! Not to my broker. Not even to my beloved wife. Client confidentiality is the cornerstone of this business. It's the cornerstone, Mrs Beecham. Without it, I have no business at all!'

34

Another telegram awaited her when she reached her rooms, this one sounding more impatient than the last, and it made her smile. Butch never did like to be kept waiting.

I AM WORRIED ABOUT YOU BABY STOP URGENT YOU CALL STOP B

'B.' Who was always so good to her, who had tracked her down to a hotel in Reno, who was worried enough to send her not one wire, but two. She missed him, suddenly.

Her mind turned automatically to Max. Between all his other concerns, had he missed her? Did he wonder where she was? Had he paused, for the briefest moment, to try to find her? Somehow, she couldn't imagine it.

She booked the call to Butch's number at Lionsfiel and waited for him to come on the line. It would be good to talk to him. God, it would be better than good—it would be wonderful.

'Butch? Is it you?'

'BABY!'

At the sound of his voice, five hundred miles away, crackling warmth and concern across the line, all the way from Hollywood—from home—she felt a rush of love and gratitude for him. Butch, who was always there for her, who was so strong and calm. Who knew her better than anyone. Except for Max, who knew her absolutely—almost—but who didn't care for her any more. It was a beautiful thing to be loved and desired.

Suddenly, she longed to give up the fight. To surrender all her secrets. To surrender, altogether. She could leave Max and allow Butch to take care of her. And he would take care of her. No matter what, he would always take care of her. And maybe it wouldn't be perfect. Maybe he would lose interest once he had vanquished them both—her and Max—in a single swoop. Of course he would lose interest. She knew it. She knew him. But right then, hearing his voice, it seemed hard to believe anything bad of him at all.

She remembered the first time he had invited her to come live with him. It was not long after Max had left for Silverman Pictures, and just six weeks after she had first taken solace in his bed. That was the closest she had ever come to saying, Yes. Until this moment.

Except he hadn't asked. Not yet. All he'd said

was 'BABY!' and already she could feel the tears of defeat coursing down her cheeks.

'Butch? It's me . . . It's Eleanor.'

'I know who it is! Sweetheart, I've been so worried about you! What's up? What in hell are you doing in Reno? And don't tell me you're finally seeing sense and throwing out that lousy husband. I checked with the courthouse. Nothing. Nada . . . *Reno*, baby? Of all places! What's happening?'

But she was sobbing so hard she couldn't speak. 'Eleanor! . . . Are you *crying?*'

35

Butch was still mid-call, and still without having broached the delicate matter of her soon-to-be-terminated contract at Lionsfiel, let alone his own imminent move to Silverman Pictures. He was trying to absorb the story she was telling him, struggling to discern the words between her sobs and pauses, wondering if he must have misheard her . . . And then Max burst into the room.

God knows (Butch knew it better than almost anyone), Max Beecham could charm himself into pretty much any room in the world, but how he got through the gates at Lionsfiel, past the receptionist, past Butch's own secretary and right into Butch's office without anyone stopping him, Butch could only wonder at.

He didn't bother to ask.

'Max,' he said pleasantly, without missing a beat. Smoothly he replaced the telephone receiver, as if his ancient foe, his one-time closest friend, with

196

whom he'd not spoken in five years—as if such a man burst into his office at Lionsfiel every day of the week. 'How terribly nice.'

Max kept on walking. His eyes on Butch, he walked through the office he knew so well, between the life-size portraits of Lionsfiel stars (Eleanor included) that lined the great producer's walls, and past the innocuous little side table, which, at the press of a hidden lever, slid back to reveal a full bar: Butch Menken's not-so-secret Speak, to which only the prettiest girls in town gained access.

Max had only one thing in his sight and, too late, Butch Menken calculated what it was. Max— smaller than Butch but niftier, had learned to move like lightning in another, distant life. He'd not hit out at anyone—not once, not since that afternoon eighteen years ago. But he stepped round the back of Butch's desk, and before Butch could blink or flinch, he threw a fist into that strong, American jaw. It was something Max had been wanting to do for a long time.

Butch reeled, stunned. And again, before Butch could blink or flinch or begin to collect himself, Max came at him a second time, and then a third. For Max, who could feel the jaw give beneath his knuckles, who could feel the pain reflected in his own damaged hand each time his knuckles made impact, the pleasure was intense. *Intense.* He stopped. Stood back, slightly—but not entirely— horrified by what he had done.

He waited for Butch to recover. 'Where is she, Butch?'

Butch took his time. He put a hand first to his jaw, and then to his nose to see if it was bleeding. It was.

'Answer me.'

Slowly, Butch took a large, clean handkerchief from his jacket pocket, held it to his nose and away again, to examine the flow of blood. He rearranged the handkerchief, the better to soak up what was fast becoming a small torrent and, finally, without looking up, he said: 'Where is who, my friend? Do you mean your daughter, Max—Little Isha? Or do you mean your wife?'

Better than any punch—Max staggered slightly. He said, 'What—what did you say?'

From behind his handkerchief, Butch grinned at him. 'So many secrets!' he tutted. 'And there was me, thinking we were such close *friends*. But you guys,' he shook his head, 'you're certainly full of surprises.'

'What daughter?' Max muttered, pointlessly.

Butch stopped. Why had he said it? He registered the shock on the other man's face, and wished he hadn't. He was still reeling from the knowledge himself—from the discovery that his two good friends could have kept such a secret for so long. He didn't answer. Instead he leaned across the blood-spattered desk and buzzed through to his secretary. 'Julia,' he said, in that quiet voice of his, 'I need security in here. Please. And I need some ice. And a couple of towels would be helpful. As soon as possible. Thank you.'

He turned back to Max. 'You need to leave.'

'I will leave. As soon as you tell me. Where is she? Where is Eleanor?'

'I have no idea. We sent a script to the house on Friday and we've not heard a word from her since. Is she not home?' He didn't wait for Max to reply. 'I guess not, huh? Well, when you find

198

her, tell her to call. Her contract's up for renewal. You probably know. And Carrascosa wants to terminate . . . This is hardly a time for her to be playing cat and mouse. Make sure you tell her that, won't you?' As he finished speaking, they heard footsteps outside, a quick tap on the door. It opened and two uniformed security guards walked in.

'*Where is she?*' Max asked again.

'If she'd wanted you to know, I presume she would have told you, Max. I can't tell you where she is.'

Max said, '*Please . . .*'

One of the guards put a fat hand on his shoulder. 'You want me to call the law, Mr Menken?'

Butch ignored it. Instead, he sighed. 'You probably won't believe it, Max. But I was actually looking forward to working with you again. We could have made some great movies. *Lost At Sea—*'

'I don't give a damn about *Lost At Sea.*'

Butch said: 'Me neither. It's not your best movie, Max. And that's the truth.'

Max shook his head. Broke into a laugh, and then, as abruptly, stopped. He lurched forward, but not to strike this time, only to plead, 'Where is she, Butch? Where is Eleanor?' The guards pulled him back. They yanked him into a double arm lock so roughly he fell to the ground.

'Hey,' Butch snapped. 'Show the man some respect . . . Show him some respect,' he said again. For the briefest moment, with Max still on the floor, both men looked at one another and forgot the present, and remembered the beginning, when the stakes were low, and they were still young, and the three of them were friends, embarking on a wonderful journey together. Butch and Max and Eleanor . . . and Rudolph Valentino and Charlie Chaplin, Mary Pickford, Douglas Fairbanks, Clara Bow, D. W. Griffith . . .

It was before Prohibition, when the living was easy. *When the living was easy*, and they used to sit together at the bar of the Alexandria Hotel, Butch and Max and Eleanor—the director, the producer, and the star—hatching their plans. They had made some great films together. The best of their careers. Butch said it again. Mumbled it. 'Show him some respect.'

The guards loosened the arm lock and pulled him upright.

As they led him away, Max turned back to Butch one last time: 'Butch, please . . .'

'She's out of town,' Butch said, looking down at his desk, straightening what didn't need to be straightened. 'I haven't seen her. But she's fine. Licking her wounds. That's all. You should take better care of her . . .'

'Fuck you.'

'Yeah, and you too. Julia!' He raised his voice, just a little: enough for his secretary to hear him through the opening door. 'Sweetheart, I'm going to need a fresh shirt. Could you fix that for me, please?'

36

Max knew it was over. He didn't need to be told. Beating up the new hire, the golden boy of Hollywood, the executive producer of his own studio wasn't, perhaps, quite as heinous as leaving a butt end in the wrong place, but Butch would see to it that Silverman fired him. Of course he would. He'd said as much already.

And Max tried to care. But, after all, and to his surprise, he found that he couldn't. He stood in the Lionsfiel parking lot, hesitating, wondering where to go next. The guards hung back, watching impatiently.

'You need to get into the vehicle,' one of them said.

He nodded. Opened the driver door and climbed in. But he didn't know where to drive. Where should he drive? Not to the empty house. God, no.

He missed Eleanor. He missed her so much. Another evening stretched ahead.

Perhaps, he thought, he should call Douglas and Mary. He had forgotten to turn up to dinner last night, but they would probably forgive him, if he apologized nicely enough. Perhaps they would allow him to come round this evening instead?

Dinners at Pickfair were always the same. Douglas Fairbanks didn't approve of alcohol—or not officially—so there was never enough to go around. But the company was always good. Actually, the company was legendary. Mary and Doug gave a dinner for at least ten, almost every night and, even despite the lack of drink, the people came.

Max would call them up. See what was going on. Or maybe not. Maybe he couldn't face company tonight. There was only one person he wanted to see. She was the only company he wanted. He remembered her light green eyes, when they smiled at him; the smell of her skin, the sound of

201

her silence. He missed her. The bed, the house, everything felt empty. He felt empty. He just needed to find Eleanor.

There had been a message from his stockbroker waiting at his desk this morning. Three messages, actually. Max had been ignoring them all day. And he would ignore them again tomorrow, if he could. He tried to care about the stockbroker, the precarious state of the market, the tumbling price of the utilities, his imminent ruin. But, after all (and to his surprise), he found that he couldn't. The market would stabilize. Probably. Maybe. Maybe it would stabilize. He needed to find Eleanor.

Max had called everyone he could think of—anyone and everyone who might possibly have known where she was. But in truth, he realized, there weren't many to call. Eleanor didn't have many close friends. She was private, just as he was. Beneath the charm and geniality, the politeness and success, they had always kept the world at arm's length.

And yet she had confided in Butch.

Max glanced up. The larger of the two Lionsfiel security guards had apparently run out of patience and was approaching the window. He needed to start the engine.

Did Butch know the full story? In her weakness, would Eleanor have told him everything? Actually, Max doubted it. He doubted it sincerely. She loved him, he realized. He knew that, and he had always known it. Of course she loved him. She would never put him in danger.

Max drove east, his back to the setting sun, his car pointing automatically towards the office and, beyond that, to his empty house. As lonely as he had ever been. Lost, without Eleanor. To his left, the iron arches to the Silverman lot loomed into view and, automatically, he slowed, ready to turn in.

He should talk to Joel. He should get in there and fight for his job. He loved his work. He loved the studio. He loved Joel. There was so much to be done . . . He stopped the car in the middle of the road, ready to make the turn—and hesitated once again. The driver behind him honked impatiently, but Max ignored it.

The Silverman parking lot was already three-quarters empty. But he saw the Silverman Bugatti glimmering beneath the evening sun, in its usual spot. Silverman would be at his desk then, still working. No surprises there . . . Perhaps, at that very moment, he was taking the call that would decide Max's fate: listening to the hushed, clipped tones of Butch Menken, as Butch demanded Max Beecham's head.

Joel wouldn't want to agree to it. Max knew that. But if Butch insisted—if Butch said: It's Max or me (and of course it would come down to that eventually, no matter how elegantly Butch packaged it up), there was no doubt in Max's mind which man Silverman would choose to keep.

Butch Menken had the Midas touch. Max made some excellent movies, some good movies, and some turkeys. Plus, he destroyed his own dailies when told to re-edit. Max told himself he should turn in, drive through the damn arches, *now*. He should fight for his job. Silverman was fond of him. Max could turn it around. Of course he could. He only needed to . . .

But he put his foot on the gas and drove straight on.

Butch said she was out of town, but Eleanor never left town. Was Butch lying, then?

Was she hiding out at Butch's apartment? Probably. He should drive by. Again. For the hundredth time. Back to his spot, under the tree, where he had spent every night since she left, sleeping in his car. He would ask the porter if he'd spotted her . . . Again. Try to find a way to get into Butch's apartment. Again. And this time if the man refused to give him a straight answer, he would punch his way in.

He needed to turn the car round. He should do that—find his goddamn wife, and bring her home with him.

But he didn't turn the car around. He kept on driving, twenty blocks further east, and then a few blocks north, until his car pulled up opposite her window. And there she was, tapping away at her typewriter.

She didn't have any drapes up. She said they weren't 'modern'. It was dusk outside by then, and the light shone over her desk, illuminating her pretty face. He could see her: the little frown of concentration, and her mouth, shaping the words as she wrote them.

Cute.

She cared so much about her work. He admired her for that. He wondered—vaguely—what she was working on this evening. One day, she always said, she was going to write a screenplay. 'And it's going to be the best screenplay you ever read, Max Beecham. And you're going to beg me for the rights to it, so you can direct it.' Cute. And maybe she would do that, too. Watching her, the intensity of her concentration, it occurred to him that she

204

probably would. One day.

But not tonight. Tonight, he decided, she was putting her typewriter away. He was taking her out to dinner.

*   *   *

They never did make it out to dinner. He stood at her door, dishevelled, with a diffidence that touched her, and which washed away all the anxiety she had been feeling about him. Blanche knew already, because it was her business to know, that his wife had gone walkabout, and that the studio was looking for her. She had heard rumours that Eleanor had been spotted in Reno, which could only mean one thing.

Blanche also knew the *Lost At Sea* dailies had gone missing, too, and knowing Max as she did, she had a pretty good idea what had become of them. So much was going on in his life these past few days, and yet he had not made contact with her; and then, after the encounter last night, she suspected the worst.

There was a smattering of blood on his shirt, which raised a few questions. More questions. She had questions of her own after what happened to her last night. There was so much she had intended to ask him.

Once a cheat, always a cheat. That's what her mother used to say.

If he could cheat on his wife, he could cheat on her. And she needed to ask him.

But not right away. He had come to her door— not to the other woman's. If she *was* the other woman. Whoever the hell she was. God dammit, the bitch had lost her nerve and run away before Blanche had had a chance to ask her.

He looked terrible, standing there, like he needed her. And she loved him, very much—of course she did—and it pulled at her heart to seem him so low. But it also disconcerted her. Just a little bit.

She said nothing. She just smiled and held open the door and welcomed him in. She would ask him later. All the questions would have to wait. She sat him down on her velvet couch and she mixed them both cocktails, and they talked, but not all that much. She made him an omelette, which he didn't eat. And then they took each other to bed. And Blanche set aside her suspicions. Or she forgot about them. Or for the time she and Max were in bed together, they seemed to be quite meaningless, anyway.

37

In the morning, while the lovers slept, the world shifted. Madness took hold on Wall Street. On the trading floor, brawls erupted as the stock prices plummeted, and grown men sobbed.

When Max finally opened his sleepy eyes, two-and-a-half thousand miles away in sunny California, well on his way to being a poor man again, nothing could have been further from his mind. He saw Blanche's young, pretty, face on the pillow beside him and he felt—for the sharpest, briefest instant—a lightness he'd not felt in years, and he wondered why he'd been fighting it all this time.

38

Five hundred miles away in Reno, the ticker-tape machine was going crazy. Matthew Gregory was finding it hard to concentrate, and even harder to sit tight, albeit at a fee of $14 per hour, while his client embellished a story with so many holes that nothing about it held together any longer or made the slightest sense.

Eleanor was talking about a guy called Butch. The screenplay Matz wrote in 1918, which Butch produced, and Matz directed—or was it vice versa? He couldn't be bothered to ask. It was the screenplay for the film that turned Eleanor Beecham into a star.

Poppy Girl! He remembered that. It was a sensation at the time. Suddenly everyone was talking about Eleanor Beecham. Matthew Gregory had seen the film, along with most of America. He'd taken his sweetheart (now his wife) on what would have been their second or third date, and they'd both laughed until they cried. You wouldn't guess it, listening to her today, but Eleanor Beecham was a wonderful comic actress. Funny thing, he thought, how gorgeous she was, up there on the screen. They'd all fallen crazy in love with her. Everyone! Men *and* women! And now here she sat, while what was left of his fortunes flushed away down the toilet, telling him a story that made no sense. Because she wouldn't accept the truth. Because she thought, if she talked—what? There was still hope? *What?* What was she doing here? *Poor thing*, he thought. *Poor old girl.* For $14 per hour, he could at least try to be patient.

So while she talked, Matthew Gregory did a few sums. Tried to work out the impossible, in a plunging market: what his situation might be at the end of the day. He'd bought £9,000 of US Steel on a margin of 10 per cent. He owned $300 of General Electric, which he'd ordered his broker to sell at whatever price he could get. Since the beginning of the week their value had already halved, and this morning it was impossible to tell what their price was until the ticker tape caught up, if it ever did. That was the damn trouble. It was driving him crazy, sitting here.

At a 10 per cent margin, he owned £3,000 of a radio stock, inherited from his father, whose price had risen by 8 per cent in the month of September, dropped by a single per cent in the first week of October, and risen by 2 per cent on Thursday last. A 9 per cent increase in as many weeks! If only Gregory had sold he might have come away with a very tidy profit.

But he hadn't, had he? On Monday last he'd bought even more.

'You'll never get 'em cheaper!' the broker had bellowed into the telephone. *What had he been thinking?* On Monday last, adrenalin pumping, from having a beautiful movie star waft into his cheap little office, he had taken the broker's advice. Now, of course, the stock was less than worthless ... He thought of his wife with one on the way, and his precious five-year-old daughter playing in her harsh, green suburban back yard. *What had he been thinking?* . . . If the price fell ten cents below the margin—he didn't have to do the sums—he would be ruined. He glanced up at Eleanor. Yes, she was still talking . . .

'. . . When you sign with one of the big studios, anything is possible,' she was telling him. 'They can fix up anything for you. They have people to do it, you see. People employed to cover up the most terrible activities. And they can do it. You know? They have all the corners covered. You remember William Taylor?

William Desmond Taylor—a Hollywood director, living under an assumed name, found dead in his home with a room full of ladies' underwear, signed by their famous lady owners, and love letters in his desk from two of America's biggest movie stars . . . They never found the killer. The studio had its people crawling over the death scene long before the police got near the place. It was a scandal back in 1922 when it happened. It was a scandal still.

'Who doesn't know about William Desmond Taylor?' replied Mr Gregory. He glanced subtly at his watch.

'Well, then. You understand. The studio *looks after you*. But that kind of protection, it comes at a price.'

'I understand.'

'Butch was a studio man by then, you see. He always knew better than anyone how to work a system.' She smiled. 'For example—right now, he's a senior producer at Lionsfiel—'

'Uh-huh . . .'

'He's a big shot, no question about that. But he's not the only big shot. There are others, more senior. But he has a better office than any of them.

209

Bigger, swankier.' She laughed suddenly, thinking of his hidden Speak, of which he was so very proud. 'Butch knows how to look after himself. And he looks after the people he cares for. And he looked out for us, Mr Gregory. You understand? He fixed us up with the initial studio contracts. And he got us new papers. We had *papers* at last!'

'He got you papers. Fair enough. But if the studios can fix anything—if they can fix you up with a new identity, get their stars off the hook for murder—then why, and you have to excuse me for asking this, but why are you sitting here with a small-town detective from Reno?'

'Because they don't know. Of course. About Isha. About the half of it. They would never have signed us . . .'

'I don't understand.'

'Matz's politics . . .'

'What about his politics?'

She shifted in her seat. The time had come. She knew it. Last night, after the call with Butch had ended so abruptly, she had considered the matter carefully: what she would and wouldn't tell Matthew Gregory today. She would tell him the truth, she had decided. Because she had to tell him something. But not all of it. Half the truth would be enough.

'He was part of the socialist movement—'

Gregory sat up as if an electric current has passed through him. '*Socialism?*' he said. Snarled.

She smiled. 'Oh, you can frown if you like, Mr Gregory,' she said. 'Just as much as you like. But when you've lived and worked as we did . . .'

He held up a hand. 'Hey, lady. For God's sakes. We all have different opinions. We're entitled to our different opinions. That's the beauty of America! I'm sure as hell not here to judge.'

'But you *were* judging,' she replied. 'We can't help but judge. And yet, until we have inhabited one another's skins . . .'

'Carry on with your story,' he said impatiently.

With an upward tilt of her head, she continued. 'You may remember, as we went into the War, there was quite a virulent feeling of—a sort of patriotism bordering on mania.'

'We call it plain old "American" here in Reno.'

'Matz held a lot of beliefs which ran counter to the . . .' She paused. 'Counter to the American way of thinking at that time. We were going to war. Matz was someone who didn't believe in it—'

'HA!' The sound—an exclamation of outrage—escaped from him before he could stop it. Nor—he realized, even at $14 per hour—did he wish it back. 'You're telling me, Mrs Beecham, that your husband refused to fight?'

'Well, he couldn't have fought. Clearly. I told you he was in hiding, Mr Gregory. His name had been on a list of undesirables, and no doubt if he had come forward they would have thrown him directly in jail . . . In any case,' she added unnecessarily, 'he would never have come forward. He would never have fought. He fought for the workers— as bravely as any man fought for any cause. But he was against the War. Against America having anything to do with it. He didn't understand why we in America should fight a war in Europe. After all, we had come here, or our parents had come here . . . to the *goldene medina*,' she smiled a little wryly. 'Our parents had escaped from a Europe which had made us less than welcome. Don't you see? And

211

we had no fond memories of it. No love for it. Why would we? Matz didn't believe we should return there to die in a War which had nothing to do with us . . .'

The words bounced off him. He had lost his hearing in one ear, fighting a war that meant nothing to him. He woke each morning with a dull ache in his left shin, left over from fighting a war that meant nothing to him. He had fought. And God knew why. Because he was an American. And a man. And proud of it . . . What allowed Matz Kappelman to think he could avoid playing his part? *Always the Kikes*, thought Gregory, bitterly. Always out for themselves.

'He was a Bolshevik?'

Eleanor tried not to smile. 'He was Socialist, Mr Gregory. Yes, he was.'

Gregory laid down his pen.

Tick-tacker-tick-tacker tick tick tick . . .

He thought of his wife, with another child on the way. He thought of $14 an hour—and the market in freefall, and no other clients on the horizon. He wanted to stand on a principal: some sort of American principal, as visceral to him as it was fuzzy, which stopped him lending help and support to Socialists and shirkers. He told himself he would ask her to leave, this Kike who didn't believe in America. And even if no more clients ever came forward, and every penny of his savings was wiped out, at least then he could hold his head high. They would move to a smaller house. He would return to the police force. It would be OK. They would survive.

Fourteen dollars an hour. And more fabulously rich clients where she came from. Kikes and

Socialists . . . movie stars and millionaires. Who the hell cared? Who was counting? This was capitalism . . . It was the American way . . .

Eleanor watched it all. 'You don't need to sympathize, Mr Gregory,' she said coolly. 'I am explaining why we needed new identities. Why we couldn't allow the studio to discover our past. Haven't you wondered? Why our hunt had been so hampered . . .? And, you know, it was Butch who got them for us . . . Our new papers.'

He nodded. 'Of course,' he said. 'Of course. Please, carry on. Only please, I need you to clarify something for me.

'Yes?'

'I am confused.'

'Oh dear.'

'Matz Kappelman, the father of your missing child, whom you always led me to believe had been killed in the fire . . .'

'Did I?'

'Is not, in fact, dead after all? Is that correct? My father could find no record of a Matz Kappelman, alive or dead. And nor could I . . .'

'Well, but I never said Isha's father was dead,' she said quickly, confused by her own lies now, wanting only to press ahead. 'Matz Kappelman is dead. Absolutely. He has been dead for a long time.'

'Ah . . . then—'

'Max Beecham, on the other hand, is alive and well. Or—at any rate—he was alive and well when I left the house on Friday morning.'

39

'I think there was a lull. After *Poppy Girl!* was released, and we three—Max, Butch and I— were quite the toast of town. And I tried so hard to forget, and so did Max. We never mentioned our old life. I dreamed of Isha every night—and I suppose Max did too. But there was nothing to be gained. We never talked about her. It was too painful.'

'When was that?'

'Well, *Poppy Girl!* was released in 1918 . . . And then in 1921 . . . It was in October 1921 that I received the letter.'

He looked down at his file. 'A letter?'

'You don't have it.'

'You never mentioned a letter.'

'No. That's because . . .'

The letter had been delivered to her private bungalow at Lionsfiel. It was in the days before she asked for her post to be sifted: the early days, only three years since *Poppy Girl!* had made her into a star, and the fan letters still gave her a thrill. The letter arrived with the usual sack of them, but it arrived on Isha's birthday, 17 October 1921. Isha would have been fourteen years old.

Eleanor was waiting to go on set. There was a make-up girl in attendance, and the costume girl gossiping about somebody in the cast perhaps being in the family way. Max was in the corner of the room, as he often used to be back then: her dressing room was like a second office to him. He was discussing something with the set designer.

214

Eleanor opened the card.

It was a picture of a ship. Nondescript. A drab little photograph. Eleanor turned it over. There was a single line, a handwritten note, not addressed to anyone. Just a simple statement.

I am looking for my mother.

That was it.

She dropped it, as if it had burned her fingers. '*Max?*'

Deep in conversation with the set designer, he didn't hear her. They had been together long enough that it was often the case. On set, when he was directing her in a scene, nothing escaped him: she had the full beam of his attention. Off set, sometimes she had to stand on a chair, sing, dance, shout, just to get his attention.

Her voice, so reliable normally, seemed to disappear. She opened her mouth to call him, but only a whisper came out. She whispered, 'Max!'

And he stopped. Turned towards her. Saw the expression on her face, the light in her eyes . . . And it crossed his mind, of course it did. It was the first thing he thought of. He said:

'Ladies. Gentleman. Everyone . . . Excuse us a moment, would you please? El and I need a minute alone.'

He crossed the room as the others shuffled out of the bungalow. She showed him the card.

'You know what the date is?' she asked.

'Of course I know what the date is.'

They gazed at the card a long moment, lost in the same thoughts, the same rush of fear and hope; enveloped together in the same memories.

Eventually Max gave a lopsided smile. 'Shucks,' he said. 'She isn't looking for her papa, too?'

Eleanor laughed. They both laughed.

'There's an address—you see it? It's Brooklyn. She must have gone over to Brooklyn. It's much better in Brooklyn. I'm so happy she made it out of Manhattan. With her lungs and—'

'Baby,' he said, reaching out, and when she didn't answer, because she knew what he was about to say, he pulled her face round to look at him. 'Baby, you've got to know—'

'I know.' She pushed his hand from her. 'Of course. I'm not an idiot, Max.'

'There are a lot of cranks out there . . . It could be from anyone. It could be just a crazy coincidence. And the fact it arrived today, it's probably just a crazy coincidence.' But even he didn't sound convinced. She could hear it in his voice—all the hope they had hidden from one another for so many years.

'What shall we do?' she asked him again. 'Shall we go to her? Write to her? Maybe telegram. We should send a telegram, telling her we received the note. Telling her we're on our way. We can leave this afternoon, Max. Can't we? Butch'll kick up a stink. It's too bad. We'll go to Brooklyn to fetch her right away. This afternoon.'

'It may not be her.'

'Oh, Max.'

'I'm serious. We can't just "go to Brooklyn". Hotfoot it all the way to Brooklyn, to answer a letter from some crazy, star-obsessed crank who doesn't even sign their name . . . Hell, Eleanor, this card,' he shook it at her, almost angrily, 'you know it could be from anyone!'

Her eyes dropped to the dressing-table top. Slowly, woefully, she covered her ears.

216

'*Max* . . . Why do you keep saying it?'

'On the other hand,' he added, and as he spoke the words he could hardly believe he was hearing them, 'we have an address, El. And it could be her. It *could* be . . . couldn't it, El? It could be that she's found us . . .'

They stayed closeted in her dressing room for an hour or so, ignoring calls from the floor manager to come back onto set. They locked the door, eventually, to stop anyone coming in, and they talked in a way they'd not been able to for many years. They wondered what she might be like, how she might have survived, whether she might perhaps have educated herself, as her father had.

'It's nice handwriting,' Eleanor said. 'That's good handwriting, isn't it?'

'It's wonderful handwriting,' Max said.

'She must have been resourceful, Max. Like you. A born survivor . . .'

'She had your beautiful green eyes,' he said. 'Do you remember her green eyes?'

Eleanor laughed. 'Yes, Max. I remember her green eyes! Do you remember her beautiful hair. Thick, curly hair. Like yours. Oh! I could do nothing with it!'

'She'll be beautiful,' he said. 'I bet she'll be beautiful.'

'Of course she will be beautiful!'

They took turns to bring each other back to earth.

There are a lot of cranks out there.

It could just be the craziest coincidence . . .

They'd missed a full hour of filming by the time Butch came down to discover what was the hold-up. He didn't raise his voice. He stood outside

217

the bungalow: 'Max? Eleanor? Could you please unlock the door? We need to get you on set right away.'

When they opened the door, he knew at once they were keeping something from him. Actually, he had always known it. He hated it. They were his closest friends—his only friends. And yet they excluded him. He didn't ask what had happened. He was too proud. From the look of them, and the light in their faces, he guessed it was something monumental. Something they weren't going to share with him. He had never seen either look so happy.

'Get out there,' he snapped. 'You know how much this delay is costing us? What am I meant to say to Carrascosa?'

They finished the day's filming. At the end of it, Max said to Butch: 'Eleanor and I have to leave for New York. I'm sorry, Butch. We have to leave this evening. We'll be back on set in ten days.'

'No, Max. It's impossible.'

But they did leave. That same night. Lucky for them, their last movie had made more for Lionsfiel than any film that year. Any other star, any other director, any other day, their contracts would have been torn up, their careers would have been finished. But Max and Eleanor came and went. They returned to Hollywood ten days later, just as they had promised, and continued exactly where they left off.

In the five days it took them to cross the country, they talked about anything and everything but what was on both their minds. And somehow, by the time they reached the address in Brooklyn, though neither said a word, in their hearts they both knew

218

how the story would end.

The house wasn't much but it was a significant improvement on the tenement in Allen Street. It stood, indistinguishable from the rest, in a long row of small, unkempt bungalows with front yards and with a hundred children scampering between them. The address on the postcard was for a bungalow at the far end. Eleanor wanted to walk right up to the door but Max pulled her back, and they squabbled about it, there on the street. Max said she should hang back. They would recognize her.

They stepped up the short garden path together. Knocked on the door.

And waited an eternity. Finally, there came footsteps—light, girlish footsteps. The door pulled back and a thin man stood before them. He looked to be in his early forties, immaculately dressed, with dark hair greased back from a face so pale it might never have seen the sun. Still clutching the door, the man gazed suspiciously from one to the other. Behind him, the grey morning light fell on a hallway that was bare and unlived in, and quite silent.

Max said—he cleared his throat. He said: 'I'm so sorry to trouble you. I was looking for a young lady.'

'Aren't we all?' said the immaculate man. But his voice and manner, his beautiful clothes all belied the implication. 'You won't find any here. Unfortunately. Who are you?' He looked at them again, slowly—from one to the other, back and forth. Eleanor's mink collar was turned up against the New York chill. She wore sunglasses and a cloche hat pulled down over her forehead. Max looked dapper as ever, in pale brown wool—a winter suit, California style. They exuded prosperity and glamour. The American Dream. On a working

219

man's street on a grey Brooklyn morning, Max and Eleanor Beecham stood out like a couple of aliens.

'We were looking for a young lady,' Max said again. 'She left us this address. Her name is . . .' and as he said it, he knew just how preposterous it was. How absurd he sounded. Eleanor knew it too. 'Her name is Isha Beekman?' The name clearly didn't register. He tried again. 'Isha Beekman—'

'Or you might know her as—' Eleanor burst out

'Yes, you might know her as Isha Kappelman?' Max said.

'Make up your mind,' the man said laconically. His eyes continued to move carefully, curiously, from one to the other. He added: 'I can't say I know either of those names.'

Finally his gaze came to rest on Eleanor. He frowned slightly and then, as if a light were dawning, his thin face broke into a smile 'Well I'll be . . .' and then into a grin so broad his face might have split in half, 'It's Eleanor Beecham!'

Instinctively Max put an arm around his wife's shoulder. 'I sent you a letter!' the man cried. 'Is that why you have come?' He glanced back at Max, confusion settling on his face again. 'Why have you come here? Why have you . . .' and then, without warning, he crumpled. His slim shoulders hunched and he began to weep. 'You came to see me! You came all this way from Hollywood . . . Because you're the kindest lady—'

'No!' she muttered, horrified. 'No, I didn't.'

'I knew it! Because I could see it in your face. You have the kindest face of anyone I ever laid eyes on . . . The sweetest, kindest face . . . Won't you come in? You and your gentleman friend. Come in—please. We'll have tea . . .'

40

'I never mentioned the letter, Mr Gregory,' Eleanor said. 'Because it wasn't anything. It turned out to be from a crank.'

'But it arrived on Isha's birthday?'

She shrugged. 'Just one of those things.'

'So, what did you do?'

'What did I do? Well—everything changed. These things . . . they send you a little crazy eventually. The fan mail, the fans . . . these sort of things. You have no idea, Mr Gregory, quite how many lunatics are out there. Not until they start to write to you. We haven't touched a piece of fan mail since that day. Neither of us. We were united on that at least.'

'I can understand it.'

'But Max and I had the most horrible fight. Max wanted to forget. Everything. He never wanted to go through it all again. You see? He wanted to pretend it had never happened. Whereas I . . . The letter had the opposite effect on me. Whereas it encouraged Max to turn away. Despair. I realized *then*—that I had never given up. Maybe that letter was from a crank—a poor, sad, lonely crank,' she added, remembering briefly his crumpled face. 'Maybe so. And maybe I would never find my baby. But until there was proof. *Proof*, Mr Gregory. I would never stop hoping. Never stop looking. That was when I hired the detective. The second detective. The one before your father.'

'But you didn't stick with him?'

'Oh! I would have done. He was in LA. And he

was pretty good. But then Max discovered I had appointed him.'

'He didn't like that?'

'And there was another fight.' She laughed. 'We almost killed each other. He told me . . . the searching was going to send me mad. So.'

'So? You came all the way to Reno, huh? So hubby couldn't reach us?'

She shrugged. 'Something like that. But that was seven years ago, Mr Gregory. And we haven't come any further.'

Mr Gregory bridled. 'But, as you know,' he said, 'as we discussed . . . It's very hard to make any progress as long as you keep so much back.'

'I am telling you everything I can!'

'You say so. And yet, I still don't even know why you left New York. I don't know why the police were coming after you.'

'I told you. Matz was an activist.'

'I don't even know when Matz Kappelman died. Or even if he died. Or even if he ever existed. Nothing makes any sense.'

'Of course it makes sense!'

'Mrs Beecham,' he sighed. 'I do, truly . . . I think I do begin to understand how much you have suffered.'

'Oh,' she laughed. 'Do you, Mr Gregory?'

'Well. Perhaps I don't. How could I? But how do you expect me to make any progress when you won't tell me the truth? Mrs Beecham, this endeavour of ours is hampered, and will continue to be hampered by your refusal to tell me the whole truth.'

'Because there are things I cannot tell you,' she said quietly. 'Why won't you simply accept it? After all this time? Why won't you simply work with what we have? I don't want to tell you my life's story. What does it matter? *I just want you to find my daughter.*'

Floor Eight

41

New York, 25 March 1911

Matz had come home when his wife and daughter were already sleeping, and by the time they awoke he had already left. It's what he often did. Since the day Eleana released him from that prison cell he had become still more passionately, angrily political. Now he belonged to the radical union, Industrial Workers of the World (as popular with the authorities as its name suggests), and he dedicated every moment he could to its cause: plastering the city with IWW posters, organizing and speaking at illegal street meetings, evading the police, or sometimes going out of his way to take them on. He had become quite a dab at escaping their clutches—quite literally: once in New Jersey and once in Pittsburgh, he had leapt from a moving police wagon and disappeared into the crowd. Matz Beekman's name was beginning to resonate with authorities, and with the IWW too. Loved and loathed, he was, depending on whose side you were on. Matz Beekman could never do anything with a faint heart.

The twenty-fifth of March 1911 started the same as any number of mornings at Allen Street, with Isha unwell again, and Matz who knew where?, and Eleana, afraid of running late for work at Triangle, trying to extricate herself from her daughter's embraces.

The garment workers' strike was long since over. For a while, in the beginning, it had looked as if the strikers might prevail. The sight of the women picketers being beaten by the police had, briefly, attracted the sympathies of high society. Money had been raised. Lunches were given. But society's attention span being what it is, society soon became distracted. The Triangle owners meanwhile, with more to lose, stuck to their guns. Their stunt with the *kurve* had proved a point that hardly needed to be made. In a city with so many new immigrants pouring in every day, there would always be other workers, willing to work for less. Triangle factory employees had been at the forefront of the strike, but they returned to their work defeated, their union demands rejected

Not all of the workers returned. Eleanor returned. And with a $1 raise too, thanks to Blumenkranz. But Matz was barred from the premises. Amen. He was a troublemaker and they did not want him back.

He continued to play piano at the nickelodeon on Hester Street, but the pay was not enough to feed a family, even such a small one as his, and so Eleana continued at Triangle. Six long, back-breaking days a week. It was life. They were used to it. Matz worked where and whenever he could. He worked six nights a week at the nickelodeon—and more if he could get it. Otherwise, he was consumed by his politics. It was dirty work. IWW members were regularly battered—and to death—during their police skirmishes. And that, too, was life. Violent and dangerous. Sometimes Matz didn't come home for several nights and Eleana and her mother would sit up waiting, fearing the worst. Eleana believed in the fight. But she longed for someone else to fight it.

Sometimes, increasingly so, if Matz failed to return home in time for his work, Eleana would bundle up their young daughter and they would head round the corner to the nickelodeon together. Between them, they would sing and dance and play piano for the packed audience in Matz's stead.

The previous evening had been one such night. It was the second night in a single month that Matz had failed to turn up, and the proprietor's patience was running dry. Whether he supported Matz's cause—and Mr Listig did: what man with eyes and a mind would not?—he asked Eleana how he could be expected to run a business when one of its most vital ingredients could not be relied upon to turn up? His customers had come to watch the movie. And to listen to Matz. Not to his wife and daughter, no matter how delightfully they performed.

'Next time,' he said to her, 'next time—tell him he needn't bother to come back.' And one day, for all Matz's crowd-pulling charm and talent—one day Mr Listig would mean it. But not that night, at least. Eleanor sang and played piano as delightfully as she always did. Isha, merry exhibitionist that she was, danced with the usual vim and everybody loved her for it.

But she woke wheezing on that sunny, fateful Saturday, coughing and fighting for breath. Eleana finally left her in her and Matz's still-warm bed, and walked the familiar streets to work with her cousin Sarah. Sarah was a machinist at Triangle too. She worked upstairs from Eleana, on the ninth floor.

It was a beautiful, clear morning and it was payday. Two reasons to celebrate, the women agreed. With luck, Matz would be home this

229

evening. And with a bit more luck (they both laughed), Sarah's husband Samuel would not.

Just another morning: except it was Saturday, and sunny. So better than most. Sarah had seen a hat she wanted to buy in a shop window. They talked about whether she could make something similar for herself.

'It won't be so pretty,' Sarah said.

'No, I don't suppose it will.'

They walked in silence, thinking about the day they might afford to buy shop-made hats, until Sarah said: 'How is it with Blumenkranz then? He seems to be leaving you alone lately, no?'

'You have noticed? Isn't it marvellous!'

'I think he's looking at the new girl—the one who sits beside me. Just a shy little thing, she is. Frightened of her own shadow.'

'Yes! So I heard . . . I want to kiss her for it. Poor darling . . .'

'He was breathing all over her yesterday.'

'Thank God for that, eh?'

Sarah smiled. 'Well, you can tell Matz. The problem is finished with.'

'Ha! Except I told Matz he left. Months ago.'

'You told him that?'

'And don't go telling him different, Sarah. Or God knows . . .'

'You know his brother's in the police now—did you know that? His brother's a sergeant at Mercer Street.'

'Do I know it? He only mentions it a hundred times a day.'

'He can get away with anything, then. With a brother in the police. He can do whatever he likes . . .' Sarah slid a sly glance at her cousin. 'If he doesn't already.'

Eleana didn't reply. She didn't know how much Sarah knew, and she didn't much want to enquire. Least said on the matter, the better for everyone. Not even Dora knew the truth.

'Well,' Sarah persevered, unsatisfied. 'Because everybody knows how he trails after you, Eleana. Nettie saw him pushing you up against the cloakroom wall last month. It's a wonder you didn't scream. Except Nettie said—'

'Please, Sarah.'

'You should find work somewhere else.'

'Ha! And I should buy the mansion next to Alva Belmont, shouldn't I? And set up a school for fairies.'

'Well,' she smiled. 'It's not a bad idea.'

'If I could find work elsewhere, don't you think that I would?' Eleana snapped.

'You should tell Matz. It's not fair on you Eleana. He needs to stop fooling around with his politics and look after his family.'

'Ha! And I should buy the mansion next to Alva Belmont, and set up a school for fairies . . .'

Sarah giggled. 'It's not a bad idea,' she said again.

'In any case, I wouldn't want Matz to stop . . . Not really. He looks after us in his way. And someone has to fight—for everything that's wrong in this world, for our children, if not for us. I admire him for it. And so should you. And God forbid I allow that *schmendrik* to curtail him. Over my dead body, Sarah. I can manage Blumenkranz myself. I have been for years.'

'Well well,' Sarah sighed, losing interest. The two of them must have had the same conversation a

231

hundred times. 'Perhaps it's all finished now in any case.'

'Yes. Perhaps it is . . .' she said, with a tired smile.

And then, a little later, a few blocks further on, another familiar exchange: a maternal competition between them. Isha, it could not be argued otherwise, although eighteen months older, was not so advanced in the learning of letters as her cousin Tzivia.

'She can't help it,' Sarah said seriously, trying to be kind, but then again, enjoying it too much. 'Isha misses so much school, being sick. Poor darling.'

'*Poor darling*,' Eleana mimicked her. 'Poor darling, indeed!' She added: 'And poor Tzivia can't help how badly she sings.'

'Of course she can sing. How dare you!'

'Tzivia is a lousy singer. Probably the worst I have ever heard.'

'She's an excellent singer.'

'Tzivia's a *dreadful* singer,' Eleana said cheerfully. 'When she sings, the whole of the Lower East Side holds its head in pain.'

'*Neyn, sha-shtil!*' Sarah snapped.

And they walked on in companionable silence, smiling, thinking pleasantly about singing, and reading, and the unassailable superiority of their own small daughters.

Just another day then.

The sun was shining. Blumenkranz had found a new, shy girl to occupy his heart and mind, to push against the cloakroom wall when he thought nobody was looking. And it was payday.

42

The Triangle Waist Company factory was a productive enterprise—in fact, one of the most productive textile factories in New York. It employed 600 workers, most of them young immigrants, and it packed them all, six gruelling days a week, into the three highest floors of a ten-storey building on the corner of Greene Street and Washington Place. There was a showroom for buyers, and offices for the brother-in-law owners on the tenth floor, so the majority of the workers crowded into the two floors below.

Eleana's station was on Floor Eight. Seated in long rows all around her, cramped and bent in the heat and relentless noise, there were 250 other machinists. A section of the room was given over to the pattern cutters (where Matz had worked previously). The cutters worked at high tables, beneath long wires draped in paper patterns which looked, from a distance, like party bunting, and they worked without machines but with space enough between them to slash freely at piles of fabric fifty layers thick or more. It meant that on Eleanor's floor there was space for a hundred fewer heat-and-noise giving sewing machines, a hundred fewer bodies. Conditions on the ninth floor were more cramped, if it were possible, and hotter, and even noisier.

She worked, as she always had, beside her close friend Dora, heavily pregnant now. Dora had married a cloak-maker who made three times more money than she made in a week, and she was counting the hours until she could leave the factory for ever. As soon as the baby was born, her husband had promised her.

'It's going to come early,' Dora said that morning, patting her swollen belly. 'I know it. Three weeks to go, El! Not a day longer. I'm willing to wager it. What do you think? Do you want a wager?'

Eleanor was happy for her friend. Of course she was. But she dreaded the day of her leaving. The noise and the heat, the backaches, neckaches, headaches, the cruel monotony—it would be much harder to endure without Dora beside her. Too bad. Too bad she hadn't married Lionel the cloak-maker. Except, of course, it would have been impossible. She couldn't imagine being with anyone but Matz.

As she squeezed in beside Dora (every inch of space had to be fought for on the production floor), she pulled a face. 'The baby may be two weeks late or more, you know. Much more.' She winked. 'I swear little Isha took eleven months to come to the boil.'

'Then she must be an elephant.'

The starting bell clanged. The two women—every woman in the room—reached automatically into the trough behind their machines and took up a first piece of cut cloth for the day. Not a moment of production time was wasted.

The women were forbidden to talk once the machines had started up. The noise made it almost impossible in any case. Dora and Eleana worked in silence, without pausing, without looking up, until the bell clanged for lunch.

Another day.

43

Management might have barred him from ever working there again, but the boy at the service entrance wasn't management. When Matz turned up that afternoon, face covered in bruises, clothes covered in dried blood—frantic, desperate—it was as if President Taft himself had come to call. Possibly even better.

'Why, if it isn't Matz Beekman!' the boy cried warmly. 'I know you! I heard you speak when we striking. Feels like a long time ago now. But you fired us up, Mr Beekman. You fired us all up.'

Matz needed to get a message to his wife. He desperately needed to do that. 'You come out on strike with us, did you?' Matz said levelly, glancing behind him at the street—and then approaching the boy's raised desk.

'I sure did . . .' The boy nodded sadly. They had truly believed things were going to change, back then. And yet here he still was, and his sister too, up on the ninth floor, and his mother two tables behind her. Nothing had changed. 'You better watch out,' he said, glancing back at Matz. 'They'll be down in a bit. Early closing today . . . What in hell are you doing here anyway?' He laughed. 'Looks like you've been through something . . . You got blood all over you. And dirt. What have you been up to?'

'Nothing much. In a fight with the bull,' Matz mumbled. 'That's all.'

The boy nodded approval. 'Good for you. Seems like they prob'ly came off the worse . . .'

Matz looked away. Couldn't hold the boy's gaze. Couldn't bring himself to think about it, not yet. Even so, the image of the man flashed before him, his body slumping on the sidewalk, and the blood seeping from his head . . . and then not seeping but gushing. Like a goddamn river. How could a man's head hold so much blood? It was impossible.

'I'm in a fix,' he muttered. 'I'm in a bit of trouble.'

'I guessed it!' The boy laughed his warm, open laugh. 'Else why would you want to come back to this stinkhole?'

Matz nodded.

'Well, I hope you're not thinking you'll be getting your job back *here* any time soon. Getting to the end of the busy season already. They've been letting people go . . . And troublemakers like you, first out the door!'

'I've come for Eleana—you know her? I need to fetch her out . . . It's kind of urgent.' The boy frowned. 'Eleana?' he repeated. 'Can't say I know an Eleana. But you know how it is here, don't you. The girls—they come and they go.'

'My wife,' Matz said.

'Oh! . . . Well. You don't say, huh? . . . Your wife? And she works here at Triangle, does she?' He laughed.

Matz glanced behind him at the street again. Still nothing. 'I need to fetch her,' he said.

'You'd have thought they'd've got rid of her, though—knowing she was married to you!' The boy looked at Matz with frank admiration. Nudged him, half awkward, half playful. 'Y'old troublemaker!' he said. 'It's what you are! You want to go on up there?'

236

'I do.'

'They'll be out in twenty minutes.'

'I can't really wait.'

The boy considered this. He looked at Matz. 'Trouble with bull you say?'

'Big trouble.'

'You gonna tell me what you did?'

'Street meeting,' he muttered vaguely. 'There was quite a crowd . . . Police came in, broke it up . . .'

'And?'

Slowly, Matz shook his head. 'Turned nasty.' He indicated the door at the back of the lobby. It opened onto a narrow stairway. 'Can I go up that way?'

The boy shrugged, disappointed not to hear more. 'Sure you can,' he said. 'Only if they catch you, don't you go saying who let you in!'

44

He had been escaping his own arrest again. He had leapt from the back of a paddy wagon as they were carting him off to Mercer Street station. The others didn't follow. He was on his own and he ran—desperate, instinctive—wild. He lost the pack without difficulty but there was one pursuer who wouldn't give up. He was coming after Matz, whistle blowing, club waving, like his police career depended on it. Someone, an IWW member, perhaps, a worker, a supporter—whoever it was, they must have recognized Matz, because they passed him something heavy as he ran by. Not a rock. A brick. It was a large brick, and it was heavy. He could see the man's face as he was pressing the weapon into his hand. *Use it.* It's what the man had said. And Matz hadn't hesitated. He'd taken the brick, the rock, the heavy thing, and kept running. And mid-sprint, his pursuer's breath audible his ears, Matz had turned and hurled the thing—to slow the man down, no more than that; trip him up; stop him. But he threw the brick too hard and the man had been too close. It was all wrong. He knew it the moment it left his grasp. The policeman had dropped like a stone. Blood everywhere. The brick had landed with such force it had cracked open his skull.

Matz stopped at once. He gazed down at the man's limp body as the blood gushed from his head. He'd killed him. It was all Matz could think. Without his hat—dislodged in the chase—he didn't look like a policeman. He looked like any other man: just a man, young and dying. And Matz had killed him.

Several seconds passed. They were in an alleyway, one that Matz knew well. Matz, who knew every crook and cranny of the city, had led him down here to avoid the crowds, but in the intervening seconds, as the man at his feet rattled his final exhalations, a small group had gathered: three young men and a woman, perhaps? He couldn't say for sure. But one of them shunted him—they told him to *run*.

Run!

Get the hell outta here!

Go NOW!

And so he did. He ran, until he was alone again. And when he stopped, he heaved the small contents of his stomach across the sidewalk. The man was dead. And when they found him dead they would know at once who had killed him.

He needed to get a message to Eleana. She had to fetch the baby, and then, together—for he wasn't leaving without them—they needed to get the hell out of town.

45

'Go on up there!' the boy at the Service Gate was saying. 'Surprise her! Nobody's gonna notice you this late in the day. Hurry up now or the bell will go and you'll be lucky you don't get mowed down in the rush to get out of that hellhole!'

Matz remembered it well. The Saturday quitting bell—the sense of exhilaration and freedom that came with the first chime—and then the mad stampede for the doors. Blumenkranz used to keep the doors locked to be sure no one slipped away early. There used to be a hint of sadism about the slowness with which he opened them at the end of the day.

'Thanks,' Matz stepped toward the stairs, but the sound of a siren approaching made him freeze . . . He waited, alert as a stag: listening, waiting. They couldn't have followed him. It was impossible. He'd made a dash, zigzagged all the way here.

The boy said, matter of factly: 'Get up there! Get lost in the scrum! They'll never find you.'

'Thank you my friend,' Matz said, starting towards the stairwell again. 'I think I will.'

'Not that way!' the boy shouted after him,

239

laughing. 'Have you forgotten already? You'll climb all the way up there—and you'll find the door's locked. Take the elevator. Here. I'll call it for you . . .'

*　　*　　*

Eight floors up, quitting time was imminent. The machines continued to whir but there was a restlessness in the noisy air. Machinists were wriggling surreptitiously into position, heads and necks still bent over their work, feet still pedalling, but bodies twisting impatiently towards freedom, ready for the quickest getaway. Pay packets had already been distributed. The week was done. The sun still shone outside the factory windows. Saturday evening and all of Sunday stretched ahead. The anticipation of so many aching, restless young bodies was palpable. 'It's the best moment of the week!' Eleana yelled over the racket of their machines. Dora didn't catch the words but guessed at their meaning. Reaching over her large belly into the central trough for another piece, another shirt sleeve, she nodded and beamed in reply.

She had told Eleana during their lunch break that her husband, who made $24 a week, was taking her uptown for her birthday, to a real movie theatre, one with a piped organ the size of half a block, which blasted music beside a screen so large you couldn't, according to Dora, see the whole of it all at once, 'not without sweeping your eyes to the left and then to the right and then to the left again.' He had bought her a new shawl, too. And he was taking her to dinner . . .

Dora looked so happy it was impossible not to

celebrate with her. Work would not be the same without her. But, Eleana reassured herself once again, they would still be friends. And maybe, one day, Matz would make enough money so that she could join her friend: maybe have another child; maybe an apartment to themselves. One day. Maybe. Imagining it made her happy enough. So she packed away the pinch of envy and returned her friend's broad smile. Too late. Dora wasn't looking at her. She was looking beyond, to the cutters' tables in the far corner. A cloud had crossed her happy face. It was a look of profound irritation.

'Damn it . . .' she muttered. This would only add to the madness of the end-of-day exit scrum and delay the moment when they might finally be free of the building. 'Why now?'

In the cutters' corner, beneath the long wire clotheslines, draped like bunting, beneath the long, high wooden table, buckling with discarded fabric strips, there curled a thin but unmistakable plume of smoke.

Eleana followed Dora's gaze, felt a similar rush of impatience at the sight which greeted her. The cutters weren't supposed to smoke on the factory floor, but at the end of a long week nobody ever seemed to stop them. And now, a flick of their cigarette ash had caught onto something. Once again. It was not the first time. And there was going to be chaos.

'At least we already have our wages,' Eleana muttered, touching Dora's sleeve. She was on the point of returning to her work. They would dock her pay if they spotted her looking up from it. But she hesitated, felt a shiver of unease. Already, the plume was filling out—not such a thin plume any

241

more. It was definitely growing thicker.

And, yes, in only a second, the smoke was spreading. There was a large box to the right of the cutters' table, overflowing with fabric scraps. She could see now that smoke was coming from that, too.

Cautiously, not wanting to be spotted shirking from the last few minutes of work, the two women twisted in their seats. Over the banks of still-humming sewing machines they could spy the tip of the flames: flames which seemed to be growing taller and bolder every second.

Another fire, then. It was the third since Eleana had worked at the factory—and every one of them starting at the cutters' tables. The cutters thought they were above the rules. They *were* above the rules. Matz had been no better. She sighed, irritated, and maybe a little nervous. But nothing more than that. Not yet.

There were fire pails dotted around the room, always kept full of water. One of the cutters, Tomas, took the nearest and tossed its contents onto the flames. It had no discernible effect. The flames burned on unabated.

'Dora,' Eleana said, taking her foot from the pedal at last. 'I think you had better get to the door . . . Get ahead . . . Don't you think so? It's probably nothing. It never is. But in your condition . . .'

Dora stopped pedalling too, but she didn't move. 'If I stop now, Blumenkranz will be after me. Any chance he gets, he'll be stealing money back out of my pay packet. For a few measly minutes? I don't think so. They'll get it under control. They always do. You go ahead if you want to. I'm staying right here.'

In the far corner, the flames licked higher. Tomas began to move faster, with a hint of urgency now. He and another cutter—Eleana didn't know his name—picked up more fire pails and poured more water onto the flames, still to no avail. The dousing only seemed to feed the flames, and they grew higher still. They licked around the wooden table edge and nibbled at the piles of fabric that hung loose over the tabletop.

'Dora,' Eleana said more insistently. 'There's going to be a rush, I'm telling you. It's not under control. And you shall be stuck. You'll be knocked to the ground.'

Dora hesitated.

'Darling—GO!'

Slowly, the sewing machines around them fell silent; an eery quiet filled the room; the crackle of flames, the sound of coughing, a few murmurs of disquiet—irritation, confusion, a shout or two from the cutters' corner . . . The room had never been so still. And still, the flames licked higher and the girls sat tight, looking on. The cutters caused their silly fires: the cutters dealt with them. This fire was bigger than most, it was true. Even so. There was an assumption, growing weaker, that the men had it under control.

So the flames expanded, and flared, and stretched, and nobody moved. They reached higher, and higher still. They caressed the flimsy tissue patterns, hanging like party bunting above the cutters' heads. They teased at the paper and whipped at the wires, until the paper caught . . . And then somebody screamed. It was the first sign of panic. Smoke began to fill the room. From the bunting overhead flames began to fall, like fat

243

raindrops. This was no ordinary fire. This was not like the others.

The bunting—the wire of hanging patterns— ran the full width of the room and the flames could not resist it. They were leaping, racing, dancing from one paper sheet to the next. Then came the roar, sudden and unexpected. And in that instant, as if from nowhere, the room became a fireball. It was the moment—too late—when awareness and hysteria simultaneously took hold. Upstairs on the tenth floor, someone in Management rang the quitting bell at last, but in the panic, the thickening smoke, the soaring heat, its musical sound went unnoticed for the first and final time.

Still the flames grew. Behind the cutters' table, at the heart of the fire, a window cracked under the heat. A second later the pane exploded outwards, smashing glass onto the street eight floors below, and through the broken window came a small, lethal breeze. It didn't cool the room. It fanned the flames.

Another roar—another fireball, this one hurtling deeper into the open space. The cutters seemed to admit defeat. They stopped tearing at the flaming tissue overhead. They stopped reaching for water buckets—there was none left to reach. They dropped the fire hose, uncoiled but useless, since no water came from the standpipe. And they began to retreat.

'We can't control it!' Tomas shouted, choking through the smoke. 'Get out! Everyone—get out.'

They were already trying. By then the fear had taken hold. Flames from the bunting had rained onto the scraps of fabric which lay everywhere in the room, and onto a wooden floor long-soaked in the oil that dripped daily from the sewing machines. The floor, the ceiling, the walls—nothing was spared; nowhere was safe: everywhere, there was fire.

Into this, the elevator doors pulled slowly open, and Matz looked out.

He had smelled the smoke. He had heard the screams, and the fists beating on the doors as he rose higher, but the vision that met him was worse than any he could have imagined. He attempted to move out onto the burning floor, but workers, surging to escape, knocked him back again; and so he fought, scrambling between them, slipping through the elevator doors just as they were closing. Behind him, thirty workers, piled one upon the other and packed into a space designed for half that number, made their lucky escape: in front him, an inferno.

Matz stepped forward onto the burning floor, shouting her name.

46

In the heat, the thick black smoke, the screaming chaos, it was impossible to make out anything but the faintest outlines. Matz stood, for the briefest and longest second, stupefied by the horror, trying to think, trying to collect his bearings. There weren't many ways to get out of the room, he knew that: two slim stairways, not wide enough for two people to pass, with doors—if they were even unlocked—that opened inwards, into a crowded and panic-filled room. There were two elevator shafts, and in the enclosed courtyard at the back of the building, a single fire escape, an external metal stairway that was partially blocked—always had been—by a jutting steel shutter on the seventh floor below.

Beside Matz, the door to one of the two stairways remained tightly closed. Through the smoke, he could hear fists and feet beating helplessly against it: whether it was locked or unlocked, nobody could tell. The crush forcing itself against the door made it impossible to discover. Behind him, the second elevator juddered to a stop and the doors began to open; beneath him the smoky shapes of women, some on their knees, choking for breath. He reached for the one closest to his own feet, in danger of being trampled, and while the crowd rushed the sliding doors, he lifted her, and then another, and then a third, piling each one onto the shoulders of the passengers already inside. And then the doors closed and elevator was gone again.

Shouts of frustration from the stairway beside him. The door had opened, but only an inch, and only for a moment before the force of the desperate crowd slammed it shut again. So it wasn't locked.

'ELEANA!' he cried. Nothing. His voice died in the smoke.

He stepped towards the stairway, approaching from the back of the knot of bodies; and somehow he pushed them back, one by one, making space until the door could swing open. 'Calm! Stay calm!' he pleaded, as they threw themselves into the stairway. 'If you can stay calm, many more will get out. You will get out faster . . . ELEANA? . . . Has anyone seen Eleana? ELEANA!' But they didn't hear him. They certainly didn't answer.

At the far side of the room, Tomas led the way to the external fire escape. They could escape the fire by climbing around the steel shutter on the seventh floor and smashing a window below the fire, on the sixth floor. He climbed out, while the people watched. The shutter jutted out beyond the edge of the stairway. To get past it first he had to climb onto it, entrusting it with his entire body weight. As his second foot returned to the relative safety of the stair-rail, the shutter dislodged. He fell backwards, his body spiralling until it hit the ground eighty foot below.

And yet his friends and colleagues followed him. They couldn't turn back into the room—behind them lay certain death. The next climber passed the shutter without stumbling. She smashed the sixth-floor window and escaped. Twenty more clambered afer her, and the word spread. An escape! More bodies piled onto the flimsy metal structure, many with their clothes already alight— they clambered on from the eighth-floor window, and from the ninth floor above it where the fire had spread. The stairs were overloaded and overloading more every second. People shouted warnings, but it was pointless. There came a growl, louder than the screams inside the building, louder than the raging flames. It was the sound of grinding metal. Their escape route was buckling. And yet still more piled on: forty, then fifty, clinging on tight, until, with a deafening screech, the stairway detached completely. It thundered onto the courtyard below, landing on top of what was left of Tomas and taking fifty flaming bodies with it as it fell.

Inside, the fire raged on, the elevator cars came and went. And Matz continued to pack them high with bodies. He ventured into the room, calling everywhere for Eleana, lifting the bodies from his feet and carrying them back to elevators, piling them onto the shoulders of the people already inside.

'*ELEANA*?' he called, his voice half lost in the screaming, in his own choking lungs.

ELEANA?

The elevators weren't coming fast enough, and by now the cables had warped in the heat, which meant they came slower still. And the fire continued to rage. It lapped from windows exploded in the heat. It devoured every chair and table, every piece of fabric. Nothing could withstand it. Nothing could stop it. The heat was unbearable. Escape seemed impossible.

They stood at the flaming windows, looked down at the crowd below. And they began to jump. First one . . . And then another and then another . . .

She collided with him, in the thick of it, as he was calling her name. No time to wonder what he was doing there. There was Dora under her arm, unable to stand. 'Get her out, Matz,' she cried. 'Get her out!'

On the street below, a large crowd had gathered and they were screaming as the burning bodies fell, one by one, two by two, sometimes holding hands and falling together. The fire patrols opened out their life nets to catch them, but the falling bodies came so thick and fast that they ripped the life nets to shreds; and soon, on the street, in a lagoon of blood, there lay a thick spread of young bodies. Mostly dead—but not all. From some of the bodies there came feeble, agonized moans and the patrolmen burrowed in among them while the bodies rained down, pulling survivors from the heaps . . .

Eleana pushed Dora into his arms. He hesitated. He wanted to take Eleana too. It was Eleana he had come for, after all.

'Get her out of here!' Eleana ordered him. 'She will die. The baby will die.'

'Let me first get you out of here.'

But Eleana shook her head. 'Clara is trapped . . .'

'I will come back for Clara!'

'It will be too late,' she said simply, and retreated into the flames.

By then both elevators had stopped. The heat of the cables, and the weight of the passengers cramming in the cars would have wreaked damage enough. But now, in desperation, the doors to the two shafts had been forced apart. It was the weight of the bodies throwing themselves into the shafts and crashing onto the roof of the cars that did the rest. The roofs had buckled under the stress. The elevators had descended to the building's basement and—no matter how frantically they were called— they would not rise again.

With Dora under his arm, Matz looked towards the stairway, or to where it used to be. There was nothing, just a wall of fire. The only way out was through the window, onto the street eighty foot below, or down the elevator shaft. If Dora could hold onto his shoulders, he could cling to the central coil and carry her down.

'Hold on to me,' he shouted. She nodded, barely conscious. He stretched across the dark shaft, looked down into the drop, nine floors to the building basement. It was too dark to see to the bottom. 'Hold me!' he shouted to her again.

'Do you hear me, Dora? Hold me, and don't look down.' She nodded again.

'. . . Not such a bad man, Matz. Eleana . . . a lucky girl . . .' She smiled, faintly, though he didn't see it. They were the first and the last kind words she ever had for him.

The central cable burned hot on his bare hands—singed the flesh. But in the moment, and with the smell of burning flesh all around him, he hardly noticed it. Dora had him in a stranglehold, clinging to his neck—her swollen belly pushing her body to one side, preventing her from wrapping her legs around him. They had travelled a quarter floor, Matz's head and shoulders still within reach of the burning factory floor—he heard his name called out. He looked up—into the ashen face of Blumenkranz. Blumenkranz, twisted in pain and fear. He lay on the ground, arms flailing towards the cable, the top half of his body protruding into the shaft, as if he might lose his balance and fall in at any second.

'Beekman!' he cried. 'Help me! Help me onto the cable, and I can make my own way.'

Matz glanced at him, and looked away again, continued on his journey. 'Hold tight,' he said to Dora.

'Beekman! My legs won't hold—Help me! I am light. I am lighter than a girl. Pull me onto the cable, won't you? I only need to reach the cable.'

Matz glanced again into the face he thought he hated. It was filled with fear. Matz could help him—or not. In such a moment, with one man's blood on his hands this afternoon already—in such a moment, his hatred meant nothing to him. Taking Dora's pregnant body with him, he hauled himself back up again—just a foot, nothing more. He would take Blumenkranz's outstretched arm, carry the weight of him, until he could reach the cable and take hold of it himself.

Blumenkranz said nothing. He took the arm and clung to it tight.

Holding onto the cable with one arm, Matz reached for Blumenkranz's small, thin body, grasped it beneath the armpits and pulled.

'Take the cable!' Matz grunted. 'Take it! I swear I can't hold you for long.' Blumenkranz took the cable—but the heat singed his hands. He snatched them away and the burn marks were clear to see. He clung to Matz, refusing to let go. 'It melts my flesh,' he said. 'I can't hold it!'

'And mine too!' Matz shouted. 'For God's sake, grasp the cable!'

But he wouldn't do it.

'I cannot take you both . . . We shall all go down. We shall fall to our death.'

Blumenkranz glanced at Dora, at her small hands grasped around Matz's neck: she was slipping already, he thought. She was falling anyway. She was falling, anyway. Keeping one arm tight around Matz's shoulders, he began to pull Dora's hands apart. Matz could do nothing. He could see, but he couldn't stop it. He had no arm free to hold Dora any tighter. He saw what was happening and did the only thing he could: kicked out at Blumenkranz with all his strength. Kicked with one leg, and jerked a knee into Blumenkranz's groin with the other.

Blumenkranz howled in pain, and loosened his hold. Too late. He and Dora released their grasp together and they fell, their bodies hitting against the walls of the shaft, bouncing against each other until they landed, their battered bodies: Dora's first—her child's heart still beating inside her—and Blumenkranz's next. They landed on people, dead already, for the most part. Dora and Blumenkranz were dead on impact. The child was dead by the time the authorities retrieved their bodies.

Matz hung where they released him, and watched them fall, watched Dora's head smash once, twice, against the shaft, before her body disappeared into the darkness.

He waited, not moving, listening for a cry. But there was nothing. Nothing to be heard but the raging fire above, and the people dying below—and Eleana still up there. He clambered back up the cable into the burning room. It was quieter than it had been only moments before—disconcertingly quiet. Beneath the black smoke, wherever he turned, bodies lay: and now a jet of water was coming from the open window: they were pumping it up from the street.

'ELEANA!' he called, yet again. His voice was hoarse, and he couldn't breathe. But he could say nothing else. He stood by the open lift shaft, bent double, shirt sleeve over his mouth, gasping for breath: nobody was standing, not any more. They crawled past him, and he let them pass: to the edge of the shaft, and then to nothing—they disappeared into the black smoke. The pain of his hands, his lungs—his need to see Eleana—it was all that Matz was conscious of. He might have reached across, pulled them back from the edge of the shaft. But they were going to die up here anyway. They were going to die. And he would not leave without Eleana.

She came towards him, dragging herself on her stomach, on her knees. 'Oh thank God,' she said. 'Clara's gone. Dead. Everyone dead . . .' she choked, laid her head onto the ground before him. 'I don't think . . .' and then nothing.

From somewhere, Matz found some last residue of strength. He took her two arms and placed them around his neck. 'We will go down together,' he whispered to her. They looked at one another through that smoke, could hardly see one another, but they could feel each other, through it all; feel for certain that they were together again—perhaps one more time. Perhaps for the last time.

'I love you, Eleana,' he said. She nodded.

'No matter what,' he said.

He carried her to the edge of the shaft and, for the second time, launched himself towards the cable. As he took the weight of them both, he felt her arms go limp. He said: 'Can you hold on? Eleana! Stay awake—you have to hold on!'

But she couldn't. Her hands slipped a little further still, and he could feel her body submitting, forgetting how to fight. 'Stay with me!' he told her. 'Hold me!' But she couldn't. Softly, she shook her head and closed her eyes. Rested her head on his shoulder.

'. . . No matter what . . .' she murmured.

He held her: with his legs, with his teeth; he could smell his own flesh burning as he shifted, foot by foot, inch by inch, floor by floor . . . until the cable seemed to grow cooler, and they could go no further. A soft heap of still-warm bodies awaited them, with Dora in there somewhere, and her baby with its still-beating heart.

At five o'clock, less than an hour since that thin plume of smoke was first spotted beneath the cutters' table, the last girl threw herself from the window, and on Washington Place a crowd of ten thousand watched her flaming body fall. It struck against the building as it spiralled through the air, before landing with a slap, the sound softened by the cushion of bodies below. She was the fifty-ninth to jump. And after that, there was nothing much to see. No more falling bodies. Nobody alive up there left to fall; nothing inside left to burn. It was all over. The fire had burned itself out.

47

The day's light had dimmed, the sunny afternoon had been and gone, by the time the fire patrol released Matz and Eleana from that terrible place. Behind them, as they staggered onto the street, the top floors of the building were still smoking and the air still reeked of trauma and death, but the raging fire, at least, was long extinguished. They might have lingered, as other survivors did. They might have been transferred to the hospital. Matz's scorched hands needed medical attention without doubt.

Instead, they slipped away. They stumbled through the streets as if the fire was still coming after them, and they didn't stop until they reached Allen Street. Eleana's mother opened the door, already dressed in shawl and hat. She had heard the news and was heading out in search of them. She looked from one to the other, faces and clothes smeared in dirt and soot, a smell of burning around them. She opened her mouth to speak—but Matz and Eleana, with the faintest of nods, brushed passed her into the room.

Isha and Tzivia were at the table. Isha glanced up at them, and at once her face broke into a happy grin. She was about to climb off her chair and tumble into their arms, but she stopped short. Their faces frightened her.

Batia's gaze flitted nervously from one to other, taking in what clues she could. She noticed Matz's hands, raw and weeping, and her eyes rested there. 'It's true then,' she said at last. 'What they're saying. Is it true?'

'Worse . . .' Matz said simply. He motioned for the children to move, get out of the room, and they did so without a word. He sat down in the seat his daughter had vacated, beckoned Eleana to take the one beside him. 'It is worse than . . .' but he didn't finish.

'*Eleana?*' Her mother looked at her hopelessly. But Eleana could not even raise her eyes. She only shook her head.

'Eleana,' Batia whispered, 'where is Sarah?'

'Sarah was on the ninth, Mama. On the ninth floor . . . I don't know where she is.'

'What happened?'

Eleana only shook her head. She motioned to her husband's hands. 'We should clean them, Matz.'

'*Where is Sarah?*' her mother asked again. 'I have to tell something to Tzivia.'

'Mama,' Eleana said, as if her mother hadn't

255

spoken. 'We need the tincture—for those burns. Can you see? They are weeping. We should bandage them . . .'

'I should go down there . . .' Batia said. 'God knows where Samuel is. And perhaps Sarah—'

'Yes.' Matz agreed. 'You probably should go. I am sorry. We should have searched for her.'

Batia kept gin tucked away for emergencies. She pulled it out now, set it before them—with two cups, old and chipped. From the same cupboard she produced the tincture—a cure-all: or cure-nothing-at-all. But it was alcoholic. It would clean the wound. She placed it before Eleanor, with a cloth.

'I am happy you are home,' she said awkwardly. 'I was coming to search for you, Eleana, Matz . . .' She wondered vaguely why he had been there at all. But it was not important. She would ask later, when she returned with Sarah. 'I am going down there now. Perhaps Sarah is . . .'

'Perhaps they have taken her to the hospital,' Matz said. But the words rang hollow. 'She was on the ninth, Batia. She was on the ninth . . . It would have been worse on the ninth.'

It was far worse, as they would learn in the days to come. Up on the tenth, the owners had escaped over the rooftops, but on the ninth, the workers were trapped. One stairwell was locked, the other was impassable—a thick wall of fire—before anyone realized what was happening. Sarah was not in hospital. She had been dead for several hours. As Batia prepared to leave, Sarah's body, her burned arms clinging tight to another, was being lifted from a pile of twenty or more within a few feet of that locked door.

'You should go, Mama. Go now,' Eleana said. She turned to Matz. She hadn't asked him. Not yet. Couldn't quite bring herself to frame the words, because she couldn't bear to hear his answer. '. . . And Dora?'

He shook his head. And kept shaking it—as if he couldn't stop. She touched him gently. He didn't seem to feel it.

'I tried,' he said.

'Yes.'

'He wouldn't let her go . . .'

She didn't ask who. She didn't care.

'He pulled her off me, Eleana. She slipped from my grasp . . .'

Eleana's mother listened to this. She could not imagine what horrors he spoke of, didn't understand. She wrapped her shawl more tightly around her shoulders. 'I'll go down there then,' she said again. 'I'll find Sarah.' And then, in a hurried movement, she turned and put her arms around them both: 'I am so happy you're here—both of you,' she said. 'So happy. Look after the girls. Say nothing to Tzivia. Not yet. Perhaps they will have found her . . .'

'Batia.' As she was opening the door into the hallway, Matz called after her urgently. 'Don't mention to anyone that we are here, understand?' he said suddenly. 'Nobody needs to know.' She didn't query it, just nodded her head once, and they were left alone.

48

The crowd outside the smoking building had swelled to twenty thousand or more by the time Batia arrived, and the police had formed a cordon around it to keep people back. Behind the cordon, a continual stream of tarpaulin-covered bodies emerged from the higher floors, from the stairways and the lift shafts and from every small nook and cranny of the building. The crowd could only watch and wonder, as the anonymous bodies were laid side by side along the sidewalk.

Batia struggled to reach the front of the crush. It was eight in the evening. The sky was dark, and the authorities had yet to provide the crowd with any useful information. Was there a list of casualties? Did they know who had survived and who had not? All around were men and women sobbing openly.

But nobody knew anything. The minutes ticked by, and then the minutes turned into hours. Still more tarpaulined bodies were pulled from the building and laid out before them. It seemed to the onlookers as if it might never end, an endless supply of corpses: first one, then another, and then another, and the minutes ticked by. But nobody knew anything.

'Are there survivors?' Batia asked. 'Are there any more survivors coming out?' Her neighbour shrugged. 'We haven't seen any yet.'

'They must have some at the hospital?'

'St Vincent's Hospital. But there aren't many. Five or six maybe . . . They're all dead up there, ma'am. Burned alive. It's what they're saying. All over in half an hour . . .'

'Five or six? Is that all?'

The man nodded. 'The city morgue's not big enough. That's all I know. They're taking the bodies down to Misery Lane . . .'

'How many bodies?'

Again, the man shrugged. 'They're saying they ran out of coffins—had to send a boat to Blackwell's Island to get more . . .' He looked embarrassed. 'Sorry, ma'am . . . You looking for someone in particular?'

She didn't answer him. She pushed on through, closer to the police line, where the crowd was thicker and angrier. She could see the sidewalk now. It was strewn, still, with the trifling belongings of the people who had jumped: purses and combs, hair ribbons, pay envelopes. In the grey evening light, the ground was black with their blood.

Police officers—the very same officers who had battled with them at the picket line on this very same spot only a year before—were bent, now, over their burnt remains. Each young body needed to be tagged, their distinguishing marks noted (if any remained), and then the bodies boxed up and piled onto the waiting wagons.

The wagons came, the wagons left—the crowd waited for news. And waited. Until quite suddenly—it seemed to Batia that it came from out of nowhere—there came a great roar of anguish—a hundred voices at least—and the crowd surged forward. The police line fell apart at once and the people rushed the building. Some ran into the open hallway, others made directly to the covered bodies and began pulling recklessly at the tarpaulins.

Batia stood in the midst of it all, pushed forward

259

by the force of the crowd and uncertain where to go, what to do next . . . She had to tell something to Tzivia. How could she leave without finding out what had happened to the girl's mother? At her feet lay bodies, three deep. She did what her neighbours did—pulled back the sheet closest to her.

Beneath it were only charred remains. She forced herself not to recoil. But they were of a large man. Of someone else. Not Sarah. She pulled back the next sheet—a strange woman; the next—a body, impossible to tell what or whom. And then, frantically, wildly, nausea making her head spin, a fourth sheet. Beneath it was a young girl, less than twenty, and heavily pregnant. There was blood matted to the top of her skull, where it had struck the shaft of the lift. There was blood, oil—black smears on her face—and more blood drenching her once-white shirtwaist.

The features, so still, took a moment to come together. It took a moment for Batia to register the similarity between Dora, her face full of light and laughter, and this Dora, dead on the sidewalk at her feet.

She began to whimper. A policeman pushed her aside and, club aloft, threw her back into the crowd. By the time she could turn to look back, the sheet had been pulled over Dora's face again.

But there was no sign of Sarah. Batia would have preferred to go home, take care of her own daughter who had miraculously—thank God—survived. But she imagined Tzivia lying, waiting. There would be Isha with both her parents and Tzivia with neither. She could not return to the girl without an answer. And so she waited, until word came at last from the authorities. They were going to lay out the tagged bodies tonight, in the emergency morgue on Misery Lane, so that friends and relations could begin to identify the remains.

When the next horse-drawn wagon pulled away, heavy with its cargo of coffins, Batia joined the section of crowd that fell into step behind it.

49

Eleanor bandaged his hands as best she could. They didn't speak. Afterwards she crept into the bedroom. Isha and Tzivia were asleep on the family mattress, their arms wrapped round each other's necks. Normally, Eleana might have sent Tzivia back to her own family's room. But tonight she left her sleeping. She closed the door softly and returned to Matz.

With his bandaged hands, he was attempting to pour them both a cup of gin. She took the bottle from him and finished the task for him, slugged hers back and poured another.

'Thank you,' she said suddenly, looking down at his bowed head. 'I didn't say it. But thank you. I would have died.'

He didn't respond.

'How are the hands?'

Again, he didn't answer. '. . . Aren't you wondering why I was at the factory?' he asked instead.

'No. Actually. No . . .' she smiled. 'It hadn't crossed my mind. But now you mention it . . .'

261

'Because the police were following me.'

'Oh, well then.' She refilled his cup, not interested, not really listening.

'Perhaps, after this, it will be forgotten. It will be lost in the . . . But Eleana,' he leaned towards her, 'Eleana, I don't think it will be forgotten . . .'

'Sarah might have made it, Matz,' she said. 'It's possible, you know, Matz. It is. She is always so fast on her feet. She might have made it.'

'Eleana, I think I have killed someone . . .'

'No, darling. You didn't kill anyone.' She smiled at him. 'You saved them, Matz. You tried to save more but you couldn't save them all.' Gently, she took his bandaged hands. 'I saw you, carrying the girls in your arms. *I saw you*. You could have run— like some of the men. You could have knocked the women aside and put yourself first. But you didn't do that. You went back and you went back again . . . And Matz, you saved me, too.'

He shook his head impatiently. 'Why won't you listen to me? I mean before. Something terrible happened. I've done something terrible. It's what I'm trying to tell you.'

She sighed, dropping his hands, sitting down beside him. 'Not today. Please. Tell me what it is, but tomorrow. Let me hear it tomorrow, when we are both stronger.'

He glanced at the door to their room, where the children lay asleep, and then at the door to the outside landing. He dropped his hoarse voice to a low whisper. 'I was trying to get away from him. I didn't know he was so close, and then when I turned back and I threw the brick—'

'A brick? What are you saying, Matz?'

'There was a meeting. I was speaking.'

262

'Oh god. Please. Not now . . .'

'And of course they came with their boots and clubs. And of course they broke it up. And of course I was arrested . . .'

'Of course.'

'They were taking me to Mercer Street—and I saw an opportunity, and I fled. One of them came after me. I threw the brick . . . *And it hit him.'*

'You hit a policeman? Is he all right? What happened? Did you hurt him?'

Matz held a bandaged hand to the side of his head. 'Right here, Eleanor . . . you understand? Right here . . .' He leaned towards her and, with his bare fingertips, he touched her temple. The softness of her skin—the ghost of his touch—sent a jolt of awareness through them both; gratitude and tenderness: a physical reminder that they were still alive. Still together. Eleana fought the urge to weep. If she started, she knew she would never stop. 'Right here, where the skull is soft,' he whispered to her. 'There was no resistance, Eleana. The brick seemed to give beneath his flesh. It seemed to sink into him—does it make sense?'

She shook her head. 'No. It makes no sense,' she said.

'Eleana, listen to me!' he whispered urgently. 'He is not all right. No. I am certain that I killed him.'

'Of course you didn't,' she said, voice rising in panic. 'Of course you didn't!' she said again. 'Don't be ridiculous. You saved us—it's what you did. You saved as many as you could, and there are plenty who can vouch for you . . . All the people you saved today. They will vouch for you. You were at Triangle . . . You were at the factory all afternoon.'

'I killed a man, Eleanor—and I will never forgive myself for it. I killed a *policeman*, and *they* will never forgive me for that. No matter what else has happened today . . . They know my name. They know where I live. They are sure to come after me.'

As he said the words, the door from the hallway burst open, and both leapt to their feet, terrified.

But it was only Samuel. Tzivia's father, Sarah's husband. Putting in one of his rare appearances at home. Pie-eyed, he was, and swaying. He glanced at them, unable to focus. His eyes, loose in their sockets, swivelled lazily around the tiny room. No Batia, no children. No Sarah. 'Where is she?' he slurred. 'Where is Sarah?'

They returned to their seats without answering.

'So, it is all true . . . But you two are here. Did she come home with you?'

'Mama is outside the factory. You should go down there yourself. There will be news, soon. Perhaps they have found her.'

He made a noise, guttural and dismissive, and staggered slightly where he stood. For an instant it looked as if his large body might simply crumple, but he recovered well enough to make the two steps across the parlour. He stumbled past them to his family's bedroom. They heard the floorboards groan as he laid his weight onto the mattress—and then, nothing. Silence.

'I shouldn't be here,' Matz whispered. 'Now Samuel has seen me . . .'

'Samuel has seen nothing,' Eleana replied. 'I should think he has already passed out.'

As they listened for his breathing, she felt suddenly overwhelmed by the desire to sleep herself, as if she might collapse from exhaustion right there where she sat. 'Come,' she said. 'Nothing will happen tonight. It's impossible. The city is turned upside down with this. Let's go to bed. And in the morning we will think of something. Tomorrow we will be able to think more clearly.'

50

Matz and Eleana were still awake at two in the morning, their small daughter and her cousin entwined across the bottom of the mattress at their feet. They lay side by side, dry eyes wide to the dark ceiling, skin touching, feeling each other's breath. They heard Eleana's mother returning. She tapped gently on their door and pushed it open. In the threshold, her outline stood out against the lights of apartments opposite, up and down the street, where other families sat waiting for news. Batia's figure stood stooped.

'She is dead,' she said bluntly.

'Shhh!' Eleana ordered. She sat up. 'Tzivia . . .'

'I have seen her.'

'Hush! Tzivia is here with us.' Eleana clambered up from the mattress, ushered her mother back into the parlour. She closed the door, and sat down with her mother at the table.

'There are rows and rows of them, Eleana. Hundreds . . . So many coffins. They have their heads and shoulders showing, and if the clothes aren't burned, the bodies lie uncovered. It's to help people recognize . . . But there are so many! And they are so burned! One body, and then the next . . . Her hair was burned away. She was burned—her skin entirely scorched. Oh! The smell! The smell in that place is too dreadful. It is dreadful . . .' Her hands shook and she spilled gin onto the tablecloth as poured herself a cup. It looked odd. Eleana had never seen her drink before.

'Are you sure, Mama? Are you certain it was Sarah?'

Batia hesitated—as if perhaps there might yet be some hope; as if Eleana's doubt offered some new shred. She shook her head. 'I am certain, yes. There was a scrap of her shirtwaist sleeve peeping out from the cover, and I thought I knew it . . . With the small embroidered flowers . . . You know the one. She was wearing it this morning.'

Eleana knew it well. She and Sarah had chosen it together.

'And then there were notes beside each coffin. And there was her little locket bracelet with . . .' She bent her head, wiped her face with a sleeve. Matz crept in to join them. He sat down at the table.

'Sarah,' Eleana said. 'She found Sarah . . .'

'I am so sorry.'

'Of course,' Batia nodded. 'We are all sorry.'

They sat for a while, not saying anything. Eleana tried to think of Sarah, of the walk they had enjoyed this morning. It seemed like a memory from another life: something she might have watched on that crooked screen at the nickelodeon.

Matz broke the silence. 'What did you do, Batia?' he asked her suddenly. 'Did you make a report?'

'They are trying to make a list, yes,' she answered. 'But it's going to be too difficult. Some of the bodies are so terribly . . .' She stopped, the

266

images swimming before her eyes. 'There is almost nothing left of them. Some of the boxes have no bodies at all—just a leg and an arm . . .' She raised the cup to her mouth, inhaled, felt a wave of nausea and quickly put the cup back down again. 'And of course,' she added, 'what do they know, anyway? Nobody really knows exactly who was in there, what their names were. Nothing.' She turned to Matz. 'You never explained why you were there yourself.'

'Matz saved so many people, Mama,' Eleana said quickly, before he had a chance to reply. 'He carried them—piled them into the elevators and went back for more, and then more again. Matz saved *me*, Mama. I would not be alive now. But he carried me . . .'

'Good.' She smiled at him, more kindly than usual. 'It's what a husband should do. Where is Samuel? Is he here?'

'Samuel is asleep in his room,' Matz said. 'It will take the ceiling to fall on his head to wake him. Tell me, Batia,' he asked her, 'when you gave them Sarah's name, did they seem to question you? Or did they simply write it down—the name beside the number?'

'Yes—they put her name down. And they thanked me. I think. Why? What does it matter?'

'If Samuel had not seen us,' he muttered. He was talking to himself. Thinking aloud. 'And even if he had, would anyone believe him? Would he even believe it himself? . . . Tell me, Batia—what is it like down there? Is it madness? How many boxes, would you say? How many bodies . . . Are there men, too? Of course there are men. Batia—I have to ask you, would you go back there, one more time?'

'No,' she said.

'If our lives depended on it. I mean to say—my life. If my life were to depend on it?'

'What are you saying?' Eleana whispered.

Batia considered his words. She looked at him hard. 'What have you done, Matz?'

He didn't answer. He said, 'Tell me, Batia. Describe to me exactly what it is like . . .'

51

By the following morning, word of the fire had spread far beyond the tenements of the Lower East Side, to the front pages of every newspaper in America. The country awoke to photographs of young immigrant bodies heaped and crushed on the sidewalk. It was a national tragedy—and a national scandal: the locked doors, the broken standpipe, the feeble fire escape. The factory owners and city regulators were already tossing the blame between them. And, amid the clamour, 136 young bodies already lay in their boxes. Crowds gathered at the pier by the thousands, tens of thousands, hundreds of thousands.

But the city did not stop. A policeman had been murdered that afternoon, and the killer's identity was known.

Early the next morning, while Matz and Eleana hid away in their room, two policemen came to the door. Batia was out. She had taken the girls to fetch bread. But through the thin partition that separated their rooms, they could hear Samuel breathing as he lay abed. There came an impatient bang at the hallway door, and then another.

'Police. Open the door!'

Matz, wide awake, as he had been all night, sat bolt upright, glanced at Eleana, put a finger to his lips. There was nowhere to go. No window in the room. The only possible exit was the garbage chute at the back of the parlour, but to reach it they needed to pass by Samuel's door, and they could hear him shifting, grunting—rudely awoken by the knocks. If they tried to reach the garbage shoot now, they would perhaps collide with him—and all would be lost.

'Open the door!' Outside, one of the police gave the door a hefty kick. The flimsy wood split noisily.

Matz and Eleana climbed silently off the mattress. In that tiny, crowded room there was a single place to hide: the chest beside the bed. Together, they threw its contents onto the mattress and clambered in, one on top of the other. It was hopeless. Worse than hopeless. The police would only need to open the chest to find them. They waited.

They heard Samuel grunting again, shuffling out of his room towards the front door. 'Take it easy!' he muttered, opening the door. 'Look what you've done to my door,' he grumbled.

'Matz Beekman?'

'Huh?'

'We're looking for Matz Beekman. Is he here?'

'You want Matz . . .?' Samuel repeated stupidly. 'What do you want Matz for? What's he done?'

'Is Matz Beekman here?'

He stopped, scratched himself. *Scratch, scratch.* They could hear it, from inside the chest. 'Not enough to keep you busy this morning?' he said at last.

'Step aside.'

'Sure. I'll step aside,' Samuel said. 'But you're wasting your time. He's not here. Prob'ly down at the morgue looking for his wife . . . If he's not dead himself, already.'

One of them said: 'Why would he be dead already?' The voice sounded taken aback.

'He was in there, getting the girls out . . . That's what I heard.'

One of the police officers had a brother who worked at Triangle. A manager, not a worker. They found his body in the lift shaft.

'Is that what you heard?' the officer asked. After all, the murdered policeman had been struck only a few blocks from the factory. It wasn't impossible.

'It's what I heard,' Samuel said again. 'The guy's a hero. That's what they're saying . . . Even if he didn't get to my wife,' he added. 'Nobody did. Didn't get to save her.'

'I'm very sorry, sir.'

'Uh-huh.'

'It's a tragedy, what happened down there.'

'Well, come in if you want,' Samuel said. 'Go ahead . . .'

Matz and Eleana heard him pulling back the broken door, and the officers stepping inside, but more politely now.

'Have a look around.' Samuel chuckled. 'I can tell you, there's not too many places he could be hiding, not in this dump. But if you want to go see for yourself . . .'

'Is that his room, right there?'

'Take a look! . . . What'd'he do this time?' Samuel asked again, padding behind them. 'Must

270

be pretty serious. To get you out here, on a day like this . . . Can I get you something to drink?'

From inside the chest they heard their bedroom door open, a voice saying, 'That's good of you. But thank you—no. We should get on . . .' And the door closed to again.

Samuel saw them out with a level of civility neither Matz nor Eleana had ever observed in him before. And there it was—they were gone.

They stayed where they were, not daring to speak or move. They waited for Samuel to shuffle back to his room. Instead, the bedroom door opened again. He said, 'Don't know what the hell you done, my friend. Not sure I want to know either. But they're after you . . . And they'll be back. Take my advice. Get outta town while you can. While it's still so crazy round here. I'm telling you, they'll be back again tomorrow.'

He didn't linger for a response, nor even to watch them emerging from the chest. He just closed the door again and returned to his mattress. They didn't go after him. They stayed in their room, too shaken to talk. By the time Batia and the girls returned, Samuel was gone—no one knew where, or why—without pausing to speak with his daughter.

52

Eleana's mother would not go back to the morgue alone. She brought Eleana with her, leaving Matz to look out for the girls. Mother and daughter walked from Allen Street to Misery Lane with hair

271

covered and heads lowered. They joined the back of a line that snaked the full length of the pier and waited silently for their turn to be allowed in.

It was a simple, gruesome plan. A crazy plan, Batia argued, and a wicked one, too. 'How is it wicked?' Matz asked her. 'They are dead, and I am alive. There will be plenty of bodies nobody can identify . . . And workers who died but who nobody knows, and who nobody will miss. Tell me what is so wicked about it, Batia?'

'Because, if we claim someone's remains as our own, their family will have nothing to bury.'

'It's true,' Matz acknowleged. 'But they are already dead. Nothing will bring them back— and that is the tragedy. The rest . . . the rest is sentiment. If a family has a few charred remains to bury, it doesn't change the ending. Does it? Whereas, it would change ours . . .'

It was not ideal, but it made sense. Set against what was at stake for her own son-in-law, she could not refuse.

'You will have to leave the city. You will have to start a new life,' she said wretchedly.

But the truth hovered unspoken between them: in that crowded flat, where death seemed to be everywhere, and poverty, and injustice, and filth . . . for a moment the three of them almost laughed. It wasn't such a dreadful proposition after all.

'I have no real work here, in any case,' Matz said. Eleana added: 'Nor I.'

'What will you do for money?' her mother asked.

Matz smiled at her: 'You think I'm feckless, Batia, because I concern myself with politics.'

'I think you are feckless because you throw bricks into the skulls of policeman,' she snapped. 'You know I have nothing against your politics.'

He paused, nodded. 'What I meant to say . . .' he corrected himself. 'I have a little money saved. Enough to last for all of us, until I find some work—and then you can bring Isha and can come to live with us. As soon as we have found a place.'

'How long?' asked Eleana. 'Couldn't Isha and I come with you?'

'But I didn't mean . . .' He stopped. She had misunderstood. 'Won't you come with me?' he asked her. 'If you come with me, we will save money twice as fast. Isha is safer here with her grandmother.'

'I don't want to leave Isha. I can't leave her.'

'Of course you can!' her mother interrupted. 'And you must. Matz is right. Isha has me to take care of her. And you will make twice the money if you go with Matz. And he needs you,' she added.

'*Isha* needs me.'

'Isha has her grandmother,' Matz replied. 'And Isha needs to get away from this place as soon as she can. It's what she needs. It's what we all need. Only it's taken us *this* to know it. Come with me, Eleana, and the sooner we can take her away from here. To a place where she can grow up to be strong, where the sun shines every day. Try to imagine it! Can you imagine it, Eleana?'

Eleana smiled. She could not.

'In California they pick the oranges off the trees! And, you know, there are film companies there galore. All the film companies are going to California now. We can work on the films, why not? *Why not*, Eleana? The sun shines in California! And it is as far from New York as it's possible to be. Won't you come with me, darling? It will be a fresh beginning—I swear to it. You, me, the baby . . . and Batia.'

'You will get into trouble again,' Eleana said, shaking her head. 'I know it. As long as there are suffering workers and forbidden strikes and the police—'

'*Never*—if you come with me, I swear—I will leave it behind. All the politics—I will forget it. I will devote myself to you and to Isha—to us.'

'You had better,' said Batia.

'I will take care of us. I promise you.'

Batia nodded. But he wasn't looking at Batia. 'Eleana,' he leant across the table and took her hand, 'will you come?'

Eleana said nothing. She began to cry.

'She will come,' said her mother confidently, taking Eleana's other hand, and then taking Matz's hand, so that the three were linked in a circle, hunched together at the small table. She turned to Eleana, 'It will only be for a month or two, darling. It will be safer for Isha to stay here with me, until everything is ready. And you will both work hard . . . And then as soon as everything is ready and safe, and Isha is strong, I will bring her with me—and Tzivia too, if Samuel allows it. And we will come and live with you wherever you are.' She smiled. 'Where the oranges grow off the trees. Even if it is California.'

Batia hesitated—it might only enrage them, she thought. God was not a part of their lives, nor ever had been. But the old ritual might comfort them perhaps: the familiarity, if not the meaning. It had comforted her when her husband died, and at home as a child, when her sister died and her father.

Yit'gadal v'yit'kadash sh'mei raba

274

b'al'ma di v'ra chiruteih . . .

But as she muttered the familiar words, Eleana and Matz gently pulled their hands away, and she fell silent.

53

They found the head of the line eventually. It was a long wait—nightfall by then, a full day since the fire was put out. At the end of the pier, they reached the threshold to the building where sat a kindly looking, elderly nurse, stationed to sift out all but the genuine grievers. She stopped Eleana and her mother, as she stopped every one. Had they come to this place, she enquired softly, because they were connected to the terrible event? Had they come because they were missing a loved one or . . . Eleana replied yes before the nurse could continue. She thought of Dora, life extinguished, and tears rolled down her cheeks once again. The nurse waited to hear more, but nothing further was offered. She said, 'Forgive me. I am sure you are here for good reasons. But we are having problems keeping the crowds back . . . Ghouls and pickpockets. It's not right.'

'It's not,' Eleana agreed.

'May I ask who you are looking for?'

'My son,' said Batia. The nurse nodded them in.

It was a metal-framed hangar, painted a peeling, greyish yellow, cavernous and full of shadows. There were small, dark windows set high in the walls above, and river water lapping at three sides of the building, giving the impression they were walking onto an abandoned ship. High overhead, lamps cast their feeble, sulphurous light onto the open coffins below, and lined along the heads of the open caskets, held aloft by waiting police officers, there were lanterns, weak and flickering.

Together, Eleana and Batia stepped into the space and joined the echo of the shuffling footsteps. The cry of gulls and the lapping of water, the footsteps, the occasional anguished sob—the noises filled the silence, and yet, somehow, hardly dented it. Dora's coffin had been closed and taken away by then, her husband the cloakmaker having already seen to it. Sarah's coffin, too, had been labelled and stowed. But the rows of unclaimed caskets seemed still to be endless. Eleana clutched at her mother's hand. She was here for Matz, for her mother. And, for Isha, of course. So they could start afresh, all of them, together. But she would know the girls in the open boxes. She would know many of the people shuffling between them, searching for the people they loved. And here she was among them, under false pretences. She couldn't have spoken to them if they had addressed her, and luckily she didn't have to. From the silence, the downcast eyes, it seemed nobody wanted to talk.

So they wandered through the rows of bodies, tagged and numbered, looking for one with almost nothing to distinguish it. It would not be hard, Batia had explained. There were plenty to choose from: scores of bodies, their features all burned to nothing.

And when they found it, this indistinguishable body, they would stop and find something, some reason to say it was theirs.

That was the plan. As Batia had done the night

276

before, when she was searching for Sarah, they would ask the policeman nearest to swing his lantern closer over the coffin. And they would murmur and discuss, and they would weep, and they would agree that yes, it was Matz Beekman.

That was the plan.

Eleana wasn't up to it. Within a few moments of walking through the corpses of her friends, she began to shake: so violently she had to lean on her mother, to prevent her knees from buckling. Her mother patted her, shushed her, waited. Eleana's breathing became heavy. She began to rasp, and it rang out over the hush.

Batia whispered, 'Eleana, for goodness' sake. You will draw attention . . .'

Eleana nodded, but her breathing somehow grew louder, and she clasped her mother's shoulder so tight that Batia had to pull her daughter's fingers from her, and bite her lip to stop crying out.

'Can you walk?' Batia asked her. 'I think you should leave. Go home. You don't need to be here.'

'I want to be here,' Eleana whispered.

'Nonsense, you are only slowing me down. Go.' Eleana did not move.

'Go home, Eleana! At once. I don't want to stay in this place a moment longer than I need to, and you are only delaying us. Leave now. Can you walk? Of course you can. Now go.' Batia gave her daughter a gentle push and turned away.

*   *   *

Hours later, when Batia returned to the apartment, she found the four of them, Isha, Tzivia, Eleana and Matz, seated at the small table, bowls of

277

untouched potato soup before them. It seemed even the children had lost their appetites. Batia hesitated. Seeing this family group it struck her afresh, the horror of what she had done. Too late. She had taken a decision and now there was no undoing it. There could be no question of regret.

'Matz. Eleana. Leave the girls to their soup and come into the other room with me.' It was unusual in itself, that the adults should be the ones displaced and not the children, but the adults left the table and filed dutifully into the family bedroom.

'You will be angry,' she said to her daughter, when the door was safely closed behind them. 'But there. I made the decision. We weren't thinking clearly before.'

'What decision?' Matz asked.

But she continued to look at her daughter. 'Eleana, if you had disappeared with Matz, there would have been too many questions. It would not have been safe. Not for any of us. Not for me or for Isha. Maybe not even for Tzivia. They would want to know where you had gone. Why it was I, and not you, who identified Matz at the morgue.' She stopped. Shuddered. 'I have registered you too, Eleana.'

'You have done what?' Eleana said. 'You have registered me . . . ?'

'Dead. Now you are both dead.' A long silence.

'We are both dead?' Eleana repeated finally. After the horrors of the last few days, it seemed to have no meaning. The words rolled off her as if she were talking about the weather. 'I am dead, too?'

'I am so sorry,' Matz said at last. 'If I had only—'

'Never mind that!' Eleana interrupted him.

278

'Never mind "if only"!' She was angry suddenly.

Batia said, 'Forgive me, my darling. It was a moment's decision, and I had to take it. I still believe—'

'But I am *NOT* dead. Unlike all the others, I am not dead, Mama. God knows why—but I am very much alive. How dare you say I am dead!' She was growing hysterical. Matz touched her arm.

'Nobody is saying you are really dead,' he said softly.

'Well I know that.' She glanced at his hand, touching her . . . They would need to find another bandage. Clean the wound . . . An image of his hands on the burning cable came to her, of her own arms clinging on to him, of his holding her when she seemed to slip. 'I am sorry . . .'

He squeezed her arm—as best he could. 'Never mind that,' he said, and smiled. Somehow, they both did. 'I swear it, Eleana, I swear it. Everything will be better from now. It will be better when we are all in California.'

*   *   *

They left on the day the city buried the unclaimed bodies: seven coffins in all, the seventh one taken not by a single corpse but by the parts of several— hands, arms, legs—unidentifiable and unknown. It was a fitting moment for Eleana Kappelman and Matz Beekman to take their leave of the city. They both thought so, quietly. Not that it had any bearing. Only it was a good day to slip away. With half a million mourners on the sodden streets, it would be easy for them to walk through the crowds unnoticed.

The weather could not have better reflected the city's mood that day, nor that of the broken family on Allen Street. All along the funeral procession, the rain pelted relentlessly down and, on Allen Street, as Matz and Eleana bid their daughter farewell, the cold grey sky never lifted above the rooftops.

Matz and Eleana would take the train as far as Chicago. From there, half a country away from anyone who ever knew them, they would look for work. It was what they had planned. Leaving behind all the money that he could spare, Matz had enough for the two of them to survive a fortnight. In Chicago, there were nickelodeons and bars and, above all, there was vaudeville. Matz would play piano as soon as his hands allowed. Eleana would sing. They would find work with a touring group, the better to save every penny they made, and they would make their way west, to the orange groves and the palm trees and the Pacific Ocean. And together they would make a home for Isha.

54

What does a three-and-a-half year old understand of death?

Isha's parents discussed it at length. After they were gone, the apartment felt painfully empty. Batia, suddenly terrified by what she had done, explained the situation to Isha and Tzivia in the harshest and simplest of terms. If they let it be known that Eleana and Matz had been alive after the fire, their *bubbeh* would be thrown into jail.

And with no one left to look after them, the two girls would have to go and live in an orphanage.

'What about Tzivia's papa?' Isha had asked solemnly.

'Indeed!' her *bubbeh* had replied irritably. He'd not been seen since the morning after the fire. 'What indeed?'

'He would never leave us in the orphanage.'

'Well maybe he wouldn't. And if you want to test your high opinion of him, I suggest you do the opposite of what I advise, my young friend. Go to the market tomorrow and tell everyone you see that your mother and father are alive and well, and on their way to Chicago. And we shall see, won't we? After I am put in jail and they have thrown away the key, we shall see if he comes for you both. Hm? Perhaps he will. And perhaps he won't.'

It silenced Isha. Because of course she could not be sure. She was far from sure.

'I won't say a word, *bubbeh*,' Isha said solemnly. 'And you won't, will you, Tzivia? You will remember to tell everyone my mama and papa are dead. Just like your mama. They are all dead.'

'Not really,' Tzivia said stubbornly. 'They are not really dead.'

'Well—but they are as good as dead,' snapped Batia, her own fear making her unkind. And both girls burst into noisy, confused tears.

55

But before that, on the day of the funeral of the unclaimed, Eleana and Matz shared a last moment with their daughter. Batia took Tzivia out to fetch breakfast, and the three were left alone in the apartment. They huddled together in the small parlour.

'You will be good?' Matz said to her, with brittle good cheer.

Isha said, sulkily, without looking up at him: 'I am always good.'

'Oh I know you are,' he said, nudging her small shoulder playfully, though there was nothing playful in the air.

'Of course you are always good,' said Eleana, crouching down so their faces were level, brushing away tears—her own, and her daughter's. She smiled into her daughter's green eyes. 'You are always terribly good.'

For once Isha did not smile back. 'How soon will you come?'

'As soon as we can.'

'How long will you be dead?'

'We are not dead.'

'But *Bubbeh* said—'

'You know perfectly well we are not really dead,' Matz said to her. 'Don't be foolish.'

'I know you are not really dead. But how long am I to pretend you are dead?'

'Until we come for you.'

'When will you come?'

'Oh, Isha . . .'

'Will it be a week, or a day, or a hundred years?'

'Much closer to a week than a hundred years, my darling. Just a few months, that's all. And then . . .'

Isha smiled, the smile that melted the snow on Hester Street, that banished the damp grey clouds on Allen Street, that made her mother's heart sing—and break, all at the same time. 'And then,' Isha recited dutifully, just as if it was a fairy tale, 'there will be sunshine and orange groves and coconut trees. And grapes hanging from vines, and sweet smelling flowers at every corner, and besides all that, the big yellow beach and the big blue sea ...'

It was how they left it. Afterwards, Isha's health deteriorated. Always weak, she seemed to grow weaker when her parents left. Afterwards, Eleana rehearsed those final moments again, and again, until the memory was worn thin with distortions, and all she could really remember was the smile— that brave, warm smile, and the warm green eyes, and the glow of health in her daughter's pale cheeks which signified that on that rainy day, at least, she might have been strong enough. She might have travelled with them. They might all be together still.

Matz and Eleana slipped out of the apartment soon after Batia and Tzivia returned. One final embrace, and they were gone, without looking back.

Sun on San Simeon Bay

56

Friday 25 October 1929

Soaking in her warm, marble tub of lily-of-the-valley-infused bath water in faraway Reno, Nevada, Eleanor knew nothing of the turmoil taking place on the East Coast and cared, though her own fortunes rested on it, hardly at all. It was the morning after Black Thursday, and disaster was writ large on the front page of her newspaper. But she couldn't have known it because her newspaper, delivered to her room that morning, still lay untouched on her breakfast tray.

She was due in Matthew Gregory's office at ten, and Matthew Gregory was running out of patience with her. That much was obvious. She could hardly blame him. She was running out of patience with herself. They were no closer to finding Isha Kappelman today than they were when she arrived in Reno. No closer than when she engaged Matthew's father seven years before.

Nothing had changed. She was trapped. As trapped as she had ever been. For as long as Matz Beekman could never be found, how could they ever search properly for Isha? It was impossible. And that was it: she knew it was impossible. She had always known. This morning, in her flower-scented marble bathtub, she tried to push away the single image which had ensured her discretion to this day and which, she knew, would ensure her discretion until she died. It was of Max, her faithless husband, who had

287

saved her life and then transformed it, strapped to the electric chair for an act he committed almost twenty years earlier, his eyes through the glass of the spectator box seeking her out, looking back at her, and only at her. The image, the sound, the smell, their shared pain—it came at her in a rush, so vividly she heard herself cry out.

And then came another picture, the one that woke her most nights: of green-eyed little Isha, waxy and feverish in that disease-infested tenement, lying beside a grandmother, slowly dying; beside her dying grandmother, slowly dying. Or Batia, already dead, and Isha crawling out onto the street in search of food, all alone, sick, frozen—calling for her mother, for her father, wondering why they had never come back to fetch her.

Unbearable. All of it. She jerked herself up and out of the bath, unable to stay still any longer.

She rested on the edge of the tub, eyes closed, listening to the cars on the street, the sounds of rich women's voices—fellow guests at the hotel, she imagined, chatting and laughing together, talking loudly about alimony settlements. What was she doing here in Reno? Risking so much—for what?

Isha is gone.

The words came to her very clearly. She wondered if she had spoken them aloud.

Isha is gone.

She stood up then, aware suddenly that she was shivering. It was finished. Over. All of it. Everything. She thought she had come to Reno to find her daughter. It's what she believed as she was packing her bags, as she stayed up all night in her first-class carriage, looking out into the darkness, and as she sat before Matthew Gregory's garish, tight-fitting jackets, pouring out her heart. But just then, she understood. She had not come to find Isha. Isha had died, many years ago, in a cold tenement flat on Allen Street. Eleanor had come to Reno to say goodbye to her. It was time to step out of the dark.

She dressed automatically, with the usual elegance and care. She arranged her hair and chose her jewellery. She called down and ordered a car. She checked her bag for the chequebook, and then her watch for the time. She did all this with a sense of resolve she had not felt in many years, if indeed she had ever felt it. But it did not come as a relief to her. The decision she had made—the answer that came to her so clearly—was not setting her free to begin a new life, so much as allowing her to accept, at last, that her life was already over. She would take the car to the Gregory offices, settle her bill, and bring an end to the goose chase. And then she would return to LA and bring an end to her marriage.

57

Matthew Gregory couldn't have timed his exit from the stock market with better precision if he'd wanted to assure his own ruin. His orders to sell— and to sell everything—hit the trading floor at the peak of the frenzy, and he had gone down owing his broker $5,000. Matthew Gregory was ruined, and so, too, was his Investigative Specializations Bureau. Eleanor didn't know it yet, but it changed the rules of their engagement.

Clara Davison, office secretary at the bureau since the day it opened, 22 May 1913, used once to consider herself a conservative type of woman, but in yesterday's crash she had hardly fared any better. All those months working so close to that ticker machine had worn her down eventually, and, unbeknownst to her conservative type of husband, she had been quietly playing the market for three years. Only six weeks ago, when the market was at its highest point in history, and it seemed prices could only move in one direction, she sat proudly on her secret nest-egg: swelled from $650 to almost $5,000 in just three years. Until that point she only ever bought stocks she could pay for in full. But then, it had just seemed so silly. Everyone around her was doing it. And everyone was getting so rich! She began to buy on margin, increasing her exposure more each day.

Yesterday, she lost all her savings, and half the value of her house. That Friday morning, when she arrived to open up the bureau, make Matthew Gregory's coffee, put fresh flowers in the foyer to welcome their famous client, she left the house she and her retired husband no longer owned, without quite finding a moment to tell him the bad news.

Nevertheless, she made the coffee, arranged the flowers. Both tasks took longer than usual, because her hands were shaking and because she felt sick. It was half an hour, bustling around the place, before she turned her attention to Matthew Gregory's desk.

Nine thirty a.m. He was due in at any second. She cast an eye across the desk's surface—set the coffee down, flicked some dust from the leather tabletop—and spotted the two envelopes at last.

290

One was for her, the other for Eleanor Beecham.

She lifted them both and immediately tore open her own.

My dear Mrs Davison,

I am very sorry to have to tell you that yesterday's stock collapse, which you have no doubt read about, has taken a heavy toll on my affairs. To be blunt with you, there is nothing left. The well is dry, Mrs Davison. There is no other way to put it.

I will come to the office in due course and we can discuss what we need to discuss with regard to the closing up of the business. (Please find enclosed a cheque for this month's salary. I must advise you to cash it at your earliest convenience if it is to be of any value.) In the meantime, I am afraid I am quite unwell, and my wife, who has delivered this and the other letter, has insisted that I remain in bed.

As you are aware, Mrs Beecham has an appointment with me at ten o'clock. She is generally punctual. Kindly deliver my letter to her when she comes. It is a letter explaining why I can no longer continue to help her in her inquiries. I have also enclosed an invoice. It is imperative—I must impress this upon you, and you must impress it on her—that she settles her bill before leaving the premises.

I would ask that the sum be paid in cash and, if you can manage to get this out of her, I would be very much obliged.

With my heartfelt thanks,
M Gregory

Mrs Davison had only finished reading the letter when Eleanor glided into the room, the usual cloud of lily-of-the-valley and shimmering stardust.

'Oh!' Mrs Davison cried, quite alarmed, Eleanor's unopened letter still in her hand. 'Good morning, Mrs Beecham. You're very early!'

'I am sorry,' Eleanor's husky actress voice sounded calm—no different from yesterday. 'I hope I am not disturbing you?' she asked, removing her sunglasses, seating herself in the usual chair, in front of Gregory's empty desk. 'Has Mr Gregory not arrived yet?'

'He—he has not . . . May I get you some coffee?'

'No. Thank you. What time does Mr Gregory normally get here?'

'Well . . . *normally* . . .' For a moment, Mrs Davison forgot her own troubles. She could feel herself blush, ashamed of her boss. 'Normally, he gets in about now. I mean—generally, he's very prompt. It's one of those things about him, you know? A characteristic . . .' She fell silent.

'Are you all right, Mrs Davison?' Eleanor inquired politely. 'You look pale this morning.'

'Oh! Do I? I am sorry. Yes, I'm absolutely fine.'

'My driver tells me there's been Armageddon in Wall Street.'

'Oh, yes . . .'

'I hope you're not affected?'

'Goodness. It's very kind of you . . .'

'Or Mr Gregory? I think he has some interests, doesn't he? I hope his stocks haven't suffered?' She laughed, a languid laugh that jarred rather with Mrs Davison. 'You know—I hardly dare to call home myself. I imagine it's . . .' It was Eleanor's turn to fall silent. Actually she didn't care what it was—not even enough to finish the sentence. Instead she glanced back at Mrs Davison, who stood before her, clasping Mr Gregory's two letters.

She spotted her name. 'Is that one for me?' she asked, putting out a gloved hand.

'Oh gosh. Why yes, I think it is,' said the secretary. 'I mean to say . . . *why, yes*. It is. It is from Mr Gregory. He has asked me to give it to you. He has written to me, too. And I don't think he will be coming in to see you. Not today . . .'

Eleanor didn't reply. Slowly, she removed her gloves, leaned forward to take a letter knife from Gregory's desk—silver plated, with two small revolvers crossed at the nozzles by way of a handle.

'He's not feeling terribly well . . .'

58

Dear Mrs Beecham,

Please accept my apologies. I am laid low with headache and fever and have been ordered by my good doctor not to leave my bed under any circumstances this morning. It is my greatest regret, therefore, that I am unable to deliver this painful decision to you in person.

I am sorry to tell you that, after much consideration, I cannot continue to work on your case. As Mrs Gregory eloquently put it when I discussed the case yesterday evening (leaving out all names, of course), we are 'chasing shadows'. I fear Mrs Gregory has put her finger on it.

According to public records, your mother,

Isha's grandmother and guardian, passed away in the winter of 1913, during an outbreak of tuberculosis in a building so dangerously overcrowded and with such minimal sanitation that it was later deemed unsafe for human habitation. The outbreak that killed your mother took the lives of many others, including several who were never formally identified. This, you do not deny. In all the years since that time, and despite energetic inquiries both by my father and myself, there has never been a single shred of evidence to suggest that your young daughter survived beyond that date. By your own admission young Isha was always an extremely sickly child.

Taking this into account, in conjunction with all the evidence collected and collated by myself and my father, and having had the good fortune to have spent these last few days with you, I now feel able to state, with absolute confidence, that in my opinion your beloved daughter passed away, alongside her loving grandmother, in the winter of 1913 in that dangerously overcrowded building, at that same tragic time. There is no other possible answer. My only hope is that one day you will accept this terrible truth, and find a way to continue in your life in the knowledge that your daughter is with God and at Peace, in a place where you, her Loving Mother, will one day surely join her. I grieve for you in your suffering, Mrs Beecham, I surely do. There is always a price to be paid for great fame and fortune, and you and your husband have certainly paid it.

With respect to the work my father and I have

*conducted over the years, with an additional
percentage for the discretion, so important in all
detective agency work, but especially essential in
such a case and with a person such as yourself,
please find enclosed an invoice, to be settled
with Mrs Davison immediately, before leaving
today. I must also request that you settle the
amount in cash.*

*As you can appreciate, your most particular
case, with all the secrecy required, past, present
and future, has been an unusually troublesome
one, and this has, understandably, been reflected
in my final bill.*

*Wishing you only the very best of luck in the
future. Mrs Gregory and I shall continue to look
out for all your movies.*
Matthew Gregory

Eleanor read the letter from top to bottom with
Mrs Davison standing, bird like, beside her,
nervously awaiting the response. But Eleanor's face
was impassive. She laid the letter onto the top of
Mr Gregory's desk and turned to the invoice folded
inside it. Without looking up at the secretary, she
asked her evenly:

'Do you know the contents of this already?'

'I understand there is an invoice . . .'

Eleanor arched one of her finely sculpted,
studio-approved eyebrows. 'My oh my, it is quite
some invoice,' she said.

'He wrote me you might like to settle in cash . . .'

'Yes. He wrote it to me too, though I'm not
certain what it is I am paying for exactly. Are you?
Since he's not been exactly helpful.'

'Well I think for his time perhaps . . . But I

295

know nothing about the case itself, of course,' Mrs Davison added hurriedly.

'Oh,' Eleanor smiled at her. 'But you must have a small idea. I have been looking for my daughter.'

'Well yes. Indeed. Of course, I am aware . . . so to speak. I think—if I may say so—in Mr Gregory's defence . . . Mr Gregory mentioned to me that perhaps you were searching for your daughter because . . . perhaps . . . it was so very difficult for you—or for any mother—to accept . . .'

Eleanor turned her cool gaze upon Mrs Davison, daring her to finish the sentence. Clara Davison thought better of it.

'There is no breakdown of the costs,' Eleanor continued, after a short silence. 'And I am not too clear how he reached this final figure. Are you?'

Mrs Davison wasn't sure whether to admit to the client that she didn't know what the final figure was—let alone how her employer might have reached it. So she didn't reply.

'Added to which,' Eleanor observed, 'he has crossed out the original figure . . .' She brought the paper closer. 'Which was rather lower . . . five thousand dollars lower, if you please. And put this new one beside it. He has asked me for twenty thousand dollars! Wouldn't you agree—'

Miss Davison gasped.

Eleanor nodded: '—that it's rather steep?'

'I think—may I see? It must be an error.'

'Clearly an error,' Eleanor said. Her mind was racing. He had underestimated her, of course. People often did. In his clumsy way, Matthew Gregory was attempting to blackmail her. Of course. He'd been wiped out in yesterday's crash— and the poor dub was trying to recoup what he

296

could, wherever he could. Almost . . . she felt sorry for him. What a fool he was! And what a fool *she* was—to have imagined for a moment that he might hold any answers for her, any comfort whatsoever.

He knew nothing. Not really. But he knew enough to be dangerous. With a little intelligence and effort (unlikely but always possible) he could perhaps discover more, cause unimaginable damage. It was true, on the other hand, that she had taken up some of his time. She owed him for that, and she would pay him generously for it.

She would also deal with the other matter.

'Tell Mr Gregory, would you?' she said, still without looking at the secretary, 'that I will pay him in cash. But he is to meet me, and take it from me, face to face. I need to go to the bank, of course. I'm hardly likely to carry that sort of cash around with me. Tell him I will come to his house in an hour's time.'

'Oh! Well, he might prefer to come into the bureau—'

'At his house. In an hour's time.' She stood up, put back her sunglasses. She looked down at Miss Davison. 'You need to give me the address.'

'Yes . . . Yes of course.'

'Is he ruined, then?' Eleanor asked, as an afterthought. 'Is it all over for him?'

Mrs Davison said: 'I really don't know. I think perhaps it is.'

'Has he paid you?' she asked.

'He has written me a cheque for the month, but he sounded as if he wasn't sure it would be honoured.'

Eleanor laughed. 'You've worked here for many years, I think?'

'I have, Mrs Beecham. Yes, indeed. Since the bureau opened.'

'Well. If you come with me to the bank I will give it to you in cash. Three months' wages, I think. No. Six. And I will deduct it from his final figure.'

'Oh! That's very kind of you, Mrs Beecham. Very kind.'

Eleanor brushed it aside. 'Thank Mr Gregory.'

'Are you really going to pay him as much as he is asking? If I may say, it seems a tremendous figure.'

Eleanor was already at the other end of the room, sweeping past the infernal ticker machine, still tick-ticking away. 'Certainly not,' she replied. She turned back to the secretary. 'Are you coming or aren't you?'

59

Matthew Gregory stood at his front parlour window in pyjamas and dressing gown, sweating less with the fever than with acute discomfort at his own conduct. He waited impatiently for her car to arrive. Clara Davison had called to tell him Eleanor Beecham was on her way, but would she really come, he wondered. And with so much cash? His secretary hadn't wanted to talk. She'd delivered the message and ended the call before he had a chance to question her. Now, all he could do was wait.

At length, a taxi drew up outside the house. In a flash he was out of his front door and trotting nervously down the neat garden path towards it. Under no circumstances did he want Eleanor to meet his wife and daughter. Not now. Nor ever. He wanted the business over and done with. He wanted the money and then for her to be gone, preferably never to be seen or thought of again.

He was beside the car before she could climb out. He opened the door himself and stood in such a way that it was impossible for her to step down.

'Mrs Beecham,' he said, beads of sweat at his forehead. 'How very kind of you to come . . .'

He was nervous, she noticed. More nervous than she was. Eleanor stayed where she was, settled in the back seat of the car.

'I received your letter.'

'Yes. Indeed.' He looked around him, unsure quite what to do next. He wanted to apologize.

'Why don't you climb in?' she suggested.

His shoulders—his face—softened in relief.

'Well—if I may,' he said.

'I just this minute suggested it,' she snapped. 'Of course you may.'

'Excuse my attire. As you know,' he mumbled, climbing in, 'I am feeling a little unwell.'

What had possessed her, she wondered, as she watched him, fussily tucking his robe around him, to confide in such a man? What idiocy, what desperation, what loneliness? It didn't matter anyway, not any more. She waited as he settled himself.

'It's hot today,' he said. 'Very, very hot. Or is it only me who feels it?'

She didn't reply.

'Well. And first of all, Mrs Beecham, thank you. Thank you for coming out this way. I would invite you in. But the little one has her cousins around—I think you would find it too noisy.'

'I think you are quite right,' she interrupted him.

'I am "chasing shadows", as you put it.'

'It was Mrs Gregory—'

'Strangely enough, I was coming to your office this morning having arrived at much the same conclusion myself.' It amazed her that she could voice it so evenly, her morning conclusion that all hope was gone. 'I have been chasing shadows,' she said again.

A heavy pause. Torn between financial desperation and (confronted now by her actual presence) simple, human sympathy for a grieving mother, Mr Gregory lifted a hand, small and hot, and placed it gently upon hers: cool to the touch, he noticed, fragile, bony, even through the gloves.

She snatched it away. 'I have brought you some cash.'

'Oh!'

'You sound surprised.'

'No! That is to say. It is not just about the money. I wanted to say how sorry I was . . .'

'Yes, of course.'

'I mean it,' he said. And so he did, at the instant. 'I am so very sorry.'

'You asked for fifteen thousand dollars. And then added another five thousand. In the same letter.'

'Yes, I . . . there were some incidentals. Expenses and so on, which I had failed to take into account.'

'I have decided to pay you six thousand dollars. I think it's more than generous.'

He glanced at her—a slithery, sidelong look, hoping not to catch her eye. But it seemed that she was gazing at him quite coolly. Or he thought she was. It was hard to tell, behind the sunglasses. 'I can't really see your eyes,' he complained.

300

'Of which,' she continued, 'I have given one thousand dollars, in cash, to your secretary. It seems the least you could give to her, after all her years of service. I understand the agency is kaput.'

'I am afraid so.'

'What will you do? Return to your job at the police force?'

'I think so. If they'll have me . . .'

She shrugged. She hardly cared. She passed him a large envelope. 'Five thousand dollars. In cash,' she said. 'Do you want to count it?'

'Hardly! No. Gosh no. I'm sure it's correct . . . But I asked for—'

'You asked for too much.'

'Yes,' he said. She wondered what kind of a man he was, to crumple so quickly. 'I suppose you are right.'

She leaned forward . . . *Lily of the Valley, shimmer and stardust* . . . He felt a little faint. She dropped her voice to a low whisper, removed her sunglasses, fixed her fathomless green eyes on his. 'Understand this, Mr Gregory,' she said quietly. 'I have told you things nobody else knows. Nobody in the world . . .'

'Yes . . .'

'If I hear a word: if a hint of a whisper of a word of what I have told you ever comes out—'

'No!'

'I will come after you . . . Understand?'

'Yes, yes. Yes, of course . . .'

'I will find you. And your little daughter. And your wife. And the new one, on the way.'

'Of course.'

'And I will send a man to kill you.'

He stopped, as if, for a moment, he might have

301

laughed. But then he looked at her again, through the haze of shimmering stardust, into the green eyes that had seen so much. And he nodded. Patted the envelope. Without another word, he slipped out of the car and scampered up his garden path, to his beloved daughter and to his wife with another-on-the-way, closed the front door behind him and didn't look back, not once, nor ever again.

60

Sitting at his well-ordered desk in the swankiest office at Lionsfiel, fiddling idly with a fountain pen of heavy gold, always so pleasant to the touch, Butch Menken reflected, briefly, on his considerable achievements, and felt dissatisfied.

Reflection of this sort was always a bad idea. Normally he was clever enough to avoid it. But on this occasion, on the cusp of so much, and with nothing urgent to distract him, he could hardly help himself. Time was crawling, according to his platinum watch. He missed Eleanor.

He missed Max.

It was all very well, a man's life going according to plan. And on every front, it appeared, he couldn't put a foot wrong. Even now, while America floundered in confusion and debt, Butch Menken was making money. He hadn't sold his interests in the stock market. For a man who liked to pit his intelligence against the world, it would have been too simple. He was still out there, still buying and selling. But he was betting on a falling market. He was selling short, and cleaning up.

302

Black Thursday was a golden Thursday for Butch. He made $250,000 in a single day. And now, since money itself never had been a driving force, he had more money than really interested him.

And Max was down and out. For the moment, at least. Butch had seen to that.

And he was about to embark on the job he had always wanted. He was going to create a super-studio in his image. He smiled, struck briefly by the inelegance of his insatiable ambition. It would be only be a matter of time, he calculated—five years, let's say, before the studio was renamed Silverman & Menken Pictures. Menken & Silverman. Menken.

In any case, this morning, he had achieved it all, he had it all—more than he knew what to do with—and he felt lonely and empty and (which was more unusual) even a little bored.

A man could be too clever. And he wanted Eleanor home.

It was noon. He'd sent her another wire early this morning, and she ought to have received it by now. Why didn't she call? Did she not realize how much she needed him? Damn her.

It was just then, just as he was damning her for not needing him enough, that the call from Reno came through. Eleanor. He could tell from the way she spoke his name—one single syllable—that something inside her had shifted.

'Butch?'

'Baby! I've been worried! Where are you?'

'I am still in Reno. I'm coming home.'

'You're coming home! Thank God! Are you all right? What happened?'

'Nothing happened. I went to see my detective,

that's all. I gave him a lot of money. And it's over. I know it's over. I'm coming home.'

He felt a leap—of triumph, perhaps. Or was it disappointment? Was it possible, he wondered, to feel both at the same time? 'What's "over", baby? What are you saying? Are you OK? You sound strange.'

'I'm saying . . .' And then she said it. The thing she needed to say—what she had called him to say. To practise saying aloud, before she said it to Max. She had said it to the mirror. She had said it to Mr Gregory. And now she said it again. 'That I have accepted it.'

'Accepted *what?*'

'That my Isha is gone. She is dead, Butch. She died. A long time ago.' And this time, as she said it, though her voice was level—she sounded to Butch almost conversational—the tears coursed down her cheeks.

It wasn't what Butch had been expecting to hear. He had almost . . . it seemed absurd, but he had already almost forgotten about the child. Isha. *Isha* . . . Of course, she was in Reno to find the child. He didn't know what to say. What was he meant to say? Or to feel? Until yesterday he'd not even known 'Isha' existed.

'I'm very sorry,' he said, and could hear how inept it was. 'Are you all right, darling?' He wanted to talk about the new contract. There was so much he wanted to talk about—things that were relevant. Things that weren't *dead*.

'She died in 1913. With her grandmother. I think they must have died together—at the same time. On the same day. I think so.'

'I guess so . . .'

304

'It's OK.'

'Yes . . . Is it?'

'It's OK.' But of course it wasn't. She was weeping. 'People die. Children die. People die every day, don't they Butch? People die . . .'

'Honey?'

She didn't answer.

'Baby, I think you need to come home.'

'I'm coming home. I told you.'

'You sound—'

'I'm fine.'

'You want me to come out to Reno?' he asked, gently. She was not fine. 'I can come and get you, baby. If you need me. I can rent a plane and bring you home. It would be easy—'

'No. Thank you, Butch. I'm leaving some things here, and I'm taking the train. There's stuff I need to say to Max . . . And then I'll come back here. It'll probably take a few weeks, won't it?'

This time, he knew what she meant. He felt another skirmish of emotion: triumph tinged with sadness. And alarm. His landscape was shifting, he wasn't sure quite how, nor if he liked it quite as much as he had always supposed he would.

'Baby—listen to me,' he said. 'There are a couple of things I need to tell you. A couple of things that have happened since we spoke. And a couple of things I meant to tell you, which I should have told you before. But you need to know them, before you speak with Max.'

'I know about the crash,' she said quickly. 'I suppose Max and I have lost a lot of money . . .'

'Well,' Butch shrugged. 'I don't know about that . . . You said he was in pretty deep.'

'Have you?'

'Have I what?'

'Lost money?'

'No.'

'Oh.' Eleanor let his answer settle. 'Well. That's good,' she said kindly. 'Clever Butch.'

'Max got fired.'

'Hm?'

'He's lost his job. Silverman had to let him go . . . I fought for him. I did what I could . . .'

Eleanor listened, confused. Why would Butch fight for Max? Why would Butch have anything to do with it? Why was Butch telling her this—now? She said nothing, waited for him to continue.

'Joel didn't like the final cut for *Lost At Sea*,' Butch continued. 'And he was right. It was unreleasable. He said Max had to go back to the edit—and Max wouldn't do it. He destroyed all the dailies. God knows what he did with them. But they're gone.'

'He did that?' In spite of everything, the deadness in her heart, Eleanor smiled at the story, at Max's indomitable spirit. 'He loved that movie,' she said.

'It wasn't his best.'

'It's a good movie, Butch.'

'Well, we have to disagree on that.'

'But you never saw it.'

Another hefty pause. Finally he said: 'Actually, I did. Actually—this is what I've been trying to tell you. This is my final day at Lionsfiel, El. Next week I start at Silverman. If you'd been in town this past week, you would have heard about it before, but it was announced in the trades day before yesterday . . .' Butch couldn't keep the small trace of pride from

306

his voice: 'Executive producer, El . . .'

A crackling silence on the line.

'Look out Irving Thalberg, huh?' he said.

Still, she didn't speak.

'It's good news for you too, El,' he continued quietly.

'I'm sure it is,' she said vaguely. 'Well done, darling.' But why was he talking about Thalberg? She had called to tell him about her daughter.

'. . . need to know that Carrascosa isn't going to renew . . .' he was saying. 'But you realized that, didn't you? Your contract with Lionsfiel ends month after next, and they're not renewing.'

'I didn't know that,' she said.

'I told you. I warned you . . . El, did you even look at the script they sent?'

'Script?'

'*PostBoy*.'

'*PostBoy* . . .' She sounded the word. 'I didn't see it, no.'

'Well . . .' He sighed, frustrated with her. Even now, she didn't seem to care. 'El—I know things are difficult for you right now. I understand. But, baby, your contract's been up for renewal. Your numbers have been lousy. You didn't think the script might have offered you an indication?'

'Indication of what?'

'Come on, El! Your future here at Lionsfiel.'

'I left in a hurry . . .'

'You should've read it, baby. You would've been prepared.'

Eleanor felt an urge—inexplicable—to laugh. She said: 'Prepared for what?'

'You don't even come in until midway through Act Three! You play the girl's *mother*!'

307

It wasn't something she wanted to think about. Not right now. It was the last thing on earth she wanted to think about. 'Butch—can we talk about this when I get home? I know it's important. Of course it's important. Everything is so important, isn't it? Oh poor Max! I must speak with him. Have you spoken with him, Butch? Is he OK?'

Butch pictured Max as he'd seen him last, spatters of Butch's blood on his shirt, pleading with Butch to tell him the whereabouts of his wife as he was dragged from this very room. 'Max is OK,' Butch said impatiently. 'Max'll be just fine. Baby, it's you I'm worried about. Are you still there? Your voice is terribly faint.'

'I'm here.'

'What's that?'

'I said I'm here.'

'Baby—can you hear me? Listen El, I'm going to get you a new contract. A nice, watertight contract at Silverman. It's the first thing I'm going to do. Understand? You're going to be OK. I'm going to look after you and we're going to make some great movies together! . . . El? Can you hear me?' The crackling was getting louder: a precursor, normally, to the line cutting off altogether. So there was an urgency in Butch's voice. He wanted her to travel back to LA comforted by the knowledge that, in spite of everything, she would be all right. He would take care of her.

'What about Max?' she asked.

'Max?' Butch smothered his irritation. 'I told you, Max can look after himself. Better than anyone else I know,' he added bitterly.

'Except you, Butch.'

'Huh? What's that? I can't hear you! Baby, can

308

you hear me?'

'Yes! I can hear you. But I have to go. Or I shall miss the train.

'El?'

'Yes, Butch?'

His voice lost its edge. 'Take care of yourself,' he said softly. An image of her supple body, warm and giving, floated through him: all the passion she revealed in his bed. Damn, he missed her. 'I want you home . . .'

She sighed. A long, low sigh, audible above the crackle. It could have meant anything. She hardly knew what it meant herself. But she missed him, too. In all sorts of ways.

Perhaps, she thought. *Perhaps . . .*

And the line went dead.

61

Saturday 26 October 1929

She sent a wire to Max before she left Reno, telling him she was coming home. But he wasn't at the station to greet her.

She took a taxicab to the *Castillo*, the house they had built together, and as the car turned up the short winding drive she knew, somehow, that he wouldn't be there. She gazed at it—her home. In all its redundant grandeur, it seemed to mock her: for the hope it once represented, for everything she and Max had once invested in it. It offered the opposite of comfort.

Teresa and Joseph came out to welcome her as

if she were a forgotten soldier returning from the front. In the few days since Eleanor had left, the world had turned upside down. It said so in every paper. Max had all but vanished. And they were frightened for their livelihoods.

'Where is Mr Beecham?' Eleanor asked, as they unloaded her cases for her. 'Have you seen him today?'

Teresa shook her head. 'We haven't seen him. Not for two days at least. It's been so quiet here. And then, with all the stories . . .' She stopped, uncertain if it was her place to continue, but unable to resist. 'The big stock market crash. It's all anyone talks about. Somebody is ruined. Somebody else is ruined. They are throwing themselves off the top of buildings, Mrs Beecham! I say to Joseph, and Joseph says to me: "We sure hope Mr and Mrs Beecham aren't ruined!" But you're not ruined, are you, Mrs Beecham?'

Eleanor smiled. 'Of course not,' she said wanly. 'And whatever happens, Teresa, you and Joseph mustn't worry. We will look after you.'

They had come into the house and were standing together at the foot of the grand stairway, the stairway Max had designed. He had come home to the little bungalow on Poinsettia, where they were living while the *Castillo* was being built. He was carrying some early sketches, something he had drawn in ink on the back of a linen restaurant napkin, just as he sometimes sketched the sets for his own films.

There would be black-and-white marble floors, he said, and, from the marble floors, the stairs would sweep in two expanding spirals: like a stage set, he said, like something Cinderella might have swept and spiralled along herself, in her magical dress, on her way to the prince's ball. It's what Max had said when he first showed her the drawings.

'You can pretend you are Cinderella,' he said. 'Every single morning, when you come down for breakfast!'

She had laughed. 'Who? Me or you? We are both Cinderellas, aren't we?

'Certainly not!'

'Well then, who are you, darling? If not someone who has hauled themselves from the gutter and the dust . . . And the cinders . . .'

'I, my love,' he kissed her tenderly, 'I am a phoenix. Risen from the cinders without any help from any goddamn prince. Thank you. And so are you.'

It wasn't true, though, and she knew it. Without Max, she would still be in New York, probably bent over a sewing machine, probably counting the hours and the pennies . . . It was Max who had turned her into a star.

In any case, there was no phoenix, nor any Prince Charming awaiting her at the *Castillo* this morning. She wondered why the memory came to her today, of all days. The house was too painfully empty. Maybe that was it. It had been built with hope, and today she returned to it with none.

'Teresa,' she said. 'Could you run me a bath? And perhaps could you ask Joseph to prepare the car? I think I'll change and go straight into town.'

'Will Joseph be driving you?'

'No. Thank you. I shall drive myself.'

Eleanor knew where Blanche Williams lived; she knew the block and the apartment number. She knew where Max was. She intended to drive

311

directly to the address, to sit outside the building's entrance until she could slip in unnoticed. How she would get into the apartment itself, she had yet to consider, but after so many years of looking away, it's what she intended to do. She wanted to walk right in there and catch them at it.

As she turned from Teresa, she pictured them, tangled together—Max and Blanche.

Eleanor and Butch.

Him, eyes glazed, shoulders glistening, a moment passing; watching the two of them being lost in each other . . . Blanche seeing her first, perhaps. Max turning, glazed eyes unglazing. Snapping into focus.

No. There was no need for that.

'You know what?' she said to Teresa. 'Don't bother Joseph.' She smiled. 'On second thoughts, I prefer to track down Mr Beecham via the telephone.'

62

Their limbs were not tangled. Far from it. They were hunched over the newspapers at Blanche's sunny breakfast table, reading reports on the Wall Street meltdown. It was the second consecutive night—the only two nights—they had spent together, and they had resurfaced this morning to a changed world.

Blanche, at Max's urging, had engaged his stockbroker, but she had gambled less heavily than he. She had held out against buying stocks on margin and, this morning, looking at Max's handsome face, grey beneath the California burnish, she was more grateful for it than she could say. She would rather die (so she said) than turn to her parents for financial help. Now—thank God—she didn't need to. Her savings had taken a knock but she was still solvent.

That Saturday morning the papers seemed to be convinced that the markets would stabilize. Readers were being urged to snap up bargain stocks while prices were dipping.

'What do you think?' she said to Max, pouring them both more coffee. 'You think they're right?'

But he didn't answer.

'Max? What do you think?'

'I think,' he said, 'that I'm probably not the best person to ask.'

She frowned. It didn't sound like Max.

They had both spoken to their broker that morning. Blanche, only briefly, but Max at some length. Blanche had tactfully retired to the bedroom while the conversation went on. And on. When he finally joined her he looked shell-shocked. She didn't ask how the conversation had gone. It was clear it hadn't gone well—and she could have guessed in any case.

She looked at him now, sitting at her small breakfast table, not yet fully dressed. His white shirt was hanging undone, strong chest, lean stomach casually exposed. A sight for sore eyes, he was. Except, it struck her, he did seem rather *big*. At her little table. *Too* big, in her pretty apartment, with its red velvet couch, and no room to swing a cat. She'd never noticed before how small her living room was. But after two days with Max's shoes by the tiny hearth, and his jacket in a messy heap by the bookshelf . . .

313

She'd thought, when she asked him about the other girl—the girl with the movie-star looks who'd followed her home from the grocery two nights earlier, who'd asked for him by name with eyes welling, as if she were about to burst into sobs any second—that no matter how well he lied, she would never believe his denials, and no matter what he said, it would be like a knife in her heart . . . But then somehow, when it came to it, the conversation came and went. Max, of course, denied any knowledge of the woman, and though Blanche didn't believe him, not even for a second, somehow her heart had never felt so terribly involved. Once a cheat, always a cheat . . . If he could cheat on his wife, he could cheat on her . . . and he did look *so* terribly *big*. In her little home.

'What are you going to do, Max?'

He didn't answer.

'Max?' A hint of impatience now. 'Darling, I want to help you. Are you going to be OK? Are you . . . I mean to say: what are you going to do? You were talking for ages. How bad is it? Max?'

Ostentatiously, he turned a page of his newspaper.

'Max! Come on! I can help you! Why won't you answer me?'

At last he looked up. 'I would tell you, baby, if I only knew. But it's hard to calculate. There's stock I haven't sold, but he's telling me I have to sell it. I suppose I could give you a rough idea of just how bad it is. Only why would I? Why do you want to know?'

'*Why?*' she repeated, outraged. 'Because, of course I do, Max. Because . . .'

Why did she want to know?

314

Maybe he was right. Maybe it was better not to know. Maybe, if they simply carried on as if—

'I'm cleaned out, Blanche,' he said abrupty, folding his paper, watching her face. 'Bust. Done. Dusted. Screwed. Fucked. What do you want me to call it? I don't much mind. Not really . . .' He sounded surprised to hear himself say it. 'But the fact is I'm sitting here now, baby, drinking your coffee . . . and I swear, I haven't got a pot to piss in! How about that?'

Blanche gazed quietly back at him, and he at her. 'Huh,' she said at last. 'That's pretty bad.'

'You think?'

'What are you going to do? I can—'

Already, he was shaking his head. 'Sweetheart,' he said, 'you have enough on your plate, taking care of your own affairs. Don't you go worrying about me.' He flashed her a smile, not a warm one—but he covered it up by stretching across her dainty little breakfast table and dropping a kiss on her cheek. 'You'd be amazed, the scrapes I've got myself out of before now.'

'Oh. I know it!' she said.

But she didn't know, and she would have been amazed. And at that instant, in her ignorance, she lost a little faith. Because of the row over the dailies for *Lost At Sea*, and then the fist-fight with the new executive producer at Silverman Pictures, and then the fall in share prices on Wall Street, Max appeared before her not quite the all-conquering king of Hollywood and king of her dreams; but as a man, rather older than she, and too big for her breakfast table. 'I love you,' she said. Because just then, at that instant, it occurred to her for the first time that perhaps she might not.

315

He observed it. He leaned over towards her again; slowly, lazily, ran a finger along her forearm and enjoyed the effect of it in her eyes. She shivered. Looked away. 'You never have to worry about me,' he said softly, his voice caressing, his gaze peeling away her irritation, her concern, her reservations, making her wonder if, after all, they couldn't just forget about everything else—stock exchanges, missing wives and pots to piss in—and go back to bed. She was about to suggest as much but, just then, as abruptly as he turned his attention upon her, he turned away again. He dropped his hand. 'I can look after myself,' he said. 'Been doing it since before you were born.' And he picked up his newspaper again.

For several minutes they read on in silence, or pretended to read. The window onto the street was ajar, and they could hear traffic below. It sounded angrier than usual, more like New York than California: honking horns and drivers' voices raised. The markets had already closed for the weekend but the mood of uncertainty permeated. Everyone was on edge.

Blanche regretted having riled him. At that instant she didn't give a fig for her savings, or his. If he didn't want to talk to her about his wife, his work, his finances—what did she care? As long as she could work, and keep her little apartment. As long as Max would take her back to bed.

'Max . . . ?' she murmured.

He looked up—thinking: yes, absolutely. Hell, why not?

The shrill ring of Blanche's telephone broke through the silence, making her jump. 'Leave it,' he said softly, leaning in.

But she couldn't leave it. She simply couldn't. Because—in the end—who knew who it might be? It might be anyone!

She couldn't leave it ringing.

So up she stood, neat and pretty, tripped round the table, playfully swiping his hand away as he reached for her, and picked up the telephone.

She answered in a silly voice, because she knew Max was listening, and because she was faintly ashamed that she had been unable to resist the call. It would ruin the mood, of course. And afterwards they might not go to bed after all. Damn it.

'Well howdee-doodie out there!' she sing-songed, idiotically. 'This is the Blanche Williams residence! One and only Blanche Williams speaking. How may I be of assistance to you on this beautiful-though-turbulent-in-Wall-Street morning?'

'Hello, Blanche. This is Eleanor Beecham.'

'Oh!' Stricken, she turned back to look at Max, watching her with lazy desire. 'I am . . . I am very well,' she said, though Eleanor hadn't enquired. 'Thank you. Eleanor . . . It's so good to hear from you.'

'Would you please put Max on?'

'M-Max? Max Beecham, you mean?'

'Could I speak to him please?'

'He's not . . . That is to say, Mrs Beecham,' she turned away from him, the better to deliver the lie, 'I don't know what makes you think . . . Mr Beecham really isn't here—'

Before she could say any more, the telephone was snatched from her hand. Max had already crossed the room and taken it.

'El? *El? Is it you?* Where in hell are you?'

The shock of hearing his voice stunned her for a

moment. Even though she had been certain where she would find him, even though she had known all this time, all these years, the *fact* of his being there, the fact of his failing to hide it . . . should have changed nothing at all, but it changed everything.

In the silence, he guessed all that. He wished, more than he wished anything, that he had held back. He said: 'Eleanor, are you OK?'

'Of course I'm "OK",' she snapped. 'Why does everyone keep asking me if I'm OK? Yes, I'm "OK". I'm alive, aren't I? You can hear me speaking.'

'Where are you?' he asked again. 'Where have you been all this time?'

'I am . . .' She was going to say 'at home'. But it didn't feel like home. Nowhere felt like home. Nothing. She said instead: 'I am at the house. Do we still own it?' But she didn't wait for an answer. She didn't care. 'Perhaps—you might be kind enough to join me here for breakfast?'

'Yes—*yes!*' he said. 'Eleana . . . yes. I'm on my way.'

Eleana.

'Matz,' she murmured, but not really to him. And there was so much sadness in her voice he could not bring himself to reply. He nodded, dumbly, into the telephone. 'Matz,' she said. 'We have a lot to talk about.'

63

By the time he reached the *Castillo*, Eleanor had bathed and changed. She had sent Teresa out with

318

a list of groceries, and, for the first time in many years, she had cooked.

She was wearing a simple dress, older than her marriage and not worn since. It was a sunshine-yellow crêpe affair, looser fitting than when last she put it on. Max recognized it at once, of course. She'd worn it for the breakfast scene in *Poppy Girl!*, the first movie they'd made together. He'd thought she looked beautiful in it then. This morning— perhaps because he'd missed her, perhaps because he sensed this might be the last breakfast they ate together—he thought she looked more beautiful than ever.

She didn't glance up as he came in. She was spooning cheese blintz into her mouth, sitting alone at the head of their ebony dining table (commissioned in a different life, to complement their black-and-white marble floor). Sunlight flooded through the French windows behind her, and spread out on the tabletop in front was a feast: a traditional Jewish breakfast the like of which Max had not eaten, nor Eleanor provided, since their wedding day, ten years ago. *Latke* and honeycake, apple fritters, apricots, bagels and warm challah . . . there was enough to feed twenty people. The heady scent of it churned up memories, a wistfulness he generally kept under tight control. It made his eyes and his mouth water, and his stomach turn with misery.

'Eleanor?' he said, staring at her, not quite sure where to start. His hands ached. 'What's with the feast? I thought you didn't like breakfast?'

'*Es tsegeyt zikh in moyl.*' She pushed the blintze towards him, still not looking at him. 'I made them myself, Matz. Everything else is bought . . . Eat!

319

They're good.'

'They smell good,' he said. And they did smell good. Of youth and happiness. She cooked them last, he remembered, to greet Isha and Batia to Hollywood. She had laid out the food before they left for the train station that morning, and there it still was when they returned, and there it stayed the following day, and the day after that. Like Miss Havisham's wedding feast. He felt sick.

'Are we ruined, Max?' she asked mildly. 'I imagine we are. I suppose we probably are. Teresa's very worried. But I've told her we'll take care of her. She has nothing to worry about.'

'Teresa has nothing to worry about.'

'Good.' Silence, while she ate some more. And then: 'What have you done, darling, with all our money?' She looked up at him at last. He dropped his gaze, ashamed to catch her eye. He pulled back an ebony chair, built to match the ebony table, to match the marble floor, and dropped himself into it.

'It's easier, isn't it?' she said. 'We can talk about the money.' She spooned in another forkful of blintz, too big for her mouth. 'And then we can talk about the rest of it,' she said, through the food. 'We have a lot to talk about. Don't we?'

He broke off some challah, held it between finger and thumb, scrutinized it as if it would help him to phrase an answer. 'What have I done with our money?' he repeated, at last.

'Oh God! Never mind the money!' she said impatiently. 'I assume it is all gone. Never mind, Matz. We made it once. We can make it again. Money is nothing.'

He nodded. 'We shall have to sell the house.'

'Good.'

He smiled, eyes still on the challah. 'Where did you get all this stuff?' he asked at last. 'I thought you didn't like this food?'

'I hate it,' she said, reaching for honeycake. 'But it's delicious, isn't it?'

He nodded. 'Of course it is.' There was a glaze in her eyes, almost, Max thought, as if she were sleep talking. 'Eleanor, darling, are you all right?'

'Stop asking me that!'

'I'm sorry. But baby, you're acting crazy . . .'

'Crazy?'

'Well—'

'What kind of crazy?'

'I don't know—I don't know, El. It doesn't matter.'

'How should I act, Matz? Tell me that. How am I supposed to act? Under these difficult circumstances? We have no money left. Shall we start with that?'

'I'm just so goddamn relieved to see you . . .'

'Oh. Really?'

'Of course, *oh really*. God dammit, Eleanor . . .'

'God dammit,' she muttered back.

'Where the hell have you been this past week? I've been worried to death.'

'Yes. I can tell. It certainly seems that way . . .'

'Baby—if this is about Blanche . . .'

Suddenly, like a wild creature, she leapt from her seat, thumped her fist onto the table; honeycake jumped, coffee cup rattled. 'Of course it's not about BLANCHE!'

'Because if it is—'

'Don't you hear me? I said of course it's not about *Blanche*. You think I give a damn about

321

ridiculous "Blanche"?'

'Well I . . .' He shrugged, looked at his wife. 'I guess . . . I sort of hope you do . . .' He sounded less confident now: truly, out of his depth. 'Where have you been, baby?

'Tell me . . .'

As abruptly as she had lost her temper, she collected herself again. 'Butch tells me you've been fired,' she said, sitting back in her seat. 'I'm so sorry about that. It's a bad time for that to happen. On top of all this. He says he fought for you. But I somehow doubt it.'

'*Butch* tells you . . .'

She brushed it aside.

'What else does *Butch* tell you—'

'*Matz,*' she interrupted. '*Matz* . . .' She leaned forward and reached for his arm, eyes so full of sadness; he caught his breath.

The thought whistled through his head before he could stop it, *If we could capture* that *for the camera* . . .

'Matz,' she was saying to him, 'how often do you remember Isha? How often do you wonder where she is, what she is doing, what became of her? We never talk about her. Never. Do you think of her at all?

'Do I ever think of Isha?' he repeated softly.

'Do you?' she leaned closer. 'Tell me . . .'

'*Do I ever think of Isha?*' he said it again.

There it was, at last: the question she had never asked. The question she never asked, because she already believed she had the answer. It was the reason she hated him. The reason for everything. He looked back at her then, leaning towards him, asking him for comfort with her fathomless green

322

eyes, because she imagined that the suffering and the guilt, the loss and the pain and the darkness which never lifted was hers and only hers. And he hated her for it. After all these years, how dared she ask him such a question? How dared she imagine that she alone suffered with their grief? He wanted to lash out, not quite at her, but—yes, at her: at those wild eyes, swimming in sadness. It's what he wanted to do, and with one swipe, destroy the memories, all the years of silence between them.

He smiled instead, while his head throbbed with anger, and he made a sound that might almost have been mistaken for a laugh. 'You ask me that?' he said to her. 'After so many years?'

'Why?' she spat back, misreading him—not reading him at all, drawing from the well of bitterness that had coloured everything between them for so long. 'You think it wrong of me to mention Isha's name? *Is that it?* I can't even mention her now? I cannot mention my own daughter? Damn you, Max. I *shall* ask you that! Tell me! Do you ever think of our daughter? The little girl we left behind—the little girl *you* left behind. YOU left behind.'

He shook his head. 'You are cruel, Eleana . . .'

'I hope so.'

Silence again.

Distantly, from the bottom of the drive, came the sound of the iron gates opening. Joseph should have oiled them, Eleanor thought. He usually remembered.

The iron gates banged closed again. An engine was purring up the drive.

'Where have you been all week?' he asked again,

323

his tone changing. 'You still haven't told me. I have been worried to death. I have missed you.'

'I don't think so.'

'Were you with Butch?'

'No.'

'I don't believe you.'

She shrugged. She said, 'I was in Reno. With a detective.'

'Detective?'

She tore off a corner of honeycake, rolled it between thumb and forefinger. 'I forget his name,' she said. 'It doesn't matter.'

Outside, the car came to a stop. They could hear Teresa's heels tack-tack-tacking across the marble to attend to it.

'I went to Reno to see a detective. I thought he would help me to find her. But nobody can. You can't find someone who is already dead. Can you? No. And Isha is gone. You have known it for a long time. Only I have refused to accept it . . . but she is gone. I accept it now.'

Matz let the words fall. Shook his head. He didn't want to hear them. As long as Eleanor had hoped, he realized, then he could hope too. But with his wife's acceptance, what faint light still remained would be snuffed out, once and for all. Darkness. The lid of that small coffin would be closed shut. He stood up, crossed the room to behind Eleanor's chair. He pulled at her so that she stood up, and he turned her round to face him, put his arms around her, and they embraced. Tired, so very tired, she rested her head on his shoulder.

He held her like that, and she held him, while the bell clanged, the front door opened and closed; and Teresa tack-tack-tacked across the marble towards them.

'Max,' Eleanor said, her words muffled by his shoulder. 'I want a divorce.'

'Of course,' he said wearily. 'Of course. And so do I.'

64

Teresa tapped on the dining-room door. 'Mrs Beecham?' She sounded excited. 'Mr Beecham? . . . I am so sorry to disturb you, but I have a letter . . . Mr Randolph Hearst's driver is here. He is waiting for a reply . . .'

A memory stirred in Eleanor. She moaned. After all these years of hoping for the wretched thing, here it was—and she had completely forgotten. They were expected at San Simeon this Monday. Day after tomorrow. She didn't move.

'Mrs Beecham?' Teresa tapped once again. 'Shall I leave the letter out here for you?' Eleanor shrugged herself away from him, and Max went to the door.

He took the envelope and turned back into the room. Marion's initials were engraved on the outside. He held it up to Eleanor. 'Is this what I think it is?' he asked.

Eleanor nodded. 'She's expecting us Monday. I had forgotten. We'll have to cancel.'

Max tore it open. Enclosed, along with the traditional tickets for the first-class sleeper, leaving the following evening, there was a handwritten note from Marion.

Darlings,

I haven't heard a squeak from you since your wonderful party and I know it was all such terribly short notice, added to which the entire world has gone stark-staring crazy since. But you sweetly agreed to come stay with us up at the Ranch this Monday. Do you remember? I'm not at all sure you do remember, darlings, since it was awfully late in the evening when we discussed it, and now the world has gone topsy-turvy.

I know it's been a rotten week for all of us, but I do believe it's vital we put on our jolliest faces now more than ever. I hope so much that you agree with me.

Here are the train tickets, darlings—because I'm simply praying you haven't forgotten and you do agree. And by the way, since you're both between movies, I insist you stay on until at least Thursday. It's only a small house party, but we shall make a wonderfully merry band. And you know how I detest to be a bossy-boo, but could you be terribly sweet and leave a little note with my driver, just for my peace of mind? Because I simply have to know that you're coming because if you aren't then I shall probably cancel the whole entire thing.

The train leaves tomorrow evening and your tickets are in the envelope. I have a wonderful surprise for you both. You simply MUST come!

X Marion

Max glanced at Marion's postcard, the tone of which seemed so jarring to him. He passed it to Eleanor without comment.

326

'Too bad, huh?' he said, crossing to the French window, looking out onto the terrace. He turned and smiled at her.

She nodded. Dropped the card onto the table. It landed on her cheese blintz: 'Too bad.'

'I wonder what's the surprise?' Max said.

'Do you?'

'. . . Not really. No.'

'A party. Or something. Probably. Or a screening.' Eleanor smiled. 'Maybe she found the dailies for *Lost At Sea*. Maybe she's stuck 'em all back together . . .'

'Huh.'

A long pause. It seemed unbelievable, what had passed between them only moments before.

'So,' she said, looking at his back, willing him to turn around. 'What do we do now? Shall you . . . ?' She couldn't bring herself to finish the sentence.

In the long journey from Reno, when she knew what had to be done, why hadn't she considered such questions?

Where would he go? Would he return to Blanche now? Would they lock up the house and sell it and forget everything and forget each other and move swiftly, smoothly to the arms of their lovers? 'God, Max,' she said. 'Help me. What do we do now?'

He said, automatically, what he always said when he saw that anxious face, heard the anxious voice, saw all the sadness churning behind those eyes. 'It's going to be OK, El.'

'Is it? How?'

He didn't answer. 'What do you want to do?' he asked instead. 'I guess . . .' He stopped. Forced himself to finish: 'I suppose Butch knows about this decision?'

327

'No.'

He nodded, wondered if it was true. 'So,' he tried again. 'Maybe I should go fetch some stuff. I guess that's what I'll do.' But he didn't move.

It's one thing, deciding on a course of action, another one setting it into motion. For an instant, it seemed to be quite beyond them both.

'You know,' she said, 'you never actually answered . . .'

'Answered what?' But he knew what. He sighed. How could she ever have imagined it would be any different? 'She is never away from me, Eleanor. Never. And nor are you . . .'

She nodded. 'It's too late for us now. Isn't it?'

A long pause. 'I think so,' he said at last.

So they stood there, unable to move forward, unable to go back.

'Right then,' Max said.

'I suppose you will live with Blanche?'

He shook his head. 'I'll find a hotel. And you? What will you do? Move in with Butch, I suppose?'

It occurred to them both, the absurdity of the exchange: of all the things they had to say to each other, the things that had been left unsaid, all the ways they could have helped each other, yet these were the words they exchanged. Eleanor didn't offer an answer. She didn't have one, in any case.

There came another tap on the door, and then Teresa's voice, calling through from the hall. 'Mr Beecham? Sorry to disturb you.' Max and Eleanor glanced at one another. 'Mr Hearst's driver is still waiting for a reply. What should I tell him? Should he come back later? Only he's waiting for a letter from you, and I'm not sure if I should tell him to wait or if . . .' Behind her came the sound of the

328

telephone ringing in the hall. She tailed off.

Eleanor said, through the door: 'Teresa, give me a minute, and I'll write a note for him. Tell him I will be just a minute.'

It was something to do. Something to break the spell between them. She walked away from Max, to the door that connected to the drawing room. There was a small table in there, decorative mostly, but Teresa kept it stocked with Eleanor's stationery. She would write a quick, gracious note, explaining to Marion that they couldn't come. It was impossible.

Max followed her into the room. She settled at the table, pen and card before her, heard his footsteps behind her, felt his presence, smelled his scent, heard his breathing; knew he was standing beside her, hands in pockets, scowling.

'El, I think we should go,' he said suddenly. 'I think we should accept.' She paused. 'Whatever for?'

'Because . . .'

'We can't possibly . . .'

'We can't? Why not?'

She didn't have an answer. But the question infuriated her. She was doing something at last—something decisive. Why did he have to make it any harder?

'I think we should go,' he said again. 'Eleanor—this needn't have anything to do with the way things are between us.'

'How's that?' she asked. She laughed in disbelief, felt a surge of too-familiar rage flare up inside her, and welcomed it in. Max's ambition had been at the root of so much that was rotten between them. She had always known it. And yet, even now, he

329

couldn't keep it in check. 'Damn you, Max. Does *nothing* stop you?'

'You know the kind of people they have there. All the big shots. The way things are, El, we can't afford to turn it down.'

'Never mind we can't stand to be in the same room together. Never mind—anything else. We could pretend, just as we have pretended all these years. Is that what you're suggesting?'

'Yes,' he said bluntly. 'The situation we're in, it is exactly what I'm suggesting. We'd be stupid to turn it down.'

'Yes, and you can sit beside Mr Hearst, can't you? Telling him what a wonderful, misunderstood director you are—and perhaps Blanche will be there too! Gosh, why not? Shall we bring her along? And I can call Butch—don't you agree, Max? Because otherwise it would hardly be fair . . . and then you two can fuck in one corner of the castle, and we can fuck in another . . .'

'It's not what I meant. You know that.'

'Which bit? Which bit of it didn't you mean?'

He stared at her: at the anger and bitterness in that beautiful face. She was unrecognizable, he thought, from the woman he loved. 'Gee, Eleanor,' he murmured, as if seeing her for the first time.

'*Gee*?' she mimicked. '"Gee", *what*?'

'*Gee*. When did you get so mean?'

'When did I . . . ?' She didn't like the question. She didn't like the way he asked, as if he really did wonder. She gave a brittle laugh. 'You really want me to tell you?'

'You think everything is my fault, don't you? Everything that went wrong in your whole, long existence. That's what your problem is.'

330

'No I don't,' she muttered.

'It's why you limp through life. Expecting me to make everything OK. Expecting me to spend the rest of my life apologizing.'

'It's not true . . .'

'So, yes, Eleanor. I do want you to tell me. I would love to know when you decided you would cast yourself as the world's greatest victim. In your fancy house. With your husband and your lover and your five-thousand-dollar-a-week contract with the biggest studio in Hollywood.'

She turned back to her postcard.

Darling Marion—' she wrote, with her film star flourish: bold letters, thick black ink curling this way and that—as deceptive as everything else about her. It struck her—it struck them both, simultaneously, the vulgarity of it all.

'Da-aa-arling,' he mimicked her, reading it aloud: 'Daarling, darling, daaaarling!' She stopped writing. Laid down the pen.

'Max . . .'

'I think we should accept,' he said again. 'I think we should go to San Simeon. Definitely. Try and salvage something out of it. I think we should say yes.'

'No.'

'And we can come back here, and we can never speak to each other again. If that's what you want. Never speak to each other. Never set eyes on each other again.' He fell silent, and she looked away. 'Maybe it's what we have to do,' he said quietly. 'Because, after all, together we can never forget, never move on . . . But Eleana . . .' He touched her cheek.

She brushed it away.

331

Another tap on the door. 'Mrs Beecham? You have a telephone call. It's Miss Marion Davies. She says it's urgent. She says if Mrs Beecham is unavailable she will talk to Mr Beecham.'

'I'll talk to her,' Max said, moving towards the door.

'No . . .' she said.

He ignored her, as she knew he would.

'Tell her, Max, won't you?' She turned back to the desk. 'That it's absolutely impossible.' But she muttered the words without conviction. 'Tell her how sorry we are.'

But she knew even as she said it that he would say nothing of the kind. Nobody said No to Hearst Castle. Nobody said No to Marion Davies.

And somehow, even now, Eleanor never could say No to Max.

65

Dear Miss Davies,
I hope sincerely that you will forgive me for intruding in this way upon your precious time. I have long been a fan of all your movies and I adored you in Tillie the Toiler which I have seen now five times and I adore it more each time I watch. However, it is not why I am writing.
I have a most unusual request . . .

Charlie Chaplin was one of the few guests allowed access to the private sitting room that adjoined Marion's bedroom on the uppermost floor of the castle. She would have much preferred to be showing him the letter up there, away from the prying eyes of servants. But Charlie Chaplin, reflected Marion Davies—and not for the first time—could be exceptionally annoying, and he claimed his delicacy forbade it. He had no such qualms at the Beach House in Santa Monica, but here at San Simeon, he always refused see her in her private rooms, unless WR himself was present.

WR (Mr Hearst to everyone but Marion) was not present. He was in Hollywood, due to arrive at San Simeon in time for dinner, bringing with him a nurse, and the six-year-old Veronica, Marion's adored niece. Until then, Charlie and Marion had the run of the castle. And really, all things considered, Marion thought it would have been far more delicate for the two of them to be entertaining one another in her private sitting room. As it was, they were together, drinking champagne and eating peaches, in Charlie's private rooms in the best guesthouse, a hundred yards from the main house. Looking as delectable as ever, Charlie thought, in turquoise satin day pyjamas and little shoes with an arrangement of coloured feathers attached to them, she was lounging across the foot of his bed.

Charlie sat in an armchair by the fireside a few feet away. He held the letter in his hand—between finger and thumb, actually—as if it were contaminated. Charlie didn't share Marion's enthusiasm for the fan letters. On the contrary, he always advised her to throw them directly in the trash; failing that, onto her secretary's desk. 'They will send you mad eventually,' he said. 'Never read personal letters from absolute strangers, no matter how harmless they appear. And never read your own press.' But she didn't listen, not on either count.

She'd been longing to show him this letter for weeks, ever since she'd received it. But knowing he would disapprove, and sensing he might dismiss it or, worse still, try to forbid her from pursuing her delightful plan, she had clutched its secrets to herself. Now—with the scene set, and the cast all making their way to the stage—she was nervous. Horrified, actually, by the prospect of what she had set in motion. She needed Charlie's wise words to make it feel all right again.

'It's a hoax!' he said, 'and you are playing with people's hearts, Marion. Can you not imagine it—the pain you may be causing?'

'You know I can imagine it, Ch-Charlie. You know just how much it means to me . . . And I told you I have especially said nothing to the Beechams, so as not to get their hopes up.'

'Well I suppose that's something.' He softened a little. 'Even so, I'm amazed you could be so fickle with other people's hearts . . . when I know you have feelings of your own.'

'I am trying to help.'

'You are trying to amuse yourself.'

'I am not! Hell, Charlie! You haven't even read the letter!'

'Because I don't need to.'

'Why, yes you do. How can you be such a know-all, when you haven't even read the letter? . . . B-besides. Imagine . . . Just imagine if I am right—only imagine it.'

He read the first few lines again and spluttered with renewed disdain.

'*A most unusual request?*' he snorted. 'I tell you what, Marion. As soon as she arrives, I shall test her on *Tillie the Toiler*. Mark my words. Honestly darling—you were blinded by the flattery right there.' He tapped the letter. 'Nobody could sit through that wretched movie even *once* without wanting to throw themselves off the nearest bridge. But five times? It's a lie! Either that, or she's a simpleton.'

Marion rolled her eyes. 'You're b-being horrid again, Charlie. I don't think you're being clever, whether you liked the movie or you didn't.'

'You know I love almost all your movies, sweetheart. You know how highly I rate you as an actress. But *Tillie the Toiler* was a stinker. And you know it.'

'Oh shhh!' Carelessly she tossed her peach stone at his chair, missed it by half a room-length. 'It's not about the movie, anyway. J-just read the letter, will you? T-tell me what you think. I th-think it's for real. I do . . . And if it is—y'know?' She rolled onto her back, gazed up at the gilted ceiling—it had once belonged in the chapel of a fourteenth-century Sicilian palazzo, or something. WR had told her before, but she could never remember. Marion thought, not for the first time, that it might have looked better if it had been left there. 'Only imagine though Charlie, if I am right, how happy they will be!'

'You shouldn't have meddled.'

'Oh! Just read the letter, will you?'

'Do Max and Eleanor know what you have in store for them?'

'I told you, no!'

'What did you tell them?'

'I said . . .' She looked at Charlie slyly. 'Well, I guess you know Max got canned from Silverman?'

335

He chuckled. 'Broke into Butch Menken's office last week and beat the hell out of him, so I heard. Blood on the carpet all the way up the corridor. God knows, there must be a hundred people in this town who would like to do the same thing.'

'And you know why?'

'I could think of a million reasons.'

'No. B-but you know the actual reason?'

Charlie hesitated. 'Presumably Eleanor. If you believe the rumours. Oddly, I never did. Not until Max broke into his office and beat the hell out of him.'

'Butch and Eleanor?' Marion cried, aghast. *'You're kidding me!'*

He laughed, pleased by her reaction. 'Ha! You see? You don't know everything that goes on in this town, Marion.'

'As a matter of fact, I don't think you're right about that,' she said, recovering herself. 'No. Definitely not. Max? Maybe, just a l-little bit. OK. So what? But Eleanor? I don't think so, Ch-Charlie. He and Eleanor are the h-happiest couple in Hollywood. Everyone knows it.'

'So you always say.'

'You got that rumour wrong, Charlie. And definitely not with Butch.'

Charlie shrugged. 'If you say so, sweetheart.'

'It's because . . .' She rolled back onto her belly, the better to share her gossip. 'Max hit Butch *because . . .*'

'Yes?'

'But Ch-Charlie. You mustn't repeat it. P-promise me you won't.'

He looked at her, deadpan, and crossed himself.

'I'm serious,' Marion said.

336

'Sweetheart, I promise. I won't breathe a word.'

'Max hit Butch, because Butch, before he went across to Silverman and got rid of Max—before he did *that*, he got Eleanor canned from Lionsfiel!'

'No, really?'

'He sure did!' Marion nodded, triumphantly. 'Can you believe it? He fired Eleanor from Lionsfiel. She's out of contract! So now they're b-both out of a job.'

'That's too bad!'

'You're telling *me* it's too bad. It's about as l-lousy as it gets! I never liked Butch Menken! I always said he was a creep.'

Charlie thought about it. They would have taken a knock from the stock market, too, no doubt. 'Poor devils,' he murmured. 'What are they going to do?'

'They're going to come to San Simeon, and I'm going to give them a great time. And I'm going to seat them beside WR on one side, and Joseph Kennedy on the other.'

'I'm sorry you invited him. Joseph Kennedy is a snake. I think he may be the nastiest man in California.'

'I didn't invite him, Charlie. WR invited him.'

'Is he bringing his wife?'

'God no! I already told you, Gloria's coming.'

'Without the marquis, I presume?'

'She's dumped the marquis—so it's b-back to plain old Miss Gloria Swanson.'

'Ha!'

'In any case, you may think Joseph Kennedy's a snake—'

'Because he is.'

'He's a snake who owns one of the biggest studios in Hollywood. And if M-Max Beecham

337

is half the man I think he is . . . I told him on the telephone that "Joseph" was gonna be here. But you know what, he wasn't himself—he didn't even ask *which* Joseph.'

'Perhaps he just assumed.'

'He thought I was talking about his driver!'

'Goodness!'

'He wasn't himself, Charlie,' she said again, shaking her head.

'No. Well. It's been a bad week. I don't suppose he was.' Charlie glanced down at the letter, still held between his dissapproving fingers. It was written on cheap yellow writing paper, in a tiny, looping, girlish hand. 'Do you really want me to read this thing?' he asked.

'I wish you would. I've not even met her yet, Charlie. We only talked on the telephone, but she's arriving tomorrow.' Marion shuddered. 'She's living in Los Angeles, if you can believe it. Trying to be an actress . . .'

'You don't say.'

'I sent her first-class tickets. But for the earlier train. Oh Ch-Charlie! What have I d-done?'

'I hate to imagine,' Charlie muttered, looking down at the flimsy paper. 'I had better read it then.' He sighed. 'Well here goes . . .'

66

Dear Miss Davies,
I hope sincerely that you will forgive me for intruding in this way upon your precious time. I have long been a fan of all your movies and I

338

*adored you in Tillie the Toiler which I have seen
now five times and I adore it more each time I
watch. However, it is not why I am writing.*

*I have a most unusual request. It is
complicated and I shall try to be brief.*

*I have seen your photograph in a thousand
magazines, and you always seem like such a
merry sort of a girl, gay and laughing with so
many friends around you. I suppose it cannot
always be so, even for a girl who is quite as
splendid as you—*

'Oh for goodness' sake,' Charlie Chaplin muttered.

'S-stay with it,' Marion said, sucking on another
peach stone, staring through the window at the
distant waves. 'She takes a while, but then she
hits her stride. You g-gotta stay with it, Charlie. I
know you *p-pretend* to think I'm just a floozy—but
I wouldn't be going to all this trouble if I didn't
believe there was something in it. Now would I?'

He didn't reply.

*I am a young woman, twenty or so years old,
by my calculation (I cannot be certain). And
like most girls my age, I am infatuated with the
movies. Especially the talkies. I think they're
quite wonderful. It's such a thrill to hear the
stars' voices.*

*Well, and like most girls, I could tell you the
names of a hundred different stars—I could tell
you almost everything about any of them: the
names of their pets, what cars they drive, where
they grew up and so on. Of course I know that
not all the stories we are told about the stars
are true stories. In fact, I wonder sometimes if*

339

there is even a grain of truth in a single word of
any of them. Nevertheless, the stories are always
entertaining, and I simply love to read about
them. I suppose I am afraid to get to the point.

In last month's issue of Photoplay I spotted
a photograph of you with one of my favourite
stars. The photograph amazed me. I must
have seen a hundred pictures of Mrs Eleanor
Beecham over the last several years and almost
as many of her husband, Max Beecham, but it
is the only one I have ever seen in which she is
smiling. In fact, it looks as if the two of you are
firm friends—

'Firm friends?' Charlie repeated aloud. 'But you're not, are you?'

'W-well th-that's just what I thought, Charlie. Eleanor doesn't really *h-have* any friends. Does she? When you really actually *think* about it. Well, and I looked up the photograph in that magazine. And it's true, we do look as though we're sharing the most terrific little secret.'

'Huh.'

'It's a trick of the light, I guess. I don't imagine we were. It was a terribly dull evening. Remember the Academy Awards back in May. Do you remember?'

'No.'

'At the Roosevelt. You must remember! All the fuss! Dougie gave a d-dreadful little s-speech. At least I thought it was dreadful. The whole s-silly evening was dreadful. But you know they've decided it was such a success, God knows why—they're going to do it again next year! Did you know? They're to be an annual thing.'

'Sweetheart,' Charlie sighed. 'It's hard enough concentrating on this drivel.'

'It's not drivel, Ch-Charlie. It's quite fascinating. And she's j-just a kid, y'know? Give her a break. And it's really a t-terrible story . . .'

Until I saw the picture of you two laughing so gaily, I thought that Eleanor Beecham was not like you, not merry and cheerful, but a lonely sort of a person, similar to the sort of characters she plays in the movies and, truthfully, it broke my heart. That might seem odd to you. But if you are still reading, I shall explain.

I understand from your interviews that you grew up in New York. But not (I think!) in the slum areas of the Lower East Side of the city. It's where I was born and where I spent the first several years of my life. I remember almost nothing of it. But I think we lived on Allen Street because, you can see for yourself, that is the name written on the photograph. And we lived together in a great crush, with cousins and aunts and uncles and just about anyone who could pay a few dollars for board, all of us squeezed in together. Of course, there were so many new people coming into America in those days—before the quotas came in, and every day there were more. I was so young, I remember so little. In my long search to uncover the mystery, I have looked at the newspaper reports and my mind sometimes confuses what I have <u>read</u> with what I truly <u>remember,</u> but I remember the hot summer nights, I think, when the heat and the crush were so terrible, we used to sleep side-by-side, like sardines, out there on the fire

341

escapes. It has changed now, of course. This was some years back, around the time of the fire at Triangle.

I remember the fire. I was very young—still just a baby: two or three years old. That is to say, I remember there was talk of a terrible fire—and I remember the smell of it filling our small living space that night as the adults came and went. I remember the weeping. So much weeping. And the streets filled with more people weeping and then, after that, nothing. Everything changed. Death seemed to be everywhere, and only my grandmother left. I wish I could be more exact. It seems so flimsy when I see it written it down. And yet and yet and yet.

In my memory it seems to be part of the same day, but I know that it cannot be. They said my grandmother was sick. People were dying, there were bodies carried down the stairs under gray sheets. I remember she lay still for so long. I remember being pulled from her arms: and then a journey, and another, and another. All this I remember but only in the smallest of flashes. And perhaps I will tell you more, one day, if you ever reply to me. But this letter is too long already. I lived at an orphanage in Brooklyn for a short while, and then at another, that one in New Jersey. I know this, because I have documentation. And then there was another and another—and here I am: more fortunate than I dared to dream; far more fortunate than the many I left behind. But along the way I lost my name.

At the first orphanage, the very first one, we arrived in a small group. The woman who

342

*collected us up must have been kind. I don't
remember. There were two or three children—
not only me. They were collecting up the
lost children. She packed me with a small case
with some clothes. I had a chamsa which my
grandmother gave to me from her own neck—
and which I have worn every day since, and
which I wear today.*

*I left the apartment with only that and a
photograph. It was the photograph that hung on
the wall by the door. I saw the lady take it down
for me: at least I think I saw it. It left a mark on
the wall behind, a small, clean square, which the
city grime couldn't reach.*

*And here it is. It is my only clue. It is only a
copy of the photograph, of course. On the back
of the original, which I have kept with me, it says
in ink:*

Eleana and Matz Beekman, 2109 Allen
Street, 1909

*I can find no listing of their marriage and no
listing of the baby anywhere. It is as if the baby
had never existed. And yet—there you see the
three of them, mother, father and child—as alive
as any you could hope to lay eyes on.*

*In all my research, I found one or two
mentions of Matz Beekman—in police records,
which I won't go into here. Apparently he was
active in the unions. There were charges. He was
arrested on the day of the fire, at a workers' rally.
And there the trail stops. It's impossible to know
what quite happened next. Because you see, in
all the records, I could find only one mention
of Eleana and Matz Beekman of Allen Street.
According to official documentation, both*

343

*burned to death on that same terrible day, in
that terrible fire: 25 March 1911.*

*I hardly dare to write what I am hoping:
it seems too absurd. But there were so many
deaths on that day of the fire, and many remains
were so badly burned they were unrecognizable.
Some were never identified at all. Do you see
what I am trying to say? Perhaps they escaped,
after all. It's possible. Isn't it? If the police
were after him, and they wanted to start afresh.
Perhaps they came back to fetch me and they
never found me again. I keep telling myself it's
absurd. But then I look at the photograph. And I
know it's possible.*

*Look closely at the photograph—won't you,
please? Also, please, at the photograph I have
sent you of myself, taken three weeks ago.*

*Am I imagining resemblances that simply
are not there? Or are they as I think they are? I
cannot see beyond them . . .*

'But I don't understand,' Charlie burst out, laying
the paper on the bed, 'why she wouldn't have
contacted Max and Eleanor herself? Why is she
sharing all this nonsense with you?'

'Well, that's just what I asked her, Charlie, when
we spoke on the telephone. Except I didn't say
"nonsense". Of course I asked her that.'

'And?'

Marion hesitated. 'She has tried. She says she
has tried on countless occasions . . . She has written
to them and received no reply. She has camped
at the bottom of their drive, Ch-Charlie! Almost
been crushed to d-death by Max, in his auto, but he
wouldn't stop. Why—on the night of the party, she

344

dressed as a waitress, but they threw her out before she had a chance . . . And then again—only last week—she approached the girl, the little reporter girl Max is so friendly with . . . I f-forget her name . . .'

'Blanche Williams.'

'That's right. She spoke to Blanche. Or she was about to say something to Blanche. But . . .'

'Well?'

'She lacked the courage,' Marion said simply. 'Each time it got so c-close. But she lacked the courage.'

'Oh, well then.' It was sarcastic. 'So she writes to a strange woman whom she happens to see smiling in a magazine.' Charlie laughed. Shook his head.

'W-well, you can ridicule that if you want to.'

'I'm not ridiculing it.'

'She's alone in the world, Ch-Charlie . . . Think back—why won't you do that? And remember yourself. It's not so completely different from your own life, now is it?'

'I didn't write to unknown movie stars suggesting they were my kin.'

'When they took your ma away from you. And then they took you and your brother and put you into the poorhouse.'

'Thank you, Marion. I know what happened. I wish I had never told it you.'

'But Charlie, of course you should've told me!'

'And if you don't mind—'

Marion leaned towards him. 'All right, then. Just imagine it. This poor little kid, she's been tossed into who-knows-how-many orphanages—she gets an idea in her head that maybe she *isn't* so alone after all. Imagine that! Imagine it Ch-Charlie! I

345

know you can! Can you imagine how precious it would be? That there might be somebody out there in that big, wide, cruel world who l-loves you, after all? A mother and a father—'

'Far-fetched.'

'And not just any mother and f-father, Charlie, but these guys! M-Matz and Eleana Beekman: Max and Eleanor Beecham. The happiest married couple in Hollywood! Rich and beautiful and famous and—'

'*Dead*, by the girl's own admission.'

Marion reached into the pocket of her satin day pyjamas and pulled out a second envelope. She tossed it across to him, missing her target by half a room once again: 'Look at the photographs, Ch-Charlie.'

Charlie Chaplin hesitated. He resented being asked to grovel on the floor to pick anything up. It was a hangover from his workhouse days, no doubt. Marion knew him well enough to know it would infuriate him and moved to fetch them for him herself. But Charlie's curiosity got the better of him before she had a chance. He swooped down and scooped them up.

Inside were two photographs. The first, of a young woman. *Pretty*, he thought. *Big, sad eyes, just like Eleanor. Thick dark hair, wide mouth—like Eleanor. So what?*

He turned his attention to the formal portrait of a young couple holding a small child. The girl, in clothes that looked worn and dated: a shirtwaist, a long skirt, a wide-brimmed hat and a sash across her chest, the word PICKET emblazoned upon it, sat in the foreground. The young man—wearing a jacket that hung together, a waistcoat too large for his skinny frame and a cloth hat half covering his eyes—stood behind her, one hand on her shoulder. And on the girl's lap sat a toddler swaddled so tight in raggedy blankets as to be hardly visible: Charlie Chaplin looked at the raggedy, hungry-looking young couple and let out a gasp.

Marion, watching him closely, smiled at his reaction. She stood up and crossed the room to look at the picture again. 'Y'see?' she said. 'Who's the floozy now, huh?'

67

It's hard to know what not to pack for a stay at such a place and in such elevated company. Joseph, the Beechams' driver, couldn't fit the Beecham luggage and the Beechams into a single car journey, so he delivered the cases to the train first. Max and Eleanor, waiting for him to return, tried to talk to each other as they normally did, just as they had for years.

'Marion said Joseph Kennedy would be there,' Max said. He was sitting in the early evening sunshine, on the stone balustrade at the edge of the Italianate terrace where, only a week or so earlier, he and his wife had entertained the cream of Hollywood, King and Queen of all they surveyed. Now, of course, the house would be put up for sale. Soon they would be homeless, jobless, broke— and divorced. But Max and Eleanor kept the conversation light.

'Joseph Kennedy!' Eleanor groaned, sitting on a sunny stone bench nearby. 'Joseph Kennedy is a dreadful man. I hope I don't have to sit next to him. Is Rose coming?'

'I doubt it. Rose never goes anywhere. Marion said Gloria's going to be there.'

'Without the marquis?'

'He's been shipped off, back to Paris.'

They fell silent. It was too quiet. They both knew how absurd it was, to keep up this pretence, and yet neither knew how to stop it. Last night, they were too tired to fight. They ate at different times, in different rooms. Max slept in his study. And now, today—it was a Sunday. They had read the papers in separate rooms.

Eleanor asked: 'I suppose it's too late for us, is it? Financially. Even if the markets recover?'

If Max could only have persuaded his broker to hold off while stock prices readjusted, as everyone said they would, he told Eleanor, their finances might have weathered it. But yes—it was too late. Their broker had forced him to sell everything they owned on margin, which was almost everything. It had wiped them out.

'We'll be OK,' he said, automatically. He looked about him at the cool green lawn, the trickling fountains, the granite statues of Neptune behind them. It was beautiful, this place they had built together. But it was too big and too empty. He wouldn't be sad to see it go.

'You know Lionsfiel are cutting me loose, don't you?' she said suddenly. 'I'll bet you do know.' She smiled. 'You probably knew before me . . . They sent me a lousy script—I haven't looked at it.' She shrugged. 'So, it's goodbye Lionsfiel. Did you know?'

'No,' he lied automatically. 'I didn't know that.

348

How do you know it's a lousy script, if you haven't even looked at it?'

She glanced at him, disconcerted. They caught each other's eye, the two habitual liars, and quickly looked away again. She could have admitted that Butch told her so—he would have guessed it anyway. But what was the point? 'Well, I did skim through,' she said, aimlessly. 'I mean—it's a lousy script for me. I don't come in until the third act.'

'May I see it?'

'Oh . . . It's upstairs somewhere. Really Max. I can't be bothered.'

'So. What are you going to do?'

She thought of Butch: he'd told her he would look after her. She wondered, suddenly, if she believed him. Once she and Max divorced, Butch would have won. And that would be it. There would be no cruelty on his part, just a switch of gaze. And it would sadden her—of course it would, deeply, after all these years of loving him, leaning on him, bathing in his desire and care and admiration. Except she had known it all along: that his love for her, and for everything in his life, was really only a private thing, between himself and himself. He didn't know how to love. Any better than she did, any more. It was no doubt what had drawn them together in the first place. 'I really don't know,' she said, gazing steadfastly at the fountain. 'What about you?'

'I suppose Butch will bring you over to Silverman,' he said lightly.

She didn't reply.

'You should let me take a look at the contract before you sign, El.'

'Nobody's said anything about a contract.'

'Trust me, they'll screw you if they can.'

'Butch hasn't said anything about a contract,' she lied again.

But Max knew Butch. He smiled. 'Yes, he has.'

Eleanor stood up. 'Well. I certainly haven't seen it,' she said. 'As far as I know, Max, we're as washed up as each other.'

'We're not washed up,' he said automatically. 'Absolutely not,' he reiterated, for his own benefit.

'In any case,' she stood up, 'God knows why you said yes to this bloody awful trip, Max,' she said, changing the conversation. 'It's the last thing I want to do. Why are you making me do this?'

'I'm not,' he said, '*making* you do it.'

'It's going to be hell. Everyone knowing our business. And don't say they won't because they will.'

'Well, honey,' he murmured, 'I don't know what else you've told Butch . . .'

'I haven't told him anything,' she said.

'But once a cat's out of a bag . . .'

'I haven't told him anything,' she said again.

'Really? Well that's all right, then.' He flicked her a cold smile.

'They'll know about you being fired,' she said, looking away. 'And about me being dumped by Lionsfiel . . .'

'Probably.'

'They'll know about your ridiculous fight with Butch. God knows what you were thinking . . .'

'I would be disappointed if they didn't.'

'In any case, Joseph Kennedy gives me the creeps. And Gloria Swanson's a terrible bore. Mr Hearst is so shy he's impossible to talk to . . . Marion will be closeted with Charlie. And I dread

350

to imagine who else will be there . . . Oh God, Max—what's the point of it? What are we doing? We can't even speak to each other without—'

'Lying?'

She turned without another word. They waited in separate parts of the property that would soon no longer be theirs, until Joseph, who would soon no longer work for them, returned with the car they would have to sell. They climbed into it from separate sides, gazed out of opposite windows, never more conscious of each other, and didn't speak until they reached the station. As Joseph stepped round to open Eleanor's door, Max took her gloved hand, resting limp on her lap.

'It's going to be OK,' he said. 'We're going to be OK.'

She pulled her hand away.

As they walked side by side the short distance to the train, Eleanor wished, if she wished anything at all, that she was back in her room at the Riverside Hotel, still free and foolish enough to dream about a different future. She pictured herself only a week earlier at this same station, setting off for Reno. What madness, she wondered, had persuaded her to believe the impossible for so long? And now she believed in nothing and there was no turning back. And it was far worse.

Mr Hearst provided first-class berths for each of his guests, as well as a private dining and drawing room on the train. San Simeon house parties began as soon as guests climbed aboard the train, and there, just in front of her, fifty yards ahead, Eleanor spotted Greta Garbo being helped up the steps.

'Oh God, Max,' she whispered, 'I can't do it.'

'Yes, you can.'

351

It was worse. Behind Greta, booming orders to the porters, yelling frantic greetings at Garbo, Max and Eleanor spotted the gossip columnist Louella Parsons. Louella, whose poisonous words were syndicated in newspapers coast-to-coast, and who was loathed by everyone who ever met her, except her employer, Randolph Hearst. She too was climbing aboard.

'It's going to be fine!' Max said weakly.

Twenty yards in front of them, the doors to Mr Hearst's drawing-room carriage had been thrown open. On the platform outside it, a collection of some of the most celebrated names in America were jostling for attention, preparing to embark the train. Louella was shrieking hello to Buster Keaton; Elinor Glyn was shaking hands with Charles Lindbergh; Gloria Swanson was offering a chilly, perfumed cheek to Will Rogers; Joseph Kennedy was leering at Peggy Hopkins Joyce . . . Bustling porters came and went between them. Max and Eleanor stood back.

'Matz? . . .' she asked him, her beautiful, trained voice carrying, soft and clear, above the station hubbub. *'Why are we doing this?'*

But the answer seemed so obvious to him. And he knew it was obvious to her, too. He knew she understood. Or else why would she still be standing there? He might have come back with any number of comforting replies, but for a moment the thought of adding yet one more lie to the mountain of lies between them seemed to be beyond him.

He said it coldly: 'Because we've been poor before, Eleanor. We know what it's like. We don't have any choice.'

She didn't argue with it. They turned towards the

train, to face the mob.

68

A small fleet of limousines awaited the dawn arrival of Hearst's house-party train, and by 10 a.m. that Monday morning, guests were all comfortably ensconced at the castle on top of the hill. Transported from the station, through the vast Hearst Estate and the Hearst private zoo, they had been shown their quarters, introduced to their maids, had their belongings unpacked for them, and were seated at one end of the long refectory table in the dining room, with Marion and her six-year-old niece, Patricia, side by side at the head, tucking into breakfast. Only Mr Hearst had yet to make an appearance. But no one expect him. He generally kept to himself, his desk, his newspapers, and his telephones, until the house party gathered in the great hall for evening cocktails.

Ten o'clock on the West Coast was already lunchtime in the East. Wall Street had been trading for several hours already, and indications were far from good. The much-vaunted Monday recovery had not materialized, brokers were selling at an ever-increasing rate and prices continued to drop. Where, on Black Thursday, the President of the Exchange had jauntily stepped in and thrown his own money into the bear pit to help stabilize things, there were no signs of big business riding to the rescue today. The market was on the edge of freefall. All this, the guests had discovered on arrival. As well as a stock ticker, there was a news ticker, tick-tacking away in Mr Hearst's private study, and it was announced to the table that on this one occasion, in these peculiar circumstances, guests would be allowed access to the room, at specific intervals during the day. They were also invited to use the telephone, should they need to call their brokers at any point. Max had no need to call his broker. There was nothing left for him to sell—and for that, at least, he was quite grateful. If he'd been allowed to hold out, he would have been even poorer this morning.

'B-but other than calling your brokers if you really, truly and absolutely *have* to, gentlemen,' Marion Davies declared, resplendent in raspberry pink at the head of the table, and with a newly acquired bracelet of pink diamonds to match, 'the s-subject is absolutely banned.'

There was a groan of protest from the guests.

'And you know,' she said, holding up her glittering wrist, 'if I hear a s-single word about the s-tupid stock market at this table, or on the t-tennis courts or *anywhere*, I shall insist on imposing some dreadful sort of forfeit. Don't ask me what it is, because I haven't thought of it yet. But it might easily involve the b-bell tower. And a couple of zebras.'

Nobody much felt like laughing (except young Patricia, who didn't understand), but duty required that the guests join in. Joseph Kennedy laughed louder than anyone. He had been shorting the market on a scale that made Butch's clever efforts seem paltry. While his fellow guests tumbled into bankruptcy, this man, or snake, the father of a future US president, was one of a small handful of Americans making an unimaginable fortune in

354

the stock price collapse. Joseph Kennedy laughed merrily at Marion's amusing diktat, his hand, beneath the table, caressing Gloria Swanson's thigh the while. He would spend just as much time as he felt inclined, gazing at the castle ticker machines. Marion knew it. She didn't look at him as she was laying down the house-party rule. She tried to avoid looking at him at all.

'So then!' Marion continued, breezy as ever. 'What shall we all do with ourselves this morning? Patricia—darling,' she turned tenderly to her small niece. 'We're going to the ch-chimpanzee house directly. You and me. This morning. B-but first you have to give me a half-hour, baby . . .' She smiled and stroked the little girl's cheek. 'And you, Charlie,' she continued, 'I know you fancy yourself the tennis champion . . .'

'Hardly,' he said mildly, eating kedgeree.

'Well, I happen to know Mr Lindbergh is quite the whiz—not just up there in the air, but on the tennis court, too. Isn't that so, Mr Lindbergh? And Mrs Lindbergh—I heard you had the most terrific, swinging forehand!'

Charles and Anne Lindbergh looked at their plates. Marion, fine hostess that she was, didn't offer them a chance to reveal their shyness. 'Don't you go denying it!' she continued cheerfully. 'I know it perfectly well. So. And if you g-give me a hundred bucks I'll even tell ya who told me! Which only leaves a partner for you, Charlie—Peggy? Fancy a run about with your old b-beau? I'll bet you can hit a ball!'

'Gosh, I shouldn't think so!' cried Peggy Hopkins Joyce, laughing very loudly. Nobody knew quite why. 'How about Greta?'

Greta didn't speak. She sipped on some black coffee and looked airily above her hostess's head.

'She wants to be alone,' said Buster. 'She told me so on the train.'

'Nonsense,' announced Marion. 'Else why's she even bothered to come all the way up here for the party? Greta—darling—*say something*, won't you? It's no good b-bringing your black mood up here. I tell you, we shan't allow it to last!'

But Greta still didn't speak.

Marion sighed. Glanced at Eleanor. 'Mrs Eleanor Beecham?' she said softly. 'A thousand bucks for your thoughts!'

Eleanor jumped.

'Ha! Honey, you were a m-million miles away!'

'Was I?' Eleanor sounded apologetic. 'I'm so sorry! You need someone to make up the tennis? Well I can certainly—'

'No, darling,' interrupted Marion. 'I told you—I told your husband . . . I have something I want to show you.'

'Oh?' Eleanor glanced at Max.

'You, Max and I are going for a little walk, Eleanor. WR's put in a too-delightful little *ha-ha* below the Neptune pool—And I b-betcha don't know what a ha-ha is—'

'Isn't it a—'

'Oh gosh,' Marion waved her words aside. 'Never mind. I'll just betcha *do* know. Anyway I know you'll want to see it, too. I've been longing to show you *all yesterday*. Miss Glyn,' without pausing, Marion turned to the other Elinor: the ageing novelist, Elinor Glyn, 'how about some tennis? Will you partner with Charlie? He's awfully good, you know.'

356

'Certainly not!' Miss Glyn's patrician English cut through the large dining room, making everyone in the room sit up a little straighter. 'I'm far too old. I intend to spend the morning looking at the giraffe—if there's anyone willing to accompany me?' She looked meaningfully at her fellow scribe, Will Rogers. Too late, Louella Parsons piped up. 'Oh, I should love to see the giraffe, Elinor darling.'

Elinor sighed.

'Natalie?' Charlie Chaplin turned to Buster's wife. 'Want to play some tennis?'

'Not really, no,' she said, scowling at her husband, as if the question were his fault. 'But if I must I suppose I must.'

'Excellent!' said Charlie, rubbing his hands together. 'We have a match!'

'Well then. I think I shall take a swim,' muttered Buster.

So the guests were found activities to keep them occupied until luncheon. There was a tour of the zoo for some; a small pool party for others. Will Rogers wanted to try his hand playing the bells in the bell tower; Max, Eleanor and Marion would examine the ha-ha; Joseph Kennedy and Gloria Swanson would retire to their adjoining quarters, and Greta would wander the grounds, alone.

'Well, that's all settled then,' said Marion, satisfied. 'Everyone has something planned. And this afternoon, we must make a little movie—don't you think? Charlie and I have it all written out. And we c-can show it to WR in the theatre tomorrow evening. He simply l-loves all that . . . And later on, we may have another guest joining us.' She glanced nervously at Charlie, the only one present who was aware of her immediate plans. But he was careful not to look at her. 'Least, I think we may. It really depends . . .'

As they were rising from the table, Charlie leaned across to Max. 'Marion has a surprise,' he said.

'A nice one, I hope. You know what it is?'

There was a pause. Max wondered what it was Charlie seemed to be on the point of saying. He looked, just for a moment, unguarded, thoughtful— sad. He shook his head. 'No idea.'

'Max darling, won't you hurry up?' Marion was already shepherding Eleanor up from the table. '*Hurry*, Max. Follow me or I think I may die of impatience.'

'*Die?*' laughed Max, following her into the hall.

'Well, but you know what I mean . . .' She sounded horribly nervous. 'Now come with me.'

69

Everywhere, sculpted from the steep hillside, there were curling paths and little steps, fountains and statues, gazebos and mazes, ha-has and follies. Trees had been uprooted and transported from every corner of America and some from as far away as Europe, and everywhere, in the salty air, the distant sound of waves crashed softly onto the bay below. The garden at San Simeon was magical. Beautiful. Spectacular. Two hundred acres of paradise. So the three of them set out through the castle grounds towards the new ha-ha, Marion holding on to her large brimmed sun hat, briskly leading the way. In her other hand, she carried with

358

her a small wallet.

'What do you suppose it's about?' Max muttered to his wife. Eleanor shrugged.

'Something's got into her.'

Eleanor said: 'As long as we don't have to look at a giraffe with Louella Parsons, Marion can walk us to San Francisco and back, for all I care.'

Just then, abruptly—and without a ha-ha anywhere in sight, Marion stopped, spun round to face them. She took off her sunglasses, looked from one to the other and then peered about her, as if checking there was no one approaching.

'I sh-should apologize,' she said, gazing at them intently. 'I know I should apologize. I have taken the most t-terrific liberty. Charlie says it's out of . . . B-but never mind what Charlie says,' she corrected herself. 'He doesn't know anything. About anything . . .' Beside her was a small enclave, a plateau cut into the hill. It was framed by thick rose bushes and, in the middle, two curving, marble benches formed a semicircle, looking out to sea. She sat herself at the furthest bench and indicated that they should sit on the other.

'I have something to show you,' she said. 'It's why I bought you down here.'

'All right then,' Max said, slowly, seating himself beside his wife. 'Well. Why don't you show it to us then?'

Marion hesitated. She said: 'I want to show it to you, Max. It's something somebody sent to me . . . But I think I may have lost my nerve.'

'Well? What is it?' Marion's uncharacteristic discomfort had roused Eleanor's curiosity at last.

'It's something somebody sent me,' Marion said again. 'Eleanor, I w-wanted to show it to you

359

last week. I thought I would. But then—it's such a tremendous . . . thing . . .'

'What can it be?' Max teased her. 'This "tremendous thing"? Here we are, Marion. You might just as well show it to us now.' He indicated the little wallet. 'Is that it?'

She glanced at the file in her hand as if she had almost forgotten it. 'W-well. Yes. I guess it is. It's part of it. There's another part . . .' Max put out a hand to take it from her.

'Except I think,' Marion said, pulling the wallet closer to her chest, 'I just want you to know that I am g-giving this to you with only the very best intentions. Eleanor—I have always liked you. And M-Max . . . The kid sent it to me, and I couldn't *not* pass it on to you. Now could I? Well, don't even answer that b-because of course I couldn't. I don't care what anyone says. And I've not shown it to *anyone*—you understand that? Well, I sh-showed it to Charlie.'

'For heaven's sake!' Eleanor laughed. 'I'm not sure I can stand this suspense any longer.'

Marion clutched the wallet tighter still. 'Of course, I showed it to WR. But you know—you couldn't have a more sympathetic supporter than WR. There's nobody in this world kinder the WR. Apart from anything, you know—he was all for the Triangle workers—'

Before Marion could prevent it, Eleanor had left her seat and snatched the wallet from her hand.

'People say such t-terrible things about him. About WR,' Marion babbled, only to fill the space. 'But you can trust him. Of all the men in the world, that man has a heart of gold . . .'

Eleanor pulled open the file and Marion,

watching her, fell silent at last.

'What is it?' Max said.

Eleanor muttered something under her breath. Marion couldn't make it out. *'Vey tsu mayn yorn . . .'*

'El?' he asked her again. *'What is it?'*

Beneath the tawny skin, her face had drained of all colour. 'It's not possible, Max.' He looked over her shoulder, saw the photograph— the picture of the three of them together; the picture neither had laid eyes on since they ran from Allen Street, and his face, too, seemed to drain of blood. His expression froze. They gazed at the photograph together, without speaking.

Eleanor ran a finger over the image. And then, so did Max. She sighed: the saddest sound, of resignation and loss, a wound that would never heal. Max put an arm around her shoulders and she leaned into him.

'It *is* you . . . Isn't it?' Marion said softly. 'I knew it was. I knew it couldn't be anyone else. It had to be you . . . Is it?' she wanted confirmation. 'Is it really you?'

'Is it us?' Eleanor said. She looked up into Marion's blue eyes. After so many years of caution, her answer came to her automatically. She smiled and collected herself. 'They look just like us, don't they? A younger version. It's uncanny . . . But it's not us, Marion. No—'

'It's not?' Marion's shoulders sagged.

'What's that?' burst out Max.

'Max, darling,' Eleanor laughed.

'But of course it's us!'

'Max. No, you are mistaken . . .'

He ignored her. 'Well of course it is us,' he said again. 'And that, Marion, that beautiful baby you see there—that is our daughter, Isha. You can't see it there—but she was beautiful.'

'Darling . . . you're confused . . .'

'She had the most beautiful eyes. Like her mother. You can't see it in the photograph. She was beautiful.'

'You have a daughter?' Marion asked.

'*No*,' Eleanor said.

'We do,' Max said. 'Called Isha. Twenty-two years old last week. The seventeenth of October.'

'Isha . . .' Marion repeated.

'It's a beautiful name.'

'Isn't it?' Max smiled.

'Only. Forgive me, will you? I'm a little confused,' Marion said. 'Is it you in the picture? Or isn't it you?'

'Of course it is us,' said Max. 'How could it be anyone else? Eleanor! Tell her! Of course it is us! How could you be in any doubt?'

And finally, Eleanor nodded. 'Us, perhaps . . . But in another lifetime, Marion,' she said.

'I knew it!' Marion cried triumphantly. 'I *knew* it!'

'And yes, we had a daughter once,' Eleanor continued. 'But we don't have a daughter. Not any more.'

'We had that picture taken—d'you remember, El? The night of the rally at Union Hall—you in the sash . . .'

She ignored him. 'It was very cold. And there was an infection. It killed my mother. It killed half the block. You know how cold it gets in New York. Especially—well.' Eleanor looked at Marion, and in her low, flat voice, there was a murmur of the rage she generally kept so closely in check. 'Of course

362

you wouldn't know. In any case, Isha is dead, Marion. Where did you get this photograph?'

'But you keep saying that, Eleanor,' Max said desperately. '"Isha is dead". As if by saying it, the pain will simply go away.'

Again, she ignored him. 'Tell me,' she said again to Marion, 'where did you find this photograph?'

'But we don't *know* that she's dead,' Max persevered, looking across at his wife, anger tingeing his words. 'We don't know it for sure . . .'

Eleanor shook his arm from her shoulders. She stood up. 'Marion. Tell us, please: where did you find this picture? Who sent it?'

'I told you I was—'

'Who sent it?'

'Except I don't think—'

'*Shiksa!* Why won't you speak?'

'Give her a chance, Eleanor . . .' muttered Max.

'What do you want from us, Marion?' Eleanor asked her. 'Why do you bring us here, to show us this? You think it's a game? A little parlour game?'

Max took Eleanor's hand. She tried to snatch it away, but he held it tight. '*Eleanor*,' he said. 'Let her speak.'

* * *

Marion looked from one to the other; the colour drained from her own face now, too. She had not expected this. She had not expected . . . anything. Had it only been a parlour game, she wondered? It's what Charlie thought. But he was wrong.

'No—n-not a p-parlour game, Eleanor. I know myself how much a mother can miss her child.'

'Ha!' Eleanor spat it out. 'I don't think so.'

363

'You can believe it or not.' Marion shrugged. 'In any case, there's a letter. I have the letter with me right here. From the girl. It explains everything, I think.' Her hands were shaking as she produced the envelope from her pocket. 'I'm going to leave you with this. And when you're done, I'll s-send the kid down. If you would like me to. I'll s-send her down here. All right?'

'What's that?' Max whispered the words. 'What "kid", Marion?'

'She's up at the house right now. In her bedroom. Waiting for you to read the letter.'

'*She?*'

'Read the letter,' Marion said. 'I'll send her down.' And she was going to leave it at that, but then the thing seemed to be so momentous, suddenly, so much more than she had ever imagined it would be, she couldn't resist turning back. 'Honey,' she said to Eleanor, 'I don't think she's dead. I don't think your daughter is dead . . . *I think we have found her.*'

70

Marion had asked the girl to stay hidden in her room until she came for her. Now Marion hurried through the castle grounds to the smaller of the two guesthouses to seek her out. There were sixteen guests in the house party altogether, and Marion had left the guesthouse empty especially for her. As she passed the tennis courts, she broke into a trot, ignoring cries from Natalie and the Lindberghs, asking her to stop and adjudicate. Charlie was a notorious cheat, in any case. And Natalie was convinced the Lindbergh's line calls could not be trusted. Marion simply waved, and ran on.

She was panting by the time she reached the girl's rooms. She found the girl pacing the carpet like a wild thing. There were patches of sweat on her cotton dress and her bobbed hair stuck to her cheeks. Marion wondered if she should lend the girl something more flattering to wear . . . She looked lovely as she was. Full of life. But even so.

'Honey!' Marion panted.

The girl spun round and almost collided with her, almost exploded with questions.

'What did they say? Did the picture seem to mean anything? Will they meet me? Is it them? What happened? Am I mad? Have I imagined it all? . . . Oh won't you just tell me please, IS IT THEM?'

Marion waited for the questions to stop and finally, still out of breath, she nodded. 'It's them. They're reading the letter now. Sweetheart, you need to pull yourself together. Collect yourself. G-give them a few minutes and get on down there.' She beamed at the girl. 'Y-your name is Isha . . .'

'Isha.' The girl tried it out on her tongue. Frowned. 'Isha.' Something stirred—the faintest of memories.

'Isha,' the girl whispered. 'Yes. Yes, of course . . .'

'Beautiful name,' Marion said.

'It is. Yes it is. Did they say anything else?'

'They think you died. The time you write about in your letter—when the w-woman came to fetch you. Your parents think you died then. At the same time as your grandmother.'

The girl said nothing.

365

'They've been searching for you all this time.'

'They didn't find me,' she said. 'I guess they didn't look hard enough.'

'Honey—how could they find you? You disappeared.'

'I didn't disappear. I was always here.'

'You changed your name.'

'I didn't have a name. How could I change my name when I never had one?'

'*Hey*,' Marion said, and it sounded sharp. 'If you're j-just going to go d-down there and make my friends feel b-bad, don't bother. I'll wish I'd never got you here.'

'No!' the girl cried. 'No, no. Of course not.'

'They've been searching for you. And n-now they've found you. That's all there is to it.'

'I don't want to make *anyone* feel bad . . .'

'Well then.'

'Truly,' the girl was aghast. 'After all this, it's the very last thing I would want to do.'

'Now,' said Marion, taking control. 'W-what are you going to wear?'

The girl didn't reply. 'Isha,' she muttered again. 'Isha Beekman . . . Isha Beekman. I had better get down there, I suppose.' She walked towards the door, and only as an afterthought turned back to Marion. 'Where am I going to find them? Will you take me there?'

'Not yet.' Marion shook her head. 'Give them a moment. It's quite a letter you wrote—and this is the first time they laid eyes on you, honey.'

'But they'll want to see me.'

'L-let's straighten you up a bit first, shall we? Got to make a good impression . . . Your dress is looking kind of sweaty. Have you anything else to wear? If you don't, I'm sure I do. You're slimmer than I am, b-but we can find something . . . C-come with me.' She took the girl by the hand.

'Can't I just go out there?' the girl said. 'I'm so damn nervous.'

'D-don't curse, honey. It's n-not nice. And, no. No you can't. You're gonna come with me. I'm going to get you fitted up just perfectly.'

She led the girl out of the guesthouse, up the hill to the castle, and up to her private rooms.

'Nothing too sophisticated,' Marion said. 'You're only a kid.' She handed the girl a blue silk dress, too loose for the girl, like everything in Marion's wardrobe; matched it with a little cloche hat and some pale gloves and a pair of sunglasses.

'It's bright out there. You don't want to arrive s-squinting.'

'All right.'

'But I think,' Marion added, scrutinizing her carefully, 'maybe you should lose the gloves.'

'Yes, yes, yes,' said the girl, tearing them off impatiently. 'I think it's OK now. Isn't it? I look—'

'You look lovely, kid,' Marion said. 'Just like your mama.'

The girl smiled uncertainly. 'You think that?' she said. There were tears in her eyes. 'Is that what you really think?'

'I just know it,' said Marion. 'Now go on out there! I'm going to p-point you in the right direction. M-much as I'd love to watch the beautiful reunion, I'm going to leave you to it. I'm taking Patricia to see the chimpanzees.' Marion smiled. 'That little k-kid—she can never get enough of those chimpanzees, y'know? She just loves 'em.' She stopped. Looked at the girl. 'Come on. They'll be waiting for you. Are you ready?'

'Am I ready?' The girl laughed, and her eyes danced. It was the lightest, prettiest, merriest laugh: and it reminded Marion of Patricia. 'Gosh, Miss Davies,' the girl said, 'I've been waiting my whole life!'

71

They read the letter together, side by side, in silence. And when they had finished it, they laid it aside, and turned to the other photograph—the one of the girl as she was now.

'It looks,' he said at last, 'a little like a casting card. Doesn't it? Maybe she's an actress. She's very pretty . . .'

Eleanor smiled. 'She's lovely.'

'She looks like you.'

'*You think that?*' Eleanor said. 'Is that what you really think?'

She sprung up, unable to sit still any longer. 'It must be her though, mustn't it? If you say she looks like me? And she has the photograph. Oh, Max how long must we wait for her? Why doesn't she come?'

'She'll come—I guess. She'll come any minute.' Max tried to be calm. But it was impossible. He stood up too, and began to pace back and forth. 'Should I go and fetch her?'

'What will we say to her? 'Eleanor stopped. 'We've waited so long and now all I want to do is run, Max. What if . . . what if—'

'It may not be her.'

'I think it is, Max. I think it is.'

'But Eleanor,' he said at last. 'You know, whoever it is, she is *looking for us*. She has come all this way to find us. All the way from Allen Street.'

She had made the same journey. They tried to imagine it—found it impossible. When Eleanor spoke, she noticed he held her hand. She turned it over, stroked the scars on his palm, and he watched her doing it. Eleanor said, 'She might be terribly angry with us. If it is really her.'

'Well then, why would she come to find us? Why?' he cried. He feared just the same thing. '. . . She has a small fortune waiting for her, you know,' he added. 'I sent it every month to that post-office box. Batia's box in New York. You remember? I just kept on sending it and never stopped. Every month, no matter what. So. And, she'll know it when she sees. Every envelope, every month. She'll know we didn't forget her.' He smiled. 'I was thinking of it on the train. All that money, just lying there in that box . . . and I was thinking, with the money, Isha's money, if it's still there . . . Maybe we could just go back to the way it was—you and me; we could rent a little bungalow. We could make a film on our own. Wouldn't you like that? You and me . . . and maybe even our daughter. It's how it was meant to be . . .'

Eleanor imagined it, and it was magical, irresistible. Of course it was. She shook her head. 'It's too late.'

'No it isn't. It's a fresh start. Another chance . . .'

'What if she isn't Isha?'

'I don't know.'

Eleanor looked again at the letter in her hand, at the photograph of the baby, and at the photograph

369

of the woman. 'She must have been looking for us a long time,' Eleanor muttered.

'Not as long as we've been looking for her.'

'Maybe not.'

A long silence—and then Max suddenly said: 'El—when this weekend is over . . .' And Eleanor laughed. She already knew what he was going to say. And she already knew, as well as she knew anything, that no matter what, no matter how this ended, it could not possibly be the end for them.

'Yes?' she said, smiling. 'What, when this weekend is over?'

'I have a script I wanted you to look at . . .'

She laughed aloud. 'No,' she shook her head. 'Really. I don't want to talk about scripts, Max. Not right now.'

'It's about the fire. About Triangle. You didn't know I was working on it, did you?'

'How could I have known, when you never told me?'

'I've been working on it for years.'

'Max—'

'It's about the fire. It's about you and me. I mean to say . . .' He gave a dry laugh. 'A version . . . A *nice* version. They come back for the kid, in my story. And she's right there, waiting for them. So there's a happy ending. My film has a happy ending.'

'Every movie should have a happy ending— *Shhh*! Did you hear it? I think she's coming.'

They waited, but they heard nothing more. Only the distant tock-tock of the tennis ball. Calls of 'cheat!' And the rustling of wind in the rose bushes behind them.

'I wonder,' Max broke the silence again. He was

370

gazing at the girl's photograph. 'D'you suppose she's any good. As an actress?'

'She might be.'

'I bet she's good,' Max continued, not really listening. 'If she's anything like her mother.'

'Her mother,' Eleanor smiled, 'was never as good as people said she was.'

'Her mother,' corrected Max, 'was—still is—far, far better than she ever realized. She just doesn't care about it enough . . .' He glanced across at Eleanor, and then back to the photograph in their hands. 'She looks just like you, El. Remember the green eyes? Those big, warm, green eyes gazing back at us. *Melting the snow on Hester Street*, you used to say. No matter what. No matter how ill she was . . .'

'I picture them every day.'

'Just the same as yours, El . . .'

Eleanor stood behind him and looked again at the photograph. 'Maybe,' she said. 'It's so hard to tell . . . But she resembles me . . . just a little bit. Maybe?' He lifted a hand, ran it along the hip of Eleanor's dress, left it there. She didn't move it away. After a while she lifted her arm, and rested it around his shoulders.

Another rustle, and then footsteps—definitely footsteps this time, coming from the pathway behind them. Light, girlish footsteps . . .

'They sound just like yours!' he whispered. And they did.

'Hello?' he called out. 'Is it you?' The footsteps stopped abruptly.

'Hello there?' Eleanor moved towards the path, but Max pulled her back.

Slowly, the footsteps restarted: light and girlish

still, tripping down the steps *one-two-three* . . .

Eleanor wriggled free of Max and ran towards them. The two women collided on the bottom step where the path turned in. They stopped. Stepped back. Considered each other.

Same willowy height. Same slim build.

Same short shock of thick, dark hair. Same light footsteps.

'Mrs Beecham?' Same soft, low voice.

'Eleana Beekman. Kappelman. Call me Eleana . . .' She laughed. 'Call me whatever you like! And you must be . . . You signed yourself, Hannah. Hannah. *Hannah!*' Eleanor leaned forward, gently, took the girl's silver *chamsa* between finger and thumb. 'Oh, Hannah. It is a sight for sore eyes . . .'

The girl turned to Max. 'And you are Mr—'

'Matz Beekman,' he said. 'You look . . . Can I say it? You look just like your mother.'

'Well, I . . .' The girl retreated a small step. 'Mr Beecham. Beekman. Please. We mustn't be too hasty . . .'

'Look, Max. Mama's *chamsa*,' Eleanor said. 'You remember it?' He nodded. Though he didn't remember it. Not really, not at all.

'Is it really you?' Eleanor said. 'Max—*Max*—Is it really our little Isha returned to us?'

'How can we be certain?' the girl asked. 'I remember nothing. *Nothing.* Except what I told you in the letter . . .'

'It's Mama's *chamsa!*' cried Eleanor. 'I know it is!' And it was, she was sure of it. Or if it wasn't, it was similar—so remarkably similar.

'And you have the same footsteps,' Max said.

The girl took off her sunglasses and gazed at them: her father, and then her mother. They gazed

372

back, both recognizing her at once.

'It was you,' Eleanor said faintly. 'The night of the party . . .'

Max reached for Eleanor's hand, and squeezed it so tight she might have screamed, if she had only felt it. It was going to be all right, and they knew that. It was the end of the longest search . . . It was the start of a new beginning. That was all. They needed each other. And now they had found each other.

'We have so much to catch up on,' the girl said. 'Where do we begin?'

'Let's begin,' answered Matz; and suddenly he laughed—soft and light, like a young man, almost, 'from the part where you remember . . . All the rest we can make up as we go along.'

'Welcome home,' Eleana whispered.

The girl smiled. And her smile was brighter than the sun over San Simeon Bay. And her dark brown eyes shone with hope, and love, and the beauty and joy of living.

AUTHOR'S NOTES

The Triangle Shirtwaist Company factory fire of 1911 remains the deadliest industrial accident in the history of Manhattan. My description of the fire—the roofs on the broken elevators, buckled from the weight of the bodies, the locked stairway, broken fire escape, burning bodies throwing themselves from windows to their certain death— are drawn from the many articles, photographs and books which document the tragedy.

One hundred and forty-six workers were killed. Six bodies were buried unidentified in a ceremony for which, in pouring rain, hundreds of thousands lined the New York streets to pay their respects. Thanks in part to the campaigns conducted in William Randolph Hearst's newspapers, the tragedy marked a turning point in industrial safety laws.

Max Blanck and Isaac Harris, the two owners of the factory, having escaped the fire over the rooftop, were prosecuted for the manslaughter of the workers, locked in on the floors below. They were both acquitted.

Marion Davies's 'niece' Patricia was a regular visitor at San Simeon and at the Beach House in Santa Monica. When she died in 1993, her family confirmed rumours which had always circulated, that she was in fact the birth daughter of Marion Davies and Randolph Hearst. In 1924, Patricia's adopted father disappeared in France, taking the girl with him. Randolph Hearst employed detectives to track her down and bring her home again.

ACKNOWLEDGMENTS

Many thanks to Sarah Ritherdon, Louise Swannell, Kimberley Young, Clare Alexander and Alona Mingueto.

Thank you Panda, Zebedee and Bashie for putting up with my obsessions and accompanying me on a fine road trip to Hearst Castle.

Thank you Panda for your insights (and gentle delivery).

Special thanks to Sharon Coussins and to Dr Khayke Beruriah Wiegand for checking over my attempts at written Yiddish.

And finally, as always, thank you to Peter.